Dance Like You Mean It

OTHER TITLES BY JEANNE SKARTSIARIS

Surviving Life
Snow Globe

Dance Like You Mean It

Jeanne Skartsiaris

BROTHER MOCKINGBIRD

Library of Congress Control Number: 2021943659

Cover Design by: Alexios Saskalidis
www.facebook.com/187designz

For information please contact:
Brother Mockingbird, LLC
www.brothermockingbird.org
ISBN: 978-1-7344950-8-9 Paperback
ISBN: 978-1-7378411-0-4 eBook

To Mom.
On the wings of angels.
Thank you for the inspiration.

Chapter One

"Life is short, ride your best horse first."
~ Anonymous

The ambulance roared into the emergency bay, sirens wailing. I ran toward the entrance and heard the clatter of the stretcher's wheels clacking hurriedly on the floor. Annoyed by racket, I admonished the paramedics racing beside the gurney. "Do you have to make so much noise?" My job as the nursing supervisor was to maintain calm in the ER.

"Sorry, Cassie, couldn't resist," said the tall paramedic as he gave me a wink and smile.

I glanced at the stretcher. A dingy white sheet covered lumps, and thick brown ooze stained the sheet.

"Oh, man," Adam, one of the nurses, said. "I can smell that from here." He stood at the nurse's station in the small emergency room. "Should we order a cardiac work up?"

"Please let Dr. Taylor know about this," I said, staring at the blotched sheet as I helped push the stretcher.

Christine Taylor and I had been best friends since seventh grade, and she expected first dibs on what was buried under the sheet.

The paramedic wheeled the bed in. "The rest is in the truck. I'll be right back."

By this time all the crew in the ER hovered in the exam doorway where the stretcher was parked. A patient in a wheelchair rolled herself near the door. "Ohh, that smell! What is it?"

Kathy, another nurse, rushed in front of the pack.

"Please take care of that patient," I said to her, grabbing the soaked sheet.

"I don't want to miss this," she whined, eyeing the globs of rust colored goop.

"There's plenty for everyone," I said. "Please." I nodded toward the patient.

Kathy huffed and turned to leave.

I pulled the sheet back, took a deep breath, and revealed our delicious lunch.

Adam came in and helped me unload trays of barbecue beef and ribs.

I licked a drop of sweet, sticky sauce off my fingers.

"Thank you, Dr. Taylor." Adam nodded at Christine who was waiting with an empty plate.

"My pleasure," Christine said.

I closed off the exam room, heaped some brisket on a plate, and headed into my office with Christine. "I hope we don't get busy," I said closing the door.

She pulled up a chair. "Just eat and enjoy." She nibbled on a baby back while I pounced on my barbecue, trying to remember to chew instead of inhale. "Why are you reading the obits?" Christine nodded at the newspaper spread out on my desk to catch the drippy sauce.

"I hadn't planned to, but noticed all these people who died. Some are my age." I leaned back in my rickety hospital-issued chair and burped. I pushed my empty plate away and a drop of sauce fell on a photo of a young woman who'd died "unexpectedly."

"This is what I was reading," I said between bites. I handed her the article that had sparked my interest.

She leaned back in the chair, her flat belly barely bulged from the pile we'd just eaten she looked over the article. I could feel my middle age tummy rolls cut through the elastic on my scrubs.

"A writer?" she asked.

"It's about writing a romance novel," I said, taking a chug of sweet tea. "You know I've always wanted to write a book."

"Cassie, the silly love stories we made up in high school don't count as reading material, much less novel material."

"Look," I said, pointing to the paper. "It says if a writer can tell a good story, create good characters, and rip a few bodices, they'd find an eager audience."

"So are you going to write a sex book about a nurse in an emergency room? Because if this is about your life I know how boring you are."

I laughed. "Yeah, look at all the material I have to work with." I waved toward the staff in the ER. "I'm not sure I can make a middleaged nurse a seductress." I batted my eyes. "I don't know, Christine, sometimes I feel like I have more to offer in life. Doesn't everybody have a book in them?"

"It's getting it out of them that's the challenge."

"My life is moving so fast, like, the finish line is closer than the starting gate, and I haven't started to run the race yet."

"You've always been a dreamer." Christine tossed her plate in the trash. "Are you going to do it?"

"I'd like to try." I crunched the obit section into a ball and tossed it in the trash. "I need to start checking off my bucket list."

"Or get a bigger bucket." Christine stood and opened the door.

I fanned my face from a hot flash, not sure if it was

brought on by hormones or the spicy barbecue sauce. "I still want to storm a castle, but I've lost focus." I considered my life. It wasn't all mine especially with family and job responsibilities.

"Then storm away, my liege." She bowed dramatically. "Just keep your butt in the saddle." She turned to go but looked at me. "It's all about the journey, right?"

"Right." I gave a thumbs up.

After Christine left, I turned the newspaper to the horoscope page to find out how the rest of my day was supposed to go. *Take time to dream. Watch your finances.* Didn't they always say that?

I'd harbored a dream of being a writer since college, but my husband, Mitch, told me I'd be chasing a rainbow—it wasn't practical. But after reading some of the books I'd read, I thought I could do better.

I read the article again and felt a stirring of optimism.

From Baker to Love MakerLocal Writer Sells
Romance.

Ida Thornton, a baker at a local grocery store, just learned her novel, *Buns in the Oven*, won the Romance Writers' Gilded Pen Award. "I've always loved reading romance novels and thought I'd spice up my life some by writing one," Ida said. "I still can't believe I got it published and it's been a bestseller for three months." Ida's agent, Beverly Burton, says that romance novels are a billion dollar industry. "Even during an economic crisis, readers buy romance. We can't get the books to publishers fast enough. Ida's book, about a wedding cake baker looking for love, has enjoyed brisk sales. The sequel, *Hot Crossed Lovers*, is due out next week." Romance editor Abigail Huller, confirmed the high demand. "Our lives are so busy, most readers just want to get lost in a fun read. Exciting, sexy characters appeal to consumers and help sell books."

I carefully folded the article and slipped it in my pocket. I spent the next hour on memos and scheduled compliance testing for the employees. Before the shift change, I walked through the emergency room. Out in the bright ward, the antiseptic smell was familiar. It reminded me of the rewarding days when I was able to help an expectant mom or start a stopped heart, when it felt like I made a difference. Now I saw more paper than people. As a supervisor, my medical training too often hinged on how well I wrote and responded to memos. Part of me missed the one-on-one with the patients.

I chose nursing to help people, to be an angel of mercy, and the math was easier than medical school. Plus I'd always been good at it.

Driving home that evening, I thought about my dreams. I needed a spark. I had a good life, two beautiful girls, and Mitch was a wonderful father. But something was missing. I yearned for more.

I reached into my pocket and touched the article, suppressing a smile at the thought of writing a novel. It could, at least, be a diversion. I leaned back in my seat and sighed. Who was I kidding? I barely had time to finish *reading* a book, much less write one.

Chapter Two

"Imagine." ~ John Lennon
"Imagine." ~ Barney

Tapping my pencil on my desk the next morning, I wondered how my dreams got sidetracked.

I considered my life. *What mark will I leave on this world?* After the flurry of college, marriage, and children, I was living a static lull. Mitch and I spent more time juggling schedules. I'd lost myself somewhere. My two girls were my light, but they were busy. This week would be the same as the next. It was a good life, but predictable. Where was the excitement? I needed to go out and chase a shooting star.

On impulse, I grabbed the phone and called Christine. She'd seen me at my best and worst and was one of the few people I could confide in.

"Hey," I said, when she answered. "Listen, you know me better than anybody, right?"

"Is this a trick question?"

I reminded her about the article. "I may need some help with this book."

"Like what?"

"Will you be my proofreader?" I asked. "Help with editing?"

"You need a strong command of writing, Cass." "You remember I didn't study journalism because you and my parents said it wasn't practical. The only reason I got bad grades in English was because my grammar sucked."

"And your vocabulary."

"In romance people want sex, not grammar."

She chuckled. "You're really going to do this?"

I shrugged and smiled.

"Sure, I'll be happy to read it," she said.

"Thanks," I said, as my other line rang. "I've got to go. I may start writing today."

After a few meetings and memos, I left the clinic for lunch. Luckily, we only had a few patients, so I wandered out to the hospital courtyard and found a quiet bench. I took out a small spiral notebook and jotted down notes. First, I had to think of a character, a name, a life. It was going to be fun creating someone else's existence on paper.

Wow, the power. I'd create a person. Any excitement my life lacked I could make up for in my protagonist.

But where to start? Back at my desk, I jumped on my computer and quickly ordered a book on how to write romance.

Mitch called later in the afternoon, telling me he was going to work late and then play basketball with the guys. I encouraged him to go. Sometimes it was easier when he was out, and I had the girls and the evening to myself. Mitch and I were good together when we were young, but the years had pushed us apart like opposite magnets. When had that changed? He'd rather spend weekends with his friends watching sports or playing poker, while I yearned for movies and family nights.

He'd always been able to make me laugh. That's why I was attracted to him. He had a devilish smile and was a great father. But, lately, his jokes seemed to cut. We'd lost something.

That night, after the girls were in bed, I sat at the computer to begin writing. I wanted a main character who was an exotic beauty with a successful job as a photojournalist—a career I'd always been fascinated with—and, of course, a healthy sex drive. With all the sexually transmitted diseases now, I set the stage in the seventies when promiscuity was a badge of honor without the ball and chain—or antibiotics.

I had created a beautiful, promiscuous but nameless photographer. I checked a website of popular baby names to find the perfect moniker for this luscious character. But I could only envision giggling babies, not a sexy seductress. She needed a name that would embody a spellbinding vixen who generated an empowering mystical aura. She had to have both strength and gentleness. No problem, right?

I scanned through names till my eyes blurred. Nothing sounded good enough for my new imaginary friend. The Smiths and Jones were boring. I flipped through a tabloid magazine, but didn't find anything—although I managed to get caught up on the Hollywood gossip. I was suffering writer's block on a book I hadn't even started. After two hours, I gave up and checked on the girls before I headed to bed.

Ashley, my fifteen year old, turned, sleepy eyed toward me. "What?" She could sound sarcastic even in slumber.

"Sorry to wake you," I whispered. "Go back to sleep."

"Whatever."

She looked so sweet all snuggled in her bed, holding her

favorite stuffed teddy bear, threadbare from many years of hugs. It reminded me of one of her favorite childhood books.

"What is real?" asked the Rabbit

"It's a thing that happens to you," said the Skin Horse. "When a child loves you for a long, long time—then you become real."

Ashley, so distant from me now—her indifference cut deep. I loved both my girls more than life itself, my bright shining lights. Thankfully, I was still in Gabby's light. But was left in the dark about Ashley's life. Since I worked so many hours, I'd often wondered if she held resentment toward me for not being home for her when the final bell rang.

Before Ashley I was going to prove a woman could have it all—motherhood *and* a successful career. But the night she was born, and I held her for the first time, I fell deeply in love, the emotion so pure it amazed me. There it was, the meaning of life—answered.

As I gazed at her brand new face and hands, tracing the fine lines of veins through her tender newborn skin, I began to sob hysterically.

A concerned nurse rushed to my side. "What's the matter?"

Choking back sobs, I wailed, "I don't want her to go to daycare!"

I've felt that way since.

I smiled, remembering. I wanted to tuck Ashley's blanket over her shoulders and hold her like I used to.

Ashley pulled the covers up. "What?" she groused.

"I was thinking how much I love you, and how beautiful you are all tucked in."

She rolled her eyes but smiled a little. I knew it was hard for her to admit that she still liked me, even if only a little.

I tiptoed into Gabby's room, my eight year old, sleeping sweetly on her stomach, feet and legs kicked out of her blanket. She slept with as many stuffed animals as would fit in her little twin bed. I gently pulled the covers up and kissed her cheek. It amazed me how big she looked. It didn't seem so long ago she was just a little ball of love, not easily distinguished from some of the stuffed animals she slept with. Now she was almost half the length of her bed. Time was going too quickly. I felt both my girls growing up and away from me. I wanted to hold them close yet set them free. Like holding air. Such is the conflict of motherhood.

Chapter Three

"A journey of a thousand miles begins with a single step."
~ Confucius

Later that week, I met Christine for lunch. I needed to pick her brain and get ideas for my smutty novel.

"After sitting at the computer for two hours, I couldn't even come up with a name for the main character," I whined, as we ordered our salads.

"Maybe you should take a writing class or join a writing group."

"Oh, sure, I have all the time in the world for that," I said.

"Do you know how many would-be authors are out there trying to get their books published?" Christine lightly drizzled dressing on her salad. "It's an incredibly competitive business. You'll be lucky to find a publisher or agent to read your manuscript, providing you even get one written."

"Don't try so hard to encourage me." I picked up a crusty roll and slathered it with butter. Since I was eating salad, I figured the butter balanced out the meal. "I hope you don't shrink talk to your patients like that."

"Sometimes I wish I could. Cass, I love you like a sister, and if I can't be honest with you, no one can. Don't underestimate the challenge of writing a book. PhDs have written romance novels that were rejected. You have to be able to tell a good story and keep the reader engaged." She delicately dabbed her mouth with a napkin. "And, it must have a happy ending. I'm not saying you can't do it." She touched my wrist. "I don't want to see you disappointed."

"Thanks, but I still want to try." I chewed on my hunk of bread. "I have to come up with a name first. Any good ideas for a heroine?"

She looked around the table. "What about naming her after a flower or food, like Willow or Peaches."

"Or maybe I could just name her after a tree, since that is what I am: stumped."

"What about Hyacinth?" Christine said. "Or Chrysanthemum," she suggested with an exaggerated flourish.

"I can't even spell Hyacinth or Chrysanthemum. Plus, I can't picture someone calling out in sexual ecstasy, 'Yes! Yes! Oh, yes, Hyacinth!'" A few people turned and looked at me. I lowered my voice. "It doesn't have the impact I want. But I do like the food idea. Maybe a spice, considering she is going to be a spicy, hot character. What about Chile or Poblano?"

"How about Cumin, isn't that what she's going to be doing most of the time?"

I laughed. "What about a strong male name? I can't just have a normal Bob being the handsome, sturdy, manlyman to sweep her off her feet. Something like Drake or Adonis, a good Greek god's name. Maybe use astrology like Scorpio or Gemini."

"How about an animal?" Christine said. "I know, a snake—Python, Dick Python? Visualize that!"

"That's a little too metaphorical. I thought all you read was educational material or classic literature."

"Oh, please! I love a good romance." She took a sip of water. "Look, why don't you just cut to the chase and name the male character Dick Bigg, or P. Ness?"

I laughed bread crumbs across the table.

That evening, I sat down at my computer to begin my literary endeavor. *Her* name would be Rosemary Christi. Rose or Rosie were good nicknames, and Rosemary was a multiuse spice, one I'd seasoned the chicken with at dinner tonight. Her last name, Christi, was for Christine. Poetic justice, I thought. I titled the book *Wild Rose*. The book was to be steamy but also allegorical. Good and evil, coming together—and having wild sex, topped off with a happy ending.

Now, where should I begin...?

Wild Rose
By Cassandra Calabria

Damn! I forgot. I intended to write under a pseudonym. Oh, great, another name to come up with by daybreak.

The author's name had to come from the heart. I thought of romantic or stripper names, like Luvy Harlequin, Roman Tique, Candi Kane. Since I was looking for heartfelt, I thought it would be appropriate to use some anatomical names from the heart. I tried to use Atria, Mitral, or Ventricle, but none of the names screamed romance. *His thrusts pumped like the heart in systole.* Nah. Didn't work. Finally, I settled on the name Cardia Loving and started my journey to romance.

Wild Rose

– FROM CHAPTER 1

The light shimmered off a thin veil of morning mist hovering over the ocean's pulsating waves. Rosemary Christi framed the scene in the lens of her Nikon. She squeezed the shutter knowing instantly what the photograph would look like. Film was her life's canvas.

Rosemary knew every picture told a story and was glad she chose photography as a career instead of nursing—a job her parents strongly favored.

She gently laid her 35mm camera on the worn teak table and admired the deck of her Venice Beach cottage near the ocean. The surf view was partially obscured by bright pink bougainvillea vines, cascading over her secluded porch. The California sunrise was spectacular with oranges and pinks tinting the marine layer. The cool, crisp morning invigorated her more than the hot coffee she put to her full ripe lips.

Rosemary's thoughts were interrupted as last night's date, Drake Longweenie, stepped on the deck wearing a pair of jeans that looked poured over his body like a second skin, the top button undone, inviting her lingering gaze.

"There's coffee," Rosemary said to his pants.

"Don't you have anything stronger?" he asked as he stretched his lithe body.

"No, unless you want some of this," she said, sliding her

silk robe from one delicate, sensual shoulder.

"What dreams are made of," Hugh said, as his jeans tightened against his zipper, causing the metal teeth to click apart one by one from the pressure.

Click.

Click.

Click.

Rosemary stood, her robe falling to the bougainvillea mantled porch. Her seraphim beauty stopped people, though she hated the double takes and catcalls.

"Come on." She brushed past him, grazing her hand over his expanding jeans, his zipper growled like a tiger and her mood ring blazed violet fire.

Inside, he grabbed her covering her mouth, neck, and body with kisses.

Hugh's hands followed her curves and finely sculpted shape. He slid his fingers down her spine. Goosebumps trailed his touch on her soft skin. Rapacious, he took her into his ropy arms of steel. Their bodies moved together in a heated embrace. His fortified steel rod probed her molten hot muffler as he assaulted her with his mouth. Rosemary claimed his hard body as they descended onto the couch. Her hand skillfully reached between the sharp biting teeth of his zipper and freed his engorged manliness. He peeled off his clothes like a python shedding its skin.

"You're a goddess," Hugh hissed through kisses. Rosemary took charge, guiding Hugh's big diesel engine to seek her tailfins of desire as he drove her to bliss.

Afterward, the batik gauze blanket lay crumpled, much like the two lovers basking in the afterglow.

Their relationship was borne of convenience and desire. Both wanted no commitments, yet they reveled in their physical attraction for each other.

"I need to get ready for work," Rosemary said.

Today, her job was to photograph a methadone clinic. If she did well, maybe her agent, Beck, would send her on more cutting-edge jobs. It was the seventies and she wanted the same opportunities as her male colleagues.

Naked, she went to her closet and considered what to wear. She grabbed her favorite sex, drugs, and rock-and-roll T-shirt, but settled on a black shirt and denim bell bottoms.

Hugh took Rosemary in his arms. "C'mon, Rosie, one for the road."

"I'm not a 'roadie.' Go write a song about us." Rosemary pulled her shirt over her lean body. "Till next time."

"When will that be?" he asked.

"I don't know. The shoot is in Santa Barbara. I may take my camera up the coast and see what's happening."

"Good luck finding anything as good as this." Still naked, Hugh stood to his full height and beauty.

"It'll be here when I get back," she said, walking out. She waited until Hugh was ready, so they could leave together. She did not trust a key to anyone.

They shared a deep kiss before Rosemary climbed into her red '71 MG. Gunning the engine, she made sure Hugh was in his airbrushed "love van" before she sped away.

"Longweenie? You named him Longweenie? Are you out of your mind?" Christine dropped the first few chapters of my meager attempt at writing on my desk. "And you didn't like Dick Python, *why*? You can do better. His name should be subtle, not rammed down your throat. Metaphorically speaking, of course," she said.

"Okay, I was thinking about Longfellow, but it's too common. How about I change it to Long. Or Dick. Dick's Long...you know."

"I think you could be a bit more creative."

"What about Huge Hard, or Huge Dick?" I held my hands up. "I've got it. How about Hugh Hardick?

She rolled her eyes. "Better. You know, Cassie, I'm wondering if Rosemary is your alter ego."

"Don't try to psychoanalyze me. You know me too well for that. Rosemary is nothing but an inkblot of my imagination," I laughed. "But she *is* fun."

"So, I shouldn't be surprised if you decide to chuck it all and take a camera across the United States?"

I shook my head. "I'm too practical." I flipped through the pages, wincing at all the red marks she'd slashed across them. "You didn't like it?"

"I didn't say that. It was good. All that sex. Impressive."

I looked at her hopefully. "So, you liked it?"

"Yeah. Read my comments, and let me know when you're done with the next chapters."

"You'll be the first to read it." I glanced at her. "Actually, you'll be the only one."

I picked up the pages and looked over her notes. I glanced at my calendar. School was ending in a few weeks.

I'd try to spend as much time as possible through the summer banging out a story. Metaphorically speaking, of course.

Chapter Four

"Mothers, food, love, and career: the four major guilt groups."
~ Cathy Guisewite

We were well into the hot Texas summer, and the start of the school year was coming too fast. It had taken me weeks of lunchless lunch hours and little sleep at night to write the first rough draft of my novel. I'd picked up more "how-to" books on writing and read as many romance novels as I could get my hands on.

At night, after the girls were in bed and Mitch was snoozing in front of the TV, I came to life, spending hours at the computer outlining and writing. It was work, but it exhilarated me, put me in another place. I loved structuring the story. Mitch barely noticed my absence, probably happy to have the remote control to himself.

Heading home from work one evening to pick up Gabby from after care, I'd mulled over plot points and couldn't wait to get the new ideas on paper.

I greeted Gabby and told her to grab her stuff. As she skipped to the door, she said to her teacher, "Bye bye, Mommy—I mean, Miss Susie." She giggled at her mistake.

I felt the twist of the knife in my chest. I hated that my child spent more of her waking hours with her teacher than me.

I tried to shake off Gabby's slip of the tongue. "How was

your day?"

"I don't know."

"Who did you hang with?"

"I don't know"

"Did you have fun?"

"I don't know."

I sighed as the minivan's engine belched to life. She was only eight, but was starting to act like a teenager. Perhaps she got it from me. I rarely told her about my work day. It's hard to explain to a child about people who overdosed on drugs, or who suffered from a sexually transmitted disease, or, why they couldn't make a boom boom in the toilet.

"How about we play soccer when we get home?" I asked.

"I have homework."

"Homework? What homework?" I glanced at her as we waited at a light. "You just spent two hours in after care. Didn't you get it done then?"

"I don't know. I'm hungry. What's for dinner?"

"I don't know," I answered.

The apple doesn't fall far.

We rarely got home before most families on our street sat down to dinner. We lived in a neighborhood where most of the mothers stayed home or worked part time. Since the kids were in for the evening, Gabby became grumpy because she wanted to play. I envied the women who were home organizing play dates and making pretty, shiny things with glue guns.

When we pulled up, Mitch and Ashley were in the front yard talking to Tina Arpino, one of the neighbors, who was out walking her well-groomed terrier. She probably spent more money on her dog's coiffure than I did at Supercuts.

We got out of the car. I was loaded down with a briefcase, Gabby's book bag, and groceries.

Gabby ran to Tina. "Can Lindsey play?" she asked excitedly.

The girls were the same age and had become great friends, as long as they could play at school and before sunset.

"I'm sorry, Gabby, but Lindsey's getting ready for dinner. Maybe another time."

"Hi, Tina," I said, barely able to see over my armload.

Tina and her family lived down the block. She was a stay-at-home mom with two well mannered kids. I'd always felt guilty around her. Like I knew I shouldn't work—that it was not best for the children. To rub salt into the wound, Tina was one of the kindest people I knew. She always had a smile yet managed to make me feel inadequate when I was around her.

"Are you just getting in from work?" Tina asked, seeming sympathetic, but if I could sniff the air, I knew I'd smell disapproval.

"What's for dinner?" Mitch interrupted.

"Chicken Cordon Bleu. With pomme frittes and homemade truffles for dessert," I said sarcastically.

"Yum, we had that the other night," Tina said. "Let me know how you pound your chicken breasts. I hate that part of the recipe."

"Actually, Tina, I'm not sure what we're having. I haven't gotten inside to look in the refrigerator." I didn't mean to be so snarky.

Gabby was trying to convince Ashley to push her on the swing in the backyard or play another outdoor game. "Let's play soccer," she said enthusiastically. "Mommy, can't you play in your work clothes? It takes too long for you to change."

"It won't take me that long, honey. Let me get inside, start dinner, and change. Daddy and Ashley can warm you up."

"I can't play in these shoes," Ashley mumbled. She was wearing platforms with four inch soles. How she even walked in them was beyond me.

"Well, go change your shoes," I said. "Are you afraid I'll beat you?"

"Doubt it." She turned to go inside. "I have to call Teresa anyway."

"About what? What you both did at school?" My briefcase fell from my shoulder to my elbow, and I almost dropped the grocery bag. "I haven't seen you all day, and you just spent the whole day with her."

"Mom, why do you always have to start?" she whined, ducking inside.

Tina watched our exchange. "I'd best be getting home. It was nice visiting."

My maternal prowess failed before her eyes.

"C'mon, Daddy," Gabby yelled, soccer ball in hand.

"Coming," he said. "Why don't you see if you can say something nice to Ashley?" he muttered to me, as he followed Gabby.

After getting in the door and emptying my armload, I headed to Ashley's room and knocked. "Hey, doll. I'm sorry if I said anything to upset you. I'd just love to spend some time with you," I said to her closed door.

"I'll be out later." Her voice sounded muffled, far away, much like our relationship.

I reached for the doorknob and then pulled my hand away. I yearned to open the door, sit next to her, and find out what was going on in her life. But I was supposed to "respect" her privacy. I could hear her laughing on the phone. About what? She was my daughter. Shouldn't I have some idea what her interests were? I hated our family time was condensed and squished into a few hours at night.

With a deep sigh, I raced to the kitchen, shelving the milk and eggs I'd just bought, grabbed some frozen chicken breasts, and threw them into a pan with oil. With minimal seasoning, I tossed the food in the oven, deciding to forgo the microwave thaw. The preheat setting was part of my cooking time, and dinner baked until we were done playing. Some nights it was cooked okay, but most nights, whatever was in the oven turned into a hockey puck. Frozen vegetables went into the microwave and rice got boiled in ten minutes—the life of a gourmet. Pounding chicken breasts, my ass. The only breast that got beat was mine when I did a Tarzan imitation to signal dinner was ready. I threw on some play clothes and was running outside when the phone rang.

"Hello," I answered.

"Hi." Mom's familiar voice greeted me.

Mitch stuck his head in. "Hellooo. How long are you going to be on the phone? What's for dinner?"

"Frozen chicken and whatever else you can find."

"Cass, It's almost seven o'clock. You haven't made dinner yet?" Mom asked. "Why don't you go and take care of your family and call me tomorrow. And, put on a little lipstick for Mitch."

"What? Why? I'm exhausted after working a full day. I have no idea what we're having with our chicken, and you're telling me to make myself pretty for my husband, who doesn't lift a finger to help?"

"A little effort can go a long way," she said. "Plus, it will make you feel better."

"I'd like to be able to take off my first layer of makeup before I add another."

Gabby came running in. "Is that Gams?"

"Okay, honey, just a sec," I told Gabby, while she jumped up and down at my feet begging to talk. "Mom, do you read any romance novels?" I asked.

"I've read a few. Why?"

"I—I—just read one that was fun," I hesitated and then decided not to tell her I'd written a book in case I never got past the first draft.

"Well, they're good to get lost in. I especially like the racy ones."

"Mom!" It was weird thinking about my mother having anything to do with sex.

"I'll let you borrow a few if you want. Now let me talk to my precious grandbaby."

I handed the phone to Gabby, thanking portable technology. During our conversation, I'd moved into the kitchen, opening pantry doors and the refrigerator to see what looked good and quick to eat with the hockey pucks. "How about rice?" I yelled into the pantry.

"Gross!"

"Okay, pasta?" I asked, as I poured penne noodles in a pot of water.

"Don't we have any meat?" Mitch came in and looked in the refrigerator.

"I have frozen chicken in the oven," I said, grabbing the garlic salt.

"Let's order pizza. We can have chicken tomorrow." He gave me a peck on the cheek. "I'm hungry now."

"By the time we get takeout, dinner will be ready." I handed him a spatula. "Here, stir the pasta."

He did a quick swirl and walked out of the kitchen.

I could hear Gabby jabbering on the phone with Mom. Ashley came in and took the phone from Gabby. I heard her say, "Thanks for the advice with Bradley. You were right. I ignored him, and he talked to me." She giggled into the phone like a schoolgirl.

Okay, she *was* a schoolgirl, but I wished she'd talk to me about this stuff.

"Ashley's got a boyfriend," Gabby sang and danced around Ashley. "His name is Bradleeeee!"

I couldn't help but smile.

"Shut up, twerp!" Ashley handed me the phone and stomped out of the kitchen.

"Don't say 'shut up,'" I yelled at her retreating figure. "It's not nice." Then I said to Mom, "I'm starting to sound just like you."

"I can't tell you how much satisfaction I get hearing that," She laughed. "Call me tomorrow."

I threw Gabby in the bath while the food cooked. So much for our soccer game.

Since I'd started writing, scenes and dialogue would pop

into my head. I felt slightly schizophrenic most of the time, with characters' voices running through my brain.

I left Gabby to soak and went to the kitchen. I grabbed salad fixings and began to wash a cucumber, giggling at nasty thoughts about Rosemary and Hugh's mighty piece of "produce." I held the large, firm vegetable erect and thought, *if Hugh's penis were the size of this cucumber, it would feed a family of six.* I laughed as I peeled and sliced.

Ashley came into the kitchen and stopped. "What are *you* laughing at?"

I felt my face flush. "Nothing."

"I'm starving. When are we going to eat?" Ashley took a slice of cucumber and ate it.

I choked down a laugh and tossed the salad into a bowl.

"Mommy, can I shave my legs tonight?" Gabby yelled from the bathroom.

"Shaving" consisted of putting foamy soap on her legs and using a spoon as a razor.

"Not tonight, honey." I walked to the bathroom, drying my hands on a towel. "We haven't eaten yet. Let's just hurry and get cleaned up."

"Why not? I'll do it fast." She looked at me with such pleading eyes my resistance broke. It seems I spend too much time saying no, rushing from one activity or responsibility to another. We rarely got the chance to play. I let her foam up her legs and spoon off the soap.

"It's beauty parlor night," she said.

I sat back and watched my little baby playing like a grownup, and was reminded again how quickly time was moving.

"Mom! I think the chicken is done!" Ashley yelled from

the kitchen.

I left Gabby in the bath and rushed to the kitchen. "Ashley, please go keep an eye on your sister. I don't want her decorating the bathroom with pink foamy soap.

I opened the oven door. Sure enough, the chicken was burnt. It was probably still raw on the inside, though.

"Gross, Mom. We have cookbooks, you know. Maybe you should try one." Ashley made a face at the charred breasts.

"I know how to cook chicken, thank you. It's hard when you have thirty minutes for an hour's worth of cooking." I tried not to lose my temper and blow up like the split breasts. "Now, please help and get Gabby into her PJs."

"Mommy!" Gabby yelled from the bathroom. "Come here.""Are you all right?" Concern laced my voice.

"I don't want to be alone."

I cast a look at Ashley. She rolled her eyes and shuffled out to help Gabs.

"Don't drown her," I said, as she ambled to the bath. Luckily, she was a pretty good big sister, but only if I wasn't watching.

"Mom! You let her use my good soap," Ashley yelled from the bath.

"I didn't know it was yours, honey. Sorry."

I worked to salvage the carcasses. Deciding we'd have stir fry instead of baked chicken. Then, with a sizzle, the pasta boiled over onto the stovetop. I was sure the frozen veggies in the microwave had little wrinkles by now, too.

Mitch walked into the kitchen. "Dinner's not ready?"

"I could use some help." I flipped the halfcooked chicken into a sizzling pan.

He took a spatula and stirred the chicken, and then

grabbed cucumber slices from the salad and popped them in his mouth. He went back to the TV.

Later, I showed Mitch the now well-creased article about romance writing. By now I was pretty much finished with the novel, and I still hadn't told anyone but Christine. "What do you think about me writing a book?"

"You?" He dropped the article on the TV table without reading it and flipped channels.

I picked up the slip of paper and looked hard at him. His eyes never left the TV. I wondered if we would ever have a meaningful conversation again. I knew he was under pressure at work. His sales quotas were down—no, dismal—so he'd been working long hours. We'd been relying more on my paycheck, which was being stretched to the breaking point.

I reminded myself what attracted me to him in the first place. Before, he made me feel special all the time. He'd surprise me with flowers and chocolates, often for no reason. And he could always get the girls to laugh—a pure sound that nourished my soul.

There were still occasional flashes of romance and fun. But lately, the magic had dissipated, like I could see behind the curtain. Both of our schedules were hectic. It was like we were playing tag all the time. Who's getting whom at what time and from what activity? Seven days a week, we were running.

As I sat at the computer that evening, I questioned whether I could really publish this book. If I could make a little money from it, maybe I could spend more time with the girls and take some financial pressure off our family.

Wild Rose

– From Chapter 2

Rosemary drove up the coast from Los Angeles to Santa Barbara. Her long, silky hair caught the breeze through the open window. She studied the stunning ocean view with a photographer's eye and imagined capturing the wake of surf and the glistening sand.

Her ex-boyfriend Richard lived in Santa Barbara. She'd left a message for him. Though one of her "ex" men, he was still good for an occasional romp. He'd wanted marriage, but expected Rosemary to quit work and be a housewife. Hell no, she wanted a profession and loved photography. Rosemary planned to be on top, so to speak.

The methadone clinic wasn't in the worst part of town, but not far from it. Rosemary parked close to a dilapidated building. The photographs were to be part of a feature story in the Sunday paper about clinics and Vietnam vets. A great way to showcase her work.

She grabbed her bags and double checked the locks on her car before carrying the camera equipment into a graffiti marked building, that had once been elegant. Sculpted stonework lined windows now had rusty bars bolted in front. The rock was mottled a dirty gray, and the heavy wood door was nicked and sprayed with paint.

Rosemary opened the creaky door. Disheveled patients sat in the grimy anteroom. The smell of used up people assaulted her. Most of the addicts were young men, unwashed, roadworn, and aged beyond their years. Wheelchairs and missing limbs singled out the vets. The only common link was they were all dazed.

Rosemary checked in with a handsome doctor wearing an expression as gray as his lab coat. He stood behind an opened window, which partitioned him from the patients. "Can I help you?" he recited more than asked, never looking up.

Rosemary noticed his voice was accented with a soft French cadence. His dark hair was straight and pulled in a ponytail.

"I'm Rosemary Christi, the photographer asked to document this clinic for the news."

"I forgot you were coming," he said wearily, eyes still focused on his work as he jotted notes.

She metered the light near a window. "I'd like to take pictures of you with the patients."

His eyes turned to Rosemary and his expression changed from apathy to desire. He quickly stepped to the front. "Well, bonjour."

Rosemary smiled and moved away noticing a glint of desire in his cerulean eyes.

He followed, gently taking her hand, and staring, his eyes alight. "You look like a fashion model." He devoured her, taking time to look stem to stern. "I'm Dr. Francois Armand. It's a pleasure." He bent gracefully, displaying broad shoulders as his lips grazed her hand. "Please, I am at your service."

"Thank you," Rosemary said, pulling her hand away.

She studied the room. Patients sat in various degrees of stupor, each holding a small Dixie cup.

One patient couldn't take his eyes off Rosemary. He raised his cup for a toast and slurred, "Man, this is some good shit today, Doc, can I have another hit?"

Dr. Armand slung a protective arm around Rosemary. "I am sorry a beautiful woman such as you is exposed to such degradation."

Rosemary moved from his embrace. Often men felt some primal need to protect her when she was capable of taking care of herself.

"No need to apologize," she said, unpacking her equipment. "I'll shadow the patients' faces to protect their identity."

"I doubt they'd care." Dr. Armand's eyes followed Rosemary like a puppy looking for a treat.

"What's your role here?" Rosemary slung her camera strap over her shoulder pulling out a small pad and pencil. She gave him the same treatment, looking at his body from head to toe, making a point to let her eyes linger on his pants. Let him see how it feels, she thought, and then looked him in the eye. He may be solicitous, but he was also cute.

"I'm working to pay my student loans," he said, running a hand through sleek hair. He squirmed under her intense gaze.

"Can I photograph you giving methadone to the patients?" Rosemary metered and calculated settings.

"Why do you want to photograph this ugly place? I'll be off in a few hours. We can take a walk, and I'll take pictures of you." He swept toward her. "You are captivating, bon cheri." He took her hand again and kissed it gently.

Rosemary pulled her hand away and gripped her camera in front of her, tired of people reacting to her looks and not her talent. Why do men always try to take charge? This time, she'd flip the coin and show him a few tricks. He was attractive and seemed willing. The world was hers, and she was going to ride it like a Texas cowgirl.

Chapter Five

"If we don't succeed, we run the risk of failure."
~ Dan Quayle

Monday mornings were usually chaos. No matter how early we started, we were always late.

"Ashley!" I yelled. "Get up, unless you want to go to school in your pajamas."

What is it about teenagers and sleep? They have the metabolism of a flea, with more energy in one day than I'll have in my entire adult life.

I sat Gabby in front of the television with a waffle. She was a lump in the mornings, hypnotized by the TV. I could dress her, move her arms and legs like a puppet, and brush her hair until it was time to turn the TV off. Then she popped to attention, upset I'd put the wrong outfit on her, making it clear she didn't want to wear the pink bunny shirt; she wanted to wear the blue shirt that had been in the laundry under a damp, smelly towel for days.

Ashley, sleepy eyed, shuffled into the kitchen, fully dressed. Long gone were the pink bunny shirts. Now she wore tiny T-shirts with "fashionably" shredded hems, and skinny jeans too low for bending. I stared at her as she foraged the fridge for food.

"Nice outfit," I said.

She held her hand up. "Don't."

I bit my tongue, not wanting to start the day with an argument. But with those clothes, it was ironic she was embarrassed to be seen with me.

I checked the time. I was only half dressed, and we were already running behind. Luckily, a hospital emergency room is easy to dress for—scrubs. Gabby's bunny shirt was the biggest fashion decision I wanted to make that morning.

While Gabby brushed her teeth and Ashley picked at a piece of toast, I ran into the bathroom to put on makeup and brush my hair. I checked my line of roots. They looked like a plowed field of white, and I thought of Rosemary's beautiful silky blonde locks. I pulled my hair back hoping to hide the gray.

I yelled for Mitch as I headed to the door. "You have to take Ashley. I'm running late."

"I was hoping *you* could. I need to get to work." Mitch walked out of the bathroom. Ashley tossed her backpack on the couch. "Fine, if no one wants to take me to school, I'll just stay home." She crossed her arms and hitched a hip.

"Mitch, please." I knew he was stressed at work, but too often I bore the weight of everyone's schedule. There was that nudge of wishing I could work parttime.

"C'mon, Ash." Mitch walked to the door and held it open. "I can't be late."

"Thanks," I said.

We grabbed our bags and raced out the door. Our Dallas neighborhood was known for its decent school system. I hoped so, since Ashley's math was too hard for me by the time she was in second grade.

Mitch turned to me. "Don't forget, I'm going to watch the

Mavs game with some of the guys later."

"No, Mitch. Don't you remember I asked you to pick up the girls today?" I've got a meeting that may run late."

"You never asked me."

"Yes, I did, last night. Can you miss part of the game?"

"Oh, great. Do I need to bring clothes for tomorrow?" Ashley slung her backpack over one shoulder. "Like, am I going to have to spend the night at school? Sorry if we're so much trouble." She rolled her eyes so far back that it reminded me of Linda Blair in *The Exorcist.*

Gabby looked at me and Mitch, a pained expression on her face. "Please don't forget us, Mommy," she whispered breathlessly.

I hugged her. "Oh, sweetie, I'll be there." I'd have to dash out of my meeting.

I tried to give Ashley a kiss on the cheek, but she backed away and waved the air. I told her I loved her, and one of us would pick her up from school.

She threw her backpack in Mitch's car. "I'm old enough to come home alone!" she whined.

"The bus takes forever, and I don't like you coming home to an empty house. Besides, you can get your homework done there."

I was glad her school still allowed high school kids to stay supervised at the library after hours. Some afternoons she went to the Y to help with the young children. She hated that, too.

"*No fair!* It's me and the detention kids," she complained, as she plopped in the seat and slammed the door.

Gabby crawled into her seat, sipping her unfinished chocolate milk. I fought with the buckle of my beat up minivan. I wished we had a reliable car, I thought repeatedly tugging to retract the frayed belt. We patched up our old vehicles, praying they'd make it another year.

We made a decent living, but we were smack in middle class with mortgage payments, college savings, and insurance premiums that whittled down our salaries. We still lived from paycheck to paycheck.

I clicked the buckle and watched Mitch and Ashley drive away. It wasn't the first time he planned his evening—his life—without considering us.

Fighting school zone traffic, I scored a spot, pulled over, and dropped Gabby off. "I love you, honey." I kissed her cheek.

"Look, there's Jenny. Bye." She clambered out of the car without even a glance back, her backpack bouncing heavy against her bottom. I prayed my meeting would be short, and I wouldn't be late picking up the girls—again.

Walking into the ER, I automatically glanced at the electronic board indicating the patient load. "What do we have this morning?" I asked Adam, the seven-to-three shift nurse.

"So far, a stiffie and a threatened miscarriage," he answered, typing on the computer.

"A stiffie?" I sighed. "I hope it's not going to be one of those days. Did you notify the morgue?"

"Not that kind of stiffie." He winked. "A Viagra overdose." I smiled.

Adam was one of my favorite nurses. He had a comforting bedside manner and his calm-during-a-storm attitude during traumas made him invaluable.

"Who's the doc today?" It was a rhetorical question as I looked at the schedule. *Good*, I thought, *Dr. Boran*. "Has he seen the patients?"

"No, but he ordered some tests on the pregnant woman," Adam said.

"I'll take care of her." I opened her digital record. "I'll get the labs ordered"

"Okay," he said. "But Viagra man is in room three, begging for a cute nurse."

We were taught not to refer to a patient by their diagnosis, but it would be nearly impossible to differentiate them otherwise. Working in the ER was like cheap sex. Patients were in and out, remembered only as a body part. Tawdry, I'm sure, but efficient.

I glanced in the patient's room. "Do you need help?"

"I can handle it." Adam took the chart. "I told Kathy about the pregnant woman, but she went to the cafeteria anyway."

"She left when there was a patient to be seen?" I asked.

Adam shrugged and headed in to see Mr. Viagra. "And Jennifer won't be back until tomorrow."

Kathy was one of those worthless employees who always had to be told what to do; otherwise, she'd troll Facebook all day. Her review was on my desk—one of many tasks I needed to take care of. Since becoming a supervisor, I missed working with patients, when I felt useful, but the siren call of administrative work kept me tethered to my desk more than I liked.

"Have you seen Kathy?" I asked Gail, our receptionist.

Gail raised an eyebrow.

"Page her STAT, please. Dr. Boran and Adam are in with another patient."

"I'll call her."

"Thanks. Please send Kathy in as soon as she gets here."

I headed to see the woman suffering with the miscarriage. I knocked and opened the door. She lay on the bed clutching a box of tissue. Her boyfriend stood away from the bed on the phone.

"How are you? I'm Cassie, your nurse."

She shook her head and tears spilled on already wet cheeks. "I'm cramping and bleeding. I hope I didn't lose the baby."

I went to her and put my hand on her arm. "It's very common to bleed in early pregnancy. We're going to order tests to see what's going on. Can I get you anything?"

She shook her head and looked at her boyfriend who was still on the phone, his back to her. I noticed he had a French accent. What bothered me was he didn't look at her at all.

"He's the father?" I asked.

Fresh tears flowed as she curled into herself.

While I took her history, he stayed on the phone speaking loudly. "Sir," I said. "Can you please talk in the waiting room?"

"Hold on," he said. "This is an important call."

"Benjamin, hang up," his girlfriend whispered.

He rolled his eyes and spoke in French to the caller. "Oui, I will call you back." He pocketed his phone. "So, is she losing the baby?" He leaned against the counter, not showing any tenderness toward her.

"We don't know yet," I said, a little harshly. Turning to the young woman, I took her hand. "We're waiting on lab results to see how far along you are," I said gently. "Then we'll get you in for a sonogram."

She nodded and softly put a hand on her abdomen. "I'm scared to lose the baby."

"I understand." And I did, having suffered a miscarriage between Ashley and Gabby. The pain layered both physical and emotional was immeasurable. "As I said, this is common often with a good outcome. I'm going to check on your blood work." I handed her the nurse call button. "Will you be okay?" I shot a glance at her boyfriend. Although handsome, he seemed cold and indifferent.

"You'll sit with her?" I asked him.

"Oui. But how much longer? I have a meeting."

"Benjamin, please," his girlfriend pleaded.

I stepped out to the desk and asked Gail, "Did you ever find Kathy?"

"She's back. I told her you wanted to see her, but she's in the break room eating." Gail read the look on my face. "I'll call her again."

"Thank you."

A few minutes later, Kathy ambled into the triage area, crumbs on her cheek. "You wanted me?"

"You had a patient," I told her. "We needed you on the floor. Jennifer's off today."

"I didn't have time to eat breakfast before I came in."

"You'd only been here five minutes. Adam's been working since seven. Please call ultrasound and see when they can get my patient in."

"Okay, okay." Kathy slouched off.

I really needed to get her review finished. There was no way I could fire her without enough documentation. I cringed, thinking about all the memos and emails I needed to deal with today on top of my regular paperwork.

Keeping up with work and home was often a Sisyphean chore. I longed to spend more time with my girls, but also wanted to be a successful role model, hoping they'd find a career they loved.

I used to love nursing—until it became less about patients and more about bureaucracy.

The labs came up on the patient. It wasn't good news. Her levels were too low for her to be as pregnant as she thought. "I know when it happened because Benjamin went overseas the day after we had sex," she said.

The sonogram would no doubt confirm the labs. I headed to her room to let her know she was next for her scan, and I saw her boyfriend in the hallway on the phone again. Jerk. I went to tell him to take it to the lobby when I overheard him whispering, "I'll see you later. You know I love you, but my hands are tied right now. Soon, baby, soon. I'll tell her it's over." His accent almost lulled me into his web.

"Sir," I snapped.

He jumped, but then held a hand up as if telling me to shut up.

"Hang up or take the call outside." I wanted him to leave.

"It's important." He waved me off again.

"I can see that. Outside, or I'm calling security." I wasn't usually so sharp, but this guy was working my last nerve.

Kathy and Adam both stopped in their tracks. Kathy smiled a little, expecting some drama, but Adam stepped in. "Sir, I'll escort you out."

Benjamin shook his head. "I'll call you back in a minute." Then he turned on me. "Who do you think you are? I'm busy.

How much longer?"

"As soon as all the results are in. I don't know how long that'll take." I was tempted to ask him how long the other woman was willing to wait for him.

Some days the pressure of the job bore down on me. How many more years could I do this? But what other job was I capable of?

How would Rosemary handle it?

I took a breath, shook it off, and went to find a doctor.

Dr. Boran stood at the desk, signing charts. I approached him. "Can you help me with this patient?" I asked. I explained her history and how rude her boyfriend was.

"I'll take care of it." He glanced at her chart. "We have results from her tests?"

"She's back from her ultrasound, and her beta levels were really low." I showed him the labs. "The sono results should be in the computer."

"Bummer," he said, as he walked toward the room. "Come on, Cass."

I liked Dr. Boran. He had skipped the asshole course offered at most medical schools. Plus, he was easy on the eyes. Dark wavy hair that just grazed his collar and eyes the color of Texas bluebonnets, he was probably ten years younger than me. *Dare to dream, Cassie*, I mused, noticing how well his scrubs fit.

He stopped to read the chart and shook his head. "Sonogram shows a missed ab."

I hated for her to get the news the pregnancy wasn't viable. I'd hold her hand while Dr. Boran told her. I knew her boyfriend would probably welcome this tragic news.

Chapter Six

"Caution: Cape does not enable user to fly."
~ Batman costume warning label

I spent the next hour sitting with my patient while she absorbed the bad news, all the while clutching her abdomen as if she could hold the baby in. My heart broke for her losing, not only a baby, but hope. Even if she was better off without the jerk. I grabbed an overdue cup of coffee and escaped to my office, still pissed at her insensitive boyfriend. He never offered sympathy, only tried to get her to leave as soon as possible. I hoped Kathy and Adam could handle the patients long enough for me to get caught up on the backlog of paperwork.

I thought of Rosemary and her photography, fantasizing about chucking it all to make a living and following a dream of doing something I loved. But didn't I love nursing?

As I answered memos and responded to emails, I couldn't help but daydream about my book and hoped it would add a little cha-ching to my life and bank account. It was fun to invent a life and live vicariously through her.

After an hour of rearranging piles on my desk, I went for a refill in the break room.

Dr. Boran and Dr. Aaron Novak, a gastroenterologist, were in deep conversation, hovering over coffee.

"They wouldn't take it as a trade in because it'd been in an accident," Dr. Novak was telling Dr. Boran.

"Are you going to sell it?"

"I guess so. I hate to go through the hassle of listing and showing it. You sure you're not interested? It's a great drive."

"Here's someone who could use a new car," Dr. Boran said as I entered. "I've seen what you drive."

My clank bucket minivan had generated many jokes among my coworkers. A few months earlier, cars were broken into in the employee lot. I'd gone to check on mine and Adam asked, "Being optimistic, are we?"

Dr. Novak smiled at me. "It'd be great if you'd take it. It's beautiful, just a little damaged. Susan doesn't have time to list it either." I knew Susan was Dr. Novak's gorgeous trophy wife.

I fired off questions: "What kind of car? How many miles? What's so wrong with it you can't trade it in? Forget the last question. If it looks good, I don't care."

Dr. Novak laughed. "It's a Lexus, only two years old. It was in an accident a few months ago, the frame got bent a little, but it runs great."

"How much are you asking?" I asked.

"Less than half what I paid."

"I'd love to see it." I sounded hopeful, and probably like a welfare recipient.

Adam and Kathy came in.

"Cassie is thinking about buying Dr. Novak's car," Dr. Boran said.

Adam patted my shoulder. "About time."

"If you ever decide to sell your car, Dr. Boran, let me know."

Kathy slicked her overly highlighted hair back dramatically. "I'd look pretty hot in that lipstick red Porsche." She turned to Adam. "Why don't you get rid of your Honda and get a Porsche? They're a real 'babe magnet.'" She grinned at Dr. Boran.

Adam rolled his eyes. "Thanks, Kathy." He leaned in to her raising his eyebrows. "I'll just get a penile implant instead."

Her flinch was almost imperceptible. My laugh was not.

Dr. Novak and I agreed to meet that evening at his house. My stomach churned, wondering how I was going to convince Mitch, but we'd probably never get an opportunity to buy a car like this again.

I called Mitch to tell him about our "appointment" with Dr. Novak.

"Cassie, your car runs fine."

"Come on, you know we need a better car. And Ashley will be driving soon."

He sighed. "I'll go look, but don't get your hopes up." His voiced was clipped, like a fish gasping on a hook. He was trying to get off the phone.

I wish I could buy it myself, I thought as I hung up. I dreamed of hopping in a shiny new car and take a solo road trip, checking off another bucket list item. But real life was demanding. I was juggling too many balls, and I feared if I miss one, it would land smack on my head. It was, however, a nice daydream.

I thought of the poor patient and her awful boyfriend, dashingly handsome, with that seductive French accent, lulling like a serpent. A wolf who only fed *his* needs. Her pain would be tough—losing the baby and dealing with that jerk. I hoped she'd have the strength to leave him.

I sighed. I wanted better control of my own life too—one I could write with a happy ending.

Wild Rose

— FROM CHAPTER 3

Rosemary cradled her Nikon squeezing off a few exposures. Maybe her photos would make a difference.

"Our clinic is usually their last stop."

Rosemary hadn't noticed Dr. Armand. He handed her a steaming cup of coffee.

She looked at the paper cup warily. "What's this?"

"It's my special brew—only coffee, though," Francois smiled. He directed her to a small clinic room. and pulled wax paper over a battered examining table.

She felt the paper crinkle under her as she sat.

"You're too beautiful to take such pictures," he said.

"I'm a photojournalist." She sipped the coffee. "This is delicious."

"French roast." He set his steaming cup on a stained, cluttered counter. "Rosemary, I am captivated by you. I'd never believed in love at first sight—until today." He took her cup and put it next to his.

She laughed and considered having a little fun. His eyes were deep and his dimples adorable. *Maybe I could teach him a few things.* "Why, Dr. Armand, you don't waste time." She glanced at her watch and thought she had time to find out.

"Please, call me Francois." His dark eyes sought hers as his mouth found her lips.

She took him in her arms, giving in to her curiosity. *He's* cute and sweet, she thought, but not my type for the long haul. She slipped his lab coat from his broad shoulders.

He seemed taken aback by her assertiveness, but let her take the lead.

She unbuttoned his shirt like picking petals from a flower and cupped his taut waist, teasing with her fingers.

He trembled at her touch. "Rosemary..." His hands danced quickly over her body as he hastily joined her on the table.

"Slow down, Romeo." She unzipped her jeans and invited him closer by wrapping her long legs around him.

He hurriedly tried to peel Rosemary's pants off. She kicked them off then opened his belt slowly sliding the supple leather out like an uncoiling cobra.

He began shaking with anticipation. "Faster!" he cried.

"We've just begun," she whispered in his ear, nibbling on a lobe.

Goosebumps raised the little hairs on his scalp. Rosemary thought it was cute.

"I can't stand it," he moaned, and scurried out of his pants.

Rosemary finished undressing and brought him to her. He was as excited as a puppy with a bone. A decent sized bone, Rosemary noted.

"Now, take me now," he whimpered, stroking and grabbing hastily.

Rosemary climbed aboard and encouraged him to find her sweet spot.

His movements became frantic. She was not ready for him to finish; he'd not even begun to satisfy her. She glanced at her watch again, wishing there was a second hand on it.

"Oh, Rosemary! I want you..." His bleating grated on her.

"Oh, oh…" His cry of desire turned to a cry of satisfaction.

Sighing and unfulfilled, Rosemary pushed off him and untangled from the waxy paper. She looked at Francois, who was gazing affectionately at her. "So, Francois, is your medical specialty anesthesia?"

"Why, yes. How did you know?"

"Call it a hunch." She picked up her clothes and dressed.

"You're amazing," he said. "We'll be great together."

She laughed. "Francois, I'm flattered. But this was just fun." She slipped her shirt on.

"That's all I am to you?" He tried to cover his nakedness with the crumpled paper.

"You're a nice guy, but I'm not ready for commitment." She grabbed his clothes, handing them to him.

"Please, give us a chance." He gazed longingly at her. "I need someone like you."

"Why don't you give me your number?" Rosemary said. "I'll call when I'm in town."

"You won't call." Shame clouded his eyes.

Rosemary slipped into her clothes, took her camera, and left him to dress. What was it with these needy guys? Smiling, she tried to imagine herself married to him. Of being tied down, changing dirty diapers and cooking while he was enjoying his career. Rosemary was sure kids would leave no time for her profession, and she'd lose all sense of herself. She wanted to take meaningful photographs—not family snapshots.

Chapter Seven

"You can't have everything. Where would you put it?"
~ Steven Wright

"MOM-MYYYY! Come quick!"

Gabby sounded panicked. I ran to her, not sure if it was a serious emergency or if her broccoli was touching her mashed potatoes.

"Gabs, where are you?" I shouted, ears and instinct perked in the direction her screams.

"In here. *Hurry!*" Frantic, I followed her voice to my bathroom and found her up to her elbows in my new makeup. "Don't I look like a princess?" she asked sweetly, posing at her reflection in the mirror.

Exasperated, I grabbed the blush and eye shadow out of her hand. "Gabby! I just bought this."

She had ground my new blush to a fine powder. It was all I could do not to scream. But as I watched her dancing and singing happily, I swallowed my anger. These were the moments in life that could go either way. I decided to let it go her way.

Ashley came in and laughed. "You are so toast, Gabby."

"Do me a favor and grab my phone, so I can take some pics," I asked.

"You're joking." She stood, arms crossed in front of her.

"If I had done something like this, you'd have grounded me for life."

"Don't you remember you did the same thing? Those pictures of you are in the blue photo album," I teased.

Granted, I was not happy about it. The credit card bill had just come in, and Mitch and I argued about the balance. But life was too short to make a bad situation worse. I opened my camera, thinking of Rosemary. She was the antithesis of me, a true artist who'd never reduce herself to family photography. I snapped a few frames of Gabby, who was more than willing to pose. Afterward, I scolded her about using my things, hoping I got the point across—at least until she found something else new and expensive to play with.

I made her scrub her face since we were going to Dr. Novak's house. I didn't want people to think I let my eight year old wear blush, smoky eye shadow, and Luscious Lover lipstick.

Mitch grumbled about going, but we piled the family into the van. I gave Gabby some cheese and crackers to keep her happy.

Reluctantly, Ashley crawled into the back seat. "This is *so* stupid. Why can't I stay home?"

"It's nice to have us all together," I said.

We drove into the beautiful neighborhood of Highland Park, where huge homes sat on tiny lots, towering trees lined the streets, and children ran and played outside. Ashley sat up a little straighter and took an interest in the setting.

"Can you imagine living here?" Mitch asked.

"Yeah, I can imagine." I played with a daydream of walking through one of these houses and calling it home.

"I wouldn't want to vacuum that house," Gabby said, looking at an exceptionally big Tudor.

I smiled. "Thanks for putting it in perspective."

"Don't be such a dweeb." Ashley sneered. "Anyone who lives there has lots of people to clean their houses."

Gabby's face lit up. "Do they live with the people? Could I have my own maid like a princess?"

"Ashley, can we please say nice things?" I glanced in the back.

She sank farther down in her seat but still looked out the window.

We pulled up into the drive of an elegant Georgian style home. I became self-conscious of our old dinged up van, imagining it lowering property values in the neighborhood.

I rang the bell, half expecting a butler. Instead, a cute boy about six or seven opened the door, took one look at us, and yelled, "Mom! It's for you." Guess he didn't want to play with us.

Susan Novak came to the door. Her blonde hair was colored to perfection, her legs and arms were well sculpted, and her smile was beautiful. I exercised, but still felt fat and sloppy next to her. *Those* could be Rosemary's arms and legs.

I sucked in my stomach and made a small, squeaky noise when I said, "We're here to look at the car that's for sale."

"Oh, sure, come in." She looked past us at our car in the drive.

"Aaron," she called. I expected to hear an echo. The home was lavish, but tasteful, like a page from *Architectural Digest*.

I wondered what our living room would look like painted

the soft seafoam green her room was, along with fresh cut flowers and light wood trim. I knew our house couldn't pull off the same elegant effect.

I'd have to find paint to match the stains on the carpet.

I introduced my family.

"It's nice to meet you." She held her hand out. Susan had a large, sparkly diamond that glittered as if alive. "You'll love the car," she said with a smile. "Aaron insisted we get all the bells and whistles on it."

I glanced at Ashley. She looked around in a state of awe, eyes glazed over like Gabby's watching morning cartoons. I was tempted to wipe drool off her dazed face.

Aaron Novak, holding a drink, appeared in the entry-way and introduced himself to Mitch. "Can I get you something?" He held up his glass. "Good whiskey. My favorite." He downed it in one gulp.

Mitch glanced my way. "No, thanks."

I hoped Novak wasn't planning on driving us.

Dr. Novak turned to Susan and handed her his empty glass. "Hit me again." He looked at Mitch. "Sure you don't want one?"

Mitch shook his head.

"Can I get you anything?" Susan asked as she headed to the kitchen. "Water? Soft drink?"

"No, thank you," I said.

Two kids peeked around a corner at us. Gabby smiled, waved, and asked to play. They obliged, and the kids ran off laughing.

Susan returned and handed her husband a fresh drink. Mitch and Dr. Novak talked about the car. She said she'd be happy to keep an eye on Gabby while we looked at the car.

"We don't really need a new car since ours is running just fine," Mitch said, arms crossed tight against his chest.

I jumped in. "Well, I'd like something safer to drive my children in," I said, my eyes shooting daggers at Mitch.

"It would be really cool to have a Lexus," Ashley swooned. "I'm getting my license soon."

We followed Dr. Novak to the garage. He was telling Mitch about car stuff: horsepower, RPMs, drive shafts. When we saw the car, I smiled. Ashley put a hand to her mouth, and her eyes lit up like dancing fireflies. The car was shiny, black, and absolutely immaculate. I could picture Gabby's cheese and cracker crumbs wedged deep in the seams of the leather interior.

"Oh, wow," I said stupidly.

"Can we take it for a drive?" Ashley asked.

"Sure," Dr. Novak said, chewing a chunk of ice. "Let me get the keys." He walked inside.

"I don't want him driving us," I whispered. "Not after having at least two drinks."

"I'll test drive it, but don't get your hopes up." Mitch looked at me sternly. "We can't afford it. You know Ashley's going to college in a few years."

"And I'll be driving in less than a year!" She sparkled almost as much as the car.

"Oh, come on, where else can we find a Lexus at this price? And we can keep the van for Ash."

"Daddy, please. It's beautiful," Ashley gushed. "Can I drive this instead? There's no way I'm driving a minivan to school."

"No," Mitch and I said simultaneously.

Aaron came back with keys and another fresh drink. "Why don't the four of us go? Susan said the kids are no problem."

I didn't know Susan, but I hoped she wasn't drinking like Aaron.

A young male voice yelled from inside. "Hey, whose heap is that in our driveway?"

I heard Susan shush him.

A handsome teenager stuck his head into the garage and waved. "Hey." He flipped a shock of hair off his face.

"The heap is ours," I said, oddly embarrassed. "We're here to look at the Lexus." Why was I uncomfortable talking to a teenager? I got in the back with Ashley.

As Novak introduced us to his older son, Andrew, Ashley's eyes widened.

Andrew looked in the back seat and seemed surprised to see Ashley. "Hey, I know you. You're in my English class."

"We go to the same school," Ashley said quietly.

"Oh, you go to Constantine High?" Aaron asked Ashley.

"Yes, sir," she answered.

Highland Park, the Novaks' neighborhood school district, was considered one of the best in Texas, whereas our school's unofficial nickname was Constant High. I wondered why Andrew went there.

"Andrew's mom lives in the Constantine district," Novak answered my unasked question. "We'd love for him to go to our excellent public school, but neither he nor his mom wants to change now that he's in high school," he said. "Ashley, do you go to the football games?" Aaron puffed out like a peacock. "I'm sure you've seen Andrew play. He's the quarterback."

I noticed Andrew didn't know Ashley's name, and it bothered me. He looked like the typical high school jock, sure of himself, the kind of kid who picked girls off him like lint.

"I'm sure you're very proud," I said to Dr. Novak. "Do you want to go for a drive with us?" I asked Andrew, biting back a snarky tone. *Or do you want to take that "heap" in the driveway and let your friends see you in it.* I couldn't help but hope his first car was a real clunker. But I knew it would be better than one we could afford. It broke my heart we'd probably never be able to buy our girls new wheels.

"Nah, I'll go see what Susan's up to," he said, ducking out as fast as he had come in.

Ashley appeared uncomfortable. She wouldn't look at Andrew as she sat in the back seat. Ashley had been a gifted soccer player, and many coaches tried to recruit her for club teams. But Mitch and I found it difficult to get her to practices and games with our busy work schedules. She had to give up something she loved, While I knew Andrew would be handed anything he wanted. I sighed. He was from a broken home and, considering how his dad was snarfing down whiskey, maybe his life wasn't all that great either.

I was tempted to ask Ashley about him but decided to wait. Maybe I could offer some sage mommy advice. I looked at her beautiful profile and wished she'd ask me questions about growing up, about life. Would she even listen? I wasn't sure.

Novak guzzled his third drink and set the glass on a well organized shelf in the garage. He and Mitch got in the front seat. Ashley and I ran our hands over the leather in the back.

As we drove through the neighborhood, Mitch's attention turned to the numerous buttons and switches, not paying close attention to the road. I wanted to enjoy the ride, but since Mitch was distracted, I made sure to watch the road for him. I felt better knowing that if we were going head on into an accident, I'd get a good look at it.

"Step on the gas," Novak told him.

Mitch did, and the car accelerated so fast I felt the skin on my face stretch back. I could almost feel my lips flapping from the g-forces. "Mitch! Slow down," I gasped.

"Cool, Dad, do it again." Ashley sat up, excited.

"No, don't," I said. "We won't be going that fast in it anyway."

Everybody laughed at me and Mitch became animated. He dropped his voice and started asking questions. I heard a dollar amount. I shook the g-forces off and listened.

Ashley and I looked at each other, crossing our fingers at the same time. They talked about the accident the car had been in and the issue of the reconditioned title. Novak dropped the price, and before I knew it, they were shaking hands. I swear I heard a chorus of angels singing "Hallelujah!"

When we got back to the house, I looked for Gabby. Andrew seemed the type to kick small children out of his path, but when we walked into the house, the kids were happily playing in the den. Andrew was nowhere to be seen.

Susan came in from the kitchen. "How'd it go?" She bent over to pick up some toys, and Novak smacked her butt.

"Did these shorts shrink, or are you putting on the pounds?" He laughed and elbowed Mitch. "Gotta keep on them, or they'll let themselves go."

Susan's face reddened, and she held the toys close to her.

She turned to me, ignoring her husband. "I hope you liked the car." She fought to stay composed.

"I—I think we made a deal," I said. I had a hard time looking her in the eye.

She nodded. "That's great. You'll enjoy it."

I didn't know what to say. I looked at Mitch to check out his reaction to the butt slap, but he was turned away from me.

Novak leaned toward Mitch. "God knows I've put enough money into that body, so she better keep it up." He laughed then grabbed her arm playfully. "I love ya, honey."

He tried to kiss her, but she pushed him away and left the room, still hugging the toys.

Ashley came into the room, breaking the tension. "I'll wait in the van."

I went to the playroom to get Gabby. "It's time to go." I gave her "the eye" when she protested, begging for five more minutes. I had to drag her out.

We finally got into our heap and headed home. Gabby asked when we could go back and play with her new friends. Ashley sat quietly in the back. Was it because of Andrew, or had she heard Novak's comments to his wife?

"Is Andrew a friend of yours?" I asked.

"No. He's a nobody," she answered.

"What do you mean a nobody?" Mitch chimed in. "He plays football, doesn't he? When I was in high school, anybody who played football was somebody. And always popular. What kind of girls am I raising here?"

I wanted to tell Mitch to stop. Sometimes his sarcasm bit. She'd never open up to us if we made her feel bad about her friends.

"I guess you don't hang out with him, huh?" I asked.

"No. Okay. I hardly even know him. We don't have the same friends." Ashley made it clear she did not want to talk about him or anything else. She clammed up in her usual curled position in the back seat.

I couldn't help but worry. She was a beautiful girl, but being fifteen was difficult. There was impending womanhood, her body dealing with change, and the independence of knowing it all, when "all" was such a smaller world than what was really out there. She was hitting the best years of her life, though she'd be in her thirties before she realized it.

I wanted to scoop Ashley up in my arms and have her talk to me the way she used to, when she would prattle on about life and clouds and rainbows. When Santa was real, and on Christmas Eve, she would be too excited to sleep, knowing he was going to swoop down our chimney bearing gifts. I missed the magic in her smile when I would pick her up from school, and she'd be excited for me to see the crayon drawing of her family wadded in her sticky hand. Now, I was on the outside looking in.

Mitch derailed my thoughts. "What do you think about the car?"

"I'm thrilled. It just hasn't sunk in," I smiled. "It still seems like a dream. I don't want to get too excited until the inspection."

"We're going to have to cut back on expenses," Mitch warned.

I considered Mitch's spotty, shrinking paychecks and hoped we could afford it. I thought of Susan Novak. Saving money probably never crossed her mind, although I wondered what price she paid living with Aaron Novak. "We'll have to take our lunches to school and work," Mitch said, addressing the girls in the rearview mirror.

"I'll starve before I brown bag it," Ashley said. "Or maybe I'll just bring a stupid Smurf lunch box. That'll crush any chance of making friends."

"You can borrow my Hello Kitty lunch box. That's cool, right?" Gabby asked, seeming concerned for her big sis.

So these were the outside influences we had to deal with. It didn't seem so long ago when Gabby sat on my lap while we watched *Sesame Street*. At first, I thought I'd throw up listening to those syrupy songs while watching the kids overact. But before I knew it, I'd catch myself at work singing the bouncy songs, feeling all happy and gooey inside. *Why can't we hold on to those years?*

Mitch laughed. "I'm sure the babes are going to be hanging off the car when they see me in it."

"Well, what are you going to do when you drive the van? Head to a trailer park?"

"Look, I wouldn't trade you in just 'cause you're old and dinged up." Mitch looked at me, almost seriously. "And you *are* getting to be higher maintenance than you used to be." Then he laughed.

Did he think that was funny?

Chapter Eight

"Life is what happens when you're busy making other plans."
~*John Lennon*

I often feel as if my life revolves around the expiration dates on a milk carton. I wondered if, on my epitaph, I'd be remembered by how many rolls of toilet paper I'd bought or how many loads of laundry I'd done.

With the bustle of the ER behind me, I sat at my desk and gazed at the flat matte wall, imagining I was behind the wheel of the new car. My thoughts shifted to how life could have been different if I had only made some changes along the way. If I'd known how seemingly small decisions would set life's course, I'd have spent more time thinking and less time jumping. Maybe even realizing my dreams of being a writer. I loved writing, but that dream got shot down because it wasn't practical.

From my briefcase, I pulled out my revised chapters. Wanting to go over Christine's feedback. Rosemary was becoming real to me. Now, when faced with a decision, I'd wonder what Rosemary would do. Maybe I was becoming delusional.

Kathy stuck her head in my office, and I surreptitiously covered the papers.

"We're pretty slow. I'm heading to the cafeteria for lunch."

"Who else is here to cover?"

"Well...you."

"Let's schedule a time for your review."

Kathy shrugged and walked out.

I hated the thought of confrontation. I knew all she'd do is blame everybody else for her shortcomings.

"Cass, line one." Gail's voice came through the intercom. "It's your mom."

"Okay, thanks, Gail."

"Hi, Mom." I leaned back in my chair. "What's going on?"

"I just got off the phone with your sister, and she told me you're buying a new car. Was I going to be the last to know?"

The love triangle seemed to work this way: I called my sister, Brenda, she called Mom, and Mom called me.

"Mom, I was going to call, but it got too late."

"So what did you have to do to get Mitch to agree?"

"Mom, I can make my own decisions," I said indignantly.

She laughed. "I'm glad for you. You deserve so much more," she said, sighing. "I just want you to be happy."

Mom still felt guilty that, as a single mother, she couldn't provide Brenda or me with extras, though she would gladly give us the shirt off her back—and had tried on many occasions. When Brenda or I complimented her on a new outfit, her first reaction was to start undressing. "Oh, do you like it? Here, it's yours."

"Mom, you know me too well."

"I know, dear. I'm a mother. That's my job. Now put Gail back on the phone. I have some information for her."

"What kind of information?"

"An herb for infertility. I told her I'd check into it for her."

"You're giving medical advice to our employees? Mom, I could get into trouble, especially if she keels over with a re-action. Please, don't embarrass me."

"Loosen up, Cassie. Gail's a sweetheart. Maybe you should spend a little more time with the people you work with. Sometimes you come across as a bit of a snob."

"Mom!"

"I know you're exhausted, working as much as you do and trying to keep up with the girls and their schedules. But I'd like to see you enjoy life, too."

I thought of Rosemary and her gusto for life. "I do, Mom."

"You should put yourself first more often."

"You're one to talk." Mom was famous for offering help to anyone. Always thinking of others before herself. She couldn't pass a homeless person or a stray animal without feeding them. She made friends everywhere she went.

"Let me speak to Gail, please."

"So, what is this magic herb?" I asked.

"It's a combination of plants that will help clear out im-purities in the blood."

"Mom, where do you find this stuff? And are you still drinking that awful box wine?"

"Yes, but don't get on me about it right now. I'm not in the mood."

"You're never in the mood," I whined.

She devoured tofu, juiced, and insisted on organic veg-etables. She took megadoses of vitamins and chugged pro-tein shakes, but she could go through that cheap, sugary vino like water.

"Are you going to transfer me to Gail, or will I have to call back?" Mom asked, peeved that I mentioned her "cardbordeaux" habit.

"Hang on, but call me later," I said as I transferred her. I wondered what else they talked about. Knowing Mom, she probably told Gail all my embarrassing childhood stories.

I snuck around to the triage area, so I could steal a glance at Gail, who was laughing heartily on the phone. Adam stood over her desk. "Is that Cassie's mom? I need to talk to her too."

I headed to the admissions desk behind Gail, who must have transferred Mom to Adam since she was no longer on the phone. Dr. Sandoval sat nearby, charting in a computer. She was my favorite person in the ER, a single mom in her late 40s, raising two daughters by herself. One was already in college and the other a high school senior. We often commiserated about the joys of working and parenting and finding time for life.

"Anything interesting?" I asked, even though as the supervisor, it was my job to know.

"No. It's pretty slow." Dr. Sandoval looked up. "What's up with you?"

I sat next to her. "I just got off the phone with my mom. It seems all the employees here have a relationship with her. She's giving Gail fertility advice, then Adam wanted to talk to her—about what, I don't know. I mean, she couldn't even tell me about the birds and the bees when I was a kid."

"Everybody loves your mom. Oh, do me a favor and thank her for that great crumb cake recipe she emailed me. I made it for my girls, and they loved it. They couldn't even taste the chia and flax in it."

"She's sharing recipes with you?" I was dumbfounded. Mom was more connected to the staff than I was. I leaned close to Dr. Sandoval. "Hey, how well do you know Aaron Novak?"

She looked up from the computer. "Professionally, I've known him for years. He's the type who'd sell his mother if she'd bring a good price." She looked at me quizzically. "Why?"

"We just bought a car from him."

She raised her eyebrows. "Make sure you get it inspected. I'm not sure I'd trust him."

"It's at the car doc now." I put a stack of papers in neat piles. "Have you met his wife?"

"Sure. Susan, right?" She continued charting as she spoke.

"Yeah. She looks like a Barbie doll, store bought, if you know what I mean." I was being catty.

"I've only met her a few times, but I remember thinking she's way too pretty for him. He's balding, overweight, and in desperate need of a back wax." She shivered dramatically.

"Dr. Novak did something weird." I told her how he smacked Susan's butt and said she'd been putting on weight. "She's perfect and seems to have everything. When he did that in front of us, it gave me the creeps."

"Who knows what she sees in him?" Dr. Sandoval shrugged. "But think about it. She stays home with two young children. What would she do if she left him? Get a job and an apartment? Try to make ends meet and support her family with who knows what kind of job?" She looked up from her computer. "Or she can stay with him and take care of the kids that way."

I hadn't thought of that. "Maybe she's living in a different kind of prison."

Dr Sandoval nodded. "I hope she's happy, but—" She grimaced. "—getting between the sheets with him..." She put her hand up and laughed. "No, thank you."

"Don't take me there."

We both giggled.

Gail called for Dr. Sandoval. "CT's on the phone with a stat report."

"Thanks, I'll take it in my office." She grabbed her laptop and stood to leave. "You know, Susan may look like she has it all, but you couldn't pay me enough to put up with him."

The car passed inspection. The mechanic found the bent frame, but it was minor. So now the Lexus sat gleaming in our driveway. Gabby and Ashley walked around the car, admiring it. Gabby jumped up and down. Ashley nodded, and said, "Yeah, I'll look real good in this when I get my license."

Mitch came outside, dangling the keys. "C'mon, gorgeous, Rocky Piston wants to take you drag racing." He spoke with such fun in his eyes I smiled. He winked at the girls. "You two chicks hop in back."

Ashley and Gabby scrambled into the back seat.

"I love the smell of leather," Ashley breathed, as she buckled herself in.

I turned and smiled. "A step up from the vinyl and velour in our old car, huh?"

"We have new rules in this car," Mitch said. "No food or drinks, muddy shoes, or even dirty underwear. If you're not wearing clean undies, then you can't ride in the new car."

The girls giggled.

"I guess that means I get to drive it more than you," I said.

"Not necessarily, 'cause I'm not wearing any!" he answered.

I glanced at the girls. "Mitch," I warned.

Ashley looked genuinely disgusted. "Gross, Dad!"

"Can I take my underwear off?" Gabby asked.

"No!" we all yelled.

I thought about our early, pre-kid years, making love, whenever, wherever we wanted. Now we hid sex from the kids. The open mind of my youth closed when I started having children. I looked at Mitch and remembered his wicked smile and devil-may-care attitude. When Mitch and I first met, we were madly in love and needed little—just love and an unmade bed. Pregnancy changed the world for us. Suddenly, a home with a good school district was more important than a small apartment with macramé window coverings, or making love in the efficiency sized kitchen. Now the kitchen was bigger and the sex efficient.

Pulling out of our driveway, I hoped the neighbors were outside, so they could see our new car. My thoughts turned to Rosemary. She'd attract attention zipping around in her cute MG, the car a mere accessory to her stunning beauty. I rolled down my window and flipped my hair back, letting the wind blow through it, pretending, for a carefree moment, to be someone else. I drank in the moment and savored the breeze until Ashley grumbled at me to roll the window up.

Wild Rose

— FROM CHAPTER 4

Rosemary sped out of the clinic's lot and threw the crumpled slip of paper with François's number into the back seat, hoping the wind would pick it up and toss it out. Her needs were too insatiable to be quelled by his quick finish. Imagine a future after just one roll. Rosemary laughed.

At a stoplight, she checked her image in the rearview mirror. Her hair was tousled in a tangled ball from the clinical roll. With a deft toss of her head, her silky tresses fell perfectly into place. Satisfied, she put her car into gear and screeched off. Fog settled over the Santa Barbara evening. Rosemary hoped to meet Richard for dinner. She was famished and her brief, disappointing interlude with François had left her hungry, craving more.

Rosemary wondered if Richard had changed much since he moved here to finish his residency. Their romantic trysts during their days at UCLA would have won gold medals. He was pre-med and she studied fine arts. She discovered her love for photography, and he discovered his love for anatomy.

She pulled in to a 7-11 to use the payphone. Hoping Richard had received her earlier message.

Rosemary dialed, not sure he'd be there since it was close

to six o'clock.

He answered on the first ring.

"Recognize a voice from the past?" Rosemary asked.

"'A Rose is a Rose is a Rose.'" He quoted the Gertrude Stein poem. "I've been waiting for your call."

"I had a shoot in your lovely city today." Rosemary paused, thinking of François. "How's your residency?"

"Busy as ever. I've decided to become a plastic surgeon."

"Plastics? I thought you were doing general surgery."

"Actually, you're the reason I switched."

"Me? Why?"

"Can you meet me tonight? I'll explain then."

"What's this? A lonely doctor in need of a patient?" Rosemary chided.

"It's been a long time. I've missed you."

"Not that long. Remember our moonlight skinny dip at Big Sur? We lost ourselves under the stars."

"How could I forget? I look at the pictures often."

"As long as they're not hanging on the walls of your office for all to see, I'm flattered."

"I do use them at work, but it's not the real thing."

"Use them?"

"Never mind. Like I said, I'll explain later."

Rosemary's stomach growled. "How about dinner?"

"Okay. But let's meet near my office, we can come here after."

Rosemary decided she needed a hearty meal in case dinner turned into an all nighter, although twice in one day on a clinic bed didn't appeal to her.

He gave her directions and begged her to hurry.

Chapter Nine

"Without Elvis, none of us could have made it."
~ *Buddy Holly*

I sat in my office as Christine leaned on the doorjamb, fanning open the new chapters I'd given her.

"Cassie, this is a little too tongue and cheek. Rosemary's nothing but a ball breaker. Are you looking for campy?"

I shrugged. "Too much?"

"Maybe a little. There are plot formulas you should stick to. You don't want to offend your readers." She flipped through the pages. "You know, I could really psychoanalyze you after reading this."

"Don't take the fun out of it. And what makes you such the expert on writing?"

"I've done research on the romance biz. Remember? I got into psychology so I could analyze characters. The DSM is my bible."

I smirked. The Diagnostic and Statistical Manual of Mental Disorders had always been her favorite read. She categorized our high school population with it.

"Uh-oh," I said. Over Christine's shoulder, I saw the hospital's administrative assistant, Nelda Stucko, marching toward my office. Nelda was five feet and 200 pounds of pure stock. She walked like a soldier and wore pantyhose two sizes too small.

I was afraid she might spontaneously combust from the friction the nylons created when she walked.

She loved the power she wielded, and she treated Ron Starnes, the administrator, as if he built the hospital himself, brick by brick.

Christine, who was an independent employee, tried to avoid confrontation with her. "Call me later and we'll talk. I'm outta here." She rolled the papers in her hand and acknowledged Nelda with a nod as she ducked out.

Nelda stopped and pointed to the papers in Christine's hand. "Dr. Taylor, I hope that's your speech for our next medical conference. You know Mr. Starnes likes to read the material before it's presented."

Christine glanced at me slyly.

"I'll be happy to give them to him." Nelda's pudgy fingers opened.

Christine slowly opened the stack of papers and began to hand them to Nelda. I held my breath.

"They're not quite ready yet." Christine rolled the papers again and stifled a laugh. "I'll email him later." She waved at me with a wink and hastily took off.

Nelda turned her attention to me. "Mr. Starnes saw one of your patients at a party last night. He was *not* pleased about the service here." She gave her tight skirt a tug. "It was Benjamin Bennett. He was here with his girlfriend."

I recalled the two timing jerk.

"He said the nursing staff kept them waiting and were rude to him. Mr. Starnes was put on the spot, and he hates that." Nelda's frosted highlights glowed green in the fluorescent lights.

I groaned inwardly. "I'm sorry. I wasn't at the cocktail party. I could have told my side of the awful story."

"Cassie, don't be sarcastic." Nelda's face scrunched when she talked. "Mr. Starnes wanted me to bring this to your attention so you'll be more considerate to our patients. I'll let him know we've had our little talk."

With that, she turned on her plump heel and started to march out, but turned and said, "Oh, and don't forget the Joint Commission inspection. Make sure you memo Mr. Starnes with your patient information. You know how important it is for our hospital to keep its high rating."

I took a deep breath. I was running out of time to do my daily work, much less the multitude of reports I needed to turn in before I picked up the girls. The Rolling Stones' "Nineteenth Nervous Breakdown" ran though my head. I spent the next thirty minutes working on the memo for the Joint Commission's inspection. I'd been spending too much time on Rosemary's story instead of doing my job. I needed to focus, to buckle down—so I went to get coffee. As usual, most of the staff was in the kitchen.

"This was the greatest restaurant," Dr. Sandoval was telling Jennifer Cho. "I begged for the recipe, but they wouldn't give me even the slightest hint what was in this dish."

"What's the name of this place?" Jennifer asked, looking at her iPhone.

"Desiree's," Dr. Sandoval answered.

Jennifer punched at her keyboard. "I'll get you the recipe."

"Hello, this is Jennifer Cho from Community Hospital. I have a patient here who's suffered a severe allergic reaction after eating at your restaurant. She had the chicken special. Could you quickly tell me what the ingredients are?" Jennifer winked at Dr. Sandoval.

Dr. Sandoval had to cover her mouth not to laugh. I rolled my eyes. "Don't get us in trouble," I whispered.

"Okay, uh huh, curry and garlic... Slow down, please; I'm writing these down," Jennifer said. "Yes, she'll be okay, but I need to be accurate and make sure I get all the ingredients." Jennifer rolled her eyes. "Look, we haven't ruled out food poisoning yet," she said threateningly.

"I saw trouble with a capital Nappy Nelda in your office. What's up?" Dr. Sandoval asked me.

"We had a patient the other day who complained about our service. A guy whose girlfriend was losing a baby while he was setting a date with another woman." I sighed. "Starnes only heard one side of the story. The guy was a toad."

"Sometimes it's hard to maintain a neutral tone with patients like that. Starnes's job is to keep the finances up, and your job is patient care. It's ugly, but sometimes we have to kiss the ass we examine."

"Thank you for that."

Jennifer hung up the phone and turned with a triumphant smile, waving a piece of paper, and told Dr. Sandoval the ingredients in the recipe. "I wasn't able to get how much of each ingredient, but I got what was in it. You'll have to experiment."

Adam came in. "Hey, am I the only one working around here? We have patients in the waiting room, and I could really use some help."

"Is Kathy working?" I asked.

"Yeah, on the same one for over an hour," Adam answered.

"Do you need my help?" I asked.

"No, if we can just get Jen out of the kitchen for a change," he said jokingly.

"Shut up! I was doing Dr. Sandoval a favor." She explained the story to Adam as they walked out, laughing.

"Sometimes I feel so disconnected," I said to Dr. Sandoval, watching Jennifer and Adam leave. "I miss the patient care and camaraderie with everyone."

Dr. Sandoval laughed. "Being a working parent and a supervisor can spread you pretty thin."

I sat at the table and wiped some crumbs to the floor. "If I'm not careful, something's going to fall through the cracks."

"I know. Most of the time I feel like I'm forgetting something."

"You?" I asked, surprised. "You always seem so organized."

"It's all smoke and mirrors. I guess I'd better hit the trenches too," Dr. Sandoval said. "Boran is in radiology checking on some films."

Chapter Ten

"Success always occurs in private, and failure in full view."
~ *Murphy's Law*

Had I known how bad the next day was going to be, I would have stayed in bed with the covers up to my ears. Mitch and Gabby left early to celebrate "Donuts with Daddy" at her school. When Ashley and I got into the new car, she slunk down in the front seat, quiet and distant. Reaching over, she turned the radio to an awful rap station. I gritted my teeth and swallowed my criticism. I remembered when my mother berated the music I listened to as a teenager. I swore I would never do that to my child.

"So what are you working on in school?" I yelled over the racket.

"I don't know," she shrugged. "Just school stuff."

"What's your favorite class?" My words sounded stilted, as if making small talk with a stranger.

"Why? Can I listen to this song?" She shot me a look, turned, and stared out the window, unwilling to discuss her day-to-day activities with the one person who loved her more than anybody. I would gladly lay down my life for her, yet I was sure I would still manage to embarrass her by whatever dying words I chose. As I stared ahead at the traffic, I felt the wrench of Janis Joplin's "Take a Little Piece of My Heart." Now *that* was music.

As we neared the school, Ashley pointed to an intersection a block away from the sprawling campus.

"You can drop me off at that corner."

"Honey, I'll be happy to take you to the front. Don't you want people to see our really cool car?" I smiled, wishing she would too. "If you want, I'll duck way down so none of your friends can see me."

"No." Not even a smile. "Just drop me here."

I pulled to the curb, noting a police officer monitoring the school zone. I was sure the high school kids who drove loved to see his radar gun pointing at them.

As Ashley opened the door, a new red BMW drove through the speed trap. The young driver arrogantly waved at the police officer.

"Hey, isn't that Andrew, Dr. Novak's son?" I asked.

She glanced indifferently at the sleek car. "Yeah, so?"

"If he's in your English class, he must be the same age as you. How can he drive?"

She gathered her books. "I don't know. He's probably flunked a few times. Or started kindergarten when he was ten." She started to open her door. "I'll go home with Teresa today, so I'll call you later." She managed an entire sentence with no inflection whatsoever.

"Hey, look, Ash. The news is shooting something here." The Channel 11 news truck was parked in front of the school, and a reporter I recognized from TV was talking to a cameraman. "I wonder what's going on."

She shrugged, "Who knows? We all probably flunked the state test or something."

"Why don't you go to the after school program and get your homework done? Dad or I will pick you up there."

"Mom, I'm fifteen. Dorks go to aftercare. I'll do my homework in study hall and be home by six."

"Ashley, I don't know Teresa's parents well, so I—"

"Well, I know them. Her mom's there, so it's cool. I gotta go." Ashley jumped out, slammed the door, and took off without even a wave goodbye.

"I love you, Ashley," I said to myself as I watched her walk away, hating the void between us and jealous of Teresa's stay-at-home mom.

When she reached the school property, a young man with long, dark hair and low slung jeans fell in step with her. I saw her glance over her shoulder at me. From a distance, I couldn't tell if the boy had any tattoos or piercings, only that he didn't look like the type of person I wanted Ashley to hang with. Actually, nobody was good enough for my girls, but I worried about who her friends were.

Before I pulled into traffic, I reached for my purse in the back seat and, to my horror, a giant cockroach flew from somewhere. Like radar, my peripheral vision had identified it in a split second. My nemesis—the cockroach. And it was on me, or near me. I had to escape. I jumped from the car, screeching and thrashing as the police officer approached, radar gun in hand.

"Ma'am." He reached toward me. "Calm down, ma'am."

"A roach!" I tripped and almost fell in the street.

"Roach?"

I tried to explain, but I looked down and saw the bug on my leg. I shrieked and kicked. I must've kicked the cop because he grabbed his knee and doubled over. "Are you nuts?" he said through gritted teeth.

"There's a roach—" I tried to say, working to keep my balance.

"Are you high, lady?"

"No! Bug!" I stamped and danced to make sure the critter was off me.

"You just kicked a police officer," he gasped, rubbing his leg, his radar gun pointed toward me like he intended to clock my dance. Traffic had come to a stop.

Cockroaches were the one thing I was absolutely phobic about. Ever since Girl Scout camp when a roach crawled up my leg. The zipper to my sleeping bag stuck and I panicked, much to the delight of the troop. They wanted to award me with a special patch—the "Big Bad Bug Badge."

I hopped and squirmed, afraid to look in the car. I'm sure I looked like someone who couldn't decide whether to pee or disco twerk in the street. Then I saw it. The roach was crawling up the officer's sleeve. I screamed and hit his arm.

"Hands against the car, lady." In one step, he was on me.

"What?" I shot my arm up. Before I could say anything, he shoved me hard against my car. Panicked, I tried to push him off.

"Don't resist." The radar gun dropped to the street. The digital readout flashed a pair of zeros. "You attacked a police officer," he said through gritted teeth.

"What are you doing?" I shrieked, my words slurring because my face was plastered against the window. "There was a cockroach in my car." It sounded like "Hersha cokrosh insh my urr." With my unsmushed eye, through the car window, I could see the news crew watching and kids encircling. "Robocop" wrenched my arms together painfully. I heard a click as handcuffs squeezed my wrists.

I took a deep, shaky breath and tried to enunciate my words. "There was a cockroach on me."

His grip loosened a smidge.

"It fell in my lap." I tried to turn my head to regain lip function.

"A cockroach?" The officer stepped back but kept an arm on my back. "You wigged out and kicked me because of a bug?"

"Yes." The window was slimy with drool.

Ashley had slowly ventured back to the scene. "Mom?" She looked scared.

I was able to raise my head now that the officer had backed off a bit. "I'm okay, honey. A misunderstanding."

Still handcuffed, I turned and faced the officer. "Take these things off me!" I glanced at Ashley.

She looked mortified, quickly spun around, and ran toward school, her posture stiff and unnatural.

The officer shook his head. "A little high-strung?" He turned to the crowd and told them to go on about their business as he took the cuffs off.

"*Me* high-strung?" He was armed, and his muscles bulged under his uniform, so I tried to keep smart remarks to myself. "Look, I may have freaked, but *you* handcuffed me. I hate cockroaches."

"Yes, ma'am, I can see that."

Andrew Novak and his friends were laughing and whooping at the scene, while Ashley ran for cover. "I thought we already worked the 'bugs' out of the car," Andrew yelled.

I looked up to see Ashley retreat into one of the side doors. The hippie boy she met earlier followed behind her. To make matters worse, Tina Arpino drove up and asked if there was anything she could do to help.

"No thanks," I said. "There was a giant cockroach in my car. I'm sure it's waiting for me to get back in, so it can scare me again."

"Cassie, maybe you should get out of the street," Miss Logical said. "The traffic is backed up."

"Good idea," the officer said. He looked at Tina and rolled his eyes. "I'll take a look to make sure it's all safe."

I glared at him. "Don't make me look crazy. You threw me against the car and shackled me."

Before he let me go, he took my driver's license and wrote down my information. "Everything looks okay now. Why don't you go on your way? And have a nice day, ma'am."

He held my car door open for me, and I had no choice but to get in. I feared the roach had crawled back and was waiting to jump me as soon as I started driving. I took off nervously and drove to the nearest store to buy Raid, where I did my best to fumigate the car.

My new car smelled of pesticide. I drove with the windows down. My hair was completely wind whipped by the time I got to work.

Chapter Eleven

"Laugh and the world laughs with you.
Cry and the world laughs louder."
~ Anonymous

"Cassie, where have you been?" Adam scolded as I raced into the ER. "We have a school bus accident on the way in."

"Sorry, rough morning." I said, still upset.

Adam turned his nose up. "What perfume are you wearing? It smells like Raid."

No sooner had I put my stuff down than the victims of the school bus accident arrived. Fourteen children with various injuries. We stabilized the more serious and sent two kids to Children's Hospital.

It broke my heart to work on children. I thought of the parents who would get the awful phone call that would change everything. I said a silent prayer as the two were taken from the ER to the ambulance.

Dr. Boran and Dr. Sandoval assessed and treated the others. The team was on top of the emergency. We tended to a broken arm, lots of stitches, a bloody nose, contusions, and scrapes, but mostly we just held everyone together by letting them know they were all right.

Problems started when the kids who were not hurt decided to explore a working ER. We found two kids playing hide-and-seek with the linen cart. An eight year old boy had blown up a latex glove and was making flatulence noises by slowly letting the air out of it. Then he went in and told a young girl who was waiting for stitches in her head he overheard the doctors saying her brain had fallen out and they were looking for another one to sew in.

We finally got the two off the linen cart and into a room, where they decided to play "push the crash cart into each other."

You would think a group of professionals could handle the rampage, but trying to treat, comfort, call the parents, and move other patients in and out made it impossible to supervise all the kids.

The tip of the insanity came when the flatulence kid and another troublemaker ran into a room where a geriatric patient was sleeping on a stretcher. One of the boys screamed, "A dead body!"

The elderly woman sat up and screamed, "Where?" She held her sheet to her chin, looking scared out of her Depends.

I grabbed the two kids by the collars of their shirts. While I was trying to round up the other "injured" kids, Mr. Starnes strode into the ER with a group of important looking people, bragging about our efficient Emergency Services. Nappy Nelda waddled close by.

She looked full of herself, having squeezed all size twenty into a size fourteen, brightly colored silk suit. There I stood with the kids, some bandaged, some with dried blood on them, and one having used a roll of gauze to wrap himself like a mummy. There were supplies and linens scattered everywhere. Nelda looked smug, as if this was exactly what she expected.

"Cassie," Mr. Starnes stopped his conversation mid-sentence. "What happened here?"

"There was a bus accident. I'm just making sure the kids are all right," I said, tightening my grip on the ringleader. "I was taking them into a room to treat their boo-boos." I smiled sweetly at the obstreperous group and gripped tighter on their collars, praying they didn't turn blue and pass out.

"Well, don't let us stop you," Mr. Starnes said curtly.

I marched the kids over the ransacked sheets into an exam room. As we passed the room with the young girl getting stitches, we heard her wailing to Dr. Sandoval, "Did they find my brain yet?"

The two boys in the front snickered but shut up when I gave them a don't-even-think-about-it look. I overheard Mr. Starnes excuse himself from the group, and I held my breath as he strode over to me.

I shoved the last of the kids into the room and ordered them to sit quietly and not touch anything. I shut the door and turned to Starnes.

"Cassandra, can you please tell me what's going on?" he hissed. "It looks like the bus crashed in here. I'm taking the Joint Commission staff through the hospital today. You were supposed to have this place cleaned up and tour ready."

Great. *That* memo was probably under a stack of papers on my desk.

"I'm sorry, Mr. Starnes. We were treating the more seriously injured, and a few of the less injured kids took advantage of the situation. I have it under control now."

I glanced behind me at the room the kids were in, praying they weren't playing with the defibrillator.

"How do you expect us to get any funding if we can't treat and control the few patients we have now?" He looked around at the mess.

I loved his interpretation of a "few patients." *He* didn't treat them. He was never around when we were short staffed due to budget cuts.

"Where is the dead body? Don't leave me alone!" The elderly woman wailed from the room next to us.

"What dead body is she referring to?" Starnes jerked his pinhead in the general direction of the voice. "Are there more surprises in store for us?"

"No, sir. There's no body, just some traumatized kids." I backed toward the exam room door. "I should be getting back to them."

"Please do, Ms. Calabria, but I intend to visit with you again about this." He marched toward the group of suits. A few were scribbling furiously on clipboards.

Adam came out of an exam room and asked if I would take the history and physical of a patient.

"Sure, but first let me get these kids under control. Have their parents been called?"

"Gail was helping a school official make the calls. I think they've managed to contact everybody," he said.

"Thanks. Then tell your patient I'll be in there in a sec." I headed to the kids' room, afraid of what I'd find.

Surprisingly, the little darlings were sitting calmly, comparing their real bruises and bandages. A moment later, Gail brought in some frantic parents. As soon as the children saw their parents, they all broke into tears, even the toughest troublemaker.

Once the tears were dried and kids were assigned to their parents, Adam handed me a chart. "Do you mind seeing this patient? She wants a female nurse."

I looked over her chart as I went into the room. "Hi, I'm Cassie. Sorry to keep you waiting." The notes indicated the patient, a young woman, was suffering with right lower abdominal pain, and her white count was elevated. My first thought was appendicitis, but when questioned, she told me her appendix had been removed years ago.

"Could you be pregnant?" I asked.

"No, my fiancé and I are virgins." She pushed her long hair away from her face looking away.

"You've never been sexually active?" I asked, checking her age again. Twenty-nine was a commendable time to wait these days.

"Well, we're born again virgins," she told me.

Gail paged into the room and asked me to come to the front desk. Nelda wanted to see me immediately.

"Excuse me, please."

Nelda looked as if she were about to explode. Her puffy face, red and pink, offset her neon blue eye shadow.

"Mr. Starnes wants to meet with you at four o'clock. I don't have to tell you he was disappointed. He wanted me to tell you that if we do not get an exemplary rating from the Joint Commission, he will hold you personally responsible."

She turned and huffed out. I sighed. There was no way I'd be able to get my work done, meet with Starnes, and pick up Gabby.

"Cassie," Gail called to me. "Your mom's holding on line one, and Channel 11 News is on line two."

"The news? They're probably calling about the bus accident. Transfer them to administration for a statement, and please tell my mom I'll call her back."

Gail got on the phone, and I returned to my patient.

"Cassie." Gail stopped me. "Sabrina Dee from Channel 11 wants to talk to you about something else, not the school bus accident."

"What would the news want with me?" I wondered, taking the phone from Gail. "This is Cassie."

"Is this Cassandra Calabria?" a female voice asked.

"Yes."

"Do you have any comment about the incident at your daughter's school today? About being handcuffed in front of a school?"

"What? Who *is* this?"

"Sabrina Dee with Channel 11 news. We were there shooting another story. We have the exclusive video of you with the police officer," she said excitedly.

I gulped, remembering how stupid I looked. "I...um, well...I don't want to talk about it. It's all pretty stupid, really, and my daughter will be embarrassed if this goes on TV, so don't run it, okay?"

"Your daughter is Ashley Calabria?"

"I don't want her name mentioned." I was becoming angry and nervous about the whole thing. There was a catfight in my stomach and my voice trembled.

"It's a special interest story. A police officer handcuffed you—in a school zone." She snickered. "Because of a bug."

Whatever happened to impartial journalism? I thought, as I rubbed my sore wrists.

"I think our TV audience would enjoy it," she chirped.

"There's nothing to talk about. I'd rather forget the whole thing."

"But it did happen, and we are here to report interesting events in our community." She sounded way too perky.

"It was stupid—" I stopped myself. She'd quote me. I thought of Ashley. "Please don't run the story, okay?"

"Are you saying you have no official comment on this?"

"I'm saying that I'm very busy now, and I don't have time for this!" I slammed the phone down.

"Whoa, what was that about?" Gail asked.

"Something happened. I don't want to talk about it." I stormed back to my patient's room, nerves crawling.

I tried to concentrate on the patient but couldn't shake off Sabrina Dee's questions. I took a deep breath.

"Nurse? Do you want to ask me some questions?

"Yes, I'm sorry. It's been a hectic day."

She sat up straighter on the bed. "Well, before you ask me anything else, I should probably tell you that, though I am a born again virgin, I had sex before my rebirth."

"I see. Have you ever been pregnant?" I asked, writing, afraid to look her in the eyes.

"Yes."

"How many times."

"Well, I guess three times."

"How many pregnancies have you taken to term?"

"None."

"How did you lose the pregnancies?"

"Do you really need to know?" she asked, upset. "I don't want my fiancé finding out."

"Don't worry. Your medical records are confidential."

"Okay. I had three abortions. One was five years ago, then about two years ago, and the third was four months ago."

I documented she'd had three therapeutic abortions. "Did you have any problems with the surgeries?" I asked.

"No."

"When did this pelvic pain start?"

"A few months ago it started hurting a little, and it just keeps getting worse."

"Has it been since the last abortion?"

"Well, I never really thought about it, but now that you mention it, yeah, maybe." She looked worried. "I hope the abortion didn't cause this. How am I going to explain it to my fiancé?" She got teary eyed. "I hope I can still get pregnant. He really wants children."

"Let me have the doctor talk to you, and we'll order some tests," I said, standing. "I'll be right back."

At the front desk I asked Gail to page a doctor. She told me Sabrina Dee had called twice, and my mom wanted to know if that really was me on the news.

"What happened?" Gail asked. "Your mom said she saw you on TV. You had a cockroach in your car, and a police officer handcuffed you?"

"It's on the news?" I gulped. "A roach fell on my lap right after I dropped Ashley off at school. I sorta freaked out, but the police totally overreacted."

Gail started laughing so hard she couldn't answer the phone. "Adam, did you hear what happened to Cassie?" She called Adam and Kathy over, leaving the phone still ringing on her desk as she ran to the waiting room to look at the TV.

"Gail, please answer the phone and tell one of the docs I need them in Room Two." I put my head down, trying to hide my flushed face, and went back to my patient.

A few minutes later, Dr. Boran came into the exam room, convulsing with laughter.

"Gail just told me. That's the funniest thing I've ever heard."

The patient sat up, angry. "You said my medical information was confidential."

"He's not talking about you." I gritted my teeth, shaking my head. "Please. I'll never live this down. Can we just forget it?"

"No way! I haven't laughed this hard since you walked in on the chief of surgery in the bathroom." He turned to the patient. "Make sure you watch the news tonight," he said in his best bedside manner.

Chapter Twelve

"If you can't laugh at yourself, make fun of other people."
~ Anonymous

When I was through with the patients, Gail flagged me down and told me she'd transferred a bunch of calls to my voicemail. My cell had been vibrating all afternoon, so I checked those messages first. Mitch had called numerous times. Then Ashley left a frantic message, saying the kids at school were laughing at her. My sister Brenda called twice. And mom called. No doubt she'd already talked to everybody at work about me. The last call was Nelda, who moved the four o'clock meeting with Starnes to four thirty.

I called Mitch first making sure he could pick up both girls, so I'd have time to get my beating from Starnes.

He answered on the first ring. "What the hell, Cassie? Ashley is hysterical and wants to change schools."

"Mitch, it's a long story. You know I hate bugs. But the officer had no right to handcuff me." Even to my own ears, my explanation sounded lame.

"I saw the news, Cass. Ashley was in the school office all afternoon, crying. Being a teenager is hard enough without having one of your parents go off the deep end. *On TV.*"

I imagined grown up Ashley speaking on some sleazy

talk show about her horrendously embarrassing mother.

"I know." I squeezed my eyes shut. "Look, I have to meet with administration later." I told him about the bus accident and Mr. Starnes.

"What if you lose your job?"

"I won't." Although I wasn't sure.

"Cass," he sighed heavily. "You need to grow up."

I bit my trembling lip. "You'll have to pick up Gabby, too. I don't know how late I'll be."

I considered not going home for about six months.

Mr. Starnes's sallow office overlooked a hospital courtyard. I watched a wheelchair bound patient trying to hold his gown from a gust of wind, while taking a drag from a cigarette. His IV bag hung loose on a pole he'd parked between his legs.

"Cassie, if the Joint Commission downgrades our hospital based on your actions, I'm holding you responsible." He sat behind his desk and angrily shuffled papers, never looking me in the eye.

"We had it under control." I thought of the mummy bound kid. "We're short staffed, and the bus accident tested our team."

He pulled a stapled pile of papers and handed them to me. "These are the patient satisfaction surveys." He leaned back in his chair while I looked at our ER "score."

"Ninety five percent." I smiled. "That's great!"

He raised his eyebrows. "I'll expect you to do better."

"Than this?" I held up the report. "This is a terrific score."

He shook his head. "Make up the five percent by next month's census, or we'll be looking at a department restructure."

I thought I'd better close my mouth before something flew into it.

After my meeting, I decided to seek refuge at Mom's. Brenda came over to offer condolences and cheap jokes. I let Mitch know I'd be home later. He didn't argue. The news was teasing the story relentlessly. I should have shut off the TV, but self-pity and fear compelled me to watch. Gabby called to ask me if we were going to drive our old car, the one that doesn't have any bugs in it. I asked to speak to Ashley, but she refused to talk to me.

I slumped on Mom's sofa, sipping some of her awful box wine. I knew Mom would offer support and unconditional love.

"Cassandra, you acted completely irrational."

"Mom, stop. I'm getting enough shit from everyone."

"Don't say 'shit,'" Mom admonished.

Brenda laughed. "Mom, make sure you tape the news, though I'm sure it'll be on YouTube forever. We'll be laughing about this for years. Even you, Cassie."

"Doubt it. Ashley hasn't talked to me since she got her first pimple. Now, any thin weave of a relationship we had has unraveled."

"I'll keep you updated," Brenda joked.

"It's not funny. She's really mad at me. I'm not sure she'll ever forgive me for this. Ashley already thinks I'm completely stupid."

"Don't you remember when you thought I was clueless about everything?" Mom asked.

"Your point?" I asked.

"It means Ashley's a teenager and doesn't think anyone understands her, especially her parents." Mom paused and smiled. "Granted, seeing your mother handcuffed is off the tracks." She took a gulp of wine and swirled her plastic tumbler, as if to make her point. "Ashley is becoming an adult and has enough to deal with in her world. She needs you and Mitch to set good examples and be there for her."

"Can we get off the philosophical crap and get back to embarrassing Cassie?" Brenda chimed in.

At that moment, I envied my character, Rosemary, a woman I created, blessed with confidence and ability. I'm sure she wouldn't be afraid of a silly bug.

The evening news sealed my fate. Sabrina Dee took such delight in reporting my story she glowed. Although the news spin featured the officer's hasty decision to handcuff me, it was the video of me writhing in the street that was the supreme topper. The anchors in the studio laughed so hard they had to take a commercial break.

In the weeks that followed, I tried to forget the incident by immersing myself in work and writing. I spent any spare time revising and editing *Wild Rose*. I wished life were as easy as fiction. Make it up as you go along. If you don't like the scene—delete.

The news footage of me freaking out in front of the school was shown over and over. I got some satisfaction when the officer was placed on disciplinary leave for handcuffing a carpool mom in front of the school.

But things with Ashley hadn't improved. When I tried to

talk to her, she angrily said some students replaced a school film with the news clip. The whole class, teacher included, thought it was hilarious. It embarrassed Ashley so much I was afraid she'd never get over it. I couldn't wait until school ended, hoping summer break would temper the event.

At the hospital, my coworkers took it out on me in the form of a plastic cockroach. It was put in places where I would find it, generating raucous laughter each time I did. Starnes was still on my back about the ratings, and I was micromanaged daily. I dearly wanted to put that damn cockroach on his desk blotter, so I could see him shriek and dance around like I did each time I found it.

While writing, I found the sex scenes embarrassing to compose. My only reference, apart from Mitch, were other romance novels. I was determined to put Rosemary in control of her sexual conquests and be professionally capable. My thoughts shifted to Aaron Novak and his custom built trophy wife, Susan. Why would such a beautiful woman put up with a man like that? Couldn't she see her own strengths?

Wild Rose

– FROM CHAPTER 5

Rosemary drove to meet Richard through the Santa Barbara dusk. As students, they'd planned to change the world. Richard applied to medical school to help people. She would capture the beauty of the world.

It was ironic how, almost five years out of college, their plans changed. Rosemary was assigned jobs, her creativity limited, and Richard deciding on plastic surgery.

What did he mean when he said he "used" the photographs of her.?

She found the small café. and parked. Before she got to the door, Richard was by her side.

"Rosie. You look great." He nuzzled her neck as they walked inside. Rosemary gazed into his mesmerizing blue eyes glittering behind John Lennon glasses. His shaggy blond hair fell over his finely structured face. A familiar fire ignited in her.

Soon they were nestled in a cozy corner. "I spend my days thinking about you, Rosie."

He stroked her arm, the effect like striking sticks together creating a spark. Hot flames of desire licked around them as both moved close, like a moth to flame. Suddenly Richard stopped. His intense eyes bore through Rosemary.

"I have imagined your incredible beauty. Every hour, every day." He touched her face with both of his hands, like a blind man desperate for answers.

"Stop." Rosemary pulled away from his touch. "You act as if you're examining me."

"I am. You're perfection." He leaned away from her but continued to look acutely at her. "Which is exactly why I'm going into plastics."

"Richard, your passion was helping people. Why did you change your mind?"

"You. You're a female David. If Michelangelo were alive, he'd sculpt your beauty. That's why I've chosen cosmetic surgery. I can be both an artist and a doctor."

Rosemary set her glass on the linen tablecloth, a red stain seeped into the delicate fabric. "I don't understand."

"It is my desire to create more women like you."

Rosemary shook her head, "Did I just hear you say create?"

"Yes. With surgery, I will have the ability to custom make perfect women." He pulled out a set of calipers and began measuring her cheekbones.

She recoiled smacking his hand away.

"Let me see your ankles. You know, you just can't rebuild a good ankle. I need good bone structure as an armature. With that, I can build my dream woman."

Shocked, Rosemary asked, "Are you mad?"

"Oh, don't be dramatic, Rose. I also intend to make myself a spouse, only one without the complications."

"Complications? Richard, what are you talking about?"

"You know, you're so into your career, you have no idea how incredibly beautiful you are." He continued to inspect her closely. "All you women libbers and bra burners. I don't get it. I've found a pretty woman who, thank God, has no idea who Gloria Steinem is. I intend to marry her. She just needs a little restructuring."

"Please tell me you're joking!"

"I knew you'd overreact. It's simple. I find someone make her beautiful, we have a nice family." He paused and looked away. "The problem is the children. I mean, genetically, my wife would still be imperfect. I'd hate to have ugly children. I haven't solved that yet."

"What woman would be so stupid she'd allow you to alter her to please you?" Repulsed, Rosemary turned away. "What the hell happened to you?

"It's practical." He shrugged. "After having you, Rosie, I must have the perfect woman."

Rosemary was shaken. He'd asked her to marry him. But she could only do photography as a hobby. Rosemary scoffed. They argued over whose career was more important. Rosemary felt he could practice medicine anywhere, and he felt she needed to act like a woman and a wife.

"You're sick," Rosemary whispered.

"I'm sorry you see it that way. It makes sense if you'd open your mind to it." He reached for her hand, she recoiled.

"This is too close to *The Stepford Wives*. I can't handle this. You've lost it." She walked away without looking back.

Chapter Thirteen

*"If a man is standing in the middle of the forest speaking,
and there is no woman around to hear him, is he still wrong?*
~ George Carlin

Nearing the end of the school year, I'd finished my second draft, including Christine's edits. I began researching literary agents and found the field was competitive. It was like credit: No one wanted to help you unless you were already established. Christine was right about how difficult it would be to get *Wild Rose* published. I considered self-publishing, but it seemed too daunting.

On the flip side, my writing allowed me to escape and express myself and to wonder how Rosemary might solve problems I faced everyday. Creating Rosemary was like going to a costume party and taking on a whole new identity.

I lived through the keyboard of my computer. Anything I wrote on paper came alive in my imagination. I could be as bad as I wanted, hiding behind the pages, and not suffer any consequences. Definitely cool.

I'd been so busy writing I'd neglected or ignored other parts of my life. Mitch and I had reached a comfort zone in our relationship. He could scratch anything in front of me, and I could wear my sloppiest sweats in front of him. Maybe that's why I was blindsided when he dropped the bomb.

I'd just started dinner when he came into the kitchen to "talk."

"What do you mean you want to separate?" I stammered. "Where is this coming from?"

He leaned over the kitchen sink, looking out the window, then turned to face me. "Oh, come on, Cass, do I even have to explain it? We've been growing apart for years." He quickly looked away.

My insides swirled into a vortex of confusion.

"You don't have time for me anymore."

Tears of shock welled in my eyes. "I don't have time for myself, Mitch! I don't have time for *anything*."

"I guess what I'm trying to say is we don't communicate anymore. The last time we went out to dinner, we didn't say two words to each other. And if we do talk, we usually wind up arguing." He couldn't look me in the eye. "Even after the girls go to bed, all you do is sit at the computer."

"I told you, I'm writing."

"Writing? Please, Cassie, if you're going to lie about things, at least make it believable. Are you having some kind of internet romance?"

"Is that what you think?" I shook my head incredulously. Maybe if you listened to me when I talked, you wouldn't be threatening to leave. And you're always working late or going out with your friends."

"Cassie, you act like you don't need me." Mitch folded a dishtowel over and over. "I want more out of life." He tried to look at me but couldn't meet my eyes.

"More what?" Shaking, I sat down at the kitchen table. "We have too much history, Mitch. Can we at least try counseling before we do anything so drastic?"

"I don't need to pay someone to tell me the stuff I already know. I *know* what the problem is."

"What about the girls?" Dread seeped into my chest. "How can you just drop this on me? Has our relationship changed to the point of no return?"

He did have a point that our marriage was running on autopilot. Neither of us was affectionate anymore.

"Cassie, think about it. You're more polite to total strangers. You have no problem telling the bag boy at the store to have a good day, but you never say anything nice to me." He had a slight catch in his voice.

"Mitch, don't do this." I started crying. "Don't you have feelings or compassion for your family?"

He hung the dishtowel over the faucet. "You always make sure the girls are taken care of, but you never think of me."

"How selfish are you?" I yelled through tears. "Our priorities are, and should be, the girls. We need to work together. I've got a full time job and a household to run."

Mitch crossed his arms. "That's not what I'm saying."

"You're right. We don't talk like we used to. And I'm sorry you think I don't treat you with utmost kindness—but most of the time, I run on fumes. I don't have the time to start meaningful relationships with total strangers, regardless of what you think."

"That's not true, Cassie. You'll talk to your friends and family before you talk to me."

"Mitch, don't put the blame on me. This is a two-way street. You can't just walk away from years of our life together. Think of your *family*. Think of the girls." I fought back sobs. "You're not the only one with issues, but I'm not so selfish I put my feelings first," I cried. "Why now, Mitch?"

He ran his hands through his hair, and I noticed they were shaking.

For a moment, neither of us spoke. I tried to regain some composure and was afraid to ask the next question, I made an effort to maintain a calm exterior, even if inside I was dying. "Is there someone else?"

He looked away. "That's not what this is about. We've, you know, just drifted apart."

"Then for what it's worth, I get the girls." I stood, defiant. "*And* the new car."

I stalked out of the kitchen. Gabby was due home any minute, and I didn't want her to see us fighting. Ashley was at Teresa's.

"See, there you go again, thinking only of yourself!" Mitch yelled as I retreated.

I turned, rage surfacing, a mix of raw emotions pulsating under my skin. "Just leave, Mitch. Since you think the girls and I have managed to live independent of you, then this will be the perfect opportunity to see how right you are."

A hot rush of tears streamed down my face. I stormed to the bedroom and slammed the door.

Sobbing, I ran into the bathroom. I'd thought our relationship was okay. Sure, we'd lost some closeness, some intimacy, but he'd never hinted he wanted to leave. Thinking back, I realized he rarely spoke to me. But I hadn't thrown myself at him either. I splashed cold water on my face, my tears going down the drain.

He was right. Most of our conversations consisted of coordinating who would pick up or drop off the girls. Who had to work late, deal with dinner, take out the trash. That was the extent of our relationship. We relied on each other for transport and general maintenance.

Mitch and I had little in common anymore. Maybe we *were* strangers with a past.

I heard Gabby come in, and I wondered where Mitch was.

I dreaded telling the girls. Gabby talked about a friend whose parents were divorced. She had a difficult time understanding her friend having two homes.

I washed my face, applied a little powder, and hoped I didn't look too bad. I was not ready to confront this issue with the girls. I needed time to think about how I would tell them. I wanted to talk to them together, hoping we could draw strength from each other.

After a forced normal evening and the girls were in bed, I closed myself in the bedroom and called Mom. Mitch was watching TV, acting as if life were the same. We'd not told the girls anything.

"I can't believe he would come up with this out of the blue." Mom took a slurp of wine. "Are you sure he's not seeing someone else?"

"I don't think so. He's moving to an apartment near his friend, Jon," I said despondently. "Jon divorced about a year ago, and I think Mitch has been living vicariously through his bachelorhood. He's probably harboring fantasies about being footloose and fancy free."

"He wouldn't do that. Besides, when he runs out of clean underwear, you'll be the first person he calls," Mom said.

"How could he decide to jump ship?" I was trying hard not to cry.

"What do you think should have been done before the breaking point?" Mom asked.

"We could have talked. Maybe tried to work through whatever issues he thinks we have. I don't know." I leaned against my pillows. "I had no clue he was considering this."

"Honey, why don't you talk to him tonight? You've invested a lot of life together. You're both hurting."

"*I'm* hurting. He obviously couldn't care less."

"Tell him, let him know how you feel. Maybe that's what he wants—to know you still need him."

"Oh, please." I pouted. "Even if that were the case, I wouldn't give him the satisfaction."

"And therein lies the problem," Mom said. "Maybe you both need to give a little of yourselves to make it whole again."

I hung up the phone. It occurred to me I was like a broken jigsaw puzzle. Parts of me were disconnected. What could I do to make the pieces fit? I didn't know, but somehow, it needed to be done before I gave more of myself away and the pieces were lost forever.

Wild Rose

– FROM CHAPTER 6

Rosemary sped down the highway, away from Richard. The streetlights creating a strobe effect, mirroring her emotions, flaring between anger and sadness. With the windows down, she savored the roar of the wind.

It was inevitable she and Richard would part ways, but this? His new obsession with appearance disgusted her.

Both were nineteen when they'd met. Their ideals were similar: study, learn, conquer the world. They attended peace rallies, protested the War, and were united in politics.

A VW beetle passed, its whiny engine snapping her back to reality. A yellow "I Found It" sticker was pasted on the rusted, dinged bumper. The driver glanced over at Rosemary, then slowed down next to her MG. The longhaired guy at the wheel blew her a kiss and signaled Rosemary to follow. "You're beautiful!" he yelled, his voice clipped by the wind.

Rosemary flipped him off and gunned her MG. *Asshole*, she thought. *Only interested in looks—just like the rest of them.* Then she felt bad for reacting aggressively. He was probably just looking for some fun. She sighed. If only she could find the perfect man, someone who possessed all the best qualities of her bedmates. Hugh's god-like physique and musical talent, Armand's sensitivity, and Richard's extraordinary mind—before he had gone image psycho. Perhaps such a man didn't exist. She smiled, cynically thinking she sounded like Richard. No, she could overlook physical flaws. Finding someone who was true to himself was important. Beauty was fleeting and transparent.

The cool ocean air cleared her head. Rosemary knew to find happiness she needed to rely on herself.

She would survive.

Chapter Fourteen

*"Our greatest glory is not in never falling, but in rising
eachtime we fall."*
~ Confucius

The next month passed in a blur. Mitch moved out the week after school ended. He wouldn't directly tell the girls why he left. Instead, he skirted the issue even as he stuffed his clothes in the trunk of his car. Ashley figured it out but didn't say much. I overheard her on the phone with Teresa, telling her that her dad was moving out because "my mom was bitching at him all the time."

When I tried to talk to them, Ashley snubbed me, and Gabby clung to me and cried.

During his weekends, Mitch came to the house while I stayed at Mom's. I didn't think it was fair to uproot the girls. Mitch avoided talking. I guess he didn't want the girls to know he was the one who decided to wreck our happy, dysfunctional home.

I dreaded the pass off. A link in the family chain gaped open. We were still a family but with no connecting parts.

I considered the holidays, months away, wondering how we should handle the visits. It was awkward. Should we be together for Thanksgiving and Christmas but sit at opposite ends of the table? My life was fragmented like a jagged scar.

The ER staff offered meager solace.

"I'm sorry you're dealing with this. What a drag." Jennifer poured a late morning cup of coffee while we sat in the kitchen. Her well muscled arms bulged with each lift of the cup. "Things will get better."

"Better than what?" A constant, dull ache throbbed in my chest. I'd lost my appetite and managed to lose a few pounds. Maybe I'll write a book called *The Depression Diet*.

"Do you think he's seeing someone?" Jennifer asked.

"I can't imagine." The thought of Mitch dating refused to sink in.

Adam came into the kitchen. "Caught you both loafing. Don't you have anything better to do than gossip? And if not, then let me in on any juicy stuff."

"No, just rehashing Cassie's separation. Mitch is probably just going through some midlife crisis."

Didn't Jennifer realize Mitch and I were the same age?

"Well, I have some good news about an incoming patient," Adam said slyly.

"If it's a GOMER, it's not my turn," Jennifer said.

GOMER—Get Out of My Emergency Room—was a patient, usually an indigent, who tended to show up when in need of a bath or a festering wound cleansing.

"No, better than that," said Adam. "Do you remember me telling you about a film crew working on a movie in town?"

"Yes," Jennifer and I said in unison.

"Well, it just so happens the star of the film tried to do some of his own stunts and hurt his arm while jumping out of a car or something."

"You don't mean the *star*, star? Not Hunter Ambrose?"

Jennifer jumped up and down as if she had live bugs in her underwear.

"That's precisely who I mean. He probably twisted an eyelash putting on his makeup. Call surgery!" Adam yelled dramatically.

I laughed. "Dibs."

"No way, Jose. He's mine," Jennifer countered.

"Gosh, ladies, I'd love to see a girl fight over this." Adam said smugly. "Come on, Jennifer, give it to Cass. She's going through a rough time."

She looked at me. "Tough shit. This is Hunter Ambrose. We fight to the finish for this guy." Jennifer had such a competitive spirit. No doubt from triathlon training. *Bitch.*

"Look, this case may require supervisor level management. You never know, he could be a high security risk, being famous and all," I said in an attempt at a joke.

"Then why don't you stand outside and guard the door?" Jennifer responded.

"I've got the solution," Adam said, pulling a coin from his pocket. "Jen, heads or tails?"

"No way," I said. "The way my luck is running, I don't stand a chance of winning."

"If you don't let me treat him," said Jennifer, "I'll call administration and tell Nelda he's coming in. She'd be down in a flash, and you'd have to deal with her."

"Jennifer, that's not playing by the rules. That's below the belt." A chance to meet a gorgeous movie star, my idol, my fantasy man, and I was probably going to miss the opportunity to shave his injured area.

Kathy came into the kitchen, breathless with excitement.

"Guess who's coming to the ER?"

"We know," the three of us chimed in.

"Stick around, Kathy. These two are in a catfight over who gets to treat him," Adam said.

"What about me?" Kathy said. "I wouldn't mind taking care of him."

"Sorry, Cass and I have first dibs, and we have seniority," Jennifer told Kathy, with more authority than I could express, even as the supervisor.

Gail came flying into the kitchen. "He's here. I just saw him, spoke to him. I'll never be the same."

Jennifer and I ran out the door at the same time, bumping shoulders trying to be the first out. Gail followed close, ignoring the ringing telephone.

"Gail, answer the phone, please," I called to her as I tried to beat Jennifer to the star's room.

"No fair," Gail yelled as she picked up the phone.

"There's a patient peeing in the hallway, in front of everyone," Dr. Boran said, as he headed toward Hunter's room.

"Damn," I mumbled. I gave up the race to Hunter Ambrose's room.

Dr. Sandoval cut in front of Dr. Boran as he was going into the room.

"I think I'll take this patient, if you don't mind." She took the chart out of Dr. Boran's hand.

Dr. Boran preened himself jokingly. "He may need a stunt double or another leading man to help him out in his movie."

"I think now he needs a doctor, so I'd better see to his injuries, 'Dr. Hollywood.'" Dr. Sandoval backed into Hunter's room, smiling.

I headed over to the incontinent, elderly man, who was holding on to a doorframe and his hospital gown, which was curtained wide open. He held himself with his other hand while urinating all over the floor. He looked as happy as a lark.

"Sir, please. This is not a bathroom," I said, watching the puddle of urine seeping into the main traffic area.

"Ha, sweetie, help me out." The patient winked at me, as he held his weenie.

I glanced back at the closed door that held my fantasy man, hoping it would open, so I could catch a glimpse. I dreamily wondered if he was wearing a hospital gown, the back panel open. Oh, right, who was I kidding? This was a man who could have any woman in the world. What chance could *I* ever have with him? My own husband didn't even find me attractive.

Here I was, up to my ankles in piss, throwing towels down to stop the river while guiding this horny old geezer to let go of his penis and sit in his wheelchair.

Yeah, I'm sure Hunter Ambrose would find me totally irresistible and would love to ravish me, here and now on a gurney in the emergency room. I fantasized him throwing his muscled arms around me, finding me alluring, and satisfying all my needs. I couldn't help but smile at the thought as I wiped the mess off the floor. I couldn't—*wouldn't*—picture Rosemary on her hands and knees, cleaning up bodily fluids.

A voice behind me. "Excuse me, where is the nearest bathroom? Preferably one with a door."

Exasperated, I looked up as I pointed across the hall. "Just by the linen cart, and watch your step. Omigod! You're Hunter Ambrose." I squeaked, like he didn't already know. My gloved hands were full of soiled, yellow towels and my hair was in my face.

He turned toward the bathroom. "Thanks."

I wanted to scream, *Wait, come back! I'm better than this. I could make you happy, fulfill your wildest dreams. Do you need help? I'm a nurse.* He was behind the door, not even seven feet away from me. So near, yet—

"So what do you say, honey, can you help me out here?" The pee-pee patient, back in his wheelchair, was still hanging on to his penis.

I sighed. "Let me get you a blanket and have someone get you back to your room." The dirty laundry in a heap on the floor, I grabbed a clean cover for him, and flagged an orderly to take him to his room.

Adam ran past me, his iPhone set on camera mode, straight for the room Hunter Ambrose had been in.

"He's not in there," I said, tempted to throw a urine soaked towel at him.

"Where is he?" Adam asked, looking around. He waved his phone around.

I pointed toward the bathroom door and nodded at the camera in Adam's hand. "He's probably hiding from the nursing staff trying to get a picture of him." I tossed the towels in a hamper. "I thought you were above all this," recalling how he teased Jennifer and me.

The bathroom door opened and Hunter walked toward me. "Looks like you've got your hands full."

"You're right." I laughed. "Thanks for noticing." *Great. "Thanks for noticing."* If I wasn't a geek before, now I'm a certifiable weirdo.

"Mr. Ambrose, do you mind if I get a picture of you and me together?" Adam positively gushed as he shoved the camera in my hand.

"No, I don't mind," he said, obviously minding.

Resentful, I aimed the camera and clicked.

"Now how about a picture of me and this pretty nurse. Looks like she's been working hard." Hunter Ambrose stared right at me. My knees went weak and shaky.

"R—Really?" I stammered.

I shoved the camera at Adam and practically threw myself at Hunter. He politely put his hand on my back while Adam took the picture. I'm sure the smell of urine rose from me like swamp steam.

"Thanks so much," I choked as he headed back to the room.

The ER had come to a halt. All eyes focused on him as he sauntered along. I got a load of satisfaction knowing they all saw him talk to me.

"Send me the photo right away," I said to Adam. "It's going to be my Facebook profile pic!"

I couldn't wait to call everybody to say I'd met a famous movie star. And Mitch, well, since we were no longer a couple, maybe I didn't need to tell him, though for some reason I really wanted to.

The phantom pain hit again, as it occurred to me we weren't a couple anymore. I was almost single. Not only single, but used—used goods.

I knew Mitch and I had once loved each other. When did it change? When had he stopped looking at me with love in his eyes?

I glanced toward Hunter Ambrose's room, hit hard with the realization that as a middle-aged mother, my options of dating had diminished considerably. I was no longer an object of desire. Life experience paled in comparison to youth. Life was no longer ahead of me. Instead, I was smack in the middle of it. Driving down the road of life, my map turned upside down.

That night, when I sat down to write, I made sure Rosemary fared better than I had.

Wild Rose

– From Chapter 7

Rosemary pulled into public parking along the moonlit Malibu coast, deserted except for two phone booths. She threw her 35mm over her shoulder and walked barefoot toward the undulating waves. She found a spot along a scenic cliff, close enough to feel the sea spray when the waves crashed against the rocks.

Rosemary heard laughter. Curious, she stood to investigate. Careful not to slip, she edged toward the voices.

Three people, two men and a woman, were skinny-dipping. She could only see silhouettes in the light of the moon but was impressed by one body, a finely sculpted man.

Not wanting them to think she was slinking behind the rocks like a peeping Tom, Rosemary called to them, "Hello!"

The woman shrieked and tried to hide her nakedness. Both men turned, startled by the intrusion.

"This is a private beach!" a short pudgy guy, called out angrily.

"I'm sorry. I didn't know," Rosemary responded.

"Is anyone else with you?" the woman squealed. Obviously drunk, she was trying, unsuccessfully, to cover herself with a beach towel.

"No, I'm alone. I didn't mean to interrupt—"

"Then leave!" the man who snapped at her before shouted. "You're trespassing."

"Hey, Laz, chill out," the handsome, chiseled man said as he covered himself loosely with a towel. He turned to Rosemary. "Sorry, my friend gets a lot of people trying to use his beach. If you're alone and come in peace, please join us for a drink."

"I don't want to impose," Rosemary said, already stumbling down the rocks.

"Hey, you've got a camera. No cameras!" the first man yelled, grabbing a pair of shorts, scrambled into them.

The sculpted man coolly studied Rosemary. "I hope you're not paparazzi. We're trying to enjoy the private beach."

With the threat of the camera, he tightened the towel over his front, further covering his resplendent manliness.

Rosemary hesitated midway down the rocks. "Don't worry, I'm off the clock. I didn't want to leave my camera in the car."

"Oh, you're a photographer?" the woman asked, dropping her towel.

Rosemary wished the man who had invited her for a drink would do the same.

"Yes, but I won't take any photos." Rosemary waved submissively. "I will take you up on that drink."

"Who are you?" the first man barked. "It would be a good ploy to have some scummy magazine send a beautiful photographer here to catch us off guard." He turned to the gorgeous woman. He handed her the towel she'd dropped. "Here, Nikki, wrap yourself up."

The lean, hard, handsome one fixed the towel around him. "I'm Colten Garrison." He then indicated the rude, chubby man, "This very polite gentleman is Lazarus Forrest. And this beautiful woman is Nikki Chimera." He made a grand gesture of bowing toward the drunken woman.

Rosemary gasped. No wonder this trio was so protective of their privacy. Lazarus Forrest was a well-known movie producer and Nikki Chimera, a beautiful, popular movie star. Colten Garrison was currently one of Hollywood's desirable leading men. Rosemary could not believe she'd happened upon three of Hollywood's most prominent players.

"Boy, when I crash a party, I make sure it's a good one." Rosemary laughed. "I'm Rosemary Christi." Her eyes never left Colten's captivating face. "If I promise not to take any photographs," She let her eyes wander, "may I still have that drink?"

"Excuse me. Where are my manners?" Colten smiled at Rosemary. "Laz, get this woman a drink."

Lazarus eyed Rosemary warily. "After she gets rid of that camera."

Colten smiled at Laz and pointed to the ice chest.

"How about a vodka tonic? My liquor stock is limited." Laz grudgingly poured a drink for Rosemary.

"Thank you." Rosemary accepted the drink. It was difficult for her to take her eyes off Colten.

Rosemary's attention to Colten did not go unnoticed. Laz leaned toward her as he handed her the drink. "Don't get any ideas, sweetheart. Colten and Nikki have this love hate thing going...and going. And I don't intend to let anything—or anybody—get in the way of that. Now ditch that camera."

Nikki staggered over to Colten, her large breasts bouncing with each step. She slurred, "Let's go inside now, baby. I'm getting cold."

"I haven't gone for my swim yet. Why don't you and Laz go on up to the house?" he said, while trying to hold her up.

"C'mon, hon," she said, addressing Laz. "Let's get in your hot tub."

Laz gave Colten a cautionary look as he escorted Nikki toward the cliffs.

Colten turned to Rosemary. "So how did fate bring you here tonight?"

"I drove in from Santa Barbara and wanted to unwind."

Colten had not taken his eyes off Rosemary. She felt his gaze go through her soul, stoking searing, hot desire.

"Does Laz really own this beach? I can't imagine having a stretch of sand to call your own. Public access beaches are my specialty."

She made light conversation, but her mind was on Colten's piercing eyes and the way the moonlight highlighted his finely whorled chest hairs. She imagined running her fingers through them, following the line plunging into his tightly wrapped towel. Blushing hotly, she averted her eyes, thankful for the darkness.

"Do you swim?" Colten stepped closer. "The water's great."

"Sure."

"Come on, you can leave your drink and camera here. Last one in..." He trotted toward the water, letting his towel drop as he ran. Rosemary was treated to an incredible view.

Shivering more with anticipation than cold, she stripped off her clothes and followed him to the moonlit surf. She felt exhilaratingly exposed as he watched her trek into the pounding foam. The water was up to his waist, and she wished the pull of the moon would recede the tides for a better view. He smiled and offered his hand to prevent her from falling into the crashing waves. Rosemary took his hand gratefully. She didn't know if it was the ebb and flow of the water, or the liquor, but her knees almost buckled standing next to this intoxicating man.

They heard Laz and Nikki's laughter in the distance. The cold water and her hot insides were a stimulating contradiction for Rosemary. Thoughts of Richard washed quickly from her mind.

Her beauty awed Colten, but he had many fans, including some who stalked his every move. It was best to be cautious. Her smile was captivating, and her athletic, svelte body aroused raw feelings in him like a hot flare. Thoughts of Nikki clouded his mood. She'd never run through the waves with wild abandon. Her fear of saltwater tangling her overly peroxided hair and the frightening thought of sea creatures lurking below prevented ocean swimming. No, she needed the sterile chemicals of a chlorinated pool. Sadly, Laz forced the relationship to help Colten's acting career. Colten didn't want to hurt Nikki, but there was no spark. It was strictly a business relationship with movie star benefits.

Rosemary decided to roll with the tide. She and Colten danced like dolphins in the brisk water.

Colten embraced her, said, "Let's go finish those drinks."

"Sure. What about the others?" Rosemary looked at the house and saw no sign of Laz or Nikki.

"I'm sure they're inside." He motioned to a beautiful beach cottage with a vista of the ocean. "Laz hates sand, and Nikki only dips her toes in. I love swimming alone at night."

"That's dangerous," Rosemary said, walking onto dry sand.

She stole a quick glance, impressed, even after a cold swim.

"Dangerously invigorating." Colten picked up both drinks handing Rosemary hers. She gazed over his incredible body. She wanted him.

Perhaps sensing her thoughts, he said, "Let's lie on our towels and enjoy the sunrise?"

Rosemary wanted to see something else rise, but she'd settle for the comparatively mere molten ball of sun.

Colten spread the towels on the cool sand standing so close to Rosemary she felt a visceral spark arc between them. He gently put his arm around her, pulling her close to his warmth. She responded to his touch locking their bodies together as one. Rosemary wanted to give everything.

"I know nothing about you," Colten said, breathless. He pulled back slightly, looking intensely into her eyes.

"It's okay. Maybe it's better the less you know. Just remember I come in peace, and now I'd like to come with you."

Chapter Fifteen

"Be content with your lot; one cannot be first in everything."
~ Aesop

With Mitch gone and Ashley ignoring me, my already wobbly self-esteem hit an all-time low. Even though I'd finished two drafts of *Wild Rose*, I couldn't revel in my accomplishment. I was reluctant to tell anyone I'd written a romance novel. I couldn't take another rejection.

I'd started walking and even managed to grind out ten sit-ups a night. My goal was to hit eleven by month's end. Losing a few pounds felt good, and walking calmed and helped me think. "What doesn't kill you makes you stronger" was my new mantra.

Christine remained my only confidant. She'd helped me with editing and keeping my characters straight, and she was not as brutal as she could have been. Actually, she told me she enjoyed proofing and looked forward to each chapter. Still, I wasn't sure if she was just humoring me while I was down or if she was being truthful.

My biggest concern was helping the girls deal with the separation. Ashley was closed off, but Gabby was full of questions, always asking when Daddy was coming home. When the family was together, the house seemed balanced, like the light from a warm lamp filling spaces. With Mitch's absence, shadows fell in each room.

Since I allowed Mitch to stay at our home on his weekends, I worried he was going through my personal effects. Never mind we had lived in the same home for almost seventeen years. All of a sudden, he was a stranger intruding on my territory. The current relationship between us was difficult to describe.

We had years of history, of knowing everything there was to know about each other, and now we couldn't even speak to each other. I'd hidden all my drafts of *Wild Rose* and hoped he wasn't trolling on my computer.

Friday evening, Ashley was invited to Teresa's. I'd spoken to Teresa's mom but still had not met her. I decided to take Gabby to the mall. I wanted some "quality" time with her, craving the need to stay close.

Gabby skipped through the mall. I couldn't imagine her feeling embarrassed to be with me like Ashley was. Gabs was full of love and innocence. I had to restrain an urge to squeeze her into me, grateful for her pure affection.

While Gabby pranced about in her brand new "sparkly" shoes, I noticed a group of slovenly looking teenagers. They looked cadaverous with stark black hair and dark makeup. Some wore tight tank tops and shorts rolled down to their hips.

Gabby danced too far ahead of me. I called her back, but she disappeared straight into the throng of creepy looking kids. My heart skipped out of sync with my feet. I was not able to move quickly enough.

"Gabby!" I yelled. "Gabrielle!"

I hoped there was not an exit nearby as I ran into the

group of tatty teens. They separated as if I were a bull in the ring. With a sigh of relief that came from my toes, I saw Gabby, but with her arms around one of the kids.

"Gabby!" I went to pull her off this girl. My relief turned to shock when I realized she was hugging Ashley. I stopped in my tracks, and we both stared at each other, speechless. With a surreal awareness, I felt as if I were seeing my oldest daughter for the first time.

"Mom? What are you doing here?" Ashley stood, defensive, staring at me. She wore a camouflage ensemble I had never seen before, with matching makeup.

"Y—you didn't tell me you were coming to the m—mall," I stammered, nervous, as if *I* had done something wrong. I finally regained my senses. "You were supposed to be at Teresa's."

"I was. Her mom dropped us off." She tried to unhook Gabby from her waist.

"And you didn't call to let me know?"

"I thought Teresa's mom did."

I leaned close to inspect her face. "Is that black lipstick?" I asked, referring to a dark slash staining her lips. I licked my thumb and started to wipe a smudge off her face.

"*Mom!*" She backed away. "We were just trying on makeup at the stores."

I dried my thumb on my pants. "I didn't know lipstick came in that…that *saturation.*" I looked her up and down, appraising my child through different eyes.

"Mrs. Calabria." I heard a voice behind me and turned to see the longhaired boy who had been with Ashley the day of the cockroach incident. "Hey, I'm Bradley." He offered his hand to me.

I was in a semi-state of shock finding my daughter with this group. He put his other arm around Ashley's waist. I didn't feel warm and fuzzy toward this kid. Still, I took his hand, and we made eye contact. His hair was long and shiny and his eyes kind, but I had a hard time getting past the lip ring and fatigues. I couldn't help but wonder what this "boy" wanted to do to the cute little bottom I had changed and powdered so many years ago.

"Are you Ashley's boyfriend?" Gabby asked, smiling up at Bradley.

"*Mom.* Can you please take Gabby and go? *Now!*" Ashley pleaded, mortified, fearing Gabby was going to either ruin or speed up her love life.

Bradley let go of Ashley and squatted to Gabby's level. "Your sister and I are friends. And she's told me all about you." He smiled at Gabs. "She told me you kiss all your stuffed animals goodnight."

I instinctively moved to block him from my youngest.

"Did she tell you my favorite story?" Gabs said excitedly, smitten by this kid. "I love the 'Princess Warrior' the best." She beamed.

Oh, goody, I thought. One wants to grow up to be a Princess Warrior, and the other already turned into a Warrior Princess.

Teresa came up behind Bradley. "Hi, Mrs. Calabria, how's it goin'? My mom dropped us off after we finished our homework. I guess she forgot to call you."

"Yes, I guess she did." I realized I didn't know Teresa's mother. She could be at home turning tricks for all I knew. "It's too bad Ashley couldn't find a phone to use," I said, looking directly at my daughter.

She raised an eyebrow. "I would if I had my own cell phone."

Bradley backed off, and the rest of the crew followed, leaving Ashley, Teresa, Gabby and me squared off.

"Mommy, can I stay with Ashley? You can pick out the rest of my stuff. You know what I like."

I got a quick glimpse of Gabby as a teenager. I wasn't ready. I wanted to talk to Mitch, someone I could relate to. Someone my age.

"Why don't you come with us now?" I asked Ashley.

"Teresa's mom is coming to get us at nine. I'll be home after."

"Come now, and we'll stop and get ice cream." I pleaded.

"Don't embarrass me again." she whispered. "I hardly have any friends left because of you being on the news."

I winced. Should I make her commit social suicide and force to leave? I sighed. "If you're not home by 9:30, you'll be grounded," I said, in a meager attempt at authority.

She waved her hand. "Fine."

"Have you eaten?" I asked, maternal concern radiating from me no matter how conflicted I felt about my camou-flaged kid.

"Yeah, at the food court." Ashley scooted Gabby toward me. "Later." In a flash, she was with the Mutant-Teen-age-Shoppers again.

"No fair. I want to go shopping with my friends, too." Gab-by pouted as she watched Ashley walk away.

Later that night, I decided Ashley and I needed to have the

"big talk." I'd tried before but could never get up the nerve to talk directly to her about sex. I'd use metaphors and TV shows as examples of what not to do, but I'd never sat and looked her in the eye and talked. It's pathetic, really. After all, I am a nurse who understands the mechanics of the body, including all the unpleasant things that can happen. I knew Ashley was aware of sex, but we'd never had a real heart-to-heart about giving yourself emotionally to someone. Plus, I wanted to show her some gross, oozy pictures of sexually transmitted diseases.

I waited until Gabby was asleep before I went to Ashley's room. Armed with my old anatomy and physiology books, I knocked on her door.

"Ashley, can we talk?" I fought down a flush of nervousness. She was, after all, my daughter. If I couldn't talk to her, who could? Why, then, was I nervous? It was as if I needed her approval, needed her to like me. *But I'm her mother.*

"What?" Ashley cracked open the door and stuck out her head.

"We need to talk."

Panic flashed on her face as if she had been caught doing something. "About what?" She stood in the doorway, her face scrubbed clean of the makeup. She didn't invite me in and it stung.

"We can talk in your room or go in the kitchen. I don't want to talk through a crack in the door."

Ashley stepped out of her room and closed the door behind her. "Mom, I didn't do anything wrong tonight. Teresa and I finished our homework before we went to the mall. Her mom said she'd call you. It wasn't my fault."

"We do need to talk about house rules both here and at

a friend's house. Just because Teresa's mom says it's okay for her to do something, doesn't give you permission, even if you are under her supervision. You should have checked with me first."

"Daddy would've let me go."

I hugged the books close to my chest and bit my tongue. I wanted to say her daddy had made his own choice to ditch his family and the responsibilities that went with it. Instead, I said, "If your father were here right now, he'd agree with me."

She eyed the books in my arms suspiciously. "What are those?"

"Information. Let's go sit in the kitchen." I motioned her ahead of me. As she passed, I noticed how tall she was. Fifteen was a breath away from becoming a woman. I watched her wistfully, aching for years past, wishing I could remember and feel every moment we've ever had together.

"Ashley, we're going to talk about...about adult things. You know—" I almost choked on the word. "sex."

"Sex?" She flopped into a kitchen chair. "I already know all about it."

"I know you know about *it*, but it's more than just sex." I dropped the books on the table. "How do you know about it?"

"I don't know. You, my friends, Internet."

"Well, we still need to sit down and go over some things, like the responsibilities that go along with having sex and the moral issues. I'll answer any questions you have." My confidence level was rising. Maybe we could have a meaningful mother daughter talk.

"I already know stuff." She started shrinking into herself,

playing with her hair, looking at her split ends.

"Ashley, you're only fifteen, and hopefully still a virgin." Oops, crossed that critical line.

"*Mom!*" she grabbed another clump of hair.

I attempted a more diplomatic approach to take her off the defensive. "Okay, I'm sorry. I jumped too quickly. I know there is a lot of information out there. I'm sure you're aware of more than I give you credit for, but consider the source. If you're learning about sex from your friends, remember they're only fifteen, too." I sat next to her. "You have to understand that no matter how old you get, you'll always be my little girl, and it's my job to protect you and help you make the right decisions. Have any of your friends had sex yet?" Damn. Did it again.

She went back to her split ends and shrugged.

"Ashley, your virginity is special. At your age, it's difficult to look beyond the next few months. But please, take my advice. Wait. It will benefit you more than you can ever know."

"That's what grandma told me."

"You talked to grandma?"

She shrugged. "A little."

I glanced up from an illustrated page of purulent herpes blisters. How could Mom, who had a hard time giving *me* advice talk to my daughter about sex?

"Ashley, you're bombarded with a lot of material about sex on TV and in the movies. You need to know that most of what is thrown out there is pure fiction." Much like the character Rosemary I had created.

Ashley looked over her split ends at me. "So, how old were you?"

Point, Ashley.

My insides rumbled like a nuclear bomb. It was one thing to ask my daughter about her life, but to be expected to answer about mine was out of bounds. I'm a mother. I'm not supposed to have a past, or sex for that matter. Again, Rosemary reared her beautiful head.

I took a deep breath. This was my chance to teach my daughter. Be the voice of experience. Let her know I wasn't as stupid about sex as she thought I was. I could teach Ashley with my incredible knowledge and infinite wisdom. I let out my breath. "Oh, honey, your daddy and I—" Gulp. "We prayed for two beautiful baby girls and were blessed with you and Gabby." *Breathe.* "It's late. Why don't you go to bed?" I sidestepped the issue.

Point, Mommy.

After Ashley shuffled to her room, I went to bed. I couldn't sleep, disappointed because I didn't have the nerve to talk straight with her. Was I such a coward I couldn't look my own daughter in the eye and say the word "sex" without feeling uncomfortable? Where was my confidence?

I turned on a light and from my locked briefcase pulled out my manuscript and flipped through it. Maybe my imaginary protagonist could provide a dose of much needed courage.

Wild Rose

– FROM CHAPTER 8

Working in the darkroom, Rosemary couldn't believe her fortune when she saw the images appear in the chemicals. Colten's exquisite eyes gazed at her from the developing pan. She swirled the solvent with rubber-tipped tongs, took the corner of the print, and moved it through the fluid with care.

He was more beautiful than she remembered. Did last night really happen? Shivers danced through her as she thought of Colten. She smiled when she saw how many photographs she had to choose from. Her favorite was a side view of him holding his towel in front, clearly showing his rippled back and muscular butt. He looked into the camera with a bemused expression and big, puppy dog eyes. His hair was mussed and fell over his movie star face. The photograph of him on his stomach, with the butterfly resting on his butt, made her laugh out loud. It was perfect. The mischievous expression over the crook of his elbow was priceless. Rosemary captured the butterfly's wings opened wide, looking as if it wanted to cover his nakedness. She made a few black and white photographs, taking care to print the exposures perfectly. In contrast, the images at the drug clinic were haunting and effective. She knew her agent, Beck, would be pleased. Working in the darkroom, the hours melted away. Rosemary enjoyed the solitude and peace.

When Rosemary got home, it was dark. She checked her

answering machine, disappointed Colten hadn't called. Beck, however, had called twice. After dropping her equipment, she poured a glass of wine and called him. He answered on the second ring, and Rosemary could hear laughter and happy screams of children in the background.

"Hey, Rose, I didn't hear from you last night. How did the shoot go?"

"I've already printed the job. I've got some amazing pictures for you."

"I knew I could count on you, honey. Michael, don't put the dog in the toilet," he yelled at his kids. "Sorry about that, we lost a hamster that way last week. How do you keep two kids out of trouble for even a second?"

"You're on your own. Kids are not my thing."

"Listen, Rose, you know I worry about you going out and not keeping in touch. You're a beautiful woman in a bad world. Next time, check in with me and let me know you're okay. I tried calling you all night."

Rosemary wondered if he checked on her male colleagues. "Thanks for your concern, Beck. I'll drop off the prints first thing tomorrow."

"Okay, Rosie, see ya then."

She took her wine and went to her bedroom. Her body craved sleep. A hot, scented bath accented with candles sounded delicious. As she prepared her spa, the phone rang. She turned off the water and ran to answer.

"Hello."

"This is Colten Garrison. I wanted to call earlier. I was on the set all day, and as you know, I didn't get much sleep last night. Laz was upset I looked tired. He made sure to get his money out of me today."

"I'm worn out, too." Rosemary twirled the phone cord in her fingers. "The photographs are fabulous, I can't wait for you to see them." An obvious excuse for another date.

"I'd suggest locking them in a safe until I can get there. I wouldn't put it past Laz to hire an investigator to ransack your place."

"I guess I didn't make a good first impression."

"He feels he owns me, I'm his property. Normally, I do as I'm told—until now." Anger rang through his weary voice.

"You've probably got it better than you think you do. I can't imagine it's all bad."

"Fame." He sighed. "You'd think because I'm a celebrity people would jump for me, but no. I jump for everybody else."

"So you'd give it up for anonymity?"

"Well, maybe not all of it. There are definite perks, but I can't walk down a street without being hounded. He sighed. "When can I see those pictures?"

"You tell me. My schedule is probably more flexible than yours."

"Maybe your place on Friday?"

"Friday's great," Rosemary said.

Goosebumps danced along her arms. She could hardly wait to entertain Colten Garrison.

Chapter Sixteen

"Fiction writing is great. You can make up almost anything."
~ Ivana Trump, upon finishing her first novel

Even though I'd finished *Wild Rose*, I was still editing the last of Christine's comments. I scrolled to the last page and typed "the end" with satisfaction.

I sighed. I'd done it. I wanted to celebrate, but the only person who knew about the novel was Christine.

I glanced at the clock. Too late to call her. I decided to enjoy a glass of wine, just me and Rosemary. I chuckled while I clinked my glass to the computer monitor. "Cheers, friend," I said, savoring the rich cabernet.

Working, writing, and keeping my family situation under control was a challenge. When Mitch and I talked, it was superficial and uncomfortable. We argued over stupid things.

When I told him about Ashley at the mall, he thought I'd overreacted.

Gabby's spirits stayed high, but she missed Mitch. Ashley withdrew and would not talk to me. It didn't help when, one day, I unwittingly handed her a dust rag, one of my old T-shirts that had "Sex, drugs and rock-n-roll" emblazoned boldly on the front.

"Ewww, is this yours?" She held the rag between two fingers. "Gross!"

I couldn't tell if she thought it was gross because it was a dust rag and she was supposed to use it, or because she pictured me wearing it.

That weekend, Mitch arrived, laden with gifts for the girls.

"Daddy! Daddy!" Gabby ran up to him and gave him a big hug around his waist. "What did you bring?" She was trying to open the packages, slowing Mitch down as he headed toward the house.

Ashley stood on the porch, her hands in her pockets. She smiled but was not demonstrative toward him. I got a measure of satisfaction out of that. At least she ignored us equally.

"Hey, slugger." Mitch put his armload down on the porch and hugged Ashley. She gave him a stiff squeeze back. Then he grabbed Gabby and yelled, "Group hug!"

My first impulse was to run and join in, but I stopped.

Mitch looked over the hug at me. "Why are you all dressed up?"

"I'm meeting Christine tonight." I didn't tell him we were celebrating my book.

"Uh-oh, girls night out." He kept an arm around the girls. "Where are you two going?"

"Dinner," I answered before it occurred to me that I didn't have to.

"You're pretty dressed up for dinner," Mitch said. "You look good. Have you lost weight?" He hesitated. "Are you meeting someone else?"

I crossed my arms and gave him a look that dared him to say more.

"By the way, Cass, I have a favor. How about letting me drive the new car for a while?"

"I don't think so, Mitch." I was shocked he would even ask. "Are you trying to impress someone?" Infuriated, I bit my tongue to prevent me from saying more in front of the girls.

Ashley stayed quiet and watched us with a troubled look.

I stared directly at him. "I'm driving the girls more than you and feel safer in the new car. You can use it on the weekends when you have them."

"So you get the house, the car, and the girls?" Mitch asked angrily. "Sounds like you're getting the best deal here."

"Deal? You're the one who dealt the cards. Why don't we discuss this later?"

Our budget was stretched even more with the rent he was paying in addition to our mortgage. Even if we did divorce, there would always be ties that bound us together. Relationships like ours don't end, they change.

I took an Uber to meet Christine at Guido's, a local Italian restaurant. I had caved in to Mitch about the car and was pissed at myself for doing so. While we waited for a table, we drank a glass—no, a tumbler of Chianti. It felt good to talk to a friend, and the wine gave me a pleasant buzz.

"How are you dealing with the separation?" Christine asked.

"I haven't had time to feel anything but numb," I said, the alcohol making my diction a little loose. "I'm going ninety miles an hour every day. The only time I have to think about it is in bed. I cry myself to sleep more often than not. Part of me misses him, and the other part hates him. I can't figure out when he thought the relationship got so bad we couldn't work on it."

"Do you think he's seeing someone?" Christine asked gently. "Phillip called to check on him—and of course, to fact find, but Mitch wouldn't say much."

"Because he knows Phillip would tell you and you'd tell me," I said. "I don't think he's seeing anyone. I mean, how many years have I lived with him? I'd like to think I'd be able to tell if he were hiding a relationship." I sighed. "But then, I didn't know he was planning to leave."

Before dinner, we both drank more wine until I was feeling no pain. An attractive young man in an apron came by to fill our water glasses, and I noticed how young and handsome he was.

"What's the soup today?" I asked Hydrostud, hoping he'd think of me as more than just an empty glass.

He shrugged. "I'm just the waterboy," he said without looking at either of us.

After he left, I leaned closer to Christine. "Be honest. How old do I look? Is it really obvious that I'm forty and fading? I was at a convenience store yesterday, and the parking lot was full of construction workers. When I walked out of the store, I braced myself for the catcalls and whistles." I took another sip of wine. "Not only did they not whistle, but when I glanced over, not one of them was even looking. If you were a guy, would you find me attractive?"

"Cassie." Christine put her hand on mine. "You're beautiful, smart, articulate, and funny. And you look great, especially since you've started working out." She squeezed my hand. "You just need to work on your self-esteem. Mitch will realize what he's missing."

I dismissed the comment. "You know what pisses me off?" I slurred. "These young fashion models who are considered beauty experts. They offer advice on how to look young and beautiful." I took another drink of wine. "Give me a break. Their brains and breasts are only half developed. Their only secret is youth. These girls have barely begun menstruating. Their collagen and elastin are what's holding things up."

"I'll offer some sage advice," Christine added. "You can't have firm flesh and an elder's wisdom."

"Thanks for not helping." I poured more wine. "Do you remember the Wicked Witch in *The Wizard of Oz*? She didn't really melt when the water was thrown on her. She collapsed because she took off her supportive underwear."

We both laughed loud enough to attract the other diners. It felt good to relax with Christine. Like family, she would love me no matter what.

"Cassie, this separation could strengthen you. You've accomplished a lot in your life. You're a great mom, and you should be proud you've written a novel. You committed yourself to a task and finished it. Published or not, it was a great read."

"You know what would be so cool?" I asked, trying to enunciate my words clearly. "That *Wild Rose* gets published and becomes a bestseller. That'll show Mitch." I was tipping over the edge of tipsy. "We definitely need to do this more often, Christine. I really love you."

Wild Rose

— FROM CHAPTER 9

The days passed slowly before Friday finally came. Rosemary wasn't sure what to cook. Her culinary skills were limited, so she decided on chicken breasts baked in olive oil and lemon, courtesy of *The Joy Of Cooking*, although she hoped for some "Joy of Sex" afterward.

She chose a light, gauzy shirt and soft, worn jeans. A twinge of excitement tickled when she thought of Colten.

It was fun to want someone so much.

Satisfied with her appearance, no makeup, hair loose and wavy, she checked her cottage for anything out of place.

She pulled the photographs of Colten from her portfolio, but then thought better of having them displayed. She'd wait until he was ready to see them and tucked them back in the case. She was fluffing her sofa cushions when she heard a light knock on the door.

Colten's mind raced driving to Rosemary's. Was he was betraying all he had worked for? If Laz learned of his rendezvous he'd give Colten hell. Though riding high now, Colten knew how fickle the industry was. Laz had enough influence to make Colten a has been. Though he hated this lack of control over his life, Colten feared being cast out of the studios.

He had been irresistibly drawn to Rosemary on that tempestuous evening and had thought of little else. But after a few days being back into his routine, he questioned the risks. Was she worth it? He, at least, needed to get the photographs from her. It would best if he walked away from her. To protect both of them.

Constantly checking his mirrors for any overzealous fans or studio people, he found Rosemary's cottage tucked away in a small copse of trees near the ocean. He grabbed the bottle of wine from the passenger seat of his new '77 Porsche, took a deep breath, and walked to the door. As he knocked, he decided he would let Rosemary down gently. He'd get the photos and if possible, the negatives, and get back to his prearranged studio life. It would be for the best.

When Rosemary answered the door, her beauty took his breath away. No, he was around beautiful women daily. He could easily move on.

"Colten. I've been waiting." Rosemary's radiance glowed from within. "Come in."

He looked better than she remembered, and she had spent a considerable amount of time gazing at his pictures. The smell of chicken cooking wafted throughout the living room. So far, so good. The fire department was not on the way, though the heat emanating from her body might trigger an alarm or two.

He wore jeans, leather sandals, and a loose fitting linen shirt. His dark, curly hair was freshly washed, and he smelled like sandalwood. Rosemary felt a tinge of nerves break through her amorous armor.

Colten smiled as he came in. "Something smells good."

"Don't get your hopes up. I'm not the best cook." Rosemary laughed. She nodded at the bottle. "How about some of that wine? Unless it's part of your image to look incredibly cool."

"Of course." He handed her the bottle.

Their hands touched, and an electric charge coursed through them. Rosemary did not trust herself to open the bottle. Her hands were shaking—unusual for her. Colten gently took the wine from her.

"Allow me. You look as nervous as I feel," Colten said, his eyes smiling.

"You're nervous?" Rosemary asked, surprised.

"This feels like a first date in high school." He twisted the opener. "Even if I've already seen you naked," he teased.

The cork popped. Rosemary blushed.

"Hey, it's the seventies." He poured two glasses of wine with nary a shake of his hands.

At dinner they talked about their lives. Rosemary wanted to show him the prints but was enjoying him so much she didn't want to break the spell.

Colten couldn't remember a more relaxed evening. He was enthralled by Rosemary. They made sure that some part of their bodies touched as they talked. He ran a hand along Rosemary's taut leg. "My dad left," he said. "Mom tried to keep the home fires burning while working in a nursing home." He shook his head. "If it weren't for acting, I'd probably be in prison." He pulled his hand away. "That's why I'm indebted to Laz. My loyalty runs deep."

"I thought you resented the control," Rosemary said.

"There is a big part of me that wants to own my life. But, I owe my agent and Laz for saving me from self-destruction. I can't walk away." As he spoke, he knew he needed to distance himself from Rosemary to protect his career. But it was hard to temper the burning desire that held him captive.

Chapter Seventeen

"Drama is life with the dull bits cut out."
~ Alfred Hitchcock

It was late in the afternoon on a busy day at work when I felt my cell phone vibrate in my pocket. I ducked into my office to answer it

"This is Cassandra," I said.

"Cassandra Calabria?" a voice asked. "Also known as Cardia Loving?"

My heart skipped. "Who's calling?" I whispered as I shut the door.

"Rita Tomazack, a literary agent. You sent *Wild Rose* to me. I'd like to talk about your manuscript. Are you available to meet?"

All my sphincters closed at once, and I sank into my chair. "Seriously?" An honest-to-God literary agent calling *me*. "I really didn't expect anything to come of it. It's been so long."

"So long? I've only had it a month," Rita said. "Have you signed a contract with anyone else?"

"No."

"When can you come by to talk about terms and sign a contract?"

"A contract?" I was in shock.

"Yeah, a contract," her deep voice said. "I'm in my Dallas

office. Why don't you come in tomorrow morning, so we can get the ball rolling. I'd like to shop this book to a specific publisher. Are you available?"

My heart played hopscotch. "Sure, what time?"

"Nine thirty looks good for me."

She gave me directions. As I wrote them down, I knew I'd have to call Adam tonight to cover. I hung up the phone and looked at the clock. It was already four thirty. I wouldn't have time to get my work finished before picking up the girls. But how could I get anything done after talking to an *agent?*

My mind was racing, and I couldn't concentrate on work. To get everything caught up for tomorrow, I'd have to bring the girls here tonight. Ashley hated coming to the hospital, and the two were a distraction. But I had no choice. Then we'd do pizza. I felt like celebrating.

I wanted to call Christine about the call from the agent but didn't have time. As I ran out of the emergency room, I felt a burst of happiness. It felt strangely wonderful.

I picked up Gabby first. Walking into the aftercare classroom, I was smiling from ear to ear. I scooped her up into a big hug.

"Hi, honey, how was your day?" I squeezed her as she squirmed out of my grasp.

"Mommy, why are you acting so different? You don't usually act happy." Gabby stood with her hands on her hips, but she was smiling. "Does that mean I'm not going to get in trouble for pinching Kevin Sloan?"

"When did you pinch Kevin?" I asked.

"He started it. I had to pinch him, so he'd give me the

book he was hogging."

I looked at her sternly. "Gabby, you know pinching is no way to solve problems."

"Yes, it is. He gave it to me. But then he started crying like a baby, and I had to give the book to Miss Julie." She rolled her eyes to the ceiling. "She wanted to talk to you about it, but I told her she didn't need to because you were really busy."

"Gabby, no matter how busy I am, I always want to hear about you."

Miss Julie came in and overheard Gabby telling me about Kevin. "Gabby, do me a big favor and put these papers on my desk." She handed Gabby a stack of spelling words.

When Gabs was safely out of earshot, the teacher turned to me. "Mrs. Calabria, I wanted you to know I put Gabby in a short timeout." She crossed her arms over her chest and looked at Gabby. "I understand you and your husband recently separated, so she may be acting out some of her frustration."

I let out a deep breath. "Gabby is usually very sweet. I'm surprised she'd do that. Tell me about Kevin."

"You know I can't do that. I can only talk about your child." She sighed. "Your daughter likes to tell the other kids what to do. She's strong willed."

This "teacher," a twentysomething, first-year instructor with no children of her own, was giving me a psych report on my child.

"Things are a different at home now, but she seems to be handling it well," I bristled. "She's quite mature for her age."

And smart and bright and the apple of my eye, so don't screw with me, bitch. Instead, I smiled sweetly, knowing I needed her to be my ally.

"I've seen children get through separations and divorces just fine. But I have also seen them go the other way." She fake smiled at me, obviously thinking the same thing of me that I was about her.

I felt like a beta fish looking in a mirror. "Come on, Gabs, let's go get your sister."

She danced away from the teacher's desk. I took her hand and led her out of the classroom.

"We need to go back to the hospital, you can help me work."

"Okay. Can I help you give somebody a shot?" Gabby loved coming to work with me. It was hard to get much done, but if I gave her a "job" to do, I could keep her entertained for a while.

On the way to pick up Ashley, I started to give Gabs a lecture about pinching Kevin but got distracted, thinking about the book agent. I wanted to pinch myself. My mind was racing with the possibility of becoming a published author.

We got to the YMCA, where Ashley was a counselor for the younger kids. Ashley was sitting alone, reading a book. She stuffed the book in her backpack when she saw us walk into the gym. Ashley hated it there but was making money after school a few days a week.

"I thought you left me to die a lonely, horrible death in this stinky gym," she whined.

I tried to hug her. "Hi, honey, how was your day?"

She didn't answer and dodged my hug. She grabbed her bags and headed out the door.

Tina Arpino was leaving with her kids. "Cassie, how are you?" She smiled cheerfully. Was this woman ever in a bad mood? "Hi, girls, you are both growing up so quickly and so beautifully." She looked at me. "Lindsey just finished gymnastics." She smiled at her daughter. "But we get home so late. We still haven't had dinner yet. I really admire you, Cassie, working all day and keeping up with your home at night."

I felt the knife twist a little.

She pulled me aside. "I'm sorry to hear about you and Mitch. Please let me know if I can help in any way. I'm always available to pick up the girls for you."

"Thank you," I said. "I may take you up on that if I get stuck at work."

"I get to help my mom at work now," Gabby said proudly. "Then we get to eat pizza."

"Mom, no!" Ashley looked at me as if I'd just sentenced her to a prison camp.

"It'll only be a little while," I said gently.

"Ashley, I saw you and your dad driving in that beautiful new car yesterday," Tina said. "I honked, but I don't think you guys saw me."

"I wasn't with Dad yesterday," Ashley said, bewildered.

Tina paused. "Oh, no wonder they didn't wave back." She laughed nervously. "Cass, really, call me if I can help." She took Lindsey's hand and scooted out.

"What is she talking about?" Ashley asked. "Dad told me he couldn't pick me yesterday because he had to work late."

"And I'm sure he did. He wouldn't lie to you. Do you know how many cars look like ours?" Though I wondered how many drivers looked like Mitch.

We spent almost two hours at work. Ashley slumped in a chair in the waiting room and watched TV with the sick and injured. Gabby was hard at work beside me with a stack of old computer paper. At least I hoped it was an old pile and nothing important. I didn't want Nelda waddling down to ask for the information on it. It would be difficult to explain why "Gabby Rocks!" was written over the data.

Dana Lange, the night supervisor, assured me the ER was slow enough for me to go home. Still, I felt guilty leaving her with work left to do.

"Cassie, paybacks are hell. I may need you to help me one of these days." She smiled as she escorted us out.

We picked up pizza on the way home, ate, and finished homework. By the time I got the girls to bed and the kitchen cleaned, it was after ten thirty, too late to call anyone about the book agent. Mitch hadn't called, which surprised me because he'd been good at keeping in close contact with the girls.

I wanted to call Mom and tell her about my meeting in the morning with a real live literary agent, but it was late, especially considering I'd never even told her I'd written a book. Anyway, her stomach had been bothering her, and she needed rest.

My mind was flip-flopping with everything going on, especially my meeting the next day. I had a difficult time going to sleep. I tossed and turned, mulling over what to wear and about whether Tina saw Mitch with another woman. I'd convinced myself it wasn't him when the alarm went off.

I got up extra early and called Adam before the girls woke. If they knew I was taking the day off, they would make me feel guilty about making them go to school. I thought I'd surprise them by picking them up after school, though. When Ashley sauntered into the kitchen, she eyed me suspiciously.

"Why are you wearing a suit?"

Her bra straps hung outside her tank top. "Speaking of outfits, you need to change yours."

"I'll put another shirt over this one," she whined.

"No, because I know you'll take it off when you get to school." I didn't want to get into an argument that morning. I needed my wits about me when I met with the agent.

As I applied a little extra makeup and more spritz to my hair, I wondered if I was kidding myself. Would my book actually get published?

I had a few extra minutes after dropping the girls off, so I went to get a latte and make some calls. I settled in a cozy chair at a Starbucks near the agent's office. It was 8:30, and Christine was with her first patient. *Strike one.*

Mom answered on the first ring. I was about to tell her about my meeting, but she said her stomach was really bothering her and that she'd call me back. *Strike two.*

As I sipped my latte, it suddenly hit me that I didn't want Mom to read what I'd written. All those sex scenes—what would she think? This presented a new dilemma: How could I let my friends and family read my book? I considered my own girls reading about Rosemary's conquests. What would they think?

Driving to the agent's office, I stopped at a light. The street rose into a rare Dallas hill, and I couldn't see beyond the rise. Along the horizon, the road appeared to ascend to the sky, giving the impression I could either drive into the clouds, soaring, or the road would end and I'd plummet, crashing down. I took a deep breath and waited for the light to change.

Wild Rose

— FROM CHAPTER 10

The bottle of wine finished, Rosemary and Colten sat on her sofa. Full, yet still hungry, palpable energy radiated between them.

Colten set his glass down. "Can I see the pictures?"

Rosemary fought an urge to slide closer, stroke his strong arm, and nestle into his muscular chest. She sighed. "I'll get them." But as she stood, he grabbed her wrist and pulled her to him.

His touch was like fire. Rosemary wrapped into his embrace. "It's about damn time—"

Before she could finish her sentence, he planted his lips on hers. She fell into his kiss, her body igniting as if an electric switch had sparked. She slid her hand over his chest, resting it over his heart, feeling the rhythm of his body until their hearts beat together.

Colten peeled his shirt off and helped Rosemary with her slipover. She stood, took his hand, and guided him to her room. She lit a scented candle and dimmed the lights before taking him in her arms.

Colten groaned with pleasure. "I've thought of nothing but you since that night." He held her tight and spoke between kisses. "This can't be wrong."

Rosemary pushed a lock of hair from his face. "Why would you think it is?"

"The studio." His eyes flashed anger. "For the first time, I'm falling in—"

He didn't finish his thought. Instead, he grabbed Rosemary tighter and kissed her with such passion she melted. Pleasure became one acute sense—touch, sight, smell, hearing, and feeling rolled together.

They feverishly undressed each other. Colten's strong hands were like silk touching her skin as he pulled her jeans over her curves. Because of his exploding desire, Rosemary let Colten shed his jeans. She devoured his physique. The flickering light of the candle danced over his sleek chest and muscled abdomen. As frequently as she'd looked at the pictures of him, her lens was unable to capture the three dimensional perfection of his body and the light of desire in his eyes. She shivered.

Colten wrapped protective arms around her. "Are you cold?"

She looked into his eyes. "No, these goosebumps are not from the temperature." She smiled shyly. "No one has ever reached me as you have."

He guided her gently to the bed. "This is nicer than having sand crusting our bodies." He smiled. "Though it was one of the best nights of my life."

"And this night is still young." Rosemary moved into him. Every part of their bodies touched and nestled together, fitting like a key in a lock.

Furiously, they explored. Desire flamed with each stroke. Rosemary pictured their love like time-lapse photography— the sun rapidly rising, clouds thundering across the sky, flowers opening their first tender buds under the morning light.

She gasped as the scene slowed, aching with pleasure—the quiver of a petal when a bee sips its nectar. A kiss, light as the feather of a dove. She cried out as the last scene played out—fireworks bursting amidst the stars mingling with dancing lights, the burning embers falling gently like warm rain on soft skin.

Breathing heavily, they rolled onto their backs. Rosemary turned and smiled. "I think the earth just changed direction."

Colten took her hand. "I could stay here forever."

She squeezed his hand. "You're welcome to." She breathed deeply. This was the closest she'd ever let anyone in. It felt delicious, and she let the comfort settle deep inside her heart

Chapter Eighteen

"Did you ever stop to think, and forget to start again?"
~ A.A. Milne

The door read *Rita Tomazack, Literary Agent* on frosted glass. Underneath the print, there was a handwritten note: "Leave unsolicited material here." An arrow pointed to a large trashcan.

Entering the office, I noticed a young woman on the floor amidst a sea of paper. Along the walls, bookshelves full of paper spilled off of the shelves. A partition separated her from a cluttered back office. She cheerfully smiled, not bothering to get up. "Hi, can I help you?"

"I'm here to see Rita Tomazack," I said nervously.

"You must be Cardia Loving," she said. She yelled for Rita from the floor. "I enjoyed your novel. It's nice to read about a strong, adventurous female character."

"Thank you." It felt good someone other than my best friend had read it and enjoyed it.

A large woman in a peach silk tank top that pinched pudgy, freckled arms, came out from behind a partition. If I had seen her at the grocery store, I'd have never thought "literary agent."

I shook her fleshy hand. "It's nice to meet you."

"Come back here, so we can talk." She headed to a desk by a window overlooking an unattractive parking lot.

I wasn't sure what to expect or what to say. Was I supposed to play hard to get? I decided, prudently, to keep my mouth shut.

"Have a seat." She offered a burnt orange chair, one that looked straight out of a government office circa 1972. Grateful to relax my shaking knees, I sat.

Rita got right to the point. "I've never seen your name before. My research shows that no Cardia Loving or Cassandra Calabria has ever published a book, so I am assuming you don't have an agent...?"

"No, I'm new to all this."

"Good. I'd like to sign you as my client." She began reaching for papers under a disorganized stack of documents, making little grunting noises as she extended.

"Ms. Tomazack, how did you get my book? I sent it to places in New York, not Dallas."

"I have offices here and New York. Family keeps me tied to Dallas."

"Kids?"

"No, husband." She continued shuffling through papers and then looked up. "Our marriage works better if he's here and I'm in Manhattan."

She found what she was looking for under the mountain of papers. "You understand this is not a guarantee of anything. However, I do have a publisher in mind."

"How long before I'll know anything?" I asked.

She laughed. "Don't quit your day job. I've been in this business long enough to know not to promise anyone an estimate of anything. I'm hoping we can get a small advance. Let's start from step one." She handed me a multipage document. "This is my standard contract. I get fifteen percent. I take care of fronting the job to publishers. The publisher will assign you an editor and recommend a publicist as soon as we sell the book."

Rita went on about her intentions and the contract. I didn't hear much past the first few sentences, though. My head was still reeling from the shock of the whole ordeal. I felt as if I were dreaming, and the rest of the world was moving in slow motion.

"If you want to take that to your attorney first before you sign, let me know. It will delay the process, but I want you to understand it." She looked at me expectantly. "*Wild Rose* looks like it could dovetail with a project a publisher and I are currently working on with a very short deadline. With electronic and self-publishing changing the scene of writing, we're moving quickly on this. Do you need a few minutes to look over the contract before you sign?"

I had to urge to cartoon shake my head to bring myself to reality. "I don't know enough about publishing and book agents to know what to ask."

"Good. That's my job."

It crossed my mind Rita could be taking me for a ride, but her attitude and demeanor had a ring of truth. I felt I could trust her. I took a deep breath and signed the contract, barely looking at it.

"Okay, let's get you a copy. Make sure you keep it in a safe place."

She stood up and took the contract to her assistant, who

was still on the floor sorting through stacks of paper. "Run copies on this and get this filed so we can move ahead."

When she turned back to me, I asked, "What should I expect? I mean, am I going to see my book in bookstores? Real bookstores?" I cringed. Why couldn't I just think before I talked?

"I think we can probably get into a 'real' bookstore." She laughed. "But I am going to stress, like I tell all my clients, don't set your expectations too high. Publishing is a new world, with self-publishing, e-books, and fewer brick and mortar stores. If it does sell, it will be a pleasant surprise for all of us."

"Have you represented writers who have been published?" I looked around her dingy office, wondering if she could even make the rent.

"A few." She smiled. Her assistant came back with the paperwork and handed it to her. Rita peeled one of the copies off and gave it to me. "I represent Dominique Matrix and Siren Song, to name a few."

I gasped. "Oh, my gosh! They're incredible writers. Don't they have bestsellers published, like, all the time?"

She smiled. "We try to keep them busy. I think *Wild Rose* would fit in with their genre. We're working on a special promotion that, I think, could include your book. It's a three pack *Summer of Love* novel set. Dominique and Siren have their books ready, and *Wild Rose* would complete the set nicely. I'm confident the publisher will approve, and short of some minor revisions, I hope to fast track *Wild Rose* for the set. It's a buy-two-get-one-free promotion."

"And mine would be the 'free' book? Would I be paid?"

"Yes. I bid for an advance first, and we'll see how sales go."

"So you don't know how much?"

"If I were you, I'd just be happy your book is being considered for publishing. I've known many writers who wait years for a publisher or agent to pick up their books. You could have the chance to see your novel in stores by summer."

"This summer?" I was shocked. "That's only a few months away."

"Let's get the revisions done, then get it out."

"Revisions?"

"Minor revisions you'll do with the editor. If it's approved, you'll need to sign a contract with the publisher, too." She reached in a file and brought out more forms. "Congratulations."

"I don't know what to say."

"Just don't call me every day. My assistant or I will call you with any news. As we move forward, your publicist will schedule book signings and let you know about the release party. Both Dominique and Siren hate to share the spotlight, so we'll have to work around their egos."

She shook my hand and escorted me out the door. I "came to" standing outside the building.

Driving home, I felt euphoric. I had accomplished something I didn't think was possible. I was dying to tell Christine, my only confidant. And oddly, I wanted to tell Mitch. Wouldn't he be proud? But that was in the past. For so many years, he was the first person I'd call with news. I sighed sadly, remembering the good years. Of course, I couldn't help but suppress a smile, wondering what he would think about me writing about passionate sex. Even if I did tell him, he probably wouldn't believe I had the imagination to come up with such a story.

Mom. I hesitated to call her because of the smutty content. I shuddered to think what she would think, me writing all those steamy sex scenes. Even if she did read romance, it felt wrong since it was written by her daughter. I blushed, recalling when Mom tried to tell me about the birds and the bees. For the first ten years of my life, I believed her story that babies were kept in God's pocket, and He would give one to each mommy when she was ready. I imagined a lump of uncomfortable babies, gasping for air at the bottom of His linty pocket.

Of course, some expert I turned out to be. I didn't have the nerve to talk to my own daughter about sex, regardless of all the experience I already had under my belt—so to speak.

So whom could I tell? I was bursting with happiness. If I didn't let my friends know, who would buy it? If I told the people I worked with, they might look at me differently, thinking I was visualizing the fervent sex on the beach while I was attending to a patient's personal needs. Then I thought of the school moms. Many likely wouldn't let their children play with my kids anymore. Would they think I acted out my story in front of children?

The children—my own children! How would I ever explain to them what their mother had written, or much less thought about sex? Especially when I was unable to say the word around them.

The more I thought about who would read *Wild Rose,* the more worried I became. My happiness changed into fear of being discovered. I would have to get to Christine soon and make sure she didn't tell anyone.

I still had most of the day to worry about it. I went home, changed, and threw myself into cleaning the house.

I surprised the girls by picking them up after school and taking them to their favorite Italian restaurant. A huge plate of spaghetti with meat sauce could solve many of life's problems. Ashley wondered what the special occasion was. Gabby just ate to her heart's content and asked if we could do this every day. *Sure, honey, providing my book is a best seller., and you never find out about it.*

Wild Rose

— FROM CHAPTER 11

Colten kissed Rosemary gently. "It's getting late."

Rosemary stroked his arm. "Stay tonight."

He shook his head. "I want to but if Laz is trying to call me—" He looked away. "I'm sorry." He stood and dressed.

"You should be able to run your own life."

Rosemary went to him, disappointed. She had sensed a shift in Colten's mood.

"I have much to be grateful for."

"At least stay and look at the prints," she said.

He smiled sadly and nodded. He walked to the window. "This is new to me." He ran a hand through his thick curls. "I've always been a love 'em and leave 'em kind of guy."

Rosemary thought, ironically, how she'd done the same to men. It hurt.

He looked at her, conflict in his eyes. "I can't." He turned. "I think my shirt is somewhere between here and the living room. I'll let you get dressed." He closed the door behind him.

She dressed and took a deep breath. Okay, she thought, close those stupid heartstrings. Be strong.

He stood by the fireplace and watched her walk into the room.

She barely looked at him as she pulled out her portfolio and laid it on the table. They sat close. Rosemary resisted an urge to touch him.

"Do I get the prints and the negatives if I don't approve?" he asked warily.

"I keep the negs and one set of prints, and you have my word I won't publish them." She scooted away.

"Why do you keep one set of prints?"

"Memories of a special night." Her cheeks reddened, and she thought of Richard using photographs of her.

"I see." Colten slid closer.

She knew he wanted to touch her, but he also acted reticent, like a marionette pulling him.

She handed him a set of the 8x10s. He studied them in silence until he got to the last picture. Rosemary's favorite, the one of him looking out of the crook of his arm, the butterfly in full spread on his...well...spread.

"You made me look good," he finally said. "Let me take them to my agent and Laz and see what they say. I'm not sure if they would hurt or help my career."

"Think of the actresses who pose for Playboy. These photos only show your butt. I can't imagine they would hurt."

"My body is a commodity, a business, and I have little say in how it's marketed."

Sadly, she realized what he said was true. His image and talent were his trade. She wondered if, when he looked at the pictures, he saw their evening together.

"You see these photos differently than me. I sense emotion. You see work."

He shook his head. "I can't think about the emotional aspect."

"Don't you feel used?"

"I have little control over my life. I have to be realistic."

"On the beach you seemed so confident." She turned away. "Tonight—"

"I'm an actor."

"Were you acting?" Her voice caught.

He paused and looked down., "No. All of that was real. I have to be honest. I doubt the studio would approve of us. And Nikki's career needs me. The public loves us together, and I'd be seen as a cad if I left. We're the Golden Couple."

"How sad." Rosemary pulled away, tears salting her eyes. "Do you care for her?"

He didn't answer. "I'll take these to my agent."

"Just have your agent call my agent" Rosemary said, like a petulant child.

She was crushed. Their time together had been bliss, but he became cold after he got what he wanted. She felt used, considering she offered so much of herself to him—her soul, if he'd take it.

"I've enjoyed tonight. I'm sorry," was all he said before he walked out.

Chapter Nineteen

"Dream as if you'll live forever, live as if you'll die today."
~James Dean

I watched the months flip rapidly by on my desk calendar, so I got up and turned off the fan that blew the pages.

The last few months really had been a blur. I'd hurriedly finished the revisions and sent them to Rita and then heard little from her. Mitch and I were living in a twilight zone relationship. Our conversations went from cordial to heated to stupid name calling. Like we were both standing on the edge of the high dive and were afraid to jump—or push each other off.

We'd made it through the holidays, thanks mostly to Mom. She had the ability to neutralize a ticking bomb by keeping it all about the kids. Any time one of the grown ups started acting up, she'd all but smack us on the head.

Christine peeked in the doorway at work. "Hey, author."

I smiled and raised my coffee mug to her. "I couldn't have done it without you."

She stepped in and closed the door. We both sat.

"You should be proud. Isn't it coming out soon?" she asked.

I turned the pages of the calendar back to April. "I sent the final draft to Rita a few weeks ago. She said they're shooting for a Memorial Day release."

"That soon?"

"I think *Wild Rose* was an afterthought. I wasn't even able to see the cover art. Rita said they had to make a quick decision and get it to the publisher. I feel like the unwanted stepchild to Siren and Dominique."

"Publishers don't print afterthoughts. You wrote a good book—no, a great book—and I'm happy for you. We need to celebrate the release." Christine stood to leave.

I laughed and nodded. "I'll buy the box of wine."

She grimaced. "I think this deserves a bottle. Leave the vino to me," she said as she walked away.

I hadn't told her I'd dedicated the book to her. I wanted to surprise her.

"To CT, my best friend and confidant. The person who believed in me more than I believed in myself."

Chapter Twenty

"When in doubt, wear red."
~ Bill Blass

On Memorial Day weekend, Dr. Novak hosted a family pool party for some of the hospital staff. Gabby was thrilled, Ashley was horrified, and I couldn't decide which sweatsuit would work best in the ninety degree heat. The last thing I wanted to do was wear a bathing suit in front of people I worked with.

Then there was Susan Novak's perfect body. What I wanted was to find a bookstore to see if my novel was really on the shelves. I asked Christine to be my date to the party.

"You know I hate that jerk, Novak," Christine whispered to me as we drove there. She glanced in the back seat where the girls were listening to their iPods.

"I'm not sure why he invited the emergency staff," I said. "But thanks for going with me. Gabby's excited to see his kids again."

She'd had a few playdates with them since we bought the car. I checked the rearview mirror. Ashley sulked in the seat, plugged into her headphones.

"Ashley doesn't want to run into Andrew. The cockroach incident will haunt her at every high school event."

As we drove, Gabby, lost in her music, sang loud and off key, her ear pod wires swinging as she sang.

Christine smiled. "Ashley's strong. She'll survive." She lowered her voice again, "What's going on with the," She glanced back at the girls, "you know, the book?"

"Rita said it's due out this weekend," I whispered. "I've been assigned a," I looked in the rear view mirror, "a publicist, but we haven't talked yet. I guess I'm not important enough." I checked the back seat again to make sure little ears were still plugged. "Dominique and Siren are the priorities. Rita said she was busy stroking their egos." I grinned. "Maybe later we can go to a bookstore and see if we can find it."

She laughed. "Okay. Can I be your manager?"

"Better yet, you can be me." I looked at her. "How am I going to, you know, sell it?" I glanced in the rearview mirror again. Ashley was watching me. "Besides, I'm sure nothing will come of the you-know-what."

"The you-know-what what?" Ashley's headphones weren't as soundproof as I'd thought.

Christine laughed. "Nunya business."

"What*ever*."

"Mommy, do they have a diving board? Can I have a Coke? Two Cokes?" Gabby prattled on and on, her voice loud so she could hear herself over her ear pods.

"You can have one drink, and don't go into the pool unless a grown up is with you. Maybe Ashley will swim with you."

"No way. I'm not swimming. I'm staying in the car." Ashley turned her back and looked out the window.

"Then can I have Ashley's Coke too?" Gabby asked, holding one ear pod away from her head, tinny music emanating from it.

Christine reached back and tickled Gabby's leg. "You can have my Coke."

Gabby giggled. "Yeah!"

We couldn't find a parking place close. Cars were lined up on both sides of the street.

We got out of the car. I was self-conscious about my boring khaki shorts. I never knew how to dress for parties. Christine looked great in her coordinated outfit, a pink tank and matching capri pants. She grabbed Gabby's hand and they skipped happily toward the party.

I held a tub of onion dip as I waited for Ashley to drag herself out of the car. "Come on, honey. I'm sure there'll be people your age here."

She shuffled along the sidewalk. "Dorks, maybe. I can't believe you're making me come to this stupid thing."

I'd bribed her with an evening at the mall with Teresa.

Christine and Gabby waited for us at the door, and we let ourselves in. The party was in full swing. Gabby took off running. She found the kids and immediately joined in a game of tag in the living room. They happily picked up where they left off the last time they saw each other.

Ashley wished she were elsewhere and acted like it. I tried to introduce her to my coworkers. She was more interested in the ceiling than meeting people. I felt I needed to apologize for her rudeness, especially considering she was still wearing her headphones during the introductions.

Christine and I headed out to the pool area, where people were talking, drinking, and eating. Most wore shorts and matching tanks. A few sported bathing suits with covers. As to be expected at a Texas pool party, no one was actually swimming. Christine grabbed each of us an iced beer from a cooler. We left Ashley to sulk alone at the kitchen table.

Susan Novak was quick to greet us as we stepped outside. "Hello! I'm so glad you're here." She smiled. "How do you like the car?"

It was obvious she didn't remember my name, though she was doing well hiding it.

Aaron Novak saved his wife from social embarrassment by providing my name. "Cassie, you remember my wife, Susan? And Dr. Taylor, good of you to come, too. Susan, Cassie works in the ER, and this is Christine Taylor." He held a tumbler in his hand, no doubt some of that expensive bourbon.

"Of course I remember Cassie. I was just asking her about the Lexus." Susan's beautiful, bronzed skin was poured gloriously into a black swim tank with a bright sarong wrapped around her tiny waist. "Can I offer you anything?"

Christine held up her beer. "I'm good, thanks."

"I see your daughter is having the time of her life." She gestured toward Ashley sitting at the table, thumbing through a book.

"Yes. I'm sorry about her behavior. Anytime she's forced to be with family, you'd think the world was about to end."

Susan laughed. "I understand. Andrew is going through the same phase, and it's worse for me because I'm only his stepmother. The teenage years seem to be a tragedy played out daily."

Christine sipped her beer and watched Ashley. "They'll come around before you know it." She touched my arm and nodded toward the window. "What book is she reading?"

Susan chirped. "Oh, that's mine. I must have left it on the table. It's a great book that just came out this weekend. It's called *Wild Rose*. It was in with Dominique Matrix and Siren Song's new books. I started reading it and could barely put it down to get ready for the party."

"*Wild Rose?*" I swayed a little. "Christine—no, she can't read that."

"I'll take care of it." Christine went inside to sit with Ashley.

"Are you okay?" Susan grabbed my arm and eyed my beer. "How many of those have you had?"

"I'm fine. Sorry. I'm just not sure my daughter should be reading a—a sexy romance novel." My voice raised an octave on "romance."

"Why not?" Susan laughed. "How else is she going to learn about sex?"

I hadn't even seen the book yet. None of it seemed like it had actually happened. But to see my daughter flipping through the pages of the book I'd written hit me like a slap in the face. It really *had* come out this weekend, and someone *bought* it—or bought the other books in the set and wound up with mine. And now my daughter was reading it.

I watched as Christine sat next to Ashley and took the book from her. She looked at the cover and then showed it to me through the window, her eyebrows raised: Two beautiful people clutched in a half-dressed embrace, the woman entwined in a prickly vine, with two budding roses draped seductively across her bosom a camera slung over her shoulder.

The strong male companion bared a beautiful chest of

his own—with Rosemary's long telephoto lens strategically placed in front of his pants.

I watched Ashley argue with Christine. Then she shot a heated look at me, grabbed a *People* magazine, and stormed off. I could practically hear the "whatever" through the glass.

Christine came out with the book and handed it to me. "Can you believe it? Great cover."

Susan watched us gawk over *Wild Rose.*

"So far it's a great read," Susan said. "If you're interested in it, I'll be happy to loan it to you when I'm finished." She held her hand out for the book.

I handed the book to Susan but held tight to it when she tried to take it. She finally tugged it from my grasp.

"It's at the bookstore if you can't wait," she said sharply.

The conversation stopped dead when Dr. Novak came out wearing a Speedo and challenged everyone to a water volleyball game.

"He actually thinks he looks good in that." Susan hugged my book to her chest. "It must be a guy thing. They love their physiques while we can't even face ourselves in a mirror."

"Oh, please, you look great." Next to her I felt like a burst can of Pillsbury biscuits. I kept staring at *Wild Rose* clutched close to her bosom. She probably thought I was eyeing her gorgeous body.

"You are kind." She changed the subject artfully. "Crab dip?" She offered a bowl.

Susan excused herself to be a hostess, offering drinks and food to the guests and no doubt to hide *Wild Rose* from me.

"Christine, I'm hyperventilating." I wanted to sit down. "My book really is in stores." I held in tears of happiness and shock.

She put an arm around my shoulder. "I'm proud of you." She clinked our beer bottles together.

"I should check on the girls." I stepped away from Christine. "What did Ashley say when you took the book from her?"

"She was looking for pictures," Christine joked. "You know she'll read it eventually."

"I hope not." I gulped my beer. "She'd never look at me the same again. Promise me you won't tell anyone I wrote it."

"Cassie, how are you going to hide it? Aren't you supposed to promote it?"

"No. Remember my book was a freebie, the one that didn't count. Dominique and Siren are the real authors."

"And now you're a real author, too."

I tried to let her words soak in.

Sheila Sandoval stepped outside. "Where's the beer?"

Christine pointed to the cooler. "Right under your nose."

I excused myself. "I'm going to check on my kids to make sure they didn't break anything I can't afford to replace."

"Don't bother. Gabrielle is playing fort in the living room. And Ashley's reading a magazine in the den," Sheila said. "You guys need another?" She reached into the cooler and handed me and Christine our second.

Dr. Boran came out to the pool area.

"I hear we have a volleyball challenge!" he yelled at Novak, who was bending over, offering a back-end view of his Speedo as he mounted a volleyball pole into the cement. He stood and adjusted the elastic around his legs.

Christine snorted. "If you ever catch me wearing anything

like that in front of my colleagues, take me around back and shoot me."

Sheila turned to me. "Okay, Cassie, you're next. I hope you have your bikini on under your shorts."

"Thong."

Sheila rolled her eyes. "I'm going in. Christine, you coming? We can't let these guys win." She took off her long T-shirt, revealing a modest tank.

"Count me in." Christine handed her beer to me. She dropped her capris and pulled off her shirt, looking fit and cute in her two-piece. She and Sheila jumped in the water without testing the temperature. They looked great. Mostly, though, it was their confidence and self-assuredness that shone through. They were strikingly beautiful.

I checked on the girls and surreptitiously looked for the copy of *Wild Rose*. Apparently, Susan made sure not to leave it out lest I run off with it. I wanted to go to the bookstore on the way home but didn't want the girls with me when I bought it. Other than a galley copy Rita sent without the cover art, I'd not seen my words in print. I'd hid the advanced reader copies in my underwear drawer, tucked between my granny panties.

I'd been invited to the book's launch party in New York last week with Siren Song and Dominique Matrix. The publicist made it obvious I would hold the spotlight instead of share it. She'd find a corner for me, and, oh, yeah, I'd be paying my own way. I still didn't feel like an author.

We stayed at the party and ate burgers and chips. Christine, embroiled in a close game of volleyball, told me to go ahead, she'd get a ride home. Ashley was more than ready to leave, but Gabby fussed about it until my beer turned into a headache. I did, however, totally sober up from shock when I got home and opened a letter from Rita.

Wild Rose

– FROM CHAPTER 12

Two weeks after Rosemary's disastrous date with Colten, her agent called. "Rosie, how the hell did you get nude photographs of Colten Garrison? This is big stuff, kid. It will put us on the map to glory."

"The studio approved of the pictures?"

"Approved? Hell, yeah, they approved, and Cocotte magazine is paying big bucks for the exclusive. They're doing a whole spread, complete with a centerfold. How did you do it, and why didn't you let me know?"

"I promised Colten, um, Mr. Garrison, I wouldn't let the prints out of the bag until he gave me the okay."

"The biggest movie star in the universe? Are you out of your mind? I'm your agent, Rosie, not him. I'm the one who makes the decisions about what gets printed by my photographers. You know better than to sit on something like this."

Rosemary's anger flared. "Beck, I shot them, so I have the say as to how or where they get printed."

"Hello, honey. I'm your agent. I'm the guy who gets you work and sales. Something as big as this should have gone through me. I'm happy Cocotte is printing them, but who knows what kind of deal I could have worked out with other publications."

Rosemary could practically hear the cha-ching of his internal cash register. "Well, I think my work speaks for itself. I could get anything I wanted—"

"Stop," Beck interrupted. "Don't get on your "pure art" high horse. Don't forget the chain of command. I've seen many shooters fade into starving artists trying to stay art virgins. You'll wind up screwing yourself if you try to manage your own work."

His words stung.

Rosemary understood what he was saying but couldn't help feeling used.

"I will always shoot for myself, so there may be prints I want control of."

"As long as they're of flowers, sunsets, and landscapes, fine. But the next time you get a mega movie star to pose nude, I'll expect you to call me first."

Rosemary hung up trying to justify what Beck said. In some ways he was right. He did find her work and took care of the money and distribution. But she would never lower her standards just to make a buck.

She wished Colten had called to let her know that the prints were going to be published and regretted promising him the right to use the pictures. But he wouldn't have allowed her to take them otherwise. There was a bittersweet feeling now when she looked at the photographs. That evening burned her insides with pleasure, but she also felt betrayed by the man staring out of the pictures at her.

"Pull up your boot straps," she told herself with conviction. "Life goes on."

The new edition of Cocotte magazine created a tornado of news. Rosemary was thrown in front of the camera. People wanted to know who the lucky photographer was that took the provocative photographs of Colten Garrison's naked butt.

Chapter Twenty One

*"I have an existential map;
it has 'you are here' written all over it."*
~ Steven Wright

After we got home from the pool party, I slipped Rita's letter in my purse so the girls wouldn't see it. Gabby begged me to play soccer. Ashley had gone straight to her room, asking if I'd been to the grocery store to get Pop-Tarts. I was nursing a headache from the beer.

The letter from Rita was burning a hole in my pocketbook and my thoughts. She probably wanted to let me know *Wild Rose* was a flop and that I owed her money.

"Mommy, come on." Gabby had the soccer ball in hand and was heading out the door. "Ashley won't play with me. She's calling her boyfriend, Braaadddlleee!" Gabby yelled toward Ashley's room loudly enough not only for Ashley to hear, but the neighbors, too.

"I'm first!" Gabby dashed out the back door.

"You were first last time," I said as I chased her. I loved the boundless enthusiasm of my baby. But I feared the hangover would turn sour before we got a few goals in.

It didn't take long to work up a sweat. I was grateful when I heard the phone ring, giving me an excuse to take a break. Gabby beat me to the phone.

"Gammaw!" Gabby yelled excitedly into the phone. "Guess what? I'm beating Mommy at soccer and I got invited to a birthday party for my new friend, Angela. It's going to be at her house. They're going to have a circus. Do you want to talk to Mommy?" She handed the phone to me. "Hurry up so we can play some more, I'm winning."

I took the phone from Gabby before she ran outside. "Hi, Mom. What's going on?"

"Nothing, really. What was that all about?"

"I'm not sure yet." I watched Gabby kick the soccer ball against our wood fence.

"Who is Angela?" Mom asked.

"She's one of Dr. Novak's kids. This is the first I've heard of a birthday party."

I told her about the pool party and the beautiful house we had just been to.

"Was Sheila there?"

"Yeah, she was there. Why?"

"Did she tell you that she's arranging some blood work for me on Monday?"

"No. For what? And why didn't you talk to me about it first?"

Dr. Sandoval and I had talked at the party. She never mentioned she'd spoken to my mother.

"You know, my stomach has been bothering me. I called her first because I didn't want to worry you and Brenda." I could hear the gurgle of box wine being poured.

"Since we're your daughters, you should've called us first," I said, sounding like a kid who hadn't been let in on a secret.

"I'm sure it's nothing, just all the years of eating poorly catching up with me. I'm surprised I haven't gotten an ulcer."

Mom did have a cast-iron stomach. She could eat more food than anybody I knew and yet stay slim and trim. It was not unusual for her to consume a full pint of ice cream in a single sitting.

I opened the envelope from Rita as we talked. Pulling the letter out, I was surprised when a check fell out of the folded page. Half listening to Mom, I picked the check up off the floor and gasped. It was made out to me for $2,000!

"What?" Mom asked, hearing my gasp.

"Mom, I'll call you right back. Something's come up." I began reading the letter as I hung up the phone. Rita's letter said that the Summer of Love pack had been presold to some big bookstores and that this was one of "hopefully many more checks to come."

I sat there with my hand over my mouth, in a solid state of shock. The phone rang again, shaking me from my stupor.

"So, what's the matter?" my sister Brenda asked.

"What do you mean?" I was still short of breath and shaking. I could barely hold the phone to my ear.

"Mom said something happened and you jumped off the phone."

The family gossip tree: If we all didn't know what each of us was doing every second, our lives were not whole.

"I can't talk now. I'll fill you in later." I wanted to tell my sister, but I knew it would get back to Mom, and I wasn't ready to face the music about my smutty writing. I started laughing.

"What's so funny?" Brenda persisted.

"I'll tell you later. I need to make some phone calls first, okay? Hey, what's this about Mom going to the hospital for tests?" I artfully changed the subject.

"What tests? She didn't tell me." Brenda sounded indignant, probably because Mom told me first.

"I don't know. She said her stomach has been bothering her, so she called Dr. Sandoval. I can't believe she didn't tell me about it."

"I'm calling Mom," Brenda hung up.

Gabby stuck her sweaty face in the door, "Mommy, come on."

"Okay, sweetie, a few more goals and then I need to start dinner." I felt as if I were having an out-of-body experience as I stuffed the check in my purse. Before I could get out the door to continue our World Cup game, the phone rang again.

"Now what?" I answered, expecting Brenda or Mom to tell me some late breaking news of the past minute.

"Who were you expecting?"

Mitch's voice cut through me like a scalpel. "I thought it was Mom or Brenda."

"So, it's been, what, ten minutes since you've last talked to them?" He'd always resented my family, though I never knew why.

"Mitch, you remember the novel—" I stopped, suddenly afraid to say anything about the check I had received. It was all I could do to keep my mouth shut. Something inside me wanted to scream the news to him about my sudden wealth. However, as poorly as things were going with us, I figured the divorce lawyers would find out about it eventually, though rubbing his nose in it would sure be fun.

"What novel?" he asked, without much enthusiasm.

"Never mind. I've been meaning to talk to you about the car. You've had it way more than me lately. I've heard you've been driving a woman around. Is that true?"

"No, why would I do that?" He had that tone he frequently used, like I'm a total idiot and why would I ask such a stupid question.

Duh, Cassandra. Reality seeped in. I'd been in denial, not wanting to believe. Slowly I sat at the kitchen table.

"Mitch?" I asked cautiously.

"What?" Suddenly he seemed nervous, his breathing more rapid.

"Are you seeing someone?"

He hesitated a beat too long. "What are you talking about?"

"*Mommy!* You said you'd play soccer with me. Get off the phone. You're always on the phone." Gabby stood in the doorway holding her soccer ball.

"Let me talk to the princess." Mitch evaded the confrontation.

In a state of disbelief, I handed the phone to Gabby. She ran to the phone and excitedly told him about the birthday party at the Novaks' and asked when he was moving home.

I could only stare at the floor. Had Mitch sideswiped me again? Could he really be with another woman? I never expected an affair. I wasn't jealous as much as I was shocked.

Ashley ambled in the kitchen, headphones firmly attached to her ears. She began rummaging in the refrigerator.

"Who's on the phone?" she asked dispassionately.

"Your father." I couldn't help but look at Ashley and imagine Mitch dating someone who looked similar. A fetid knot burbled in my stomach.

Gabby handed the phone to Ashley. "Daddy wants us to come over!"

"Hi, Dad." Ashley sounded so innocent and young. Could she imagine Mitch with another woman? I thought of him being a father to the girls, holding them in a thunderstorm, playing practical jokes until they laughed themselves silly.

"I don't know, it was all right, I guess." Ashley still had her head in the fridge, foraging for food. "I don't know if he was there." Even through the "I don't knows," I could tell Ashley was talking about the party and Andrew Novak. "I don't know, let me ask Mom." Ashley turned to me. "Can we have dinner with Dad?"

"Not tonight. This is your last week of school before summer break. You can see your father next weekend." *And because he could be going out with someone your age.* I winced. No, I worked to convince myself. We were still married. He wouldn't do that. Was I that blindly stupid?

"Here she is." Ashley held the phone out for me.

"What?" I said as rudely as I could muster.

"I'd like to take the girls tomorrow night. Come on, you've had them all weekend."

"Sounds like you've had your share of girls this weekend, too." I noticed Ashley look in my direction.

"I'm not looking for a fight." Mitch sighed yet still sounded nervous. "I just want to spend time with my children."

"No. Period. We'll discuss the other issue later." I was hoping my voice didn't give away my emotions.

I hung up the phone and looked at my daughters. Ashley could tell something was up, but she didn't say anything. Gabby was happily making faces at herself in the hallway mirror.

Wild Rose

– FROM CHAPTER 13

Rosemary landed in the spotlight hard and fast. She fielded calls from magazines, newspapers, and TV shows.

Beck was thrilled.

"Rosemary, at her kitchen counter, turned the glossy pages of Cocotte magazine, ticked that the pictures didn't look as good as her originals. But damned if Colten didn't look luscious.

One afternoon, a few weeks after the pictures were published, Rosemary turned on a talk show. A celebrated feminist was arguing with a conservative woman about the photographs. The feminist said it was about time men showed their bodies, women had been exploited for years.

"Oh, heavens," Miss Conservative began. "If the good Lord wanted us naked, then he wouldn't have invented clothes." She giggled. Recovering from the stupid quip, she went on. "These photographs are immoral, disgusting, and should be banned."

"Have you ever protested Playboy?" the host asked.

"No, I believe women shouldn't bare their bodies. But—" She paused to make a point. "—men's urges are stronger." She blushed so deeply Rosemary saw the woman's cheeks change hue on her small black-and-white television.

The feminist rolled her eyes. "Double standards. We have as strong sexual needs as men. We're just expected to repress it. It's the seventies. Women need to embrace their sexuality."

Ms. Conservative smoothed her modest skirt. "Only women with low standards have excessive sexual desires."

"Not true. You've obviously never had good sex," Ms. Feminist challenged.

Rosemary was glued to the television. She'd never seen anyone argue on a television talk show and was both appalled and amazed.

The ringing phone made her jump.

Holding her breath. *Colten?*

She picked up the phone.

"Hey, babe, you wanna explain those pictures?"

"Hugh, how's the tour?" Rosemary asked. Hugh was still her loyal consort. Like a tail wagging pup, he was always ready to play. And was as comfortable to Rosemary as a worn pair of jeans.

"It was going fine 'till I saw those naked pictures of that movie star and your name as the photographer." He sounded like a jilted lover. "What were you doing while this dude was naked on the beach?"

Her relationship with Hugh had always been easy, with no commitments. "Hugh we're not going steady or anything."

"I thought you were my main squeeze."

"I'm not a lemon. I don't get on your case about your groupies."

"That's different. I mean, I'm a guy."

Rosemary laughed looking at the television. There was a commercial on.

"Don't be needy," she said.

"Fine. I'll just pick a name out of the groupie hat.

"Have fun." Rosemary sighed. His rebuff stung. Not only was he an amazing lover, but also a good friend.

As she hung up, Rosemary fought her desire for Colten. Her photographs were garnering lots of attention—he was on many talk shows—yet he never mentioned the photographer. She needed to get busy and forget him. But she'd never known such yearning.

It was time to get out of town.

Chapter Twenty Two

"When everything comes your way, you're in the wrong lane."
~ Steven Wright

With the girls out of school and Ashley working at the kids' camp at the Y, while Gabby attended the camp there. Both were occupied while I worked. However, it was difficult managing drop off and pick up, now that I was a single mom.

Mitch managed to dodge questions about another woman, throwing blame back at me for being irrational. Our tenuous relationship was a tightrope ready to snap.

One evening while I was making dinner, Rita called. "*Wild Rose* is receiving critical praise. First run sales are encouraging—actually, remarkable. *Wild Rose* has pulled away from the three pack and is generating enough interest for the publisher to print a second edition of the book on its own."

I was afraid to spend the proverbial wad just yet. The checks continued to come in. Years of riding the wild wave of Mitch's sales commissions made me conservative, and besides, I wasn't sure how to explain my sudden wealth to everyone. I almost told Mom and Brenda several times, but I couldn't work up the nerve because of the sex. Nor did I want Mitch to claim his spousal share of it. We didn't talk much during our brief, uncomfortable conversations. He continued to evade my questions, saying he was trying to "find himself."

I worked to contain a molten ball of energy—I could either blow or refocus.

I opened a separate bank account and deposited the checks.

A few days after Rita's call, on a muggy summer afternoon, Mom surprised me by coming into the emergency room. To my shock and amusement, she carried a copy of *Wild Rose* under her arm.

"Mom, what brings you here? And how do you like that book?" I asked both questions in one breath.

Ignoring the book question, she sighed. "I'm getting a stomach X-ray."

"For what?" I sat forward. "I thought Dr. Sandoval said the blood tests were normal."

"My stomach is still bothering me," she said, clutching the book to her chest.

"Dr. Sandoval didn't say anything." I felt betrayed and worried. "Have you had any other tests?" All at once, I noticed Mom had lost a considerable amount of weight. Though I'd seen her weekly over the last few months, I hadn't paid much attention to her weight until I saw her standing in the doorway. Maybe it was the hospital backdrop that made her look different. "Mom, how much weight have you lost?" A searing bolt of fear shot through me realizing that something could be seriously wrong. "Why didn't you tell me how you were feeling?"

She waved her hand in her usual fashion. "Oh, it's probably just gas."

This had to be serious, Mom *never* joked about gas. She was appalled at the mere mention of farts.

I couldn't stand the thought of her being ill. "Mom, is there something you're not telling me?"

"Mrs. Ellison!" Kathy bounded into my doorway. "Long time no see." Noticing *Wild Rose* in Mom's grip, she raved, "Don't you just love that book? I finished it in one weekend. Couldn't put it down. My kids were neglected because I did nothing but read."

Kathy was so animated talking about *Wild Rose*, I couldn't help but swell with pride. I was tempted to spill the beans and confess.

"So what do you think of it?" I looked at Mom and motioned toward the copy of *Wild Rose*. "I heard it was pretty racy."

"My reading group picked this," Mom said, looking at the cover. "It's good. Mindless, but fun. You should read it. Cardia Loving must be a hoot to create a character like Rosemary. My book club is going to try and Skype her at our next meeting."

"Don't bet on it," I said, before I could stop myself. My feelings hurt a little when Mom defined my work as mindless. "I'll bet I could write that stuff," I said, miffed.

She and Kathy laughed so hard, they had tears in their eyes. I glared at them.

Mom looked past Kathy, "Hi, Sheila. I was just heading to X-ray."

"Do you have all the paperwork I gave you?" Dr. Sandoval asked as she walked in. She avoided looking at me.

"X-ray?" Kathy asked. She looked at me. "You didn't tell me your mom wasn't feeling well." She touched Mom's arm. "Don't be such a stranger here. We love to see you. I hope you get to feeling better," she said as she left.

When Kathy was out of earshot, I looked at Mom and Dr. Sandoval. "What's going on? My mom is having tests and you didn't tell me?" I directed the question to Sheila but looked at

Mom for the answer.

Sheila glanced at Mom. "Cass, you know I can't talk about my patients."

"She's my mother." My voice caught.

Mom defended her. "Honey, I didn't want to concern you, especially with everything going on with Mitch. Trust me, I'd let you know if there's anything to worry about." She gave me her I'm-a-mom-so-I-know-everything look—a look I've never been able to master though I'd borne children.

I watched them walk away. Mom's jeans hung loose and saggy. Why hadn't I noticed the weight loss? I said a short prayer the X-ray would find nothing serious. When I prayed she only had gas, I smiled, thinking Mom would be mortified I'd mentioned flatulence in my communication with God.

Chapter Twenty Three

"Drag the Joneses down to your level. It's cheaper.

~ Anonymous

The day after Mom's visit to the hospital, I took Gabby to Angela Novak's birthday party. As we walked to the door, I noted a pungent smell of manure wafting on the breeze. Ringing the bell, I wondered if they'd just fertilized the shrubs.

A grown up Tinkerbell answered the door, holding a tray of clown cups. She twirled, and her green, shimmering skirt caught rainbow light. "Welcome to Angela's party!" she said, and threw a smatter of pixie dust at us as we walked in. In the backyard, on a green patch of lawn by the pool, I discovered the reason for the aroma: The Novaks had a mini-circus, complete with a feather plumed pony.

Gabby squealed, "Wow!" and ran to the one ring circus, ignoring the sugary drinks.

Tinkerbell winked at me and nodded toward the kitchen. "Mimosas are being served for the big kids."

I was dumbstruck at the elaborate event. Whatever happened to lopsided homemade birthday cakes, pinchy hats, and wilted balloons? I wanted the best for my kids, but this was too lavish. What would be left when the kids grew up? *But what the hell*, I thought. A mimosa sounded pretty good.

In the kitchen, moms hovered over trays of food while

sipping drinks. Susan welcomed me and handed me a mimosa. "It's good to see you, Cassie." She pulled me into the group. "Try the appetizers. They're great."

I'd just started my second mimosa when Gabby came running, breathlessly excited. "Mommy, look at that pony! He can do tricks! Mommy, can I please have one? Angela said she was going to get one and it's going to live here. Please, can I?"

"We can't have a pony, sweetie. Ponies can't live in a neighborhood. They need more space."

"Angela said it was going to sleep in the backyard." Gabby's excitement quickly twisted to disappointment.

I guided her away from the group. "Gabs, Angela can't have a pony in her backyard. Horses need to be in a barn and need a big pasture to run in." I tried to hug her, but she pulled away.

"You *always* say no. I *never* get to have any fun." The sugar meltdown was starting. Cake, cookies, and cola—a sure-fire recipe to turn a beautiful, sweet child into a screaming, body slamming demon.

"Never? I can recall a few times you had fun. Let me think..."

Her lip started quivering, a tantrum welling up like mercury in a thermometer.

"Why don't you enjoy the rest of the party, Gabs? We'll talk about this later."

"I want a trick pony."

Angela ran by, screaming, "Time to open my presents."

Gabby gave me a look letting me know this discussion was not over, turned and followed Angela.

I worried about the gift we had bought, a little art set. No doubt the competition was going to be stiff. Maybe, if I was lucky, the card had fallen off in the shuffle.

I watched Angela spend the next hour tearing open gifts like a rabid dog, while the mimosas bubbled in my head.

I didn't know if it was guilt or competition, but later, I took both girls to the mall for a shopping spree.

When I suggested the excursion, Ashley acted surprised but came willingly. The possibility of purchasing new grunge clothes we could fight about must have been irresistible. Gabby threatened she would only go if she could get a trick pony. "If they have one for sale at the mall, I'll think about it," I said.

"Yes!" was her heartfelt response.

I prayed there was no petting zoo, or I'd be in big trouble.

It felt good to go shopping without worrying about money. I could buy anything, though, as we shopped, there was little I wanted. Not so with the girls.

"I'm going in here," Ashley said, indifferent. Her slouched posture fit with the pants that fell too low on her slim hips. She stood outside a store featuring shimmering, halter-top fashions and a black light sign above the doors that read "The Pit." The music blaring from inside made my fillings vibrate.

"Why don't we go somewhere together, like Penney's or Kohls?" I asked.

"Like I'd look good in anything from Kohl's? They only have old lady clothes." Ashley's slouch turned defiant as she crossed her arms.

"Cool, look, body glitter." Gabby slipped by us and headed to a display of The Pit's body creams. "Mom, can I have some black body glitter?" Gabby began smelling and sampling various body massage oils.

Without a word, Ashley went in and riffled though the racks. I shrugged remembering how I loved odd fashions when I was in high school. Mom hated most of what I wore but tolerated it. Giving me lectures about wearing classic designs, clothes that never go out of style.

"Hey, Ash. I didn't know you were going to be here." Teresa emerged from a rack of ripped, distressed shirts. "Hi, Mrs. Calabria. Man, my mom wouldn't be caught dead here. You're pretty cool."

Ashley looked at me smugly with "Kohls" written all over her face.

"Mommy, look I *really* need this." Gabby was holding a gold, fuzzy sweater. The material looked as if it had been a shag carpet from the '70s. Upon closer inspection, I think it *was* shag carpet—complete with pet stains.

"How cute," Teresa said to Gabby. "C'mon, I'll take you to the dressing room." Teresa turned to me. "It'll look really cool on her."

I didn't know what was worse—a real trick pony or a shirt that could turn tricks.

Ashley, weighed down with an armful of clothes, went into the dressing room with the others. I looked through the racks of merchandise and gasped at the prices of the junk.

By the time we left the store, loaded with shopping bags, we were all having a great time. So what if my kids looked like prostitutes? At least they were happy.

Gabby, slathered in blue body glitter—I'd drawn the line at black—wore her shag carpet sweater, and Ashley carried a bag of clothes that would probably disintegrate after the first washing.

"Mom, Teresa wants me to go to the food court with her. Can I?" Ashley started handing her bags to me to carry.

"No," I said, firmly. "We're going to have dinner together. You can call her later."

"Why not?" Ashley whined. Teresa waited nearby.

"Ashley." I tried the adult mommy look but felt like I was only scrunching up my face.

Reluctantly, Ashley acquiesced. We decided on a Mexican cantina in the mall. As we walked to the restaurant, I was shocked to see copies of *Wild Rose* featured in front of a bookstore window. My knees went weak, and I pushed the girls ahead of me. I looked around furtively, as if people knew I had written the racy book so prominently displayed, although I'll admit I had a "Mary Tyler Moore" moment— an urge to toss my hat in the air and twirl. I bandied about feelings of being proud *and* ashamed. I don't think the girls noticed me sweating like a racehorse. Gabby couldn't get enough of her reflection in the windows as she passed, and Ashley shuffled along, quietly but obediently.

I was surprised when Gabby squealed, "Daddy!" and dashed ahead.

Sure enough, there was Mitch, looking surprised.

Ashley brightened a bit. "Hi, Dad. I thought you said you had plans tonight."

I wondered when she had talked to him. "Hey, what brings you here?" I asked, disappointed. We'd been having a nice girls' night, and I didn't want any tension spoiling our evening.

"Look, Daddy" Gabby twirled like a ballerina to show off her new sweater. "And I even got blue body glitter. Smell my arm." She shoved her forearm under Mitch's nose. "It smells like blueberry."

"Well, don't you look...um...furry." he said. "So, did you get a bonus?" he asked me, eyeing the big shopping bag Ashley held. While he talked, he herded us away from the store he'd come out of.

"We're going to eat. Come with us, *pleeaase*?" Gabby said in her best pleading voice.

Mitch glanced back toward the store. "Not tonight, honey. How about tomorrow? It's Sunday, so maybe we can play and have dinner then." He glanced at me for an answer but kept us moving.

"I'm sure the girls would love that. Just let me know what time, and I'll have them ready," I said.

He looked at me. "Probably around three, if that's okay."

"That's fine. You know you're welcome to join us for dinner." I extended an olive branch to make the girls happy.

He glanced over his shoulder. "Thanks, but I've got to run."

"Okay. Come on, girls, I'm hungry." I headed toward the restaurant, glad to be leaving without a scene.

"Mitch, are these your girls?" An attractive woman appeared by Mitch's side. Her brown hair was long like Ashley's, and her hip-hugger jeans fit her slim hips like mine used to before my pregnancies. "Hi, you must be Ashley, and you're Gabrielle." She began petting my child. "What a cute sweater!"

I looked at Mitch for an explanation. All I got was an introduction.

"Girls, this is Renee Tibbits. Renee, my girls, Ashley and Gabby. And this is my—this is Cassandra.

Ashley looked as shocked as I felt. Gabby seemed confused. She stared at the woman. "Are you a friend of my daddy's?"

Renee looked humorously at Mitch. "Yes, your daddy and I are good friends," she said, a lilting emphasis on "friends." "It's nice to meet you, Cassandra." She held out her hand to me. "Mitch has told me lots about you."

I stared, dumbfounded, not sure whether to shake or slap her hand.

What had Mitch told her? Perhaps he mentioned the time when, as I was tearing my insides out bearing his children, he fainted, and all the nurses descended on him, leaving me writhing in agony. Yeah, I'll bet Mitch said a lot of nice things about me.

"Nice to meet you." Not really, but I didn't know how to act in front of the girls. There was nothing like meeting your husband's beautiful girlfriend to magnify your own insecurities.

"Mitch, this *is* a surprise." I smiled through my gritted teeth. I glanced at Ashley, who had stepped away from us. She looked as if she were ready to bolt into the depths of the mall. I could tell she was trying not to cry. It broke my heart. Gabby, unusually quiet, stared intently at Renee.

"Cassie, I'll call you tomorrow," Mitch said abruptly. "Hey, princess, how about we get some ice cream tomorrow afternoon?" He bent down talking to Gabby.

"Okay, but will she come, too?" Gabby looked at Renee.

"All right, girls, pack it up, and let's go eat." I tried to keep my voice steady. "Miss Tittits, I—I mean Tibbits, nice to meet you."

As I turned to go, I noticed she seemed to apprise me with a coolness, as if to say she had won the prize.

As we walked away, Ashley followed a few paces behind. Gabby held my arm, turned, and stared over her shoulder at Mitch. I refused to look back.

At dinner, none of us had much of an appetite. Ashley was especially upset. "Mom, who was that? How could he be going out with someone?"

"Ashley, I didn't know about her. I'm as surprised as you—probably even more." I thought about Mitch's evasive answers. I'd not pushed it. I hadn't wanted to believe it.

Ashley's eyes were wet with tears. "You guys are going to get a divorce, aren't you?"

"No, honey." But I was in a state of disbelief myself. Perhaps we *were* heading for divorce. "I don't think so. I don't know." I put my hand on her arm, as she ducked her head and wiped her eyes.

I wondered what Renee saw in Mitch, an older man. It hurt and angered me to see Mitch with another woman, but my heart broke for my girls.

"I'm not going with him tomorrow," Ashley said.

"Me either," Gabby responded firmly. Then, looking at Ashley. "Why not?"

"Girls, I think you both need to go." I put my arm around Gabby. "It will give you an opportunity to ask your father any questions you have."

I couldn't believe I was encouraging them to go. I wanted the girls with me, but deep down knew they needed to spend time with Mitch, no matter what. He was their father. I felt my food respond viscerally to that thought.

Since Mitch and I had separated, I hadn't pictured him with another woman. I'd imagined him staying up late, drinking beer, and watching sports in a cluttered apartment, alone, or with his friends. I guess I didn't know him as well as I'd thought. Or had I been in denial? It was easier not to face the truth. Our once parallel track had derailed.

Wild Rose

— FROM CHAPTER 14

Rosemary was still considering a sabbatical when the phone rang. It was Beck. "Rosie, guess who asked for your services?" He paused, dangling the carrot.

"Colten Garrison?" Rosemary asked, hope laced her voice.

"No. You've already shot as much of him as is legal." He laughed. "Better than that."

"Okay, Beck. Surprise me."

"Rolling Stone wants you up close and personal with a new rock show touring California. I mean, this is it, Rosie. People are clamoring for you. They know who you are. Pretty rare in the world of photography."

"How long is the assignment?" She hoped the job would get her out of town long enough to forget about Colten.

"Through the summer," Beck answered. "It'll be an on-and-off schedule with about 75 percent travel from June through the end of August. So don't get a pet anytime soon."

"Speaking of pets, I don't hear your kids in the background today."

"I can't wait until you have children of your own," Beck said with conviction.

"You know I don't have a maternal bone in my body."

"You'd be surprised." He laughed softly. "When the alarms start going off in your biological clock, I promise you'll start seeing children differently."

"I'll stick with my career. Keep my life simple."

"You're in the limelight now. Let's stay on this bucking bronco for the full eight seconds. You're already known in the art community, but now you're becoming a name in the media. Let's not lose momentum."

As much as she hated to admit it, Rosemary was enjoying the fame. She laughed. "Sure, Beck, I'll do what I need to keep up with the demands of being an overnight success."

"Look, Rosie, we both stand to benefit from this. The Colten story will eventually die down. If you want to stay ahead of the game, shoot, print, move on."

His tone stung, so she snapped back, "I didn't get in this business to please everybody. I don't intend—"

Beck cut her off. "This is the real world. You can't hide behind your virtuous attitude and be successful. Shoot what the public wants—not what you want. I love you, Rosie, but you're on the fence. Stay on top of it for a while, okay?"

"Okay, okay." Rosemary rolled her eyes. He was probably right, though she didn't want to admit it.

Colten sipped a full bodied cabernet on the balcony of his Malibu estate, while Nikki primped for a studio dinner. As the sun set over the ocean he thought of Rosemary, remembering their lovemaking. He'd painfully resisted the temptation to call. Laz made it clear he was not to upset the relationship with Nikki. If he called Rosemary, there'd be hell to pay. Nikki needed him as much as his career needed her.

Laz was forced to rethink the naked beach photographs when the public responded favorably. Keeping the publicity going until the movie's release was Laz's specialty.

Colten replayed memories of Rosemary, responding physically with a throbbing surge of happiness. He closed his eyes imagining until Nikki's screech brought his pleasure to a raging halt.

"No way, honey." She eyed his engorged desire tenting out of his tuxedo trousers. "I've spent all day at the beauty parlor, and the last thing I want is somebody else touching me." She waved her manicured fingernails and giggled. "Maybe later, if you don't mess up my French twist." Her hands patted her tresses as she admired her reflection in the glass. Her hair was curled, layered, and stacked. The poof seemed to defy the law of gravity.

"Do I look fat in this gown?" She turned. Her large breasts cast long shadows over the potted impatiens. She touched her face checking the glue on her eyelashes. "You're not going to wear your hair like that?"

Nikki looked at Colten in the window's reflection. "When you wear your hair natural you look like a hippie," she squealed. "Wear it slicked back like the gangster from your new movie."

Rosemary's summer rock tour featured multiple rock bands and to follow a new band, The Fakers. She enjoyed throwing her Rolling Stone press pass around working backstage.

Beck checked in telling her the magazine was impressed.

Working around the super ego rock stars made Rosemary think of Colten. She was better off without him but desire haunted her no matter how hard she tried to forget.

Rosemary's tour companion was Natalie Boyette, the wife of the The Fakers' lead singer. Natalie did a lot of drugs and was fearless.

One muggy afternoon, they sunbathed by a lavish hotel pool.

"Loosen up Rosemary." Natalie pulled her sunglasses off. "Come to the party tonight. Unless you're scared, or just too cool?"

"I'm too cool," Rosemary joked. Surprised to think people thought she was unapproachable.

Natalie poured a stream of baby oil on her thin, bronzed arm. "I don't want you to be like the sleazy parasite groupies. It's just I'm never sure if you're having fun."

"I'm not into the drug scene."

"Some of the guys don't know how to take you."She smeared oil on her face. "Ritchie, the drummer, thinks you're hot."

"I'm here for a short time. This is your life." Rosemary stood and grabbed her towel, "I've got to work. I'll see you later."

All eyes watched Rosemary walk to the lobby. She hated the attention. A young girl stepped in front of her. "Are you a movie star?"

Rosemary laughed. "No, but thank you for asking."

"Can I have your autograph anyway? You're so pretty."

"Sure." She took the girl's Disney autograph book and signed next to Goofy's.

"Thank you." The girl scrambled to her mother. Rosemary smiled and headed to the elevator. Cute kid, she thought, then stopped, suddenly aware of a strange feeling in her gut. Surely that wasn't a tick of her biological clock?

Nah. She shook off the feeling.

Rosemary went to her room, missing her little cottage. She sighed. The novelty of hanging out with famous rock stars was losing its appeal.

She called Beck.

"Rosie, I've been trying to get a hold of you." Beck's voice offered a familiar dose of comfort. "Life on the road must be keeping you busy."

"It's a great job. But I'll be happy when I can sleep in my own bed."

"Well, I've got good news. You must not have shot enough of Colten Garrison, because his producer called."

"Colten?" Rosemary couldn't keep the excitement out of her voice.

"Actually, Lazarus Forrest called. He wants you to shoot the wedding of the century—Colten and Nikki's. Pretty cool, huh? I'm telling you, Rosie, you're the photographer to the stars."

"His wedding?" Rosemary choked. "He's marrying that bimbo?" Her voice raised an octave.

"Ain't it great?" Beck gushed. "Can you imagine how many stars will be there? You get jobs like this, and there'll be no more drug clinic shoots for you."

Rosemary's spirits plummeted. "Trust me, Beck, I've done nothing but shoot a glamorized drug clinic on this tour."

"Do you know how many photographers would give their 200mm lenses to be in your shoes?"

"I don't understand why Laz wants me. He was furious the night I took the pictures of Colten."

"Probably because you've generated a ton of income for him. I thought you'd be jumping off the walls with happiness.

Jumping off the balcony to the cement sidewalk was more like it, she thought.

"I'm not a wedding photographer."

"This isn't a wedding. It's an event, a milestone, a happening. It's history, and you're the photographer." He became businesslike. "You have four weeks on the tour. That will get you home the end of August. The wedding is mid-September. I'm not going to book you for anything.

Rosemary dropped the speaker of the phone to her chin and listened to Beck. She angrily swiped away a tear. She'd been proud not to depend on anybody. But this cut deep. Though she had only been with Colten briefly, she sensed their souls were one. She dreaded the wedding and hated Colten for being too weak to take charge. And she hated herself for not having the courage to call him.

Chapter Twenty Four

"Fighting not good. Somebody always get hurt."
~ Mr. Miyagi, The Next Karate Kid

When we got home from the mall, I had two messages from Rita, asking me to call her right away. There was also another check in the mail.

Even so, I felt numb. I sent the girls to get ready for bed trying not to imagine what Mitch and Renee were doing. I fought back tears as I brushed my teeth, sure they were in the throes of passion. I wondered if, before he was sated, he made that funny squeaky noise with her. Was he thinking of his family?

In a spurt of anger, I went to the phone to call him, hoping to stop both of them mid-sex. Being visual, it was hard imagining my husband "doing it" with another, woman. I worried what Ashley and Gabby were thinking.

I picked up the phone to find Ashley on the extension. "*Mom*, I'm on the phone." Same teenage inflection in her voice as before the Renee sighting. Maybe she was okay.

"Sorry, honey, I need to make a call when you're done." I hung up slowly, tempted to eavesdrop just a little, glad she didn't have a cell phone yet.

Fuming about Mitch and Renee made me think about

my lack of a physical relationship. If I didn't have my imaginary sex life through Rosemary, I'd be celibate. It had been months since Mitch and I separated. I still felt married. Sex was nonexistent, except maybe Rosemary's conquests.

I told the girls we'd stay up late, eat popcorn, and watch a movie. Then snuggle in my bed like we used to.

Outside Ashley's door, I overheard her on the phone. "... he was with her at the mall. We were all like, totally surprised. I wonder if they've had sex. Gross! I mean, this *is* my dad."

I stuck my head in the door. "Ashley, join us for popcorn when you're off the phone."

She looked as if she'd gotten caught.

"Mommy, can we have a slumber party?" Gabby came out of her room all cute and cozy in her pajamas and bathrobe. I was happy that she looked like a little girl and not a fuzzy doormat. "Can we sleep in your bed?"

"Sounds perfect." I folded her in my arms, "Just promise you won't take all the covers." She smiled.

"Go brush your teeth and wash your face. I'll get Ashley."

"If I'm going to eat popcorn, why do I have to brush my teeth now? I promise I'll do it later." Gabby whined as I pointed to the bathroom.

"Yes, you still have to brush now, and then we'll see about later." I knew she was going to be fast asleep before she would brush again.

I knocked lightly and opened Ashley's door. "C'mon, time to get off the phone. We're going to have a slumber party in my room."

"I gotta go. Call me tomorrow." Hanging up the phone,

Ashley said, "Some lady named Rita called, said she'd call back later."

"Ashley, that was an important call," I admonished. "You need to give me my calls when they come in." I wondered why Rita didn't call my cell. Probably because I'd been ignoring her calls.

"I was going to, but she said she'd call back."

I sighed, glad she hadn't asked who Rita was. "Go get cleaned up. I'll make the popcorn."

Later, as we all snuggled in my bed watching a movie, Gabby asked me about Mitch and Renee. "Mommy, if you and Daddy get a divorce, is that lady going to be my stepmom?"

I sighed. "Daddy and I have many things to talk about before we get a divorce. I don't think that lady will be your stepmother any time soon, Gabs. Let's take one day at a time."

Ashley looked over her pillow. "Did you know he was going out with somebody?"

"No, well, I wondered when Mrs. Arpino said she saw you and Daddy driving together. But honestly, I didn't know." I hugged Gabby. "Ash, let's talk about this another time. I really need to talk to your father about a few things before I start making assumptions."

"I don't think there's anything to assume, Mom." Ashley smirked. "None of us are stupid. Well, Gabby."

"Mommy! She called me stupid." Gabby's lower lip quivered.

"Ashley, apologize to your sister. There was no reason for that."

"Just kidding." Ashley played with her split ends. "Sorry, it was just a joke."

Gabby pouted but accepted her apology.

"I'll call your father tomorrow."

Gabby began to tear up. "Mommy, I'm scared you and Daddy are going to get a divorce. When is he going to come home?" Gabby's tears streamed down her face. "I want to call him now and tell him to come home."

"You know what, sweetie? It's late and past everybody's bedtime. Let's wait until tomorrow and we'll talk to him." She nodded and pressed close to me. By the time we hit play on the DVD, she'd already fallen asleep.

Ashley muttered under her breath but loud enough for me to hear. "*Whose* bedtime?"

I opened the covers for her to lie down. For the first time in ages, she didn't pull away from me when I began to rub her back.

Chapter Twenty Five

"Behind every successful man is a surprised woman."
~ *Maryon Pearson*

I debated calling Mitch after the girls had gone to sleep. Once down, Gabby would sleep through the night no matter how loud I raised my voice to Mitch. I wasn't sure about Ashley. Her hearing was becoming more and more selective. Plus, I feared she might wake up and head back into her room. It was nice having both girls asleep so close to me.

Sinking into bed, I turned the TV off, picked up a book, trying to read, but was so wound up with the image of Mitch with another woman I couldn't relax. Was Mitch caressing her, was she taking care of his needs? As much as I tried to separate myself from him, I couldn't see myself as single. But another woman? I hadn't seen it coming. Did I live with blinders?

I thought about our relationship, wondering when the last straw broke. We had a comfort zone, a life built on routine, mostly. In retrospect, it was more of a working relationship. But we had loved each other and had been committed, we'd promised each other to be together and we'd meant it. I wondered if I'd ever be able to regain those feelings for Mitch, or even someone else.

I put my book aside remembering Rita had called. I got up to write a note to return her call in the morning. When we'd spoken before, she was happy about the success of *Wild Rose*. The few times I let myself jump up and down in her office about my newfound wealth, she managed to maintain a businesslike air. At our last meeting, Rita told me *Wild Rose* was selling better than Dominique's and Siren's books and the publisher was running a third printing. It was becoming more and more difficult for me to keep my success a secret.

Rita objected when I declined the inset photograph for the book, but she was in such a hurry to get the book out that she didn't push. In all honesty, I don't think either of us thought *Wild Rose* would do so well. Now I could consider quitting my job or taking a sabbatical, but I hadn't done anything because I didn't want to set off alarms with Mitch. Also, I needed to maintain an "in" at the hospital while Mom was being treated. Though I had friends at work, my employment badge carried more weight than my personality.

With the problems concerning Mitch, I'd not given enough time to Mom. I prayed hard that she was okay. I couldn't take a double blow: a failed marriage, and the fear Mom may have a terminal illness. The extra money couldn't buy happiness.

I must have fallen into a deep sleep, dreaming about ringing telephones chasing me in slow motion. And, of course, I was naked—a Freudian issue I'd deal with later.

I opened one eye as I reached for the phone. "Hello?" I croaked.

"Cass. How are the girls?" Mitch's voice was so familiar,

but remembering Renee, I immediately went on the defensive.

"Why? Do you want them to fix you up with their friends?" I surprised myself with the ability to be even remotely witty while half asleep. I looked at the clock. It was seven o'clock on Sunday morning.

"That's not funny. What did they say about last night?"

"If you're so damned worried about it, then why didn't you call?" I hissed into the phone. I sat up and glanced at the other side of the bed. Gabby was sound asleep and Ashley was gone. "Did you finally get rid of her this morning, so you could call your family? By the way, what high school were you trolling when you met her?"

"Cass, she doesn't mean anything. Maybe if you were a better listener, I'd tell you more, but you'd just be catty," Mitch said, his voice shaking. "Don't start. Really, it's nothing serious.

"Nothing serious? What counts as serious?" I asked in a squeaky, high pitched whisper, trying not to scream. I slipped out of bed.

"We were just at the mall."

"Do you know how upsetting it was for the girls to see you with another woman?"

Gabby started waking up.

"That's why I'm calling. I'd like to talk to them."

I grabbed my bathrobe. "And what are you going to tell them? That you were tutoring her? I don't think the girls should visit you today. They need to get over the trauma of seeing you with her."

"Mommy, who's on the phone?" Gabby asked sleepily.

"I'm hungry, can you make bunny rabbit pancakes?"

"She sounds really traumatized," Mitch said. "Let me talk to her."

I'd gotten one arm in my robe. "Not now. I'll have her call you later."

"Is that Daddy? Lemme talk to him." Gabby reached for the phone.

"Daddy." Gabby grabbed again, and I relented and sat next to her. "Hi. Did you like my new sweater last night?"

"Yes, baby, you looked like a princess." I could hear his muffled reply through the receiver.

"Who's Renee? Is she your girlfriend? Are you allowed to have a girlfriend and mommy at the same time?"

Come on, Gabby. Start crying. Throw a tantrum.

"No, honey, Renee is just a friend," Mitch said to her.

Liar, liar pants on fire. Oh, bad analogy.

"Daddy, when are you coming home to live?" Gabby cooed with her sleepy voice.

"I don't know, baby. Hopefully soon."

"Soon" by whose standards, I wondered. I got out of bed, wrapped myself in my old terry cloth robe, and went to wash up.

"Mommy, Daddy wants to talk to you." Gabby held the phone out. Reluctantly, I walked to the bed and took the phone from her.

"What time can I get the girls this afternoon?" Mitch asked. "I'd like to take them to dinner."

"Would you be including Ms. Tidbits in this outing?" I asked sarcastically.

"Look, Cass, I have nothing to hide. I told you Renee is

only a good friend helping me out right now. She listens when I talk and doesn't tune me out."

"Did you say something?" I responded angrily. "I think I've spent plenty of time listening to you and *your* problems, thank you very much."

"Yeah, and you seem to be *my* biggest problem now."

"Me? Who's the one who ran away from his family?" I glanced at Gabby, wondering how much she understood.

I could see this conversation was going nowhere. My hands shook and, for the first time, I seriously thought that our marriage was irreparable.

Mitch and I left the Renee issue unresolved. He would pick up the girls at three.

Rita called as I was making breakfast and debating about going to church with Mom. All I wanted to do was crawl under my comforter and only come up for air. I was unprepared for what she asked.

"It's time for a book tour." Rita's heavy voice dropped the bomb.

"I can't do a book tour. No one even knows I wrote the book."

"I guess they're about to find out."

"Rita, I have too many things going on in my life now. I recently separated from my husband. My mother is ill, and if she found out I wrote that book, it would send her over the edge. I just can't do it."

"Cassandra, or Cardia, I hate to break the news to you, but book tours are clearly stated in your contract."

Wild Rose

– FROM CHAPTER 15

Rosemary couldn't sleep thinking about Colten's wedding. Party noise from next door vibrated through the walls pounded in her head. She felt displaced and restless. Even ol' faithful, Hugh hadn't called. Needing a distraction she decided to join the revelry. She grabbed her camera. The party could provide some good "day-in-the-life" shots of rock stars.

She hesitated at the door. The room was packed with stoned and drunk people, and her nose tickled from the cloud of pot smoke.

Her party gene had turned off after Colten. She desired cozy now, not noisy, throw-up drunks. She turned to leave when Natalie, already stoned, grabbed Rosemary and pulled her into the crowded room.

"I'm so glad you came," Natalie slurred, falling into Rosemary.

Rosemary recognized a few faces in the crowded, smoke-filled room. "Hey, that's Mick Jagger."

He looked Rosemary from head to breast, winked, and flashed a big toothy smile.

"Pretty cool, huh? I can't believe he's still playing. He's so old." Natalie swayed. "I mean, he's got to be like thirty-five or something. How long can you be a rock star?"

Rosemary held Natalie's elbow to steady her. They cut through a throng of people, and Rosemary leaned Natalie against a wall. One familiar face didn't fit in amidst the mass of drunken people. "Isn't that Bonnie Bunnie?" Rosemary asked, surprised.

Natalie threw an arm around Rosemary. "Yeah, she always makes our show in LA."

"The host of the children's TV show?"

Natalie nodded and stepped away, took a shot of tequila, and chased it with a lime. Wincing, she said, "She's fun, but when she gets really high, she starts singing songs from her show. It's wild." She laughed, lost her footing but managed to stay standing. "I know I've had too much when I start to enjoy the songs."

"Damn. I wouldn't have imagined her here," Rosemary said.

Band members sprawled over unmade beds and piles of trash. The bass player, Scout, had a groupie on either side, each sucking an earlobe from what Rosemary could gather. She wondered what the average life expectancy of a drugged out, tanked-up rock star was. She looked around for the best light to shoot some photos.

"Hey, beautiful, come here." Ritchie fell back on the king-sized bed inviting Rosemary to join him.

"He's really got the hots for you," Natalie whispered drunkenly. "Go have fun." Her breath was strong, and her whisper loud enough for most to hear, even over the blaring music.

"Natalie, I'm fine."

Ritchie rolled off the bed and walked to Rosemary. "What's your pleasure?" He put his arm around her shoulders and pulled her close.

"How about a vodka tonic." She pushed out of his embrace.

"One vodka tonic coming up." He sauntered, shirt open, barefoot, bell bottoms slung low on his hips. He went into the main room to mix her drink.

Natalie staggered toward her, a joint in one hand and a tumbler in another. "How about a hit?" she squeaked, trying to hold her inhale.

"No, thanks. I'm going to have one drink, take some photos, then call it a night."

Ritchie came back with her vodka and encouraged her to drink up. As Rosemary took the first sip, Ritchie pushed the bottom of the glass, tipping more into Rosemary's mouth. She either had to swallow or spit. Taking a big gulp she gasped at the strong, bitter taste. Ritchie draped his arm around Rosemary's shoulders and pulled her close. She took another sip and tried to move away from his grasp.

"C'mon, let's make some music together," he whispered heavily in her ear.

"Ritchie, stop." Rosemary pushed him off. He smelled funky, and his bravado turned her off.

He released her, and she tumbled onto a large, overstuffed chair, feeling woozy. She bordered on fear and pleasure, not sure which one to hold onto.

Ritchie sat close to her. This time, Rosemary didn't resist.

"So, picture lady, how are you feeling now?" Ritchie's eyes flashed as they roamed over her body.

A lava lamp mesmerized Rosemary. The colors mixed with the music were so vivid. There was a tug of fear, but it seemed far away. "I'm feeling pretty high. How much vodka did you put in this?" She started to sway to Bonnie Bunnie's drunken song and dance routine.

"It's my special brew." He began kissing Rosemary's neck. Then Ritchie stood, leaned over Rosemary, and began to undress slowly, making a show of each item he discarded. There were cheers and claps from the group on the bed. Rosemary found the whole scene hilarious. She instinctively grabbed her camera and began shooting.

Rosemary awoke in her hotel room, full sunlight in her eyes. A sharp pain pierced her head, and her mouth was dry and rancid. Slowly, she sat up trying to piece together last night. Still dressed in the same sour, dirty clothes, she crawled painfully out of bed and went to the bathroom. Her reflection in the mirror surprised her. Her face was pale and swollen, and her hair was plastered by sweat.

A wave of nausea hit and she bent over the toilet, feeling worse than she ever had in her life.

She remembered going to the party. Natalie's face floated in and out of her memory, something about Mick Jagger, but everything else was cloudy. Slowly she reached up, turned on the shower, and undressed. Shaking, she stepped into the water. Every cell in her body hurt.

Hot water pelted her and helped shake the fog, but the headache still pounded behind her eyes. What happened? Apprehension began to grip Rosemary from the inside out. As she got out of the shower, she heard someone banging on the door. Wrapping a towel around her weak body, went to see who it was.

"Who's there?" Rosemary's voice was hoarse and dry.

"Dr. Steve," came the answer, and behind that voice Rosemary heard Natalie.

"Rosemary, are you all right?"

"Give me a second." Rosemary fought down another retch and quickly dressed before she let her visitors in.

"I'm glad you're up." A thin, lanky man holding a black bag leaned on the doorframe.

Rosemary looked at him through bloodshot eyes. "What the hell happened last night? Who are you?"

Natalie appeared from behind the man, holding two Styrofoam cups of coffee. "Rosemary, this is Dr. Steve, the tour doctor. We sat with you most of the night, watching over you. How do you feel?"

"Like a convoy of semis ran over me." Rosemary backed away from the door and let them in. "You sat with me?"

Natalie guided Rosemary to the bed and helped her sit. "You were totally high last night, man."

"High? What are you talking about?"

Dr. Steve stepped up. "Rosemary, it looked like you had a full hit of acid."

"It's okay to talk to Dr. Steve. He's cool about that stuff." Natalie pushed a strand of Rosemary's wet hair from her face. "That's why he's on the tour."

"I gave you some Thorazine last night and was about to send you to the hospital. Then you began to stabilize, so we set up watch."

"I did not take any acid last night. I don't do drugs." Rosemary looked angrily at Dr. Steve. "I had one drink."

Dr. Steve took a blood pressure cuff out of his black bag. "It's only my business to know what you took in case of an overdose. Otherwise, you guys are on your own to party." He took Rosemary's blood pressure.

"Natalie, I swear I didn't take anything."

"Rosemary, if you didn't take it, how do you explain the fact that you were so weirded out?" Natalie asked, handing Rosemary one of the cups of coffee.

Gingerly, Rosemary took a sip of the hot drink savoring its warmth. Her body ached inside and out. She felt violated and bruised, but she couldn't remember anything about the evening.

"The last thing I remember is thinking how strong that drink was because I was getting drunk really fast." Rosemary stopped, realizing what happened. "Ritchie, that son of a bitch. He must've spiked my drink." She felt the blood drain from her face. "How could I have been so stupid?"

Chapter Twenty Six

*"The capacity to care is the thing
that gives life its greatest significance."*
~ Pablo Casals

On Sunday evening, I'd fallen asleep on the couch watching TV, waiting for Ashley to come home. I let her go out after she and Gabby spent the afternoon with Mitch. She'd been defiant when she came home, and I thought an evening with her friends would be good for her.

The ringing phone woke me at twelve thirty. Ashley's curfew was eleven thirty, so I wondered, as I rushed to the phone, if she'd come in and I didn't hear her. I answered the phone and walked to her room.

"Cassie? It's Annie Gaines." Annie was the supervisor of the ER graveyard shift. We rarely saw each other but often communicated through our paperwork.

"Annie, what a surprise." I tried to shake off sleep. Ashley's room was dark and empty. "What's going on?" I asked.

"We need to talk."

She wasn't in the bathroom.

"Cass, please sit down."

She wasn't in the kitchen.

"Cassie, are you sitting?"

I felt the world slowing down.

"We have your daughter Ashley here."

My breath caught and my body went numb. "What? Oh, God, no. Is she okay?" Suddenly, I couldn't separate real from unreal.

"She's taken an overdose, and we're treating her. Her vitals are stable, but Cassie, she's unconscious and we're not sure what she took."

"No, no, my baby!" My knees gave out, and I fell into a chair. Overdose? "Annie, help her, take care of her, make her better."

"We are, Cassie. Dr. Boran, is with her now. Is there someone who can drive you here?"

My body went into survival mode. I ticked off in my head what I needed to do to get to the hospital as quickly as possible. "I'm coming, Annie. Tell her I'm coming." A sob broke my words as I ran to get Gabby.

I called Tina Arpino and woke her and her husband. She was gracious as I quickly explained Ashley was in the hospital and asked her to watch Gabby. I wasn't sure if Gabby was awake enough to realize she was at their house as I hugged her tearfully.

I sped to the hospital, running red lights, honking my horn, flashing my lights. I prayed through tears and gritted teeth Ashley was okay. She'd been admitted—an ominous sign. At the hospital, I left my car in the ambulance only parking bay and ran into the ER.

The ER at night looked different. The familiar smell and feel was tinted with green fluorescent lights, and the minimal staff gave the impression no one was there. The few patients waiting seemed more distressed and lonely than those during the day. At a quick glance, I saw a group of teenagers huddled together.

I rushed into the treatment area, yelling for someone to tell me where Ashley was. I opened curtains, interrupting exams and surprising patients until I found the room my baby was in.

She was so pale and tiny on the hospital bed. Charcoal from the stomach pump had stained the periphery of her mouth and the front of her hospital gown.

"Cassie, she's fighting, but not—" Annie came into the room behind me, her unfinished sentence piercing my insides. "We're still waiting for the drug screen to come back. We've given her Narcan and pumped her stomach." Annie put her arm around my shoulder as I held Ashley's hand to my tear streaked face. "One of the kids who brought her in said she probably was given Rohypnol."

"The date rape drug? Oh, God." I put my head in my hands. "What are her vitals?" I was playing nurse during my worst nightmare.

As Annie gave me Ashley's medical information, I heard a soft knock outside the curtain.

"Mrs. Calabria?" Teresa's voice interrupted Annie. "May I come in?"

"Teresa, what happened?" I yelled, sobbing, my eyes accusing her.

Teresa opened the curtain, her face swollen from crying. Behind her I saw Bradley, the longhaired boy who had been hanging around Ashley.

"Get him out of here! Who the hell do you think you are?"

I screamed and threw a box of gauze at him.

"He was helping her. He didn't do anything." Sobbing, Teresa squeezed between me and Annie and looked at Ashley. "Is she going to be okay? I'm so scared." She cried harder and grabbed my arm.

I did not welcome the intrusion. I wanted to be alone with my daughter, holding her close. I had never felt such pain and hopelessness.

Annie must have sensed my feelings because she took Teresa's arm and guided her out of the room.

Ashley stayed comatose while I sat with her. As a nurse, I knew this was the defining moment during an overdose. First, we weren't sure what she had taken. Second, though her stomach had been pumped, the drug may still have affected her organs via her bloodstream. I prayed with every ounce of power the treatment was started before the drugs had time to travel through her body and her brain.

People came in and out of the room, technicians checking on Ashley's vitals and employees checking on me. Someone took my keys and moved my car out of the ambulance bay. Annie was a pillar of strength and spent much of the night by my side while I stood vigil.

"Cassie, do you want me to get Mitch on the phone?" Annie gently touched my shoulder. It was almost three o'clock, and there was no change in Ashley's condition.

"Thanks Annie," I answered wearily. "I'll do it."

I pulled my cell phone out, never releasing Ashley's hand, and called the Arpinos. Tina, bless her, had been sleeping with Gabby, the phone tucked under her. She said Gabby had been frightened at first but finally fell asleep. I told her I'd call her when I knew more.

My stomach churned as I dialed Mitch. When a sleepy female voice answered, I struck out with anger. All the pain and frustration I felt could be taken out on these two.

"I need to talk to Mitch." I looked over at Ashley, desperate for her to wake up.

"He's sleeping. What do you want?"

"This concerns our *family*," I seethed. "Let me talk to him now."

Mitch grabbed the receiver from Renee. I could hear her complaining in the background.

"Cassie, what's up?" His voice sounded concerned, frightened.

Before I could get the words out, I began crying, heart wrenching sobs that came from deep in my soul. "It's Ashley."

"Oh, God. Cassie, is she okay?"

"No. She's taken an overdose of something. She's in a coma." As hard as I tried, I couldn't get all the words out. "We're at the hospital." My body began shaking uncontrollably as I tried to hang up the phone. Annie appeared at my side and took the phone from my hand.

"Annie, can you call my mother?"

She squeezed my shoulder. "Sure, Cassie."

Dr. Boran came in holding my daughter's drug panel results. "Cassie, it looks like she has Rohypnol on board with a mix of barbiturates. Her levels are pretty high, but..." His voice trailed as he checked Ashley. "I'm surprised she's still comat—um, sleeping. I'm sure her tolerance for drugs is low and her body is fighting the drugs."

He lifted her eyelid, revealing her dilated pupil under

the harsh penlight. I couldn't stand seeing her so helpless, so lifeless.

"She's stable, so we're going to observe her for another hour and then recheck her levels." Dr. Boran squeezed my shoulder. "Stay strong, Cassie."

I tearfully nodded. As I said a silent prayer, I wondered how many other prayers were embedded in the walls of this small emergency room.

Chapter Twenty Seven

"The tragedy of life is not that it ends so soon,
but that we wait so long to begin it."
~ W.M. Lewis

I didn't know my body had the capacity to hurt so much. The pain seemed endless—a bottomless pit of agony.

When Mitch arrived, I broke down. I could be strong when I had to be, but when someone I trusted could take some of the grief, I allowed myself to give it.

I couldn't answer any of his questions. "How did this happen? Who did this?"

My only concern was to be by Ashley's side, willing her to wake up—offering love and prayers. *Please, please, Ashley, wake up.*

The morning crew checked in just after seven o'clock. The news spread quickly, and the exam room began filling up with my coworkers.

"Damn. I didn't believe it," Kathy said.

Sensitivity was not one of her strong points. She examined Ashley and her attached tubes and wires as if she were a lab animal.

Adam and Jennifer came in behind her. "Cassie, I'm so sorry. Let me know what I can do to help." Jennifer took my hand and gave me a big hug. Mitch stood in the background, watching.

"Cass, you look like hell," Adam said, as he herded everyone out. Then he said to Jennifer, "Go check on the patients and keep guard outside, so no one else comes in here."

Thank you, Adam, I thought.

"Mitch, why don't you go to the cafeteria and get some coffee for Cassie," Adam said, as he checked Ashley's vitals. "I'll take care of things here."

Mitch glanced at Ashley and left the room.

"All right, Ashley, it's time to wake up. Your mother's worried sick." Adam went to the crash cart and took out some meds.

"Adam, I'd give anything for her to wake up and be okay."

He broke a vial and ran it under Ashley's nose. Her hand suddenly rose and pushed away the offensive smell of ammonia.

"Smelling salts?" I couldn't believe I hadn't thought of that. "Ashley, honey, can you hear me?" Tears streamed down my face.

"Sometimes, Cass, the answer is right under your nose," Adam said, but relief showed on his face, too.

"Mommy?"

Her tiny, weak voice was the most beautiful sound I'd ever heard. "I'm here, baby. I'm here." I squeezed her pale hands. "I love you."

"What happened?" Even though she slurred her words, I understood what she was saying. Like when she was a baby and I could always understand her little mumbles. "Where am I?" she asked weakly.

"Ashley, how many fingers am I holding up?" Adam interrupted.

She blinked open her eyes and squinted at Adam's hand. "Two."

"Good. Who's the President of the United States? Oh, forget that. Let me ask you something worth an answer. Who is the best nurse here? Now, using the alphabet, start with the letter 'A.'"

Ashley tried to smile and took my hand. "Mom, am I in the hospital?"

"Yes, honey. Thank God you woke up." I was sobbing and holding her hand tightly. I didn't want to let go.

"I have a really bad headache." She tried to scratch her face, but the IV tubes made it hard to manage. "I don't feel so good."

I gently dabbed her forehead with a damp cloth.

By mid-morning, Ashley was lucid enough to answer easy questions, though she drifted in and out of sleep. Mom came in with Gabby, and Gail took her to play on her computer.

Mom and I sat next to Ashley while she slept. "I would never have thought Ashley did drugs. It's so out of character for her," Mom said.

"Shhh, Mom. She can hear us talk."

"Don't shush me, Cassandra! We need to get to the bottom of this. I want to find out who, what, why, and when. I'm a pretty good judge of people, and Ashley doesn't have it in her to do this."

"It was the date rape drug," I said. "Someone must've given it to her."

"This is what we need to find out. Was that Bradley and Teresa I saw in the waiting room?"

"They were here earlier. I think Teresa's mother came and took her home last night. I wasn't really paying much attention."

"Maybe you should, Cassie." Mom left the room.

Sitting in the cold, sterile hospital room, I realized Mom had a point. I did let Ashley get away with her silence and teenage attitude. I needed to be more assertive and not let her call all the shots. I could still love her *and* be the mom.

Mitch came in with more coffee and put his hand on my shoulder. "I'm sorry, Cass." He began crying softly. "I've been so selfish. I love you all. I really do."

I wanted to yell at him about his girlfriend, his lifestyle, his decision to leave. To unload all my anger and fear on him, but I was too tired. Anyway, it wasn't the right time or place, not to mention it all seemed so insignificant while sitting with my critically ill daughter. But I understood what he was saying—family is what's important.

Mom came in with Teresa and Bradley in tow. "Teresa and Bradley want to talk you. Mitch, you may as well stay, too," she said.

Teresa looked as bad as I felt. Tears puffed and reddened her eyes. Without makeup she looked so young and vulnerable. Bradley stood behind her, staring at Ashley, tears in his eyes.

"Mrs. Calabria, I swear Ashley doesn't do drugs," he said. Teresa kept glancing over at Ashley, who was stirring slightly. "We don't do drugs."

"Mr. and Mrs. Calabria, I'm Bradley Collins." Bradley stuck

out a shaky hand, first to Mitch and then to me. "Please don't blame Ashley."

"Yeah, Bradley saved her!" Teresa jumped in. "We think it was Andrew Novak who put drugs in her Coke. We saw him taking her to his car. She was stumbling around, so Bradley went to check on her. Andrew started fighting with him. That's when I saw that Ashley couldn't stand up."

"Whoa. One at a time. Are you sure someone slipped her drugs?" I asked.

Bradley stepped up. "Mrs. Calabria, I'm sure Ashley didn't mean to take anything. The party started getting out of hand when some of the others brought alcohol. A group of us were planning on leaving—Ashley included—when she started acting weird. At first, I thought she'd had some alcohol, which surprised me."

I watched Bradley while he talked and got a good look at him for the first time. The long hair, grungy clothes, and flash of metal in his pierced tongue concerned me. But he was surprisingly articulate and gentle when he spoke.

"At first, I noticed Andrew and his friends were laughing and pointing at Ashley. It wasn't until I saw Andrew hitting on her...umm, you know...trying hard to kiss her and stuff. I thought he may have had something to do with her being drunk." Bradley went to Ashley and touched her arm. "Then a friend of Andrew's told me Andrew put a roofie in Ashley's Coke." He paused for a long time and wiped his eyes before continuing. "There was a bet that Andrew could... um...have sex with her."

I felt violently ill. Mitch picked up a metal tray and threw it at the far wall. Ashley jumped and looked around, frightened. After the crash, the room became deadly silent.

"Mommy?" she whispered.

"I'm here, honey." I tucked the blankets around her. My voice shaking, I asked, "Bradley, how sure are you? Do you realize how serious this is?" I began crying again. The realization my daughter's life had been threatened and her virginity put on a betting table was a gut punch.

"This Andrew, the son of a bitch, I'll kill him! I swear I will!" Mitch was venomous.

Mom walked over to him and put her hand on his back. "Mitch, take a deep breath, then call the police. Making threats is not going to solve anything." She turned her attention to Bradley. "Thank you for coming forward. "Ashley thinks highly of you. You should know that, today, you are her hero."

I was reeling from shock. Nothing seemed real or right. It was as if the whole world were out of sync. How could this boy who I had been so scared about turn out to be the good guy? How could Dr. Novak's son do something so vicious? I looked down at Ashley, now in a a deep, drug-induced sleep, and held onto her for dear life.

Chapter Twenty Eight

"The most important things in life aren't things."
~ Anthony J. D'Angelo

Tina Arpino set up a buffet in the waiting area, feeding the staff and just about anybody else who came in. Her husband took Gabby and their daughter, Jennifer, to play Putt-Putt. Later, Brenda stayed with the kids.

Between Tina, Mom, and Brenda, I knew my outside life would be taken care of while I made sure Ashley was okay.

Christine came in to comfort me. She held my hand while I held Ashley's. She looked at me with tears in her eyes. "I can't believe this, Cassie."

I entwined my fingers in Ashley's. "This can't be happening," I said. "I keep trying to wake up from this awful dream."

Christine squeezed my hand. "Ashley's still a child. I hate she's been exposed to this at such a young age, and worse, she's become a victim of it."

"She's only fifteen."

Christine looked at me sympathetically. "I know."

I wanted to take Ashley home and tuck her into her comfortable bed, but we still had to continue checking her blood levels to make sure her body was getting rid of the poisons.

The drugs had to go through her liver, kidneys, and so many other precious vital systems in her body. I prayed no permanent damage would be done.

I started to nod off but was startled awake by shouting in the main ER area.

"This is the boy, officer! Arrest him and get him out of my hospital!" Dr. Novak's voice boomed. I got up to see what the commotion was about, surprised to find Dr. Novak in the waiting room, with a police officer at his side, pointing at Bradley.

Mom stepped into the fray. "Hold your horses, Novak. My stomach is already upset. Let's not start throwing innocent kids in jail. Besides, I think you need to look a little closer to home before you start accusing others."

Dr. Novak crossed his arms and glared at my mother. "This has nothing to do with you."

"Bullshit!" Mom turned on Dr. Novak. "My granddaughter is lying in the hospital because she was given an illegal drug. Don't you dare tell me to back off!"

Novak waved her away. "Arrest this kid, officer." He again pointed to Bradley.

Bradley's face was red with fear as he fought back tears. "I didn't give her anything! I was trying to help her!"

The police officer stepped away from Novak. "Calm down. We'll take statements one at a time."

"Everybody in Cassandra's office, now!" Mom ordered, as she directed the group into my little office. while I stood by Ashley's door, my mouth gaping open.

I snagged Adam. "Adam, do me a favor and sit with Ashley for a few minutes, please. Mitch should be back any minute."

"I'll take care of her."

"Don't leave her alone for a second." I ran to my office.

The group was engaged in a heated shouting match. Mom was in the middle, holding court, clutching her stomach. Speaking to Dr. Novak, she said, "Aaron, we need to get to the bottom of this, but first let's talk about who's behind the drug use."

"Mrs. Ellison, I know who's responsible," he said, pointing at Bradley. "Just look at that hippie punk!"

Bradley started to protest, but I stepped in and blurted out, "Dr. Novak, there are witnesses who say your son, Andrew, gave my child drugs. Let's talk about accountability."

If looks could kill, I would have been a goner. "What did you say?" he seethed, turning to me slowly. "My son does not do drugs. Who the hell do you think you are, talking to me like this?"

The police officer spoke up. "Folks, I'm going to take the stories one at a time. We'll put the pieces together after we talk to everybody." Turning to Bradley, he said, "Young man, I'd like to start with you." He motioned Bradley to my chair. "The rest of you wait outside and don't leave the area unless you talk to me first."

Dr. Novak glared angrily at me as he strode off.

Mom and I walked back to Ashley's room to wait. "Mom, I can't believe any of this is happening. Why? Why Ashley? Where did they get the alcohol and drugs?"

Mom gave me a hard look. "Honey, you're a nurse in an emergency room. Don't tell me you don't know this stuff goes on at the high schools."

"I didn't think it went on here."

"Don't you remember what you were exposed to when

you were a teenager?"

"Yeah, so?" I gave Mom a weak smile. "I mean, I found out some years later you really were smarter than I gave you credit for. So, how much did you know?"

"I had spies planted on every corner." Mom laughed. "As hard as it was for me to see you make stupid mistakes, I knew deep down you needed to learn the lessons for yourself. I trusted you, Cassandra. Now you need to trust Ashley."

"Please don't make me admit you were right about everything. I'm not ready for that," I said.

"You will be." Mom looked thinner and frailer than I'd ever seen her.

"Mom, you need to get some rest. You really look tired."

"It was a tough night. I can't look gorgeous all the time. I just wish Dr. Novak and Dr. Sandoval could figure out what's wrong with my stomach."

I thought back to when she started having pain. "It's been more than a month since this started," I said. "I thought the tests showed a hiatal hernia. What about the CT scan?"

"I'm still waiting on insurance to approve it."

"If you need it done, we'll make it happen."

"Whatever. I'm just tired of feeling bad." She pushed some hair away from her face. "You just need to worry about Ashley right now. I'm going to run home, change, and come back. Hopefully, she'll be released this afternoon."

I touched her thin arm. "Go home and rest, take care of yourself. We all need you." Her weight loss worried me more than I wanted to admit.

I went to Ashley's room. She was in a deep, restful sleep, and her vitals were stable.

Mitch came in, and I sent him to get Gabby. I knew he

wanted to be here, but I was uncomfortable around him after everything he'd put us through.

Soon after Mitch left, Bradley came in with his parents. His face was red and blotchy as if he'd been crying. He politely made introductions.

Thomas and Anne looked like older versions of sixties "love children." I could see where Bradley got his looks and his style. Anne wore a big gunnysack dress, and her long, curly hair was peppered with gray. Thomas's hair was as long as Bradley's and was tied back into a ponytail. His brown corduroys were thinning at the knees.

Anne spoke first. "Cassandra, we are so sorry about Ashley. Bradley told us what happened." She held her son's arm as she spoke. "I know you work with Dr. Novak, and I don't want to interfere in your relationship in any way, but he has made serious accusations against my son. I want you to know we think the world of Ashley, and Bradley would never harm her."

"I didn't do it, Mrs. Calabria. I promise." Bradley's lower lip trembled. His dad stood behind him and placed both hands on his son's shoulders.

"We're proud of Bradley and hope he's strong enough to discuss drug use with us. We've always been open with each other," said Thomas, affectionately. "But we would expect him to deal with any consequences if he had anything to do with this."

Ashley began stirring. I tucked the blanket around her.

Bradley pulled away from his father to face him. "Come on, guys. You know I don't do drugs."

Gauging his parents, I couldn't be sure they didn't enjoy an occasional toke.

"I appreciate your concern," I said. "My first priority is to get Ashley better, then find out what happened."

"Of course." Anne walked to Ashley and me. "We've all been praying."

I tried to imagine what church they prayed in. My first impression of Bradley did not involve church—unless it leaned toward a cult with ritualistic sacrifices of small rodents. My eyes felt gritty, my body numb. I didn't know what to think. "Thank you. We need all the prayers we can get." I rubbed Ashley's shoulders as Bradley and his parents left.

Outside the closed door of Ashley's room, I could hear activity, patients being treated, and others being moved to other parts of the hospital. No one came to transfer Ashley, though. I knew hospital policy stated we could not keep patients in the ER this long, and we were getting special treatment. For once, I was thankful for the job I'd complained about so often and for the staff who allowed us this privacy.

Chapter Twenty Nine

"A successful man is one who makes more money than his wife can spend. A successful woman is one who can find such a man."
~ *Lana Turner*

We brought Ashley home from the hospital late that evening. Mitch carried her inside like he did when she was young and had fallen asleep in the car. I brought pillows and blankets for her in front of the TV and sat with her. She put her feet on my lap, and I gave her a foot massage.

Gabby wasn't sure what was wrong with Ashley, but she didn't pick on her for a change. She even offered Ashley her best stuffed animal to sleep with.

Mitch paced back and forth from the den to the kitchen, looking uncomfortable. "Hey, how about I go get some ice cream?" he asked.

Gabby jumped up from the sofa. "Yeah! Can we get Blizzards?"

Mitch picked her up. "How about we go to the store and get stuff to make our own Blizzards."

Gabby beamed. "Sprinkles, too?"

"You can get hot fudge fish egg sprinkles if you want." Mitch tickled her, reducing her to giggles.

"Ice cream sounds good," Ashley said, still pale and shaky. She looked at me. "Is it okay if I eat something? My stomach still feels kind of yucky, but I'm a little hungry."

I tucked her feet under a blanket and got up. "Let me make you some soup while they're at the store." I smoothed hair from her face. "And a milkshake will be good, too."

Mitch, looking relieved to be doing something useful, carried Gabby to the door. Before leaving, he asked if we needed anything else, like he was a guest doing us a favor.

I smiled. "No, thanks. Just make sure to get something chocolate."

After they left, Ashley turned on her side and looked at me in the kitchen. "Can Dad stay here tonight? Everything seems so weird now."

Opening a can of chicken noodle soup, I hesitated. "Sure, honey. If it'll make you feel better, I'll ask."

As I stirred the soup, I watched Ashley flip through TV channels. My heart clutched at the image of her in the hospital bed, unable to wake up. I grabbed a dishrag and wiped away tears. A small part of me also wanted Mitch to stay, but I didn't want the ghost of his girlfriend, or whatever she was, haunting our family. Like an addict, I craved normal.

With school out, Ashley had time to heal. Mom came to the house with the girls, so I didn't have to truck them to the Y. Mitch stayed a few nights but slept in the guest room. We both felt Ashley needed the family together and tried to maintain a civil demeanor. It worked as long as we kept the girls between us.

Since her overdose, Ashley and I became closer. I forced open the lines of communication, finally acting like the grown up. I would not allow her to hide behind her bedroom door and her friends. Though I respected her privacy, I started making an effort to find out what she was doing and with whom. I understood she needed independence and was trying to break away and grow, as this was the natural progression of teens. She was learning to become her own person, but without the experience to make all the right decisions. She was still a child and needed me. I think the overdose scared her back home.

One evening, a few days after Ashley came home, we'd just come back from dinner and a movie when the home phone rang. I wasn't fast enough, and the caller hung up without leaving a message. I looked at the caller ID and noticed the same person had called every few minutes for over an hour.

Ten minutes later, the phone rang again, and Ashley rushed to get it. She got a funny look on her face when she answered it.

"Can I tell him who's calling?" She glared at Mitch, indicating the call was for him. "It's *her*." She tossed the phone on the kitchen counter and left the room, giving Mitch the brush-off, although there was fear in her eyes.

The air pressure in my body dropped when I realized it was Renee. Why was she calling the house and not his cell? Mitch and I hadn't discussed her yet. I resented that she'd intruded on what had been a nice evening. I hovered, trying to make Mitch uncomfortable while he was on the phone. He walked around the corner but still within earshot. I took a deep breath and decided to wait until he got off the phone before I verbally disemboweled him. I didn't want to give Renee the satisfaction of finding out I was the psycho-alpha-bitch wife Mitch probably portrayed me as.

"I blocked your number on my cell for a good reason." Mitch hissed on the phone. "Renee, it's over. Quit calling me."

As I watched Mitch fumbling on the phone, trying to talk to her and at the same time keep an eye on me, I experienced a range of emotions—from rage and anger to pain and loss. I wondered when I was going to get that happy ending feeling you see in the movies when the victorious woman wins her man. But I didn't feel anything when I looked at him. I wondered if our marriage would be stronger because of this—or were we done? Our relationship was fragile, already cracked and close to shattering. I thought I was being generous by letting him have the guest room, but I had to consider family first. Our marriage had come to an apex. Which way it would go required time and work. Sighing, I walked out of the room to tend to the laundry, hoping it had folded itself.

Chapter Thirty

"The problem with reality is the lack of background music."
~ Alfred Hitchcock

My book was everywhere. It still gave me a jolt of excitement to see someone reading it. I often fought the urge to ask the reader what they thought. Rita was pushing hard for a book tour, and I considered my options. My best idea, so far, was to tell Mitch and the girls I wanted to join a convent to meditate for a few months until I could find the answer to the meaning of life. That would be more plausible than telling them I'd written a sexy romance novel and needed to leave town to promote it.

Mom was still suffering with abdominal pain and weight loss. Because of her insurance, she saw Dr. Novak's partner. Too close to home, I thought, since I wanted him as far away from us as possible. He'd been cold since Ashley's overdose, which was fine with me. It enraged me how hard he fought against us. And, thanks to his power and money, his son *still* was not formally charged with anything—two weeks after the overdose.

I was angling for life behind bars, while Ashley just wanted to forget the whole thing. We waited while the prosecuting attorney built a case against him.

Mom believed that Dr. Novak should be able to separate his home and professional life, so she continued to see his partner. No matter how much I begged her to find another gastroenterologist, she just waved her hand. "Novak's group is fine."

I raised enough of a stink with her insurance company to get a CT scan approved, but the imaging center couldn't get her in for a week.

Rita sent over a case of my books for me to give to my friends and family—as if I'd be passing them out like candy. Since I still didn't have the nerve or the time to reveal myself as the author, I gave a stack to Christine and hid the others. The books were easy to hide, but I feared Mitch might open the bank statement before we had a chance to talk. Even though the growing wad of money was in a separate account, he probably wouldn't think twice about opening an envelope with our bank's logo on it. Deep down I knew I needed to sit down with him and come clean, but I found it difficult to discuss much more than the weather with him. Until I could get Ashley's post-overdose life back to normal and my mother's illness defined, I didn't have the time or energy to talk. Plus, I was still embarrassed by the thought of him visualizing the erotic scenes I wrote, imagining his reaction to the gritty, sandy, sex on the beach.

Chapter Thirty One

"Where do forest rangers go to get away from it all?"
~ George Carlin

It took another week for Andrew Novak to be charged. The detective assigned to the case had to interview all the kids at the party between investigating other cases. It wasn't a priority.

"Cassie, what are you going to do about Novak's kid?" Adam asked.

Gail turned from the phones. "Yeah, Dr. Novak will probably come down screaming. I'd hate to be on his bad list. I'd file a restraining order against him."

Kathy leaned against the desk, slurping a sugary frozen drink. "You should pray. Give your problems to God."

"We're going to take one day at a time, starting with making sure Ashley is okay," I said, grabbing a pile of patient reports to file. I loved how everybody had plenty of ideas on how to resolve my problems, no matter how screwed up their own lives were.

"You got loads of problem for sure," Kathy said. "Your hubby's out catting around, and then top it off with what happened to Ashley. It's a real bummer." I sorely wished I could add one more strike to her employee review and let her go.

Dr. Sandoval came in, said, "Cassie, you need to ask yourself just how important the marriage is to you and the girls. Also, think about the future. Do you think he'll do something like this again?"

"I didn't think he'd do something like this in the first place." As I turned to go, I said, "I'm not sure where Mitch and I stand. On one hand, I want our family back, but on the other hand, every time I look at him, I picture him being with another woman." The walls were closing in on me, and I wanted to cry. "I need to get to work."

"By the way, how's your mom?" Dr. Sandoval asked walking with me. "Novak doesn't seem to be doing much for her. She's lost a considerable amount of weight."

Dr. Sandoval followed me to my office. "Cassie, I don't want to worry you, but I'm afraid your mom is suffering with more than a hiatal hernia. She needs a CT scan."

"I finally got her on the schedule for the day after tomorrow. You know she had the stomach X-rays, which showed the hernia. I've been trying to get her to another doctor, but she thinks Novak's group is fine."

"Between his son's legal problems and all his extracurricular activities, his heart's not really into his work. I'll call your mom and see if I can get her in to see Jenny Sorrel, the new GI doctor here."

"I'd really appreciate it. I'm worried, but she won't listen to me."

About an hour later, I walked to the front desk where the group had gathered again. Now they were arguing about the death penalty. I hoped they were talking about Andrew Novak.

I noticed a copy of *Wild Rose* on Gail's desk. "Hey, how do you like that book?"

"It's great. The main character is a photographer, and she's so cool. I wish I had the nerve to chuck everything and do what I really love."

"Don't you love it here?" Jennifer joked.

"You know what I mean." Gail held up the book. "I was watching one of those Hollywood news shows last night. There's this big mystery about who Cardia Loving is. Some people think she's not a real person."

"*Someone* wrote it," Jennifer said. "She must be real."

I blanched. Christine had said something to me a few days ago about an article she'd read about the unknown identity of Cardia. "It was on TV?" I choked.

"Yeah, I saw it too. And I heard the *Enquirer* is offering a $5,000 reward to the person who can find out who she or *he* is," Kathy said.

I swallowed the lump of terror. What if I was found out?

The automatic doors swished opened and a patient came into the ER. The frail woman was doubled over in pain, clutching her abdomen.

"Looks like we've got a victim," Jennifer said.

"Get a wheelchair. I'll help her," I said, glad for the distraction. Jennifer was already sprinting to get one.

I went to help the woman, who seemed to be in agony. "We're getting you a wheelchair now."

"Thanks, Cassie."

I gasped when she spoke my name. "Mom! Oh, my God! Are you okay?" She slumped in my arms. "Jennifer!" I screamed, "Get me that wheelchair *now*!"

Chapter Thirty Two

"Don't take life seriously because you can't come out of it alive."
~ Warren Miller

The day Mom came into the ER, the new GI, Dr. Jenny Sorrel, was on call. She found the cancer —pancreatic. The diagnosis hit hard. It was one of the worst kinds of cancer, extremely painful, difficult to diagnose, and lethal. Often, by the time pancreatic cancer is found, it's too late. I sat at Mom's bedside, wondering how I'd missed the obvious signs.

The cancer had already metastasized to her liver and probably affected other abdominal organs in its insidious path.

As soon as Mom was admitted to the hospital, Brenda and I started calling cancer centers about the treatments. I had Adam researching holistic therapy as I prayed for a miracle. I begged Adam, Dr. Sandoval, and Dr. Sorrel to keep quiet about Mom's diagnosis for now. I wasn't ready to have Mom's room full of visitors. I wanted, *needed*, time with her by myself. It felt as if someone had tilted the ground I was standing on, and I found myself sliding, lost, unable to keep my balance.

Because the tumor had constricted vessels that supplied blood to the abdomen, Mom immediately had surgery.

As she recovered in her room, the three of us sat close together, bound by fear.

Mom remained optimistic. "You know, I've been blessed to have daughters like you." Mom unplugged her IVAC-IV, so she could plug in her electric curlers. She instructed us to hit the stop button when the IV beeped a warning. "I'm proud of you both."

"Mom, you know we can't go on without you. You've got to get better," Brenda said, as she held up a mirror while Mom applied her makeup and fixed her hair.

"Hold it up a little higher, please." Mom was dabbing on foundation. "If I go today, I want to make sure I get my curlers in and my eyeliner is straight."

"That's not funny," I said, sitting on the edge of her bed. "And we need to plug your IV back in."

"You're right. It's not funny. But promise me girls, when my time comes, make sure the funeral home brushes my hair right and gets my makeup on. I'd be mortified if people saw my wrinkles during the wake. As far as the outfit I want to wear, I was thinking of my navy suit. Well, no, that one's too nice. One of you girls can get some use out of it."

"Mom, stop talking like that." I fought back tears. "You're going to make it. Brenda and I have been talking to treatment centers. We'll do anything and everything to get you into one. Not only do we need you, but our kids need their grandma." I thought of my two girls growing up without her.

"Let's be realistic." Mom became serious. "Jenny and I had a long talk about my prognosis. Cassie, you should know better than anybody that this cancer—it's even hard to say the word—will be my downfall. Maybe we need to go ahead and start saying the things we've been meaning to tell each other. For starters, I love you both very much."

"We love you too, Mom," Brenda and I said. I regretted not saying it more often.

We talked and reminisced, before Mom began to show signs of being weak and in pain. I had plugged her IV back in and made sure she had enough medicine, but unfortunately, with this type of cancer, there would be little relief from the pain. Still, with her hair and makeup done, she looked surprisingly well, although still thin and frail.

I don't know what prompted me, but I suddenly jumped up. "Mom, remember that book *Wild Rose?*"

"Yes. Have you read it yet?"

"*I* did, and I loved it!" Brenda interjected.

"Good." I paused and took a deep breath. "I wrote it."

If Mom hadn't been in so much pain, she probably would have fallen off her bed, laughing as hard as she was. Brenda looked at me as if I were from another planet.

"Cass, have you completely flipped?" Brenda rolled her eyes. "Why would you even say that? Oh, and by the way, Mom, my artwork is hanging in the Metropolitan Museum."

"I'm serious. I haven't told anybody because I didn't want you to give me a hard time about writing a racy love story. I mean, don't you think people would lose respect for me if they knew I wrote it?"

Mom looked at me incredulously. "You *are* serious."

"Maybe she needs a brain scan," Brenda said.

"Do you remember a long time ago, when I asked you about romance novels? I had read an article in the paper about how well they sell. Well, I wrote one, and it's really selling."

"You're so full of it," Brenda said, unconvinced.

Mom waved off Brenda's comment. "Well, if the cancer doesn't kill me, the heart attack I'm getting ready to have might." She stared at me as if I were shapeshifting before her eyes. "Cassie, why didn't you tell us?" She scooted into a more comfortable position. "So what does Mitch think about this? Is that why he left?"

"No, Mitch doesn't know. I've never had the nerve to tell him." I sat on the edge of Mom's bed. "He left before it was published. Then when it started making money, I opened a separate bank account. He's not even aware of how much money there is."

Brenda looked at me skeptically. "How much is there?"

"Lots. I never expected the book to do this well. Part of me is excited, but part of me is scared about people finding out. The only one who knows about it is Christine."

"So, how much is 'lots?'" Brenda asked. "And why so secretive? Don't you trust us?"

"Yeah, like family." I answered. "Every time I confide in you, someone else manages to find out. And Mom, you know all my coworkers better than I do. I just couldn't risk anybody finding out."

"I've never told anything that would hurt you or embarrass you, honey," Mom said.

"Remember in high school when you told your friends you thought I might be a lesbian because I didn't have a boyfriend?"

"Well, you were a late bloomer. I was worried."

"Brenda, I remember the time some man called for me and you screamed into the receiver, 'Cassie, your boyfriend is on the phone!' It was my manager at work, asking me to come in. You two would have tortured a guy if I'd brought him home. That's the reason I didn't date back then and why I've been afraid to tell you about the book until now."

"Well, I certainly enjoyed the book." Mom was starting to hold her stomach as if she were in pain.

"Maybe if you had tried some of those moves on Mitch, he wouldn't have left you," Brenda chimed in.

"Brenda, stop," Mom said through gritted teeth. "So you're the mysterious Cardia Loving? I just read an article in *People* magazine, speculations of who the mysterious author is."

It's in *People*?" I was shocked. I'd seen a headline in a grocery store rag but hadn't heard about *People*.

She smiled and nodded. "There are all sorts of theories as to who wrote *Wild Rose*—people from Stephen King to Dick Cheney's wife, to Stacey Abrams." she said weakly.

"Mom, are you okay?" I worried, seeing how much pain she was in.

"I'm fine." She rested her head on her pillow and looked at me. "How did you manage to write a book without anyone knowing about it?"

I got up from her bed and slumped in a chair next to her. "I don't know. I never expected it to get this big."

"So Mitch really doesn't know?" Brenda asked. "When are you going to tell him? Can I be there when you do?"

"My agent and publicist have been trying to get me to go on a book tour. I was able to hold off because of Ashley, but now she's pushing me hard. And I never called the publicist back."

"Your agent? Publicist?" Brenda said in a sarcastic tone. "This is too much for me to take right now."

"Didn't I always tell you girls you could do anything you wanted if you put your mind to it?" Mom's voice sounded weaker. "Cassandra, I'm proud of you. A little surprised but proud. I swear, I don't know how you found the time."

"I stayed up late nights and wrote. Mitch thought I was playing solitaire or having an online romance." I laughed at the irony.

A weight lifted off my chest after telling Mom and Brenda. It felt good. "I really wanted to tell you, Mom, but the more I thought about the book's content, the more nervous I got. I was afraid you'd lose respect for me or look at me differently."

"Honey, don't you know I'll love you no matter what? It's called unconditional love, a mother's love."

"I don't want Ashley and Gabby to lose respect for me. I mean, what am I going to tell them? That's another reason I didn't tell Mitch. I knew he'd use it against me if we did divorce. You know, a divorce attorney would have a field day with that material."

Mom gingerly put a hand over her abdomen. "I see your point. But I'd love to be able to brag about my daughter, 'the author.'"

"Mom, are you feeling okay? How much pain are you in?" I felt selfish talking about myself, ignoring her pain. "Can I get you anything?"

"Maybe a little more medicine, but not enough to knock

me out. I need to talk to Jenny when she comes in. The pain is becoming unbearable, and I'm wondering if the surgery didn't work like it was supposed to."

Brenda looked concerned. "Do something, Cassie!" Make her pain go away."

I picked up the call button and pushed for a nurse. Fear took hold as I realized there was nothing anyone could do. I told the nurses to have Dr. Sorrel paged and to bring Mom some medicine now.

"Don't bother Jenny. She's very busy," said Mom, obviously in severe pain.

"It's okay, Mom. She needs to see you," I said, as I tried to help her get comfortable, sliding a pillow under her head. I hit the morphine button on the IV.

"Cassandra, if you don't want Mitch to know about the book, tell him I gave you the money. Tell him it's my life savings and I wanted to make sure it didn't go to an estate attorney." She winced, changing positions. "I'm glad you did it, Cass. I knew you had it in you to do something extraordinary," she said before she dozed off.

Brenda and I kept vigil by her bedside, holding her hand, trying to comfort her. I was frightened. I prayed, again, with all my strength, she would miraculously survive this disease.

As the afternoon turned into evening, things began to happen quickly. First, my fear of Mitch finding out about the money was no longer a concern, since he'd opened my bank statement. But worse, Dr. Sorrel came in to see Mom, and told us the bad news.

Wild Rose

— FROM CHAPTER 16

Rosemary was so angry about Ritchie spiking her drink she wanted to play rock star and destroy the hotel room. She couldn't believe she'd been stupid enough to fall for the drug-in-the-drink trick. If he had taken her, she hoped she'd screwed the balls off the bastard. Because that's what she wanted to do to him now—only with power tools.

For the rest of the morning, Rosemary packed. She sent an assistant to develop the concert film. "Make it a rush order. I'll pick it up in a few hours," she said, as the intern took the envelope from her.

Rosemary decided to head home for a few days to regroup.

As she finished packing, there was a knock at the door.

"Who is it?" she called through the door.

"Natalie. Do you have a minute?"

Rosemary let her in. "I'm taking off for a couple of days."

Natalie's hair was wet from a shower. "How are you feeling?"

"Other than my pride being crushed and having a nasty headache, I'm fine."

"Listen, I wanted to apologize for what happened."

"Did you know he'd planned on spiking my drink?" Though Natalie was a party girl, Rosemary couldn't imagine she'd stoop so low.

"No!" Natalie looked hurt. "I thought you'd decided to get high, but when you started acting crazy, I wasn't so sure. It seemed weird for you."

"How crazy?" Rosemary wasn't sure she really wanted to know.

"Well, you were taking pictures of the group sex."

Rosemary cringed. "Group sex?"

Natalie twirled her wet hair. "Ritchie was hitting on you. You took some pictures of him naked. Things started getting a little rough, and I told Ritchie to back off. About that time, I had to save Dale from a gang of hungry groupies. When I got back to the room, you'd passed out, and Ritchie was with another girl." Natalie pushed Rosemary's suitcase to the side and sat on the bed. "I asked Ritchie, and he said nothing really happened."

"I'd like to know what 'nothing really' means." Rosemary fumed. "I can't imagine anyone—even Ritchie—taking advantage of someone who's passed out."

"You're probably right. And besides, it's not like he couldn't get any."

Natalie left, and Rosemary grabbed her bags. She wanted to get to the photo lab and home.

It was early afternoon when she left the hotel. Thank God for her work. She'd file last night under Really Dumb Mistakes.

The photo lab was on the way. As she entered, the door let out a ding.

"I need to pick up some film that was dropped off earlier," Rosemary told a clerk who appeared from a back room.

The guy looked as if he'd taken a bad batch of too many

recreational drugs. He wore white, cotton photo gloves, which contrasted with his dirty clothes. He pushed his oily hair back with his gloved hand. Rosemary worried he'd probably been wearing the same gloves all day.

"Name?" His voice was thick and gravelly.

"Christi. Rosemary Christi. But you may have them under Rolling Stone."

"Oh, yeah, man. I remember those." His greasy face brightened. "Those were from the concert! Looks like you guys had a crazy party after the show." He laughed, making gross snively noises. "Sure wish I could've been there."

"I need to pick them up." Rosemary wanted to see those damned pictures.

"You're a shooter for the Stone? What a great life, man. I could really dig that." He started sniveling again.

Rosemary wanted leave. "Can I please pick up my order?"

"It's in the back. I'll tell the guys you're here. We're all creamin.'" Rosemary wished she had worn sunglasses and a hat.

"I hope you haven't shown them to anybody!" she yelled as he disappeared to the back of the store.

When he handed her the envelope, she fought the urge to tear it open right there and see the pictures. She signed for them and dashed out. In her car, she threw the envelope on the seat and made a fast exit. She did not want a group of photo wannabes following her.

Pulling into a McDonald's lot, Rosemary opened the envelope and carefully pulled out the contact sheets. The first sheet looked great. The density, contrast, and exposure were perfect. Images of the concert and singers pleased her critical eye. She had captured the groups beautifully.

When she saw the pictures from the party, her stomach twisted. Damage control, she thought. Looking at the pictures, she was horrified she'd shot Bonnie Bunnie with Ritchie, both naked, both entwined, and both obviously high.

How could she have taken these? She looked more closely at Ritchie and smirked. She'd need a loupe to magnify his little erection, even though Bonnie was smiling. But she's used to working with dummies, Rosemary thought.

Sick, she stuffed the pictures back in the envelope. She'd need scissors and a roaring fire. Problem solved.

Colten tried to keep his mind on work and at the movie premiere, but he thought about Rosemary all the damned time. Sitting in his Hollywood living room, he looked at the beautiful Malibu vista below his window and laughed, thinking how envious people were of his lavish lifestyle. Sometimes, he considered making his own deal with the devil to live a normal life again.

Nikki was driving him crazy with the wedding. The event benefited her career more than his, yet she acted as if he owed her. She chose his wardrobe and micromanaged his schedule. He hated himself for allowing such manipulation.

He'd heard Rosemary was on the road, so he didn't get too upset when she hadn't returned his calls. He entertained fantasies about running away from Nikki, and into Rosemary's arms. How could he get out of this nightmare?

"Colten, baby, don't forget about our engagement party tonight." Nikki's voice pierced him. "Wear that Nehru thingy. It makes you look like Paul McCartney, and you know how sexy he is. I want us to make a good impression, especially for the press. You know, those naked pictures of you are a problem." Nikki's hair was up in big pink curlers, and she wore a silk robe with imitation animal puffs around the neck. "I need to go get my hair and makeup done before the party, so I'll meet you here later."

"Why are you wearing curlers if you're getting your hair done?"

"Oh, you are such a cutie," she squealed. "I can't leave the house without doing my hair first. Someone might see me!"

Colten jumped from the couch. "Oh, for heaven's sake, Nikki. When was the last time you saw yourself without makeup or those stupid getups you wear?"

"What are you talking about, sweetie?" said Nikki, visibly upset. " I need to look beautiful for you and my public." She started fanning her face with her hands "Don't make me cry, my mascara will smear."

"I'm going for a drive. I'll see you later." Colten opened the door, turned, and looked back at his beautiful house and at Nikki, standing dumbstruck. "Get Laz to take you. I'll meet you there."

Colten drove aimlessly. Speeding along Highway 101 trying to get far away from Nikki and Laz. He craved Rosemary, wanted to fall into her soft embrace. Slamming his fist on the dashboard, he screamed, "What happened to my life?"

Colten found himself on Rosemary's street. His heart pounded as he approached her tree lined drive. He knew she was working with the tour. Damn. How could he see her? It was hopeless. As he approached her house, he saw her car in the driveway and skidded to a stop.

He was out of his car when it occurred to him she might not want to see him. The last she'd heard, he was marrying Nikki, and Rosemary was asked to photograph the damned event. He'd been an insensitive brat. How could he just show up on her doorstep, after he let her go to save his precious movie star life?

Colten burned for her, he cast doubts to the wind and decided to tell her how he felt. She would probably, and rightfully, throw him out on his butt. What did he have to lose? Taking a deep breath, he walked to her door and knocked.

Chapter Thirty Three

"I don't want to achieve immortality through my work;
I want to achieve immortality through not dying."
~ Woody Allen

Mom's cancer progressed faster than any of us imagined. The tumor blocked blood flow to other organs, and emergency surgery had not been successful. After the operation, Dr. Sorrel told us Mom probably would not survive more than a few days— a week at most.

"No!" I gasped. "That's my *mother*! She has to be all right." I was in the hallway of the cancer ward, inconsolable. Dr. Sorrel rested her hand on my shoulder. Just then, Dr. Novak and another physician walked by, and I yelled at him, "You're an incompetent asshole! You shouldn't be allowed to practice medicine!"

"Who do you think you are, talking to me like that?" he shot back. His eyes burned with malice. "I'll personally see you fired from this hospital! You have crossed the wrong person, Cassandra." Then he turned to his friend. "Her daughter was recently admitted for a drug overdose. The whole family is crazy, but it's so hard to get anyone terminated around here."

I would have thrown myself on him, kicking and screaming, but Dr. Sorrel and Brenda grabbed me before I could get to him.

"And *your* son gave her the drugs!" I screamed at him.

"Prove it!" he yelled, as he retreated into an elevator.

Brenda and I spent as much time as possible with Mom. Since the blood supply to her vital organs had been shut off by the tumor, her body was becoming necrotic. There was nothing anyone could do.

We met with the hospice team and arranged to have her brought home, hoping she would be more comfortable. The hospice nurses were compassionate and took over most of the difficult decisions. I was grateful for their intervention.

Mitch was with me when I needed him and with the girls the rest of the time. Ashley was despondent about Mom and wasn't sure what to do. It hurt when I thought about Mom not being there for the girls' graduations, weddings, and other milestones. The keening loss I felt encompassed us all.

When Ashley was two, I'd told Mom how I felt about being a mother. "I can't believe how much I love her, Mom. It's a feeling that is so deep and real."

"Yes," she said. "Just like I love you."

I was still her child—something I hadn't thought of in a long time.

Mom was a picture of grace and dignity. I'd never seen anyone handle a devastating disease so serenely. After we got her home, she opened her door to visitors and played hostess from her hospital bed. By some miracle, her pain was not as intense as it had been before the surgery, although she was still suffering. Groups of people streamed in and out: children ran in the yard, grown ups sat in the kitchen, cooking and talking, people sat with Mom remembering their time together.

Mom was ready with a smile and an encouraging word. Even through her illness, she continued to shine.

I selfishly resented the intrusion of visitors. Our time together was quickly waning, and I wanted every precious second with her I could get.

Mom became weaker and required more morphine—a double-edged sword because, while the medicine helped with her pain, she was becoming less responsive.

There were moments we shared during this time I'll cherish forever. Brenda and I laid out photographs on Mom's bed. The three of us laughed and cried through the memories.

I told Mom I finally understood the many words of wisdom she had given me in life and apologized for my teen years.

She closed her eyes, smiled, and whispered, "I know."

When I asked her what other advice she could offer, she said, "Never wear black socks with white tennis shoes." She was weak but managed to smile at her joke.

I tried to make her more comfortable by arranging her pillows.

"I hope I've taught you all I can," she whispered. You two need to quit arguing. Life's too damned short." She paused, and I could tell she was thinking of her own mortality. You need each other. Don't let petty nonsense get in the way." She sat straighter. "Make sure to look for the silver lining in the clouds, never lose faith it will be there." Mom dabbed at a tear. Her voice broke as she said, "Take care of my precious grandbabies. Love them, hold them close, and remind them Grandma will always love them." She shifted and winced in pain. "And remember the line from my favorite Irish poem: 'Dance like nobody's watching.'" She took our hands in hers. "Life is short. Enjoy it."

Tears gushed down my face. Brenda was crying as hard as I was. "I can't stand this, Mom. How are we going to go on?" Brenda could barely get her words out.

"You both will go on. We're bound by love and always will be. Be proud of all you've accomplished." She looked at me. "Cassie, embrace your success, don't worry about what others think. You need to think about your decision with Mitch. Nobody's perfect. Forgiveness is the ultimate sacrifice. Look at the big picture."

I couldn't think about Mitch now. I squeezed Mom's hand and sobbed. "I know I'm supposed to give you permission to go, but I'm not ready to do that."

"Well, I'm not quite ready yet either, but I guess I don't have much say in the matter." She took a halting breath before continuing. "Both of you need to stay strong for yourselves, your families, and for me." She rested her head back on her pile of pillows. "And for God's sake, don't fight over my hot pink running suit."

Tears salted our laughter. As I held her hand, I realized how much a part of me came from her. To know love is to know pain.

Wild Rose

— FROM CHAPTER 17

Rosemary was breathing a bottle of merlot and stoking a fire to burn the negatives. She pulled out Joni Mitchell's Blue album and got ready to settle in for a pity party when she heard a knock.

"Who's there?"

"It's me, Colten."

"Colten?" Rosemary peeked out, surprised to see him fidgeting on her porch. "Why are you here?" Seeing him sent prickles of electricity through her body.

"I made a big mistake."

"Did you take a wrong turn?" She didn't invite him in. "Shouldn't you be out buying a tux for your wedding?"

He stood in the doorway, contrite and anxious. "I've missed you."

Rosemary ran her fingers through her long, silky hair. "Are you here to invite me to shoot your bachelor party, too?"

"Forget about the wedding and the studio. I've only been able to think about you. Do you think you could find it in your heart to give me—us—another chance?"

Rosemary couldn't believe her ears. She'd spent the last few months thinking of only him. Now he was standing so close she could feel heat radiating off his body.

"Come in. Why the change of heart?" She was wary Nikki and Laz were still in the circle of Colten's life.

"I've lost myself, Rosemary. When we were together, it was the first time I'd felt alive in years." He took her into his arms. "I'm sorry for treating you the way I did."

She accepted his embrace but was torn. They stood together until Rosemary remembered the photos and pulled away.

"Can I get you something?"

Colten released her. "Sure." His eyes glinted as he took her hand. "A tall drink of you ."

She winced, thinking of the drugged revelry. The fire popped. "How about a glass of wine?"

"Sounds nice."

She pulled her hand away. "I'll be right back."

"You've already got a fire going—not that I need any more flames."

Rosemary sighed.

Colten suddenly looked stricken. "Were you expecting someone? This might be a stupid question, but why are you burning a fire in the middle of summer?"

Rosemary waved him off. "No, I'm not expecting anyone. I like to enjoy a fire and a glass of wine, even during summer. It's relaxing."

A twinge tugged at her thinking of the reason the flames burned. On her way to the kitchen, she grabbed the envelope with the photographs.

"Make yourself comfortable. I'll be right back."

She hid the photos in an unused cooking pot.

"How's the tour?" Colten asked, when Rosemary handed him his wine.

"Oh, you know, busy." Rosemary squirmed under his gaze.

"The lifestyle is way too decadent for my tastes."

Colten looked hungrily at her and put his glass on the table. "I'm sorry for leaving you like I did."

"I didn't expect to see you again."

He took her glass and set it next to his, reflections from the flames danced in the crystal. Gently, he coaxed her into his arms. "You have every reason to toss me out on my butt." He held her tight. "I'm sorry."

Rosemary melted into his embrace. She let the heat from the flames and his delicious bouquet wash over her. She began to forget everything else. Slowly, tenderly, he began to kiss her face, her neck. Gentle caresses followed his light touch.

In his arms, Rosemary felt happy. She let the memory of the pictures slip from her thoughts as she stroked his muscled chest.

Responding to her touch, Colten's hands became bolder, his fingers deftly and artistically brought her out. Like a painter's soft bristles, he decorated colors of devotion with his touch. Their palettes mixed hues that no rainbow could match.

Tangled in each other's bodies, drunk with desire, Rosemary and Colten spent the evening locked together, unwilling to let go. They fell asleep, content. Nothing else in the world mattered.

They were awakened by a sharp, persistent knock at the door. Rosemary rolled away from Colten and saw that it was after eight a.m. She figured it was Hugh, after seeing her car in the driveway.

Colten sat up. "Are you expecting someone?" He turned

to her. "Let's ignore them. Stay under the covers. You look irresistible."

Rosemary stretched.

"Rosie, if you're there, open the door, now!" It's me, Beck. His voice was just outside Rosemary's bedroom window. "I mean it, Rosie. We need to talk."

"Damn!" Rosemary shot out of bed.

"Who's Beck?" Colten looked surprised. "You said you weren't expecting anyone."

"Beck is my agent. How did he know I was home?" Rosemary quickly dressed as she yelled to Beck, "Give me a sec, I'm coming."

"Your agent makes house calls?"

"He never has before." Rosemary was anxious. "He can't expect me not to take a few days off. I wonder if someone complained I wasn't there last night."

"Boy, and I thought I was controlled." Colten smiled and took Rosemary in his arms, giving her a passionate good morning kiss. "You're radiant. Don't make me let you go."

She kissed him. "I should see what he wants. He sounds angry."

"I'll hide here if you don't mind. I didn't tell anyone where I was going last night. I'm sure a search and rescue crew was sent out."

"So, I'm harboring a fugitive?"

He shrugged irresistibly. "I did miss my engagement party."

"Colten! What were you thinking?" Rosemary tossed a pillow at him. "You know the news is going to be all over that."

He raised his eyebrows and smiled.

The pounding on the door started again. "I'll be right back," Rosemary said. We'll pick up where we left off."

She ran out, making sure to close the door. She did a quick inspection and finger comb of her hair before letting Beck in. As he strode over her threshold, she glanced outside to see if Colten had parked in her drive. Relieved, she spotted his vehicle down the street under some large trees.

"What's going on? I took a few days off. The tour can live without me for a day or two."

He angrily threw a tabloid magazine on the table and pointed to the cover story. The headline caught Rosemary's eye: "Colten Garrison a No-Show at His Engagement Party, Nikki Devastated." She felt a stab of regret. "Look Beck, I can explain—" Her words caught in her throat when she saw her photographs under a huge banner headline: "Bonnie Bares Her Bunnie With Rock Stars at All Night Orgy—More Exciting Pictures on Page 3." Under the headline was a print of one of the photographs she'd taken of the children's TV star, stark naked, with certain anatomical details blacked out.

"You're fired, Rosemary." Beck looked as if he wanted to roll up the paper and swat her. "I thought you were more professional. This was your big break! To think I respected you. I sang your praises and this is how you repay me?"

Rosemary fought fear and anger but was losing the battle. "Beck, it's not what you think."

"Did you take these?" Beck looked at Rosemary like she was a four year old who had just gotten caught with her hand in the cookie jar. "For Chrissake, Rose, my kids watch her show."

Rosemary bit her lip. "Yes, but I was drugged. I didn't even know I took the pictures."

"You took drugs? Rosemary, I really had you figured wrong. I never imagined you being a stoner."

"I'm not!" Before Rosemary could finish, Beck turned and walked out.

As Rosemary followed, she heard Colten yell from behind her. "She had nothing to do with this, I came here on my own."

Beck stopped and looked at the movie star. "Colten Garrison? You're here?"

"Colten, that's not what this is about." Rosemary tried to close the door. "I'll explain later." He followed them out.

"Rosemary seems to be in the business of stirring up tabloid gossip." Beck's look shot bullets. "How am I going to explain that one of my photographers—ex-photographers—ruined the marriage of the century? Not to mention ruining the biggest rock tour of the summer. And destroyed a beloved children's star." He leaned close to Rosemary and growled, "I could have helped you sell those photos, but now that they're published, we're screwed—no, you're screwed."

At his car, Beck turned to Colten. "You leave me in the uncomfortable position of having to call Laz to let him know where his biggest star is." Beck's eyes held a glimmer of evil satisfaction. "Everyone in Hollywood is worried. Looks like both of your careers are going down the toilet."

"Beck, wait! Let me explain."

Beck's engine roared as he peeled out, leaving Rosemary standing in the dust of her career.

Chapter Thirty Four

"There are only two ways to live your life. One is as though noth-ing is a miracle. The other is as though everything is a miracle."
~ Albert Einstein

Mom's death sent me into a tailspin of grief. We had barely dealt with her diagnosis and were still in hope you're going to survive the cancer mode when she died.

The night she passed, Brenda and I held her hand, and fought to stay awake in the early predawn hour. I laid my head on the side of Mom's bed and closed my eyes. I'm not sure how long I'd rested, but when I looked up, Mom was gone.

No angels, no bright lights, not even a smoky wisp from her soul leaving her body—only a deep silence and an unbelievable hole of pain in my chest. For the first time in my life, I felt completely alone. The one person who had been constant in my life, the one I went to with problems or advice, was gone. Hers was the shoulder I needed to help me get through this excruciating grief.

At the funeral, the girls and I stood over her casket, which was closed. I couldn't bear to see her now.

I put my arms around her granddaughters. Gabby was silent and clinging; Ashley trying, unsuccessfully, not to cry. She touched the spray of flowers that draped over the simple casket.

"Remember when she used to read me *Goodnight Moon*?" she asked, tearfully.

I squeezed her shoulder. "It was your favorite. You wouldn't go to sleep without it."

"Yeah, but she'd read it to me as many times as I wanted." She sobbed quietly and ran her hand along the flowers. "Goodnight comb. And goodnight brush. Goodnight nobody. Goodnight mush." We both smiled at Ashley's favorite line. Together we whispered, "Goodnight stars. Goodnight air. Goodnight noises everywhere."

I put my hand on top of hers and grasped it tight. A few photos were nestled between the petals. Mom looked happy, especially in the picture of her sitting on the floor with all her grandchildren, hugging her.

The funeral was beautiful. Mom would have loved being the center of attention. Flowers filled the church, floral sprays surrounded the coffin. I hated to think she was in there. I wanted her back so much the pain was tangible.

Friends spoke about Mom and how she touched their lives. Dr. Sandoval was there with her daughters. She took the podium first.

"I met Jane at this church during our Christmas food drive. Being a single mom, she'd joke that she came to pick up food instead of dropping it off. We instantly became friends. I admired her ability to laugh the hardest when times were the toughest. We were both divorced moms, and she had already raised two wonderful daughters." Dr. Sandoval looked at me. "I appreciated her advice and keen insights into motherhood as well as life."

I never realized Dr. Sandoval and Mom went back that far. I knew they had met in church, but I thought it was my relationship with Sheila through the hospital that brought them closer.

"Losing Jane Ellison is a loss that cuts deep through my family and our community. I am thankful that we had the time we did. I'll leave you with some of her wise advice." Tears were streaming down Dr. Sandoval's face, although her voice never faltered. "She told me to laugh when it hurts—till it hurts. Love everybody. You'll never know who you might need to suck up to. Always be nice to animals. And take time to read bathroom walls, you just might learn something."

Quiet laughter rippled between the sniffles.

Adam surprised me when he got up to speak about Mom. He looked so different in a suit and tie—really quite dashing. His voice was shaking with emotion. "If it weren't for Jane Ellison, I would never have had the confidence to pursue my dreams. She encouraged me to try new things. She always asked, "What do you have to lose? Move ahead. You've already seen what's behind you." He paused to compose himself. "I'll always remember her telling me a quote she swore by: 'If two wrongs don't make a right, try three.' I continue to use that as my mantra to move toward my goals." He laughed, but his eyes were wet.

I smiled through tears. Mom meant so much to so many. I didn't have the emotional strength to get up in front of the filled church and speak. I was glad others were so generous.

The priest was gracious and spoke fondly of her. "She still lives on in her family and friends. Everyone she touched holds her love close."

My Kleenex supply was becoming sopped and stringy. When the cantor belted out "Ave Maria," I lost any sense of composure and doubled over in the pew, my face in my hands, sobbing.

When the pallbearers lifted the casket and walked past us, almost inaudibly, I heard Ashley, through jerky sobs, whisper, "Goodnight, Grandma."

The girls had a difficult time with the loss. I could offer little comfort, as I was suffering with my own grief. When Mitch asked why I had a new fat—not fat, *obese*—bank account, I waved him off and told him it was Mom's money. He didn't ask again. Rita was like a pit bull—sympathetic, but ready to bite. She was not happy playing both publicist and agent. She wouldn't back off.

Ashley retreated into herself again and wouldn't talk. She was still sensitive about the overdose, and losing Mom was a devastating blow. She was reluctant to discuss it with me, though I knew she'd talked to Mom. They shared an understanding I wish Ashley would share with me. Now that life line of advice was gone.

Gabby had a million questions I couldn't answer. She asked about heaven, and if there was any way God would change his mind and let Grandma come home.

About two weeks after the funeral, Gabby was really on me about getting a new pair of boots. She insisted she had to have this particular fashion statement and would not be happy until she got the real brand—not the knockoffs from Target. She sat next to me as I slumped on the couch, staring at nothing.

Gabby stuck her lower lip out and crossed her arms defiantly. "Mommy, it's not fair. Everyone has the Sparkle Boots except me."

Still wallowing in my own misery, I was not in the mood for an argument about who had the most toys. "Gabrielle, stop begging. You don't need them. Period. End of discussion." I wanted to be left alone in my grief.

"Why not?" Her lip began to quiver.

"Because you have enough shoes you don't wear."

"I promise I'll wear these every day." Tiny tears filled her eyes. "Grandma would have bought them for me."

This time my eyes filled with tears. I grabbed her in a big hug. "I'm sure Grandma would have. I wish she were still here—" I couldn't finish the sentence. We sat together in each other's arms.

"Mommy?"

"Yes, honey?" I wiped my tears off with my sleeve.

"Mary Katherine said you can talk to people in Heaven. Can you?"

I thought of all the people who told me the same thing. Every time they did, I had to bite my tongue to stop myself from telling them that not only do I want to talk, I want to listen.I want to see and feel her. Somehow, it just wasn't the same.

"Well, I suppose you can talk to people in Heaven. When you pray to God, you talk to Him."

"Yeah. And my Sunday school teacher said I could ask God for things, too."

I smiled. "In a manner of speaking, yes."

She smiled through wet eyes. "So if I ask Grandma for

Sparkle Boots, could she get them for me?"

"You can ask, maybe she'll answer your prayers." I wanted her to pray more, but not use the medium as an auction block. "Honey, you can't get something for nothing. You have to earn things, like those boots. Grandma will know if you deserve them."

Gabby became reflective. "Mommy, if Grandma does get me my boots, how will she give them to me?" She looked to the ceiling as if awaiting an answer. "Will she just drop them out of the sky?"

I had to laugh. "No, honey, miracles happen every day. I'm sure Grandma will find another way to see that your prayers are answered."

Her eyes lit up. "So it will be a miracle if I get them?"

Chapter Thirty Five

"All the world is made of faith, and trust, and pixie dust."
~ *J.M. Barrie*

I had serious issues with religion after Mom passed away. During her illness and suffering, I argued with a priest, asking how a God so loving could allow so much pain. He told me it had to do with free will, and no one knows why God works the way He does. At one point, I sniped at him, "I know God is a man because no mother would do to her son what He did."

Though I felt angry, sad, hurt, and betrayed, I had to keep my faith, for where would Mom be if I didn't? Going to church was a struggle, but I forced myself, and the girls, to go. One Sunday, a visiting priest was saying Mass. He was so ancient he could barely hold up his head. His brilliant white hair was Brylcreemed into snowdrifts. When he talked, his words were muffled, except when he said "fornication" or "sin." Always saying the two words together, it sounded like one word, "fornica-shin."

I even saw Ashley try to suppress a grin during the sermon. I almost fell out of the pew when he brought out a set of the *Summer of Love* books. Then he held up the Bible, saying *this* was the book you should be reading. He waved *Wild Rose* in the air and mumbled something about fornica-shin, pointing to the cover. The little bit of the sermon I could understand spoke of the evil content of the book, and we were surely going to Hell if we read it.

I flinched a little and cut a look over my shoulder, expecting a bolt of lightning to take me out. My face burned. I was sure my cheeks and ears were crimson. I glanced at the girls, noticing Ashley was blushing, too. Times were getting pretty bad if you felt the need to screen the church sermon for your children.

An elderly woman sitting next to me smiled. "He is such an old fuddy-duddy," she whispered. "*I* thought the book was great!"

"Thank you." I smiled back, then bit my tongue in horror.

"You're welcome," she responded, with a puzzled look.

"I read it and enjoyed it, too," I whispered back. Ashley gave me a stern "be quiet" look. I considered kneeling and pounding my chest in repentance to beg forgiveness. But I didn't want to make a scene.

Instead, I tried to understand the priest's mumbles while he extolled the sins of Rosemary and Colten. It felt as if he were attacking personal friends of mine. When I thought of the big picture, me sitting in church with my girls, avoiding a book tour because I didn't want them to know I wrote a romance novel, and watching the priest waving the damned thing next to the Bible in front of the congregation, I had a suffocating, uncontrollable urge to laugh.

I pulled out a Kleenex to catch the streaming tears of laughter. I snorted into the Kleenex, pretending to sob. "I miss Grandma," I choked.

"Mom, get a grip!" Ashley whispered, appalled.

As we were walking out of the church, Gabby asked, "Mommy, what's fornica-shin?"

I've learned when you have a problem, such as a death of a loved one, people really don't want to hear about it. Sure, many offered support, but no one's really attentive unless they've been through it. Some told me to look for signs from my mother. Most had an experience of either seeing or feeling the presence of a loved one after they died. I was looking for something more tangible, like a roll of thunder and a voice from heaven.

I'd settled back into a work routine but with a black cloud of grief hovering, ready to rain down. An elderly female patient had come to the ER, having lost consciousness at the local Walmart. I took her history and asked the usual medical questions. She had smoked for years and ate poorly. Although she wasn't overweight, I was sure her arteries were clogged with plaque, causing her blackout.

"What did you feel before you passed out?"

"Fine, as usual. I bent over to get something from the bottom shelf, and bam, the next thing I remember is seeing the bright light."

"The light?" My heart skipped a beat. This woman had been at Heaven's door. I wanted—*needed*—affirmation that Heaven existed. That Jesus extended his hand and welcomed her into eternal peace and comfort. "You really saw 'the light?' Was it beautiful? What did you feel?" I was rapidly shooting off questions. "Did you go toward it?"

She just shrugged and looked at me funny. "No. I don't

know. It was just one of those big fluorescent lights in the ceiling. Nothing too fancy."

Christine was my rock, and she was feeling the pain of losing Mom, too, having known her since she was seven. We told stories about how she took care of us growing up. There were small comforts in those talks.

Mitch helped a lot at home. He took charge of the girls and was sympathetic when they needed a shoulder to cry on. He told everybody how much I was hurting and to handle me with care. His affair/relationship with Renee was not mentioned. I don't know if he kept in touch with her when I wasn't around, but he always seemed to be there for me. After losing Mom and helping Ashley regain her strength, Renee seemed insignificant. At least to me. I wondered if she was for Mitch .

I remembered Mom's advice about forgiving Mitch. He was trying hard to save our marriage, to be the husband I'd always hoped for. But the hurt was still raw. Would he do something like that again? He seemed to regret it.

Did I have it in my heart to forgive?

I guess the one person who really forced me to snap back to the real world was Rita. She made it clear the book tour needed to get under way—*now*. She called me while I was sitting, staring at nothing, feeling sorry for myself. Her deep, bold voice brought me back to reality. "Cassie—I mean Cardia—it's time to get this show on the road. I'm sorry about your mother, but it's almost been a month. I love the press is asking who Cardia Loving is, we need to keep the momentum. Mystery is only good if you feed the fire. It's time to make the big reveal. I've got you scheduled to appear in two bookstores in Los Angeles next week. No more excuses. If you don't show, we'll have to begin legal proceedings."

"What do you mean, legal proceedings?" A tingle of nervousness seeped through the grief.

"Cardia."

"Cassie," I corrected.

"It's in your contract you'll do tours to promote the book. Sales are amazing, but they could be better if your public has an opportunity to meet you."

"My *public*?" It sounded more silly than important. "Rita, I've just lost my mother, my daughter is recovering from an overdose, and my husband had an affair. I'm in no shape to go on a tour."

"It sounds like you've already got a good storyline for your next novel." Her laugh was gusty and loud. She paused before dropping the next bomb: "Oh, by the way, how *is* your next book coming along?"

"*What* next book?" I asked warily.

"You owe me another book before the year is out. Didn't you even read your contract?"

Wild Rose

— FROM CHAPTER 18

After Beck's angry departure, Rosemary shuffled into the house. Colten met her in the doorway. "What was that about?"

Rosemary told Colten about the photographs and the real reason for burning the fire. "I didn't realize my drink had been spiked." She looked at him. "I'm ashamed and royally pissed. I can't believe the photo lab sold prints!"

He took her into his arms. His embrace warmed her, but she couldn't wrap her head around getting fired. It hung like a black cloud of despair. She'd not only lost her job, but worse, her credibility.

The rest of the morning, Rosemary and Colten perused the tabloid paper. The pictures showed Bonnie Bunnie with Ritchie in nasty poses. It was clear the TV star was enjoying herself.

There was nothing Colten could say to make Rosemary feel better. Plus, he had his own problems: The paper had photographs of a teary-eyed Nikki being held up by Laz.

The only solace Rosemary and Colten found was fleeting and carnal. Throughout the day, they poured themselves into each other until each frenetic climax brought them back to the harsh realities both faced.

"Why did I wait so long to find you again?" Colten stroked Rosemary's sweat glistened back with nimble fingers.

"I'm sorry Beck didn't let you explain. It wasn't your fault."

"Colten, it doesn't matter. The pictures are out, I shot them, I'm responsible. No one will care I don't remember any of it. How sympathetic do you think people will be when they find out I was drugged? I caused the downfall of everybody's favorite kid celebrity."

"But you didn't take the drugs. Someone slipped them in your drink."

"Look, I'm a photographer touring with a bunch of rock bands. Loud, obnoxious rockers, complete with groupies, roadies, and loads of drugs. There are risks that come with the territory. I should have known better." Rosemary rolled on her back and held Colten's hand. "These photographs will haunt me forever. I can't blame anyone but myself." She looked deep into his eyes to see if she could read any changes. "I'd understand if you didn't want anything else to do with me." She looked away. "Ever."

Colten grabbed her and held her tight. "For the first time in years, I'm happy." He smiled. "We'll get through this together, Rosemary. Together."

"Together," she repeated. "I like that."

With the last of the summer's evening light gently touching the gauze curtains, they both fell into a peaceful, dreamless sleep.

Rosemary, awakened early by the sound of running water, remembered Colten's light caresses and smiled.

Her happy thoughts were crushed when she thought of the pictures and her career's demise. She sighed and decided she'd channel a phoenix and rise from the ashes.

Jumping from the bed, she went into the bathroom, steamy from Colten's shower. His chiseled silhouette shadowed the diaphanous curtain. He sensed her, because he turned inviting her in. Rosemary joined him under the pounding hot water. Lathered with soap, Rosemary guided his hand over her body, She pressed herself to him. Ravenously, he sought her delicate petals. Together they shared a frothy, finale. Water peppering their bodies like a warm elixir.

He smiled tenderly. "I've decided to face the music. You've made me realize our actions are our own responsibility. I don't want to feel like I'm running away."

They stepped out of the shower wrapping themselves with towels. Colten sat on the bed and pulled Rosemary to him.

Rosemary massaged his neck. "Do you have to go? Why can't you just call?"

He stroked her silky wet hair. "That would be the chicken shit way. Being with you has made me feel as if a weight has lifted. I'm not afraid." Standing to get dressed, he said, "We'll be together, I won't let the bastards take me prisoner."

Rosemary gazed hungrily as he dropped the towel and dressed. "Colten, as you're driving back, I want you to really give some thought to the future."

"Are you talking about marriage?" A worried expression crossed his beautiful face.

"Yeah!" She laughed. "The one you're giving up. Walking away from the 'wedding of the century' is going to be enough of a challenge. But walking into a relationship with me could be disastrous, especially for your career. I'm going to have a lot of issues with my own scandal. I don't want to deal with guilt, too." Rosemary stood "I might be excess baggage you don't need right now."

He kissed her gently. "We'll deal with one problem at a time. Together."

She walked him to his car. With a heavy heart, Rosemary watched him drive away. She already missed him.

A few hours after Colten left, Rosemary sat in the kitchen, finishing her coffee, when someone knocked at the door. Afraid it was a reporter, she peeked out the curtained window. Hugh was standing on the front porch looking toward the street. Relieved, Rosemary let him in and closed the door.

"Looks like you've been busy." Hugh kept a distance, which was unlike him. He usually grabbed her as soon as he walked through the door. "I came by to find out if you really took those pictures."

"Hugh, if you're here to give me the third degree, you can just leave. I have enough problems without you judging me."

"Rose, what were you thinking? It's not like you." He paced the living room. "First that naked movie star and now Bonnie Bunnie."

"I really don't want to talk about it."

"I mean, *Bonnie Bunnie.* "

"Hugh, drop it, please."

"You know, I have friends on the road, and they said you were really shooting it up that night."

Rosemary felt as if she'd been kicked in the stomach

"It's over," Hugh said. But he looked as if he might cry.

It made her sad that Hugh, a constant in her life, was another person willing to toss her out like garbage. He'd always been there.

"I care about you, Rosie."

Rosemary smiled. "Thanks." She thought he'd be good for

someone, someday, if he would settle down and stop playing rock star wannabe.

She walked to the living room and pushed the tabloid paper to the floor. How had she had taken such a free fall from success? The one bright light was Colten coming back. Taking a deep breath, she whispered, "Together."

Colten decided to take the scenic route, exhilarated by his freedom and Rosemary's welcoming arms.

Rosemary's scandal did worry him. He was going to be hit with the challenge of leaving Nikki, Laz, and, likely, the studio. He hoped the studio wouldn't toss out their biggest revenue star. And, damn it, if they did he'd sign with another.

Because of the wedding, he didn't have another film lined up and thought of the numerous scripts piled next to his bed.

He smiled remembering Rosemary's embrace. Driving along the picturesque highway, Colten began to sing at the top of his lungs, "I Did It My Way." Sure, they would both deal with a storm of controversy, but he felt strong and ready for this new life. They'd weather the storm—together.

He was still laughing and singing as he rounded a curve, going way too fast to avoid the truck heading straight toward him.

Chapter Thirty Six

"Hire a teenager while they still know it all."

~ Anonymous

For the past two months, Bradley had become a fixture in our home. I was unloading groceries one evening, trying to think of a storyline for another novel. Since I hadn't accepted the fact I'd written *one* book, it was hard to come up with a plot for a new one.

"Hey, Mrs. C, let me help you." Bradley walked in with Ashley and Gabby, grabbing the grocery bags from me. "Here, Gabster, I'll throw the food, you catch and put 'em away."

Gabby squealed, delighted. Fortunately, he only tossed the foods that were unbreakable, like pasta and frozen vegetables.

Ashley sorted through the other bags to see if I'd bought anything good. "I asked Bradley to stay for dinner," she said.

"Okay, honey. That'll be nice." I glanced at Bradley as he gently lobbed a can of soup at Gabby.

Bradley seemed to buffer Ashley's depression over the death of Mom and keep her grounded with the case against Andrew.

Ashley didn't hide their relationship. She still didn't confide in me, but now I asked more direct questions and gave advice whether she wanted to hear it or not. She usually gave me the brush off, but I knew she listened. She'd roll her eyes to the ceiling and complain I was more a warden than a mother.

The more I got to know Bradley, the more impressed I became. An honor student, he excelled in science, math, and physics. Both of his parents were well educated. His mother, Anne, was a civil rights attorney, and his father, Thomas, worked as an engineer for a technical company. There were a few evenings both families got together for dinner. I enjoyed hearing their diverging views on a variety of subjects. It was as if they purposely took different sides just to have lively conversation.

I still had a hard time with Bradley's appearance. I knew not to judge on looks, but it was difficult to send your daughter out with a boy whose fashion accessories came from a pet store.

While I was cooking dinner, Rita called. Mitch had just come in from work and gave me a welcome peck on the cheek. This was how it had been since Mom died, but there was still much unsaid. He went into the den and joined the others.

"Rita," I whispered, my head in the refrigerator, looking for garlic. "I can't go."

"Cardia, you're going to California. End of story." She was relentless.

"Can I send stunt double?"

She made a noise that sounded like no. "Normally, I don't travel with my writers, but I'm going on this trip to make sure you show up."

I pulled out the garlic, tossed it on the counter, and sighed. "Let me see what I can do."

Later that night, I told Mitch I needed to go out of town on a work trip. "You know, I need medical credit hours." I couldn't look him in the eye.

"No problem. For how long?" He was cleaning the kitchen after dinner. As much as I hated to admit it I found some comfort in having him home. "A few days," I replied. I had accumulated enough vacation time, so I could easily take off work.

I didn't know what to expect on the book tour. Would I be photographed? What if someone recognized me? I was such a wimp about "coming out." I dearly wanted to call Mom and ask her advice.

On the afternoon before I left, I was putting laundry away in Gabby's room. I overheard Ashley talking to Teresa on the phone. "I want to be just like her. I think she's totally cool." Ashley's voice was breathless.

"Yeah, can you imagine going out with a famous movie star like that?" I couldn't hear Teresa's side of the conversation, so I figured they were talking about the latest teen idol of the week.

"Oh, man! Can you imagine doing that on the beach? *Outside*? I mean, what if someone walked up while you were doing it? Gross!" Ashley giggled. "I want to be a photographer just like Rosemary. I'm going to take some journalism classes next year."

Hearing the name Rosemary stopped me in my tracks, practically leaving skid marks on the carpet. I fanned myself with a pair of Gabby's neatly folded princess underwear. Surely they couldn't be talking about *Wild Rose?* They were too young to read a book like that, much less understand it. The book was written for sexually frustrated, perimenopausal women—not teenagers.

"Bradley knows a lot about photography, he said he'd help me find a good camera. Maybe I'll even be a photographer for some awesome rock band." She paused, listening to Teresa. "Yeah, and you and I can get an apartment together."

I had a quick visual of Edvard Munch's *The Scream* replaced with my face on it. The book I'd written to make money to allow me more time with my family had turned against me. I could see the irony in it but no humor. I took a folded stack of clothes into Ashley's room. She stopped talking to Teresa—her way of acknowledging me. "Okay, call me later," she said. "I'll ask my mom if she'll drive us to the mall."

"Ashley," I said. "I overheard you talking to Teresa about a book you've read."

Her face registered surprise.

"*Mom*, you were listening?"

"I just caught your comment about a book I've, um, read. It's clearly meant for adults."

"Well, you've read it. Why is it okay for you but not me?"

"Look, Ashley, there are situations in that book I don't think you're ready for." *And your own mother dreamed them up and wrote it.* How was I going to tell her about that?

"I'm almost sixteen! You treat me like I'm a kid." She crossed her arms and looked at the ceiling. "I'm old enough to understand about that stuff."

I remembered her frail body hooked up to IVs and pumps and wondered how I could protect her from outside influences. Didn't she remember Andrew Novak's sick bet? It still made me sick. I wanted to see Andrew hung by his little scrotum. Unfortunately, the court and I didn't see eye to eye.

"Ashley, at fifteen, you have a nice boyfriend, and might know *some* things about sex, but that doesn't make you an expert. You're going to have experiences and even make mistakes before you have a better understanding of how important it is to stay true to yourself. It's my job to guide you down the right path."

She uncrossed her arms and began to work at her split ends.

"I want to protect you as much as I can." I touched her shoulder. "Once that line is crossed, there's no going back." I cringed, thinking how much of her innocence was lost with Andrew. "Being a kid's really not that bad."

Her arms loosened a little, and she stared at her toes. "I'm not a kid."

I hoped my sermon was getting through to her. "I want you to be happy, but mostly, Ash, I don't want you to make mistakes you'll regret for years." I smiled. "I'm really not as dumb as you think I am."

She shrugged. "I know, and *I'm* not as dumb as *you* think. Can you drive me and Teresa to the mall?"

We both smiled, and I gave her a hug.

Chapter Thirty Seven

"We didn't lose the game, we just ran out of time."
~ Vince Lombardi

Christine almost peed her pants laughing when I told her about Ashley reading *Wild Rose*. Personally, I didn't think it was funny.

"Look, Cassie, as a psychologist, I've seen lots of situations. This is pretty minor in the larger scheme of things." She wiped away tears as she stood in the doorway of my office. "It sounds like you handled it well. Trust me, she knows a lot more than you give her credit for."

"I guess you're right. But I still have to face the fact I was the one who wrote the book she's now basing her future on. How do I tell her she shouldn't consider such a decadent lifestyle, when it came straight from her own mother's imagination?"

"It's time you come clean, Cassie. You need to tell her and Mitch you wrote it. Honesty is the best policy. Let her know your reasons behind writing the book." She gave me a big grin. "You realize your mom would think this was priceless."

"I wish she were here to help me get through this." Tears veiled my eyes. "I'm sorry. I miss her so much."

Christine gave me a big hug, "I know. We all do. She

was there for everyone and was proud of you for writing the book. Let your family be proud of you, too."

I nodded and wiped my eyes with the back of my hand.

Jennifer and Adam walked by. "Cassie, you have to hear about this new admit," Jennifer said. "This guy just brought in his wife—" Jennifer shook her head. "It's sad, really. She has cancer, and he was getting her dressed and had to put a Kotex on her." She snickered.

Adam took over. "And he put it on upside down, with the adhesive side to her body." They both laughed a little.

Christine smiled but seemed uncomfortable.

I fumed. "What in the hell is so funny about that?" The tears that had started when Christine mentioned Mom began to flow. Both Jennifer and Adam stopped laughing.

"Oh, Cass, I'm sorry. I wasn't thinking," Jennifer sputtered.

Adam put an arm around my shoulder and grabbed a box of Kleenex.

"Sorry, Cassie. You know we have to find humor in barbaric situations. We weren't thinking past the moment."

I wiped my face. "I know. But think of that poor woman and her husband. We're supposed to be here to help, not laugh at them."

"I'll go get Dr. Sandoval to assist me." Jennifer ducked out, giving my arm an affectionate squeeze before she left.

"How else can we get through a day here if we can't laugh a little?" Adam said, as he ruffled my hair.

"Hey, I understand you're finally going to take some time off."

"Yeah, and I'm going with her," said Christine.

My wet eyes brightened a little. "You talked to Phillip?"

"Turns out he's out of town a lot the next few weeks. I've cleared my calendar, so we can take a girls only vacation."

"I'll warn the airlines," Adam joked. "And as a public service, I should probably notify the mayor of the city you're going to, so they can alert the citizens." He turned to leave. "You know what we all need around here?"

"What?" Christine and I said together.

"Hospital happy hour! It's been ages. Can you guys go tonight?"

"I can," Christine chirped. "Cassie, call Mitch. Your family can survive without you for one night."

"I don't know." I was reluctant. I still had to pack for tomorrow, and spontaneous happy hours were not a part of my life anymore. "I need to make sure the kids are fed and—"

Adam flailed his arms dramatically. "Fed, watered, walked... Cass, we won't take no for an answer even if I have to call Mitch myself."

"Okay, I'll call, but what about the rest of the staff?"

"I'll take care of them. You take care of yours." Adam took off to book the party.

Mitch thought the happy hour was a good idea. "You need some time to unwind. Go and have fun."

"Make sure you feed the girls real food. Not just chips and cereal." I felt guilty and selfish, leaving my family to have a night for myself. But it gave me a little extra time that afternoon to go shopping for something new and bizarre to wear to the signing. I didn't want anybody to recognize me.

"They'll survive," Mitch sighed. "I'll do my best not to poison them or give them too much beer."

"Mitch, that's not funny."

"Have some fun, Cassie. Don't worry about us."

"Okay. Thanks."

I spent most of the afternoon with the terminally ill cancer patient. Jennifer and Dr. Sandoval had taken care of the sticky situation. I visited with her husband, too. He was beside himself with grief and exhaustion.

"I feel so stupid for putting that thing on wrong. I mean, how was I supposed to know?" His voice had a soft country edge to his Texas accent. "I'm tryin' to keep Ivy as comfortable as possible. I know she's in pain, but it's wearing me out like the dickens." His eyes looked tired and sad.

"I'm sorry. I recently lost my mother to cancer. It *is* difficult." I don't know why I felt the need to tell him about Mom, but it felt good to talk. "Let me sit with her for a while, and you can go down to the cafeteria and get something to eat."

"Oh, I'm not so hungry, but a cup of coffee sounds nice." He looked grateful. "Are you sure you don't mind?"

"Not at all. In fact, while you're gone, I'll gather some information about hospice care."

"No! I ain't gonna send her to no nursing home. I promised her I wouldn't do that."

"You don't have to send her anywhere. Hospice will send a nurse to your home. Ivy can stay in her own bed, and you can take some time for yourself. The hospice staff will help you and Ivy get through this."

"I don't know. We really can't afford much. She'd shoot

me if I went through what little money we do have."

"Insurance usually covers hospice care. They'll be able to control her pain and take care of her. I'll check on it for you while you go take a little break."

"Don't leave her alone, okay?"

"I promise." I brought as much paperwork as I could into Ivy's room and sat next to her.

Ivy's husband spent a few hours sleeping in the waiting room while I managed to get hospice set up. I felt like I had made a difference in someone's life that afternoon.

Happy hour with hospital staff is like a group of veterans telling war stories. I was impressed Adam managed to round up the whole day crew for the get-together, including Dr. Boran and Dr. Sandoval.

Gail came but said, "I may need to leave early because I'm ovulating."

"Just get drunk and loosen up, or the sperm will get scared and swim the other way," Adam said. "I think alcohol conceives more children than sex."

"What makes you such an expert on conception?" Jennifer asked.

"I might have conceived a number of little rugrats, for all you know. When I was in nursing school, I made many donations to the local sperm bank."

"And they accepted them?" Dr. Boran laughed. "Maybe they used it for research with rats."

For a couple of hours, we ate, drank, and laughed until it hurt. It was cathartic, not only for me but for the rest of the group. The crowning touch of the evening was when Adam, giving Gail a hard time about conceiving, started singing, "I am woman, hear me roar, in numbers too big to ignore..."

Everyone at the table joined in and sang as loud as they could. Dr. Boran sang but changed the word "woman" to "man."

We made a spectacle of ourselves. Other diners glanced uncomfortably at us. Some looked down, embarrassed. Others smiled and encouraged us. I noticed a waitress trying to catch the eye of a manager to see if she should boot us out, but when we came to a rousing finish, the whole restaurant stood up and applauded. Christine took a deep bow and swept her arm around to include us in her encore.

The manager stood, warily watching us, but later came over with a free plate of appetizers. "I'd buy you guys another round of drinks, but I think you've had enough."

It was the most fun I'd had in a long time.

Chapter Thirty Eight

"A doctor can bury his mistakes,
but an architect can only advise his clients to plant vines."
~ Frank Lloyd Wright

Rita made good on her threat and met me and Christine in Los Angeles for the book promotion. Having Christine along gave me strength, although I was as nervous as a gazelle in a lion's den. I knew I was going to have to "come out" sooner or later, preferably later. I couldn't imagine the reactions of friends and family. I didn't know what to expect. The thought of being a celebrity was so far out of my realm. Though *Wild Rose* had been on many bestseller lists since it came out, I didn't feel any different.

On the first morning of the tour, Rita invited—no, demanded—we have breakfast in her suite. My stomach was in knots, I couldn't bear the thought of food.

I debated whether I should invest in a wig and monster sunglasses, so I wouldn't be recognized. Rita said this was a city where no one knew me, but taking no chances, I asked Christine to give me a full makeover before we left the hotel. We slicked my hair back in a severe wet bun. It was plastered and shellacked so hard to my head that it not only hurt, but I swear, all my forehead wrinkles smoothed out. Christine slathered so much eye makeup on me that I didn't recognize myself. The fashionable eyeglasses we found at Walmart, sprinkled with little pink rhinestones, were the crowning touch, but I would have been more comfortable in Groucho glasses, complete with the mustache.

"There, finished." She stood back and appraised my new look. "I feel like your fairy godmother. Bippity-boppity-boo!" She waved the brush over my severely styled hair.

"More like bippity-dippity-doo, you put so much gel in my hair. I look like a crossdresser." The fuchsia silk suit with the serpentine turquoise scarf thrown over the shoulder was so not my style. I felt like I was suffering delusions of glamour. "I look like a combination of Sarah Palin and Tootsie."

"You look gorgeous." Christine held the door open for me as we headed to Rita's hotel room. "And look how thin you are in that suit."

"Cassie-Cardia," Rita belted. She had started hyphenating the names together. It was aggravating, but I said nothing. "Good heavens," she said, as she looked me over." How many layers of eye shadow did you put on?"

"I don't want to be recognized." I gingerly touched my crisp, overly sprayed and varnished hair, afraid it might shatter.

She raised an eyebrow. "Recognized as *what?*"

We sat in her hotel suite. Coffee and baked goods sat on a room service tray. "Okay, here's the deal," Rita continued. "We're going to get you in and out quickly. No interviews. I want to keep the mystery of who Cardia Loving is." She appraised me again. "This get up might be the ticket to keep an air of secrecy and from people finding out the author is just a suburban housewife."

I slow boiled a shot of anger and could practically feel my fire engine red lipstick bubble. "There's nothing wrong with—"

She waved my words away and went on. "Then we'll set up for publicity shots—photos only. The mayor and his wife will be there to welcome you."

"The mayor? Rita, what are you talking about?" I almost choked on my coffee, still miffed about her housewife comment.

"Don't you dare spill anything," Rita admonished. "You need to look picture perfect all day. Now, about the mayor and his wife." She took a big, crumbly bite of a muffin. "She's a big fan of *Wild Rose* and is looking forward to meeting you. The mayor is using this as an opportunity to get his face in front of the public. Plus, he's trying to get the filmmakers to shoot the movie here."

The room started to spin and the rhinestone glasses became heavy. "Movie? What movie?" If there'd been anything in my stomach, it would not have stayed long.

Christine spoke up. "Rita, slow down. You're going a mile a minute, and you're sharing interesting news without elaborating. Cassie looks like she might need a trip to the emergency room before the book signing."

"Look, we're behind schedule already. Cardia had too many issues to deal with before, and her first tour was cancelled. Books don't sell themselves, and if we don't jump now, we're stuck with a warehouse full of unsold product." Rita was talking as if I weren't there. "I'm more surprised than anybody that the book took off as well as it has. It crossed over, hitting mainstream markets as well as our loyal romance readers." She shifted heavily, smiled, then got serious again. "We don't have time to pamper the author's ego when the book is selling like hotcakes. That's why I'm here. To make sure you go." She patted my trembling knee. "This is the perfect place to get your face in public and to shake and sign."

I hoped she meant to shake hands and sign books. Getting my face out there was a whole different issue since I didn't recognize myself. Instead of being excited, I was nervous. It was funny. I could handle a trauma in the emergency room with my eyes closed, but being the center of attention stopped me in my tracks.

"So what's the deal about a movie?" Christine asked Rita. She looked at me, her eyes twinkling with excitement.

"There are a few studios fighting over it." An unnatural glint flashed in Rita's eyes. "Right now, everybody is chomping to find out who you are." She stood, signaling it was time to leave.

When we arrived at the bookstore, I was surprised to see a crowd of people in a long line that snaked around the building. "Why the crowd? Did they just open a Super Target?

"No. They're waiting for you to sign their books."

"This is for *Wild Rose*?" I asked, astounded. "For *me*?" There must have been about a hundred people. I looked at Christine and Rita. "Is there a ring of fire I'm supposed to jump through?"

Rita paused, considering. "Not with all the hairspray you're wearing," It wouldn't be safe." She grunted as she pushed me out of the car. "Remember, don't sign any books unless they were bought at this store."

We walked into a side entrance, and Rita sat me at a table. Fear gripped me as the first person shoved a book under my nose to sign. I was afraid I wouldn't be able to write my name because my hand was shaking so badly. At that moment, I regretted writing *Wild Rose*. I felt like Colten. I'd sold my soul to the devil.

After a few autographs, I was able to write "Cardia Loving" without the urge to laugh or run. I relaxed and began to enjoy the experience. Most people were gracious. Some asked to have the book signed for a friend or relative, others wanted a signature only. Like an army sergeant, Rita kept the group moving, handing me books with the covers open, ready for a signature. We managed to visit two bookstores in one afternoon.

At the end of the day, I was tired but happy. I'd been incognito all afternoon, without a hint of recognition. Of course, it helped that I didn't know anybody in California. Publicity was fairly low key, a few shots of me holding the book with the mayor and his wife and a few of me alone, by a display of *Wild Rose*.

That evening, the three of us enjoyed cocktails in the hotel bar. My high heels, tight suit, Spanx and rhinestones were pinching every nerve in my body. All I wanted was to change into something comfortable and enjoy a quiet dinner. I was glad when Rita excused herself, leaving me and Christine alone.

"After we finish our drinks, let's put on real clothes and go eat. I'm famished," I said.

"Or we could just get into our PJs and order room service." Christine stirred her ice. "I'm already feeling mellow. We can order dinner for two and wine for four!"

Thirty minutes later, we were scrubbed clean and ready to eat. It was nice to feel my skin again. It had taken two bath towels to wash the makeup off.

We ordered a feast of steak, potatoes, salad, a bottle of merlot, and a decadent chocolate cake for dessert.

"So what did you think of the book signing?" I asked between mouthfuls.

"You know, I never thought I'd see the day when you'd be a celebrity. Here's a toast to my best friend—my *famous* best friend."

"I still feel like I'm on the outside looking in or that I'm living someone else's life." Though, admittedly, I was hiding behind a disguise. "What would people think about me writing this book?" We clinked glasses. "Mostly, I miss Mom. I feel like I can't allow myself to be happy about the success."

"Your mom would've loved to have seen you signing your book." Christine took a sip of wine. "But she'd have told everybody in the world you wrote it. You know she'd never be able to keep that a secret." Christine paused. "She's probably shining down from heaven, proud as punch."

"Yeah, but I need something more solid. A real sign, like angels singing, or to be able to hold her."

"I know, Cass. How are you?"

I let out a deep breath. "There are moments I think I'm doing okay, then I get hit with a reminder. I can't tell you how many times I've picked up the phone and dialed her number." I sipped my wine. "The other night, Gabby was watching *The Lion King*. I walked in during the part where Rafiki shows Simba the reflecting pool. In the ripples, Simba sees his dead father. When Rafiki says, 'He lives in you,' I burst out sobbing." I wiped my eyes while I talked. "Poor Gabby didn't know what to do. She saw me standing in front of the TV, holding a bag of garbage, crying my eyes out at a cartoon. All she said was, 'It's okay, Mommy. It's only a movie. It's not real.'"

Christine began to tear up, too.

"You know, your eyes are going to be so swollen tomorrow you won't be able to glob your makeup on for your book signing. Let's go wash our faces and go to bed."

I could feel the warmth of the wine all the way to my toes. We did the dishes by pushing the room service tray out into the hallway. Christine went to her room, and I crawled into bed and called home. Mitch said the house was still standing and the girls were still breathing. I talked to both of them. Well, I talked while Ashley listened. Gabby, on the other hand, yakked up a storm. I loved hearing her little voice.

"Mommy, when are you coming home? I don't like it when you go on trips."

"I don't either, sweetie. I'll be home day after tomorrow."

"Daddy said I didn't have to take a bath tonight, and he's going to make a tent in my room so I can have a campout."

"That sounds like fun, honey." I knew she'd be disheveled and dirty when I got home, but as long as she was happy with me not there, I was okay. "Let me talk to Daddy. I love you."

"Love you, too. DAAADDDYYY! TELEPHONE!" she screamed into the receiver.

"Honey, please don't yell into the phone."

She giggled as she handed the phone to Mitch.

"How's the meeting going?" Mitch asked. "No, not now. Brush your teeth."

"I've already brushed my teeth, but thank you." I almost giggled as I spoke.

"I was talking to Gabby," he said, as he shooed her into the bathroom. "Are you learning new torture tricks to try on your patients? I talked to Phillip today. He said Christine went with you. You didn't tell me she was there. Since when does she need credits for emergency medicine?"

"It was a last minute decision. We thought it would be fun to take a trip together." The wine emboldened me, so I took a potshot. "You did a pretty good job of keeping secrets."

"I'm not in the mood to argue." Mitch sighed. "Let's save that for the marriage counselor you scheduled."

After we hung up, I tried to read but was so exhausted from the day's events I fell into a deep sleep.

I had a vivid dream about Mom. She looked radiant. Her hair was long and silky gray, and there was a beautiful aura of light around her. I was so happy to see her. In the dream, I asked, "Are you in heaven? Are you okay?" Peace enveloped me having her near, especially looking as ethereal as she did. "I've missed you, Mom." Even in the dream, I knew I was dreaming. Yet she seemed so real and close I reached out to touch her. "Can you hear me in heaven when I talk to you?"

She smiled, took my outstretched hand in hers, and gently shushed me. "We've said all we needed to." Her light faded a little, but before I lost the vision, she said, "I love you, too."

Then she was gone.

When I woke up, I felt as if I'd held her hand in mine.

Wild Rose

– FROM CHAPTER 19

Rosemary grabbed coffee and a pair of scissors to shred the party negatives. The irony wasn't lost on her that the nude pictures of Colten made her a celebrity, while the naked pictures of the rock group and Bonnie Bunnie had cast her so far into the dead zone she wasn't sure she'd recover professionally. She was furious Ritchie had taken advantage of her, yet she was the one paying with a fall from grace.

She clicked on the TV to watch the news. President Carter was talking about the gas crisis. The next story was about a terrible car accident on a mountain highway. There was no live footage—only black and white images of a small car crushed beyond recognition. The pictures were frightening.

The anchor's baritone voice talked over the photos. "...the truck driver was also fatally injured. The death of this popular actor will have a devastating effect on the Hollywood community. His high profile wedding had been listed as the biggest event of the year. Unfortunately, due to his untimely death, Colten Garrison will not be taking the beautiful Nikki Chimera as his wife."

Rosemary went cold.

She stared at the TV while pictures of Colten flashed on the screen. The announcer continued reporting on the fiery car crash that killed Colten "in the prime of his life and career." Shock radiated through Rosemary like a nuclear blast.

Shaking, she reached to put her coffee mug on the table but missed, and it shattered on the floor.

Rosemary wasn't sure how long she lay there in shock. The TV was droning on, with updates on Colten's death. In a state of disbelief, she rose and picked her way carefully around the broken shards of glass and congealing coffee. She'd given her love to Colten and, now her life was spiraling to darkness. This was a tragedy she couldn't distance from. An empty loneliness coiled in her soul.

The ringing phone jolted her.

"Rosie, Beck here." He sounded perfunctory. "I just heard about Colten."

"I just heard, too." Rosemary started crying.

"Laz knew he was coming from your place. I called him before I knew about the accident. He was not happy to hear that you two were together."

Rosemary felt her stomach lurch at the mention of Laz.

"Colten decided not to marry Nikki," Rosemary sobbed, "he came to tell me." Just moments before, Rosemary had wanted to talk to somebody, but now she was reluctant to confide in Beck.

"The two of you were an item?" Beck asked. "I mean, this was news to both me and Laz." The way he dropped Laz's name seemed slimy.

"Look, Beck, I can't believe he's—oh, God." Rosemary cried. "I don't give a damn about what you or Laz think."

"C'mon, Rosie. One day, you're my best photographer. The next you have two huge black marks against you. You've always had a love 'em and leave 'em attitude. Why get so attached to this dude—the untouchable one? How do you think I'm taking all of this?"

"Don't make this about you." Rosemary wiped her wet face and slammed the phone down with a satisfying bang.

Chapter Thirty Nine

"The Constitution only gives people the right
to pursue happiness. You have to catch it yourself."
~ Ben Franklin

After having the dream about Mom, I began to feel more at peace. The fact the dream happened on the book tour made me wonder if she was giving me an ethereal thumbs up about my success.

When I got home on Sunday, Gabby ran into my arms. "Did you get me something?"

With her hanging on my hip, I opened my suitcase and pulled out her much desired Sparkle Boots. She squealed and hugged them to her neck. As I kissed her, I was tempted to tell her I'd seen Grandma.

I gave Ashley a T-shirt from her favorite store, the expensive logo stitched prominently in the front. She didn't squeal like Gabby, but she smiled. "Thanks."

Mitch came out of the kitchen and pecked me on the cheek. "I made dinner."

Still clutching her boots, Gabby said, "Didn't you get Daddy anything?"

I tickled her. "Yeah. I'll do the dishes." I looked at Mitch. "Thanks for cooking."

Realistically, it was inevitable that my secret would be discovered, and I knew I had to confide in Mitch. There were times I considered telling the world. But each time I had the urge, I thought of Ashley reading *Wild Rose* and lecturing her about how inappropriate the book was. How could I reasonably explain it was okay her mother wrote it?

The checks continued to come in, and Rita called the house frequently, asking for a person named Cardia. My family thought it was a crazy lady dialing the wrong number. Then Mitch began to wonder why my investments were paying so well while our meager joint stocks were tanking.

He asked about my drastically reduced hours at the hospital, also noticed by Nelda and Mr. Starnes. Nelda happened to call my house when Christine and I were in Los Angeles and asked Mitch when I was going to return to work full time. She and Mr. Starnes were sorry about the loss of my mother and Ashley's "drug problem," but they needed to hire a full time replacement if I didn't get back to the ER." To his credit, Mitch told her I'd come back when I was ready.

I was being pulled in different directions between home, work, and my romance ruse.

I'd blamed Mom's death and Ashley's recovery as the reason for my time off.

Mitch agreed to marriage counseling while fretting about the hourly cost of saving our marriage. During the first few sessions, Mitch and I threw accusations at each other. I think the shrink, Dr. Ogden, scribbling notes, was really writing her grocery list while we argued.

Dr. Ogden was located in a strip mall, right next to a bookstore where there was a window display showing not only the cover of *Wild Rose*, but a poster with a life-sized photo of me taken in California. I was stunned to see the fully made-up reflection of myself staring out of the window. Surely, Mitch would recognize me. As we walked by the store, my breathing became shallow and my knees unsteady. This was the moment of truth. I watched him pause, look at the poster and waited for him to start questioning me. I glanced nervously between him and the image, grateful we were on our way to counseling, so we would have a mediator to temper the discovery.

He did stop and stare at the picture. I began sweating. "That's an attractive woman. She even looks a little like you," he said. "Why don't you wear your hair like that? We could probably save some money on this marriage counselor." He gave me a wink and a smile, indicating that all our problems would be solved if he could get me in the sack while I looked like a Mafia don in drag.

"Did Renee wear her hair slicked back like that for you?"

"Low blow, Cassandra. That wasn't fair."

"Well, it wasn't fair for you to have an affair."

"You're right, and I'm sorry. That's why we're meeting with the counselor." He directed me through the entrance to Dr. Ogden's office. As I passed him, he leaned down and whispered. "But I do think you'd look pretty hot in those rhinestone glasses."

We sat in the waiting room, a chair between us. I thought of the toothpaste analogy all marriage counselors seemed to use about relationships: *Sometimes, a marriage can crumble because the toothpaste was squeezed from the wrong end.* I picked up an outdated *People* magazine. If it were that simple, all those marriages could be fixed for a few bucks. They could each buy their own damned tube. I glanced at Mitch and wondered how many tubes of toothpaste it would take to fix our marriage.

I needed to give him some credit. He was trying to keep our marriage together. When I was younger, I had a one strike rule in relationships. There was no way I would have forgiven an affair. But now, with children, I was forced to see the big picture. I couldn't think of only myself; the girls were part of me. I remembered Mom's advice about forgiveness being the ultimate sacrifice. I was trying to be that person.

That I could now support myself and the girls financially was immensely satisfying. I looked at Mitch and wondered if I could singularly maintain the emotional strength the girls needed. He was a good dad.

Mitch grabbed a *Sports Illustrated* and flipped through it. I watched him reading and noticed he had more wisps of gray in his hair, especially along the temple. He'd kept fit, but had softened around the edges, his face delicately lined, particularly around the eyes. When we met, he had a hard, lean body from playing basketball in college. I loved to run my hands along his angles and muscles. Looking away I realized, with surprise, my character Colten was drawn from a younger version of Mitch.

We were finally called in to see Dr. Ogden. Her office was decorated in soft earth tones. Floor to ceiling windows overlooked a tree lined creek. I wondered how many of her patients' secrets were held in the dense canopy of trees.

She offered us each a chair facing her massive desk. "Did you both have a good week?"

I expected our counseling session to be about us. Instead, we began by talking about Ashley and how she was dealing with life after the drug overdose. Mitch brought up Andrew Novak. "I've never wanted to hurt someone like I want to hurt him. He's taken something from my daughter that she'll never get back. I can't stand it." He spoke with surprising calm, but I noticed his hands were shaking.

"And what are your thoughts on that?"

"Like I want to kill him. Don't worry, I won't. But there's this primal urge to do some major damage to him."

I looked at Mitch. "We need to encourage Ashley to show up at the court hearing to testify against him. That's the best way to punish him for what he did. Dr. Novak will hire the best defense attorneys. Andrew will get off if we don't fight."

Dr. Ogden peered over her glasses at us. "And what are your thoughts on that?" she asked.

"What do *you think* I think? Why don't you give us *your* two cents?"

Dr. Ogden clasped her hands in front of her and looked positively excited. "I'm sensing anger. This is good."

"Mitch, we need to be united on this with Ashley. She needs to pursue charges against Andrew. If not, he'll probably do it again. We can hire the best attorney money can buy. Ashley needs to do the right thing."

"How?" Mitch asked. "Using your mother's money?"

"Forget about the money. In fact, pretend it's ours. Let's just take care of Ashley."

I knew then I had to come clean and tell Mitch about *Wild Rose*. It wasn't just the money. I had my head stuck in the sand, concealed behind a façade, afraid. Here I was, spouting off about Ashley doing the right thing, when I needed to take responsibility for my own actions instead of hiding behind those damn rhinestone glasses. It had been easy writing under a pseudonym. I didn't have to be accountable.

I remembered something Mom used to say: "If you do something wrong, you'll have to suffer the consequences. So think what those consequences are before you jump in."

I had jumped without looking.

For the next hour, Mitch talked about getting revenge on the Novak family. I sat and thought about how I was going to tell Mitch and the girls about my deception.

Chapter Forty

"Make everything as simple as possible, but not simpler."
~ Albert Einstein

Life continued to be a roller coaster ride for me, mostly the stomach in your throat part. Rita scheduled more book signings, including one close to home in two weeks, even though I'd begged her not to schedule Dallas. I needed to keep Ashley grounded long enough for her to testify against Andrew.

"It's too late, Cardia," Rita said. "The bookstore is already scheduled. If you'd worked with your publicist, then the two of you could've dealt with your issues. I don't have time for your problems. We need to sell books. And I like the enigma your fake identity is creating. It should get us more TV coverage."

The news had latched on to the story about the elusive author, and it made a ruffle on the morning shows. Luckily, a tornado disaster in the midwest cut my story short.

I called Mr. Starnes and told him I needed more time off. He was not happy but didn't threaten to replace me. He did want assurances Adam and Jennifer were responsible enough to handle the administrative duties. He also wanted me to schedule a float nurse.

Mitch and I had another unproductive counseling session—unproductive because, again, I chickened out and didn't come clean. There was a part of me that felt like I was having a secret affair. My Dallas book signing was creeping up like a pair of ill-fitting undies.

I'd made reservations for us at a neighborhood Italian restaurant after our appointment with Dr. Ogden. On the table, a candle flickered, its weak flame threatening to go out. I sipped a glass of Chianti, staring at the sputtering flame, hoping its tiny light would keep burning. Taking a deep breath I blurted, "Mitch, we need to talk."

The tone of my voice seemed to scare him. He looked stricken. I gulped more wine.

"You're not pregnant, are you? Or—oh, no! Is it Ashley?" he squeaked. "Is she—"

"No, Mitch."

"What? Have you decided to divorce me?" He looked down. "I wouldn't blame you."

"No." I paused. "You know all that money that's in the bank?"

He opened his menu. "Your mom's money?"

"It's not mom's. It's mine. I earned it."

He looked up quizzically. "When did nursing become so lucrative?"

"That money is not from nursing." I was shaking so hard I had to hold my glass with two hands.

"Then where's it from?" He put his menu on the table and stared at me. "Cassie, if it's something illegal—" He looked away. "We'll get help. I don't want to see you or the girls hurt."

"No, it's nothing like that." I set my glass down. "Do you remember when I told you I wanted to write a romance novel?"

"No." He gave me a confused look. "When?"

I realized again how he never listened to me. "You waved it off."

He had a perplexed expression on his face, like a two year old who's been told Santa Claus flies around the world in one night and comes down the chimney with toys.

"I wrote a romance novel."

"You wrote a book?" he asked, in seeming disbelief.

"I did. And it's a bestseller. My agent is pushing me to do book tours—which was where I really was in California with Christine. And I've taken some day trips, too, when you thought I was working. I have to go on another trip soon." I was jumbling my thoughts and words together. "Believe me, no one is more surprised than me."

"Wait. What?" He sat back and stared at me as if expecting an alien to jump out of my chest. "Cassie, slow down. You have a bestselling book *and* an agent?"

I pulled out a copy of *Wild Rose* from my purse and handed it to him.

He looked at the cover. "It says this book was written by Cardia Loving." Mitch held it up and pointed to the cover as if I were clueless.

"Pseudonym. Cardia, for heart. Loving—speaks for itself."

Mitch turned the book over and read the back. He looked at the front again, then at me. "Wait a minute, isn't this the book we saw in the bookstore window when we went to Dr. Ogden's? There was a picture of the author."

"That was me, Mitch. It's amazing what a little...well, *a lot* of makeup can do."

He stared at me dumbfounded.

"You'd think I'd be bouncing off the ceiling for joy. I mean, the book is a bestseller. It's making a lot of money. I could quit my job and stay home if I wanted to."

"This is unbelievable." Mitch shook his head and smiled. He sipped his wine and stared at me. "You're not kidding, are you?" he asked skeptically, looking at me as if for the first time. "Are you trying to get me back for something?" He turned away, no doubt thinking of Renee.

"I did it for the girls, Mitch. To be able to spend more time with them. To take some time off work." I slumped in my chair. "The ironic thing is I don't want the girls to know I wrote it. How would I be able to look either of them in the eye when they find out their mother wrote something so scandalous?"

"Scandalous? Bestseller?" He looked at the book and then me. "Why didn't you tell me? Had our relationship deteriorated to the point you couldn't trust me?"

I hesitated. "It wasn't trust." I ran my finger along the rim of my glass. "I tried to tell you." I swirled my wine, thinking of how he'd ignored me when I showed him the newspaper article. "We'd grown so far apart. I knew you'd say it was a stupid idea."

"Forgive me, Cass." He touched my hand. "Can we try again? I love you."

Tears welled in my eyes, emotions mixed in my soul. I nodded and wiped my eyes.

"You're amazing." He leaned over and raised his glass. He

set *Wild Rose* on the table and grabbed my hand. "I'm proud of you, Cass. I know I took you for granted, didn't recognize your...I don't know...talent and dreams."

He turned away, his face pained. "I'm sorry I screwed up. You deserve better." He flipped through the pages. "Scandalous. I can't wait to read it."

I laughed, unburdened, my secret was out. "Sorry it doesn't have any pictures in it." I sipped my wine.

"Too bad," he said, as he read the cover synopsis. "Sounds like it'd be more interesting with pictures."

Chapter Forty One

"Do or do not; there is no try."
~ *Yoda*

Mitch and I fell into a comfortable but still celibate relationship. We circled around each other, keeping family front and center. We were closer, more attentive, and listened to one another. It was like we had to become friends again before we could advance.

We both decided to wait and tell the girls about *Wild Rose* after a court hearing bringing charges against Andrew. The thought of Novak's attorneys using my book as courtroom fodder terrified me.

Ashley was reluctant to pursue charges. She waffled between trying to forget the incident and pretending it never happened, and wanting to stand up for herself and fight. She'd heard a lot of her classmates were siding with Andrew, and she was convinced he'd easily win. After much coaxing and pleading, Ashley finally agreed to appear in court. Bradley promised to be with her.

At least she was angry about Andrew's version of what happened. His story was Ashley had come on to him, and she tried to commit suicide because he rejected her.

A week before her birthday, Ashley appeared at the hearing to testify. The prosecuting attorney was young and unorganized. I prayed she was good, though I didn't worry too much since the evidence was overwhelmingly in our favor. I figured it would be a piece of cake.

Unfortunately, Aaron Novak had hired the best defense attorney for his little prodigal shit. I'd seen this attorney on TV defending serious criminals.

I was more than surprised when we arrived at the courthouse and found it full of Andrew's family, friends, and coaches. I found out later they were there as character witnesses.

Our side of the courtroom had a meager showing, like an unpopular groom's side of the church—me, Mitch, Ashley, and Christine in the first row. Teresa and Bradley sat behind us, looking small and nervous in the massive halls of justice. Bradley's parents sat a few rows back. As it turned out, Bradley and Teresa were asked to leave because they had knowledge of relevant facts and were witnesses. As the victim, Ashley was not offered the same indulgences as the criminal because, after all, he was innocent until proven guilty.

Dr. Novak acted the perfect gentleman in the courtroom, except when he looked at me and Ashley. He would have shot venom from his beady, little black eyes if he could. His two-faced persona was frightening. Ashley cowered and looked away when he came near.

I noticed Andrew's loud mouthed attorney joking with the judge. For the first time, I questioned whether it was in Ashley's best interest to drag her through this.

Ashley was called to the witness stand. She looked tiny and young sitting next to the judge. Her face barely cleared the wood railing in the witness box.

The judge looked down at her. "This is just a preliminary hearing to gather facts." Then, motioning to John Roche, the defense attorney, he said, "This gentleman is going to ask you some questions about what happened that night." I thought he should rephrase "gentleman" to "that high paid attorney who would sell his soul to make sure he wins this case."

After Ashley was sworn in, Roche stood and walked to her. "State your name, please."

"Ashley Calabria." She had to stretch her neck to talk into the microphone, positioned near her forehead.

"May I approach the witness, your honor?" Roche looked to the judge, who indicated it was okay.

"You might be more comfortable if you lower the microphone." He reached into the witness box. Ashley jumped back.

"I'll do it." She grabbed the microphone and pulled it to her level, never taking her eyes off him. I was surprised at her burst of confidence.

"Do you realize the serious nature of the charges you've made against my client?"

Ashley looked straight into his eyes. "Yes."

"As you sit here today, sworn to tell the absolute truth, can you honestly say this young man, a pillar of his community, purposely gave you a drug?" Roche turned to look at Andrew. He never gave Ashley a chance to answer. "Andrew Novak is a model student, an exceptional athlete and popular with the student body at Constantine High School. Do you really think he would need to offer *you* drugs to pleasure himself?" He turned to Ashley with a look that clearly said Ashley wasn't good enough for Andrew to offer candy to.

I wanted to jump up and scream at the arrogant asshole. I think Christine sensed and put her hand on mine to calm me. I could feel Mitch tense next to me, and I wondered if he was going to climb over the railing and coldcock John Roche.

Ashley shrugged and continued to look at the attorney. "He *did* give me my soda, and it had drugs in it."

I was amazed she seemed so calm.

"Just answer yes or no!" Roche bellowed at Ashley and walked toward the witness stand.

"It wasn't really a yes or no question." Though still nervous, Ashley gave him a look similar to one she gave me when I told her to clean her room. I puffed with pride at the way she was handling herself.

"Objection! Nonresponsive!" Roche looked at the judge, shaking his head as if Ashley had just committed a horrible breach of ethics.

Dr. Novak looked at me as if I should do something to control my daughter's behavior. I gave him a look that said, *I think she's doing great, thank you.*

The judge leaned forward. "Mr. Roche, try to phrase your questions without additional commentary. This is not a trial; it's only a hearing."

Novak shifted in his seat and put his hand on Andrew's shoulder, as if to let him know everything was going to be okay.

Roche hovered over Ashley like a buzzard on roadkill. "Are you still a virgin?"

Outraged, I jumped out of my seat and shouted, "Objection!"

The judge looked over his glasses at me and said, "Ma'am, do you need to be escorted from this courtroom?"

I shook my head.

"No more outbursts. Please sit."

Christine grabbed my arm and pulled me down next to her. Mitch looked ready to take Roche outside and fight.

"Why does Ashley have to answer those questions when Andrew doesn't even have to take the stand?" Mitch whispered fiercely.

"Shhh," Christine admonished. "As the prosecution witness, Ashley has to prove her case, while Andrew doesn't have to say anything."

Roche looked me in the eye and asked Ashley, again, if she was a virgin.

This time Ashley's attorney stood. "Objection, relevance."

The judge paused. "I'll allow it."

Ashley glanced at us then looked directly at Roche and answered, "Yes."

I breathed a sigh of relief but hated that the most private aspects of her life and character were being put on public display.

Roche gave a look as if he didn't believe her, sneered. "Why do you think this handsome and well-liked young man would give you a drug?"

Ashley gave him her best *"whatever"* look. "How would *I* know? Ask him."

Such impertinence. I was so proud.

"Objection!" he shouted, looking at the judge wearily.

"Please, your honor. She's not answering the questions."

"Mr. Roche, ask her a question based on relevant facts, not hearsay."

Roche's face reddened.

The young prosecuting attorney watched the proceedings quietly.

Roche leaned uncomfortably close to Ashley. "Weren't you distraught Andrew didn't respond to your advances?"

Ashley laughed. "Are you *kidding* me? Gross! He's the last person I'd want to date."

I had to restrain myself from jumping up and raising my arms victoriously. Instead, I squeezed Christine's hand.

The hearing lasted almost two hours, though it seemed like an eternity. Ashley was asked to leave the room while Teresa and Bradley were questioned. Although I wanted to hear what they had to say, I went out to be with Ashley. Mitch and Christine stayed and would fill me in on the details later.

Ashley started crying when I approached her.

"You did great," I said, hugging her. "I'm sorry for the way they treated you, honey. It's not fair you're getting dragged through the mud when Andrew is guilty." I pushed her hair away from her tear stained face. "If you want to stop, I'll understand."

"No. Now I really want to nail that jerk. He did it, Mom. I know he did."

"I know, baby, and I want to see him punished. But I don't want to see you hurt anymore."

"I'm okay. I need to do this. He's telling lies and everybody believes him. It's wrong. I want people to know what really happened. A lot of them are treating me like it's my fault."

That comment cut to the bone. I didn't want her ridiculed when she started school in the fall. "I'm behind you, Ashley. Whatever it takes, we'll make sure justice is done."

She nodded tearfully. I handed her a tissue.

After the hearing ended, Novak's group filed out. Aaron strode over. "You'll never win. You need to call off your daughter and make her tell the truth." He looked at Ashley. "Andrew certainly doesn't need drugs to get girls, especially someone like you."

"Aaron Novak! That's a terrible thing to say, even by your low standards."

I was ready to slap him, but Ashley surprised me by saying, "I wouldn't have gone out with Andrew if he were the last person on earth—and that was before he spiked my drink. *He* was the one who tried to get *me*, remember? I didn't do anything wrong. Andrew did." She held her head high and her gaze steady.

"Dad." Andrew stood about ten feet away, looking sheepish. "C'mon, let's go."

"I'm watching you, Cassie." He pointed a nubby finger at me. "You guys don't stand a chance."

I put my arm around Ashley and said, "Yes, we do," as he retreated with his entourage.

Wild Rose

— FROM CHAPTER 20

A who's who of Hollywood attended Colten's funeral. Because of tight security, Rosemary was forced to stand outside with hundreds of his crying fans. Nikki, sobbing, hung onto Laz's arm, passed as they entered the church.

Rosemary felt some responsibility. After all, Colten was returning from her house when the accident happened. She gritted her teeth and wiped away tears as she watched the guests enter the church.

Closed in by the crowd, she left and drove aimlessly in the busy Los Angeles traffic before stopping in a church parking lot to cry. Taking a deep, sobbing breath, Rosemary decided to go into the church and light a candle for Colten, for what they almost had.

Over the next few weeks, Rosemary found small steps of strength. She kept busy because whenever she stopped, grief overcame her. It bothered her to hear her name associated with the nasty photographs, which by then had made the tabloid and news circuit. Bunnie, whose children's show had been abruptly cancelled, threatened to sue and even told the media the images were altered.

Rosemary heard The Fakers were ticked about the pictures and hated how Rosemary portrayed them. Right, Rosemary thought, they're probably the ones publishing them.

She was glad when Hugh stopped by one morning. As critical as he had been of Colten, he seemed sympathetic and supportive.

He took her in his arms affectionately. "Rosie, you're stronger than those bastards. I'm here for you."

Rosemary let him hold her. "I hope my strength lasts longer than my bank account."

"I know what you mean. My ol' man is cutting me off unless I finish college. He doesn't get it. I need my music. But I'll help you any way I can."

"If your dad is willing to pay for college, then go. I might have to find another career soon."

"No, you won't. I'll take care of you."

Though she'd picked up a few gigs, Rosemary hadn't had a decent paying job since the tour. Her pride wouldn't allow her to call Beck, begging for work.

She found a job shooting black and white headshots for a law firm. It's not Rolling Stone, Rosemary thought. But it's work. She feared her next job would be doing kiddie shots at the mall.

On the day of the shoot, Rosemary set up her gear in a lavish conference room. The office had dark wood paneling with hunter green carpet and tapestries on every wall.

She spent a considerable amount of time with the partners of the firm. Each had an ego the size of Texas. Afterward, the junior associates came in for their shots. The lineup was like a cattle call, drive-thru photography.

The last associate was a cute, diminutive woman, professionally dressed in a power suit. Her blonde hair was cut as short as some of the men's, and her smile brightened the room.

"Hi, I'm Sarah Martin, and I'm incredibly photogenic. I debated between going to law school or becoming a super-model." She posed dramatically with her head thrown back and one leg in the air.

"You're going to be easier to photograph than the other stuffed shirts I've shot today."

Sarah stuck her chest out, laughing. "Hey, you're not supposed to know I stuff my shirt! They're supposed to look natural."

Rosemary liked Sarah and was glad the shoot ended on a high note. She positioned the lights and framed Sarah in the lens. "These offices are amazing. What kind of law do you practice?" she asked as she began shooting.

"Don't make me talk while you're pointing that thing at me. I can't answer and look beautiful at the same time. You're as bad as my dentist. He waits until both hands are in my mouth before asking questions." She stuck her fingers in her own mouth and tried to grunt words. "Okay, now I'm sure I've smeared my makeup."

Rosemary laughed while Sarah repaired the damage. "You don't act like an attorney."

"I'll take that as a compliment." Sarah smiled from behind her mirror. "We practice civil law, personal injury, medical malpractice, car wrecks. We don't handle criminal cases unless we're helping a politician get elected." Sarah snapped her compact shut. "Why, someone suing you for taking an unflattering picture?"

"Actually, yeah, but it's more complicated." Rosemary repositioned Sarah and directed her. She considered telling her about Ritchie and what happened at the party. Maybe Sarah

Then we take a percentage."

could offer some advice. "Tilt your head a little to the left. Good. Smile." The flash of strobes illuminated Sarah for an instant. "Maybe I could talk to you. But honestly, I don't think I can afford you." Rosemary hit the shutter. "Nice, hold that—"

"We don't charge the client until a settlement is reached. Then we take a percentage."

"Oh, good. Smile." Rosemary looked up from the viewfinder. "Well, it's a long, ugly story. I'm not sure what to do about it. Maybe you can give me some ideas about how to screw these guys' nuts to the wall."

Chapter Forty Two

"Can't nobody lick us, Pa. We're the people."
~John Steinbeck, *"The Grapes of Wrath"*

On Ashley's sixteenth birthday, the results of Andrew's hearing were announced. There was enough evidence to charge him with drug possession and for giving drugs to a minor. This was only the first step, but a very important one. I didn't know which was worse, seeing Ashley in the hospital, suffering from the overdose, or having her credibility questioned in a courtroom in front of the world.

The days I worked at the hospital, Dr. Novak made sure to come down to the ER to make subtle threats about how he was going to make my life miserable now that his son was charged. He had the nerve to talk about me to Mr. Starnes and Nelda in administration, both of whom let me know they thought I was taking this drug thing a bit too far. "Perhaps Ashley did have something to do with it. You know, kids will be kids."

That angered me to no end and, if it hadn't been for the supportive staff at work, I'd probably have quit the hospital, kicking and screaming. But I also thought I probably got under Novak's skin more by staying than giving him the satisfaction of seeing me resign.

I'd also been avoiding the other big issue—people finding out I was Cardia Loving, but I couldn't deal with two of us in the same family having to confront questions of ethics. Mitch and I agreed it was in our best interest as a family to stay close to home and keep our noses clean. Unfortunately, Rita demanded I sell more books, and getting my overly made-up face out in public was the best way to stay on the bestseller list. She loved the speculative stories about who Cardia Loving was since there was no background record of her. Every time I saw someone with Wild Rose, I was tempted to either run up and thank them for buying it or run quickly in the other direction. Mitch, still in shock after reading the book, treated me differently. I'd often catch him staring at me with a confused look on his face.

The date for the book signing in Dallas grew close. I'd taken a few day trips to sign books but could never get my costume done as well as when Christine made me up.

The Dallas signing had me shaking in my sparkly stilettos. Wild Rose was a hot seller here. I prayed if any of my friends came, they wouldn't recognize me. I felt better that Mitch saw the picture taken in California and had no clue it was me.

The night before the Dallas signing, we took Ashley, Gabby, Teresa, and Bradley to a fun restaurant where the waitstaff dressed up in character costumes. Gabby found the place enchanting, while Ashley thought it was stupid, although you'd have thought she was riding a unicorn after receiving her coveted iPhone for her sweet sixteenth. Luckily, Bradley was good natured about it all and teased Gabby and our waiter, who was dressed as the Pillsbury Doughboy.

Mitch cautiously kept a close eye on Bradley whenever he showed any affection toward Ashley, though most of Bradley's time was spent entertaining Gabby, who was spellbound. She hung onto his every word. I'm sure it had not gone unnoticed by Mitch that both of his girls found another man.

Before we were served, I sat back and looked at my family. I felt a stab of sadness not having Mom there was the first time she hadn't been at a birthday celebration, bearing gifts and hugs. You could always count on her to call at the crack of dawn on our birthdays, singing "Happy Birthday" off key.

I missed that phone call on Ashley's birthday. I fought tears, not wanting to be a downer at the celebration. Ashley must have noticed because she smiled at me and said, "I miss her too, Mom."

The next day, I tried to mentally prepare myself for the book signing. Rita called bright and early to make sure I wouldn't back out. She was in town and wouldn't accept any excuses. Dead or alive, I'd better be there.

I called Christine and begged her to help me with my makeover. But Phillip had made plans for them, I wouldn't be able to use her or her place to change my identity.

I couldn't dress at home with the girls there. Even if I'd been sable to find a few moments of privacy in the bathroom, I'd wreck my expensive suit trying to crawl, undiscovered, out the window. I called Brenda to see if I could use her house, but she was waiting for her husband to get home and watch her kids so she could come to my debut.

"Please don't come," I begged. "I don't want to risk you giving me away."

"Give me a break, Cass. I can keep a secret. I wouldn't miss this for the world. I want to look you in the eye while you're signing my book. Oh, by the way, will you give me a discount?"

"Brenda, don't make me more nervous than I already am. You know I hate the spotlight, and I'm stressed about Ashley's trial. She doesn't need to find out her mother wrote a risqué book—not now, when our family's morals are being scrutinized." I looked at the clock. I had less than two hours to get changed and to the bookstore. "I don't have time to argue with you now, Brenda. Please do me a favor and don't show up."

"You worry too much, Cassie. I'll be as quiet as a mouse. Better still, I may dress up and you won't be able to recognize me." She laughed. "You know, Cassie, Mom would have given anything to be there." I could hear her voice catch. "So don't deny me the pleasure." She knew how to work the guilt.

"Okay, but keep quiet. It needs to be a secret until Ashley gets through the trial."

I peeked into the den to check on the girls. They were watching a movie, quiet and content. Mitch was in the kitchen making them a snack. When I told him I was leaving for the bookstore, he said he'd see me there. I think he was harboring some fantasy about those stupid rhinestone glasses.

"Mitch," I whispered fiercely. "I have to find somewhere to get ready. Please, stay here with the girls. Just tell them I've gone out with Brenda."

"Is she going to be there? Cass, I want to go, I'm proud of you. I don't want to miss it."

"What if someone we both know shows up? Don't you think you'll look pretty ridiculous buying a romance novel?"

"I'll just hang around the fix-it section." I was tempted to tell him to check out the how-to-make-your-marriage-work section.

Besides, Ashley is planning on seeing Teresa, and Gabby has a play date at the Arpinos'. Maybe we'll even have a little time after the signing to—" He raised his eyebrows suggestively.

Why did I already feel like I was getting screwed? "Mitch, please, I'm stressed. If you must go, don't talk to me, or even look at me. Think of Ashley's trial. She doesn't need the extra drama, and if I don't find a place to change my identity soon, everyone will know it's me."

I grabbed my stuff and ran to the door, blowing kisses to the girls on my way out, wondering how Superman got his pantyhose on so fast in a confined telephone booth. I decided to go to the hospital and use one of the empty rooms to change in. I could get in as an employee. It was getting out that worried me. But with the clock ticking, I had no choice.

When I got there, the day shift was leaving. I stuffed my makeup and glasses in a bag, threw my suit over my shoulder as if I had just picked up my dry cleaning, and walked into the main lobby, far away from the ER. The hospital was doing construction on the third floor, so those rooms weren't being used.

While waiting for an elevator, I heard my name called.

"Cassie. What are you doing here? I thought you had the day off." Adam walked over and took note of my dry cleaning bag.

"Uh...um...I'm going up to see Christine. Why are you here so late? You should have been off an hour ago." Answer a question with a question, right?

"I'm waiting for Jennifer. We're going to dinner and a book signing."

"Book signing?" I squeaked. "Really, what book?"

"That romance novel that's been in the news. Jennifer wants to buy a copy and have it autographed. She and Gail talked me into going. You know, something different to do. Hey, I didn't think Christine was here today. We had a psych call for the ER earlier and were told she wasn't in."

"I t—think she's getting caught up on paperwork," I stammered. "Um...what bookstore are you going to?"

He shrugged. "Who knows? I just go where they tell me. Can you join us?"

"No, I already have plans, but thanks." The elevator doors opened, and I told Adam that I'd see him later. If he only knew.

My hands were shaking so much I could hardly push the button to the third floor. This couldn't be happening. How was I going to face Adam, Gail, and Jennifer? I desperately hoped there was another book signing nearby. Fingers of apprehension squeezed my stomach.

The elevator door opened, and I peeked around the corner. It looked clear. Quickly, I ducked in a hallway and headed toward the construction area. The last time the hospital renovated patient rooms, a security guard found a homeless man living there. Hopefully, I could get in and out before I was caught.

"Cassandra?" I stopped in my tracks outside one of the

rooms. The voice was familiar, and I didn't want to turn around and confirm my fears.

"What are you doing? You're not supposed to be here." Aaron Novak strode toward me. "I was looking for you today, they said you weren't coming in."

"I was going to meet Christine, and I was curious to see how the construction was coming along." I felt my lying face flush hot.

Novak continued, seeming unaware I was sneaking around the closed section of the hospital. "I want to talk some sense into you and your daughter about Andrew. We've all been through enough. I'd like you to drop the charges." He looked down and crossed his arms. "This is no admission of guilt, of course, but the football coach won't let him practice until this is cleared up. And who knows how long that could take." He shook his head as if this whole situation were a mere annoyance. "I'll pay your legal expenses to see this go away."

I felt a blast of anger at his audacity. "It's Ashley's decision—not mine—and I support her in seeing this through." I swung my flashy suit to my other shoulder. "Why don't you put that money to good use and get Andrew into drug rehab. It sounds like he needs it more than we do."

"My son does not have a drug problem. Don't insinuate the problem lies with him. There's no doubt in my mind your daughter and all her grungy, slacker friends are behind this." His face was turning as interesting shade of red and yellow. "You won't win, Cassandra. I'll fight with everything I have on this."

"Even if you're wrong?" I got in his face, the book signing forgotten. "Even if Andrew gave Ashley the drugs?"

He looked down his bulbous nose at me. "That's not the issue."

"That's the whole issue! We'll see you in court." I started to leave, but stopped. "You have some nerve questioning the integrity of my daughter and our family." Never mind I was breaking into a closed section of the hospital so I could change into an overdressed romance writer.

"I will do whatever it takes," he bellowed angrily.

"So will I." I turned my back to him and walked away.

I knew Ashley was innocent, but the shouting match shook me. I'd seen too many times where the person with the most toys wins. Sticks and stones can break your bones, but money can buy your friends off. I was more resolved than ever to see justice done.

Looking at my watch, I gasped. I had less than an hour to get ready for my big debut. I dashed into an empty room. After running into Adam and Dr. Novak, I was jumping at my own shadow and any tiny sound. New flooring had been put down and was only half done. At least the bathroom was in working order. I quickly set to work.

No matter how hard I tried, I still looked like me but with way too much makeup. I couldn't get my hair to stay slicked back, little strands kept popping out of the thick gel like broken guitar strings. I could almost hear a twang as another one shot out from under my brush.

I threw on the same suit I had worn in Los Angeles, assessed the damage in the mirror, and dashed out, praying I wouldn't run into anyone else.

I skittered to the elevators and pushed the down button. Taking a deep breath through neon glistening lip gloss,

I told myself I could do this. I *had* to do this. It was ironic that the whole reason I wrote Wild Rose was to take some financial pressure off and to have more time with the girls, not spend time running and hiding from people like a drag queen fugitive.

Chapter Forty Three

"Life imitates art far more that art imitates Life."
~ *Oscar Wilde*

A crowd gathered in front of the bookstore. I couldn't face them—not yet. I drove around to the back hoping I could sneak in through the employee entrance. I never expected this book to not only get published but to be so popular.

Luckily, the back door was open, and an employee wearing a green apron smoked a cigarette outside.

I rolled down the window. "Can I get into the store through here?" I asked the girl.

"The entrance is at the front of the building." She looked at me as if I were lost, stupid, or both.

"I know. I'm doing a book signing here tonight, and I want to find my agent before it starts."

"Oh, my gosh! Are you Cardia Loving?" She put out her cigarette. "I'll be happy to take you inside. Just park anywhere." She indicated an area behind a trash dumpster and waited while I parked and checked my appearance.

"This is so cool! Will you sign my copy? Employees have to wait until the last person leaves before the manager will let our books get signed. The authors usually have to go before we can get them done."

"Sure. I'd love to. Thank you for reading it." I didn't know what to say. I still didn't feel like an author.

"Great. I'll get my book and see if I can find your agent. Is her name Rita?"

"Yeah, she's the one."

"She's been here bossing everybody around for the last hour. We're expecting a huge crowd tonight." She happily skipped off, leaving me in a back storage room.

I ventured a peek into the store and saw people lined up, waiting. While I looked for Mitch and Brenda browsing the shelves, Rita bustled in, upset I was late.

"I should've driven you myself. My heart can't take this kind of pressure." She took a moment to appraise my appearance. "It'll do. But for heaven's sake, you can't keep wearing the same suit. You had pictures taken in that one."

"Sorry, Rita. I've been preoccupied. My wardrobe doesn't go beyond hospital scrubs and jeans." She fussed over my hair and straightened my suit.

"We already have people waiting. But before we start, Channel 11 News wants to interview you. Come on. We don't have much time."

"Channel 11?"

I felt a new surge of panic when I saw the reporter, Sabrina Dee. She was the snot who reported the cockroach incident in front of Ashley's school. Before I could turn and run, Rita got behind me and pushed me into the store. I considered decking her, jumping over her body, and sprinting as far away as possible. I already dreaded running into my coworkers, but now Sabrina and a broadcast interview? *Damn.* Thoughts of Ashley and the trial whirled like a tornado."

Rita, I don't have anything to say to the news. I haven't had time to come up with a story about who Cardia Loving is." In a moment of suffocating terror, I pleaded, "Please, Rita. I can't do this. Get me out of here."

With the strength of a sumo-ninja, Rita shoved me under the glaring lights of the news crew and said, "You'd better think fast on your feet." Just before she stepped away from me, she whispered, "Take a deep breath. You look like someone's pointing a double-barrel at you."

The bright lights and the throng of people looked more like a crime scene than a book signing. Rita indicated to Sabrina I was ready for my close-up. "Sabrina, you only have five minutes before we need to get Cardia to the floor. People are waiting," she said in her bossy tone.

In the glare of the lights, I saw a pack of people vying to get a better view. I didn't trust my voice and was scared when Sabrina started talking. My mind was reeling with stories to make up about Cardia. This was so twisted.

"Okay. I'm going to ask you a few questions about you and your book, which, by the way, I just loved!" she cooed. "I identified with Rosemary. She's such a strong character. I saw a lot of her in me." She flipped her starched hair over her shoulder. Then hesitated, eyeing me closely. "Do I know you from somewhere?"

I shook my head. "I don't think so."

She stared harder then shrugged. "As we're talking, I'm going to show the cover of *Wild Rose* and have you sign it." She looked at the camera operator. "Are you ready, Ken?"

He gave a thumbs up and began a countdown: "In five... four...three...two..." He pointed his finger at Sabrina.

Sabrina perked up and smiled at the camera. "We're here today at Barnes & Noble with the first ever interview with Cardia Loving, the author of the amazing and successful book, *Wild Rose*." She turned to me. "Cardia, some people wondered if you even existed. Usually, authors promote their books when they're hot off the press. You haven't made many appearances, and your audience knows little about you well into the book's success. Tell us the story about that." She thrust the microphone under my nose, which felt drippy with sweat. I imagined my face looked like a road map with rivulets of thick makeup snaking down my face, my glasses steaming from hot fear.

"I...um...didn't think it would be a bestseller," I stammered. I saw movement to my left and noticed Brenda smiling and waving. Mitch stood next to her, grinning from ear to ear. So much for subtlety.

"Well, it *is* a bestseller, with talk of a movie. How did you come up with the idea of the main character, Rosemary, the beautiful and tenacious photographer? Do you have a photographic background?"

"No. I've always thought it would be a fun profession." I could feel a trickle of sweat snake down the front of my push-up bra. "I didn't know anything about photography." I was crashing fast.

"Sabrina smiled brightly into the camera. "Tell us a little bit about yourself. Where are you from?"

I wished she had given me a multiple-choice question. "Texas...um...a little town just outside of...the...uh... Panhandle." I racked my brain, trying to remember a small town in West Texas. Why in heaven's name did I say the Panhandle?

Was that even in Texas? I could see Mitch out of the corner of my eye. He put his hand over his mouth to stifle a laugh.

Before Sabrina could ask me which town, I said, "Oh, I've moved around a lot. That's what helped me create the character Rosemary."

Rita could tell I was floundering and signaled to Sabrina to move on.

Sabrina shoved a copy of *Wild Rose* at me. "Cardia, would you please sign my copy of *Wild Rose*?" She addressed the camera. "*Wild Rose* was initially sold as part of a romance summer package, along with novels by bestselling authors Dominique Matrix and Siren Song. Now the book is enjoying phenomenal success on its own." She turned to me. "If you're from Texas, why did you set the story in California?

I took the book from Sabrina. She had to see my hands were shaking. "Oh, I don't know. I just started writing about Rosemary and, gosh, I just kind of made it up as I went along."

The heat of the lights was unbearable, and I could feel the armpits of my suit becoming saturated with huge blobs of perspiration. I looked at Rita, my eyes begging for help. She stood there, arms crossed, assessing the scene—pretty much me, crumbling. Finally, Rita caught Sabrina's attention and pointed to her watch, indicating she was running out of time.

Sabrina ignored her and continued talking to the camera. "*Wild Rose* is the first novel written by Cardia Loving." Turning to me, she asked, "Do you have another book in the works?"

"No, um...not really...yet." Lying was not one of my specialties, and I was stumbling over every word. "I haven't thought of anything I want to write about." I cast a quick glance at Rita.

Rita, seeing my interview go down the toilet, decided to end it. She practically stepped into the range of the camera and let Sabrina know that the interview was over.

Sabrina was miffed Rita had horned in but ended with a dazzling smile. "This is Sabrina Dee with Channel 11 News, from Barnes & Noble with Cardia Loving." As soon as the camera stopped rolling, her smile turned into a sneer. She turned to Rita. "I wasn't finished. She didn't answer all my questions. I need more time."

"We got the book on camera. You can shoot Cardia signing." Rita ushered me away from Sabrina and into the throng of people waiting.

The next thing I knew, I was sitting at a table, having books shoved under my nose. The pace was frantic. I wondered if Adam, Jennifer, and Gail were in line, but I couldn't look up long enough to see if they were waiting.

A book was handed to me, cover opened, and a voice asked, "Can you write 'To Susan.'" I glanced up to see Susan Novak smiling at me.

I think I smiled back, probably made a funny fart noise out of my nose while trying not to scream and signed my *nom de fake* along with her name. "Thank you for reading *Wild Rose*." Aware that the profits from my book would help prosecute her stepson, I added a few swirlys to my signature.

As I handed her book back, she said, "I really enjoyed it. I even told my husband I wanted to take a photography class.

He thought I was crazy." Susan smiled. "I just might surprise him." She turned away giving no indication she knew me.

That Susan hadn't recognized me gave me a small boost of confidence. I felt better about my disguise in case the group from work showed up.

Rita kept the line moving quickly and efficiently. until Brenda appeared. I tried to give her a look to tell her she shouldn't be there, but she ignored me. "Cardia, will you sign my book?" She giggled conspiratorially. I wanted to snap the cover on her nose. Then she leaned down and whispered, "Hey, that's the same reporter who did the cockroach story."

I gritted my teeth. "Thank you," I said, shoving the book back at her. She waltzed off, laughing.

"Hey, aren't you Cassie's sister?"

Hearing my name gave me a start. I looked up and saw Adam and the gang wave at Brenda. She glanced back at me and met them in line.

I didn't even acknowledge the next few people as I signed their books.

"I'm so sorry about your mom. She was such a special person," I heard Adam say as he gave Brenda a hug.

"It's been really hard. I miss her so much." Brenda kept looking my way. "I wish she could've been here tonight."

"Why? Did she like romance?" Jennifer asked.

Gail was next in line. She approached the table and gushed, "I just loved your book. It was the best."

I kept my eyes down and mumbled, "Thanks."

Gail turned to Adam and Jennifer. "We should get a copy for Cassie." She looked at me. "This woman we work with is so uptight. She'd probably learn a lot from Rosemary."

I cut a quick glance at her. "How nice of you."

Adam put his copy of *Wild Rose* in front of me. "Don't I know you from somewhere?" I could feel him studying me while I averted my gaze. I wanted to crawl under the table. He leaned down for a closer look and said, "I know you. What high school did you go to?"

"No," I replied, biting my tongue from saying *No Adam*. "I don't think we know each other." I couldn't look him in the eye as I gave the signed book back to him. He stared at me until Rita asked him to move on.

Brenda, trying to stifle a case of the giggles, ducked into an aisle.

Adam moved to the side next to Gail, never taking his eyes off me. Jennifer gave me her book to sign. "I've always wanted to write a novel," she said. "Maybe someday I will."

"Well, good luck with it." I glanced up as I handed her the book.

"Hey, how did you know my name was Adam?" He held the book open to the signed title page. "You wrote my name." He walked back to the table and looked me directly in the eyes.

"D-didn't you tell me your n-name?" I stammered. "You must have told me." I must have moved or spoken in a familiar way. I could almost see the light bulb over Adam's head as the switch went on.

"Cassie? Cassandra Calabria? Is that you?"

Chapter Forty Four

"You're only given a little spark of madness. You mustn't lose it."
~ Robin Williams

"Cassie! What are you doing?" Adam would not shut up. "And why are you pretending to be an author?" He paused. "And dressed like that?"

I gave him a look that begged him to move on. Unfortunately, Sabrina Dee noticed the spectacle and moved in like a rabid dog ready to bite.

"Cassandra? I thought your name was Cardia. Is that your pen name?" Sabrina practically had her nose in the air, sniffing out the scent.

Rita took action and shuffled the work group away from the table. Gail and Jennifer looked at me and asked Adam, "You think that's Cassie?" Jennifer looked unconvinced. "Nah, it can't be, can it?"

Sabrina got on her cell phone and ordered the station to check on past stories on someone named Cassandra or Cassie.

"Look, there's Mitch." Jennifer pointed to the second floor. Mitch was leaning over the railing, trying to see what was going on. I saw Brenda peek around shelves of books like a mouse checking to see if the cat was out.

I kept thinking of the phrase "damage control." How was

I going to escape and deny any of this?

Rita leaned down and whispered, "Cardia, keep signing. We need to make sure everyone has your signature in their book."

The last person in line finally approached. I quickly scribbled "Cardia Loving" and handed the book back. I stood, ready to bolt, when a group of store employees brought their copies to sign. Mitch and Brenda edged closer.

As I scrawled my name on the last book, Sabrina sprinted over. "Start rolling, Ken. Don't let her leave until we've interviewed her." Ken followed quickly, surprisingly agile considering he was holding a large camera.

I looked both ways and debated jumping over the table and running out the front door. But the way my luck was going, I'd probably trip, land with my dress over my head, and have the whole incident shown on the ten o'clock news.

Rita, appeared by my side, whispered, "Get ready, act calm, and tell the truth. It'll be easier to deal with later." She walked up to Sabrina. "Set up your camera over there. Cardia will be happy to talk to you."

"Cardia or Cassandra? Cassandra Calabria, the nurse who's phobic about cockroaches? I knew I had seen you before." She obviously got a lot of satisfaction, remembering my buggy lap dance.

Mitch, Brenda, and the ER group stood nearby. Rita took me to them first. "You guys hang out here," she said. "Cassandra will need some support after the reporter gets through with her."

"How are we going to explain this to Ashley?" Mitch asked me quietly.

I don't think Adam's mouth had closed since he realized who I was. By the looks on their faces, Jennifer and Gail still weren't sure it was me.

I took my glasses off. "I guess I have some explaining to do."

Adam looked mystified. "I don't know what to say, Cassie."

Jennifer was laughing. "I can't believe it. *You* wrote *Wild Rose?*"

"Hey, I just found out about it, too," said Brenda. "When Mom was in the hospital."

Rita pulled me away from the group. "Cardia or Cassie—go talk to Sabrina. You can catch up with these guys later." Rita pointed to the camera and lights, smiled. "If this doesn't sell books, nothing will." She put me in front of the camera. "You might as well get it over with."

Get what *over with*, I thought. *My life?* I guessed my fifteen minutes of fame were not going to be as glamorous as I had hoped.

Wild Rose

— From Chapter 21

After talking to Sarah about the photographs and her overdose, Rosemary felt better. Sarah spent over an hour with her, asking questions about the night with Ritchie.

"I can't believe you're the one who brought Bonnie Bunnie to her knees. I can't even sleep with my favorite Bunnie stuffed animal anymore," Sarah said, as she took notes.

"I didn't intend to bring anybody down. I don't even remember taking the pictures." Rosemary sighed. "I'm proud of my work. But not this."

"Well, cheer up. I'm sure we have a case against the photo lab for selling the photographs without permission. However, we need to establish who owned the negatives, you or Rolling Stone. Then I'll need to talk to witnesses about what happened the night you were drugged." Sarah scribbled on a legal pad as she spoke. "Because we're dealing with drug possession, there might be some criminal issues too; however, since the tour has deep pockets, I'd like to talk to them before we file. Chances are we can settle this without going much further."

"I'm glad we talked. I'm less interested in the money than I am in clearing my name." Rosemary thought of Colten. "I want to move on."

Sarah looked over her big red-framed glasses at her. "You might move on faster with a decent settlement."

"I've never been faced with something like this and have

always been proud of my good reputation, personally and professionally."

Sarah gave her a big toothy smile. "Well, you'd just better hope my pictures turn out."

Rosemary spent more time at home, taking care of neglected projects. She started an herb garden, and the feel of working the earth gave her a measure of comfort. Hearing the phone from her garden Rosemary ran to answer it.

It was Beck. His sharp tone surprised Rosemary.

"Rosemary, I just received a call from Nate West, the manager of The Fakers. Nate just talked to some bitch attorney about a possible lawsuit. What gives?"

"Beck, my professional life is shit, thanks to that stupid drummer, Ritchie—not to mention those weirdos at the photo lab."

"You are taking this way too far, Rosemary," he growled. "What gave you the idea to sue?"

"Everybody else is riding high, while I'm stuck, unemployed and taking a beating. So let's talk about who's taking it 'way too far.'"

"Everybody? What about Bonnie Bunnie? Her career will never come back." His voice calmed. "Nate wanted me to call you before his attorneys did. He hoped I could reason with you. Drop the suit, Rosie. Trust me. You don't know how hard his attorneys will make your life. You think you know misery now, wait until they chew you up and spit you out."

Rosemary felt her confidence deflate. "I don't know what else to do. I'm the bad guy in this scenario, and I didn't do anything wrong."

"Call off the dogs, and I'll see if I can get you some work. I don't want to see you hurt anymore." But Beck sounded insincere.

Rosemary thought of Colten and the last time she saw him drive away from her house. Beck had threatened her that day. "Look," said Rosemary, "I'm sorry Bonnie Bunnie wasn't the picture of innocence she wanted people to believe. She's not my problem. What The Fakers did to me is my problem, and I intend to do something about it."

"You'll be sorry, Rosemary. Quit stirring the pot. This will go away in time."

"Yeah? They don't go away until someone is blamed for it, which, at this point, is me. I'm already having a hard enough time with Colten's death." She swiped angrily at tears. "I can't do anything about that. What I can do is clear my name from this stupid scandal. Bring on Nate's attorneys. I'll give them a fight." Rosemary slammed the phone down while Beck was still screaming.

Chapter Forty Five

"Experience is the name everyone gives to their mistakes."
~ *Oscar Wilde*

I made the lead story on the local news.

The true identity of Cardia Loving was out, and the story was being devoured, especially with the cockroach segue.

Mitch, Brenda, and I stood in front of the TV and watched me self-implode. On camera I looked like an idiot, stuttering nervously under Sabrina's lethal questioning, my eyes darting everywhere but on Sabrina. Then she went in for the kill showing the cockroach story. I looked just as stupid dancing around the car the second time around

Immediately after the story aired, the phone started ringing. Mitch answered the first call. "It's Christine,"

"Cassie, I just saw the news. What happened? I'm sorry I wasn't there."

"I got busted. I really can't get into it now." I sank into the couch. "Ask Adam, Jennifer, or Gail. They'll tell you all about it." I took the clasp out of my hair, which didn't move an inch with all the gel in it. "I need to talk to the girls before they find out from somebody else. And I'd like to change my clothes and turn myself back into their mom before they get home."

Mitch went to get Gabby from the Arpinos'. Teresa's mom

was on the way with Ashley since Mitch called and asked her to come home immediately.

Brenda followed me home to offer support in case I was tempted to jump out of our first floor window.

No sooner had I hung up with Christine, the phone rang again. I turned the ringer off and went to my room to change clothes when Ashley walked in.

She looked at me and squinched up her face. "So what's *your* deal? Where did you go in *that* outfit?"

Teresa and her mom came in behind Ashley. Her mom hesitated when she saw me. "Is everything okay? Mitch sounded stressed when he called."

"Yeah, well, no. I need to talk to Ashley. Can I call you later?" I wanted to talk to my family before I had to deal with anyone else. "Thanks for having Ashley over tonight." I walked to the door and held it open, hoping she'd get the hint that it was time to go.

Before I could get them out the door, Mitch, Gabby, and Tina Arpino walked up. I was surprised Tina didn't have a casserole in hand. "Cassie, I just saw the news. How exciting for you—"

"Tina," I interrupted, "I was hoping to sit down with the girls and talk to them."

"What? You were on the news again?" Ashley's face registered a look of dread as she swung around to face me. "Mom! How *could* you?"

Teresa's mom, sensing gossip afoot, jumped in. "The news? What about? Does it have anything to do with bugs?"

The rumor mill still buzzed over the cockroach story. "No, it's not about that. Listen, everybody. I'd like to talk to the girls before they hear about it from someone else."

"Oh, no, Mom. Can we please move?" Ashley wailed.

Gabby had been hiding behind Mitch stuck her head around him. "No, I love our house." Her lower lip trembled.

Tina looked surprised. "They don't know about the book? How did you manage that?"

Ashley looked worried. "What book?"

I shooed everybody out with promises to call them tomorrow .

"Cass, I recorded the news for the girls to see," Mitch said.

"Can we just tell them first?" I asked wearily, sinking into the couch. "Girls, sit down. We need to talk."

Gabby snuggled next to me. Ashley stood over me with her arms crossed.

"Mommy, why does your face look like that?" Gabby stared at my plastered on makeup. "I think you kinda over-did it with your eye shadow."

I had to smile in spite of everything.

"Ashley, do you remember that book you were reading, *Wild Rose*?"

She looked at me defensively. "You didn't go on the news because I read that book, did you? I'm old enough."

"No, honey." I sighed. "I went on the news because I *wrote* that book."

She rolled her eyes and looked at me, waiting for the punch line.

"Really, Ashley, it's true. I never expected it to do as well as it has, and I wasn't ready for people to see me as a...uh... romance author."

Brenda sat down. "It's true. Your mom really wrote that book. And don't be offended you didn't know about it, because she didn't tell anyone—not even Grandma. At least not until after it was published."

Ashley plopped next to Brenda, arms still crossed. "Do you guys think I'm stupid? Mom didn't write a book."

"Yes, Ashley, I did."

She stared hard at me. "Did *you* know?" she asked Mitch, who'd been standing by the door.

He shook his head. "No."

"It was published while your father was living...you know...away." I felt the need to get that point across.

"Mommy, what book are you guys talking about?" Gabby said sleepily. I stroked her hair and held her closer.

"I don't get it. You're not a writer. You're a nurse," Ashley said.

"I wrote the book at night and on weekends. I did it for you girls."

"How could you do it for me when I wasn't even allowed to read it?"

"I wanted to make some extra money to be able to spend more time with you."

Ashley sat back slowly, taking the information in. "Well, that's pretty cool. All my friends have read it." She looked at me again. "Are you sure you're not making this up? Is this some weird joke?"

"No, I'm serious. What do you mean your friends have read it?"

"So, this means you're famous?" Suddenly, her face registered shock, probably recalling the sex scenes. "Mom! *You* wrote *that*?"

I nodded. "I guess an autobiography wouldn't have been as interesting."

She averted her gaze and blushed.

Gabby looked at me funny. "Mommy's not famous. She's just Mommy."

I laughed at her candor. "I *am* just Mommy, and darn proud of it." I hugged her and addressed Ashley. "The content is racy. After it came out, I worried what people would think."

"Are we rich?" Ashley asked.

Mitch raised his hand. "Ashley, all this is great, but we have to worry about the fact this might hurt your case against Andrew.

She looked confused. "Why?"

"I can guarantee Andrew's attorneys are going to use the book against our family, you know—" He hesitated. "—about the moral issues."

Brenda spoke up. "Yeah, but the difference is the book is fiction, pure fiction, and I'll vouch that your mom is as boring as they come. What happened to Ashley is real. We're talking apples and oranges here."

"I thought you were talking about books." Gabby snuggled closer but was still listening.

I glanced at the clock and realized it was almost midnight. "Okay, everybody. It's bedtime." I hoped Ashley would still think this was cool in the morning.

I didn't want to look as if we were hiding behind closed doors—never mind I'd been hiding behind Cardia Loving. We needed to handle this head on.

This experience taught me life was not about learning how to juggle problems but how to balance them. By continuing to sidestep the issues, I'd been hiding in the shadows. I was tired of running. After all, I wrote the book. It was a good book. And I should be proud—not ashamed. Our family would survive and grow from this. I wiped my tired eyes. When I brought my hands back, they were black from mascara and eye shadow.

Chapter Forty Six

"When you win, say nothing. When you lose, say less."
~ Paul Brown

As expected, Novak's attorney, reacted to my "coming out." What we didn't expect was the venue he chose. He called Sabrina, who couldn't wait to sink her bleached teeth into the story about Ashley's overdose.

"And in another twist to the surprising story about the local mom who wrote the popular romance novel *Wild Rose*, this same mother has filed charges against a football player at Constantine High, holding him responsible for her daughter's drug overdose..."

The sensationalized story was teased as "Love, Bugs, and Drugs." I didn't respond to Sabrina's incessant calls.

I decided to keep Gabby and Ashley home from summer camp the next day. Ashley spent a good part of the morning messaging her friends, mostly to say how cool it was that her mom was a celebrity. I was afraid the novelty would quickly wear thin when she saw Sabrina's latest news story. I looked just as stupid dancing around the car the second time and was surprised the clip wasn't played backward and forward for more comical effect. That, coupled with my sweat saturated interview. The Panhandle? I cringed each time I thought of my stuttering answers.

Ashley rebuffed me for days after the broadcast, though I caught her laughing about it later during a phone call with Teresa.

For the next few days, Rita, Christine, and Brenda came over to field the phone calls and visitors. Rita handled the news. Christine and Brenda took care of the friends. The only calls I took were from work where they put me on a speakerphone in the break room. As usual, they were able to make me laugh, which helped me feel a little better. That was dashed when Nelda called to tell me Mr. Starnes wanted to talk to me immediately.

Nelda was chomping so hard I could hear the spit spew. "Cassie, I can't believe you really wrote that book. I read it and all, but you know our hospital has an image to uphold. I think Mr. Starnes is upset that you've tarnished our good name."

"Nelda, that's ridiculous. Let me talk to Starnes."

"*Mister* Starnes is not available right now, but he wants to see you at four this afternoon."

"I don't know if I can make it today. Just have him call me."

Nelda gasped. "Cassie, I suggest you find a way to come in. We don't want to upset him and his busy schedule. I think he's been very understanding with your reduced hours. You need to be here."

"Have him call me." I hung up.

I didn't know why it bothered me my job was in jeopardy. *Wild Rose* was selling like crazy. But surprisingly, thinking about quitting cold turkey and leaving my coworkers, my other family, scared me. I needed to feel grounded and not have my life undergo too many changes at once.

Early the next morning, comfortable and sloppy in my old bathrobe, I went to get the newspaper. As I bent to grab the paper I didn't notice the news truck parked at my neighbor's until it was too late. Sabrina ran out, Ken in tow with camera.

"Cassie Calabria! I'd like to talk to you. Start rolling, Ken."

Her hair looked exactly as it had on the news. Did this woman sleep standing up?

"Sabrina, don't!" I ducked my head to avoid the camera and saw my feet. I'd put on Ashley's pig slippers to grab the paper. A gust of wind caught the paper and my robe as I ran awkwardly into the house.

Sabrina rang the doorbell, waking everybody in the house. Gabby ran to the door, thinking it might be a friend."

"Don't answer the door, Gabby!" I pulled her into the kitchen with me as if avoiding an attack. We crouched on the floor, keeping our heads below the windows. "Mitch! Can you get rid of them?"

He and Ashley walked in, sleepy eyed and clad in pajamas. "Who?"

"Sabrina and her sidekick." He yawned as he pulled on his bathrobe. "I'll see what I can do."

It seemed an eternity before Mitch came into the kitchen. "She promises to leave you alone if you'll give her an interview. Also, she won't use any of the footage she shot of you this morning if you talk to her."

"What kind of evil person is she?" I hissed.

But as I sat huddled on the kitchen floor, I figured I'd better deal with it. Who knew how long this reporter would be interested? And maybe I could make amends for my poor showing at the bookstore.

"Make some coffee, Mitch. Ashley, tell her to wait outside until I'm ready." I prayed the Texas humidity would wilt her poofed hair.

I put on a little makeup and brushed my hair. I decided on tennis shoes and jeans instead of the pig slippers and Pj's.

I opened the door and Sabrina jumped out of the air conditioned van. Her hair was still cemented perfectly. She pranced up the walk and into my living room.

"Can I get you some coffee?" I sounded more confident than I felt.

"No, thank you. I've had some, but I would like to use your bathroom. Doing stakeouts is hard on the bladder." She giggled and tossed her head.

"I'd rather get this over with if you don't mind." That felt good. Besides, I didn't trust her not to go through my medicine cabinet.

"Okay, then." We eyed each other, both refusing to back down. "Ken, are you ready?"

He flipped open a tripod and turned on a bright light. It took him less than ten seconds. "Ready."

Mitch, Ashley, and Gabby watched from the hallway as I sat on the couch with Sabrina sitting across from me. Ken aimed his camera over her shoulder, pointed directly at me.

Ken gave the countdown and Sabrina began. "Many people are surprised a local nurse wrote *Wild Rose*. Why did you try so hard to hide your identity and create a huge mystery?"

"I didn't want to draw attention to myself because of the sex scenes."

That comment took her by surprise. "Why? You're an author didn't you want to sell books?"

I wasn't sure where to look, at Sabrina or the camera. I settled on Sabrina. "Sure I do, but as a mother, I didn't want my daughters reading it, and I don't relish the idea of having my life exposed publicly."

"Then why did you write it?" She looked at me, but it seemed she was already forming her next question.

I hesitated. "It started out as a whim. I guess I was realizing a dream of being a writer. It never occurred to me the book would be so popular. As I wrote *Wild Rose* I grew close to the character, Rosemary, and enjoyed creating her life. Since I was writing under a pseudonym, I thought I could write *anything*. Even after all this hiding, I have to say I'm proud of Rosemary and the book. But it wasn't me."

"Of course, it was you."

"Sure, I wrote it. But my fear about the content didn't tsurface until it was published and began selling.""Why are you so worried about the content? It's a bestseller, movie producers are interested, and it appeals to a huge audience."

"I don't know. I mean, there are books and movies more hardcore than *Wild Rose*. But I'm responsible for what the book represents. I like that Rosemary is a strong character and can take care of herself. She's a badass! But her lifestyle is not something I condone. I have to set a good example for my kids." I kept my eyes on Sabrina but was painfully aware of the camera boring down on me. "I wrote something that was out of character for me."

I paused, thinking how close I was to Rosemary. I had thought up her words, how she would say them, what she would do, and how her life would evolve. "It was fun creating Rosemary's life. But the whole thing escalated, and I was afraid it would hurt my family. I don't know why I hid. I guess I didn't want to disappoint them."

"Did you?" She started wiggling as if she were uncomfortable. Hopefully, her stakeout coffee had kicked in. "Is your family disappointed?"

"I don't know." I glanced at them. "No, I don't think so."

Mitch, Ashley, and Gabby were smiling and giving me a thumbs up.

Chapter Forty Seven

"Forget regret, or life is yours to miss."
~ *Jonathan Larson*

Once the story aired and the initial shock wore off, I tried to get used to being recognized while keeping things at home normal. People would stop me on the street and tell me how much they enjoyed *Wild Rose* and especially the story behind it.

I met with Mr. Starnes and it was decided I take a sabbatical until the publicity died down.

I relished being able to spend more time with the girls, but the calls from news stations and publications continued. I had to do some traveling for book signings and even a few talk shows.

School started. The girls settled into their new classes. Ashley's overdose seemed to be last years news. Going into her sophomore year, she seemed more confident, more grown up.

Just as I was settling into celebrityhood I received a call from the prosecuting attorney, who told me a court date was scheduled. However, we wouldn't be allowed to testify unless Andrew pleaded not guilty. I failed to see the sense in that ruling.

Ashley and Gabby had just come home from school. I

didn't want to bring up the news of the hearing yet.

I grabbed Gabby and challenged her and Ashley to a game of backyard basketball.

Gabby squirmed under my embrace. "Mommy! Let me go. I'm first!"

Ashley came out, ball in hand, and took the challenge. She tossed the ball from a three point distance. It hit the rim and bounced into Gabby's arms.

I laughed, still holding her. "Shoot it from there!"

She squirmed harder. "Mom!"

I finally acquiesced and put her down. She threw the ball backward. It sailed into the net with a soft swoosh.

Ashley laughed. "That should be a five pointer!"

"Okay, five to zero." Gabby was strutting around as if she'd scored the winning shot in the NBA playoffs.

"Let's play horse." I shot the ball and missed.

Our game was well under way when I saw Andrew walking up the drive. I stepped protectively in front of my girls. "What do you want?"

"Mrs. Calabria." He greeted me but didn't look me in the eyes. "May I please speak to you and Ashley?" He cast a glance over his shoulder, and I saw Susan getting out of a shiny red Mercedes.

"Cassie." She waved as she walked up our driveway. "Andrew has something to say to you and Ashley."

Ashley stepped in front of me. "Andrew, I don't want you here. You really screwed up my life. Leave." She stood tall, confident and looked him directly in the eye.

Susan moved next to him. "You're right, Ashley, but please give him a few minutes. How about if Gabby and I shoot some hoops while you talk."

"Where's Angela? Can she play, too?" Gabby threw the ball to Susan. "Just because Ashley doesn't like Andrew doesn't mean I don't like Angela."

I motioned for them to come inside. "Please." My insides were roiling. I had an urge to smack him on the head as he walked past.

Once inside, Ashley wheeled around. "What?"

He took a deep breath and said, "Ashley, I'm sorry. I messed up."

I bit back an I told you so retort.

She rolled her eyes to the ceiling. "Duh." She looked both angry and scared.

"I didn't know what I was doing that night. I know it was stupid."

She stood with her arms crossed. "You're just *now* figuring that out?"

He looked down, cheeks blooming red, and was on the verge of tears. "I've thought a lot about this. Susan and my mom really raked me. But they also got through to me. I'm going to plead guilty."

I stepped up. "Andrew, what about your dad?"

"Screw him!" The tears came. "He doesn't care about anything except me playing football and our good name."

This big, arrogant tough guy had turned into a young vulnerable kid.

"What about me? What about *my* good name?" Ashley asked. "Have you and your dad even considered that?"

"I'll talk to anyone you want me to and tell them the truth."

"Why the change of heart?" I asked. Although glad Andrew was taking responsibility, I was still wary.

"After I heard about Ashley being in the hospital, I got scared. Especially you being in a coma. Dad wouldn't let me talk to you. I'm really sorry." He wiped his face. "Then my mom and Susan grounded me, like, forever, and made me volunteer in the children's cancer ward this summer. Man, I learned a lot about what's important."

Ashley softened a little. "I'll try to accept your apology. But it's still going to take some time."

I fought an urge to speak for Ashley, but she was doing fine by herself. I felt our life line slack a little. I still wanted to reel her close, but it was time for her to dip her toes into independent waters.

"I don't want to be best friends or anything just because you're on some kind of weird guilt trip," she said.

For the first time, Andrew looked at Ashley. "That's cool."

His apology seemed sincere, but the wound was still fresh. "Andrew, I'm glad you're doing the right thing. It's been tough for Ashley, for all of us."

"Yeah, I'm sorry. Really. I mean, at first, I thought I was cool. But then Teresa said Ashley might die. That really freaked me out." He paused and cast his eyes down. "It made me think differently about life." His voice caught. Taking a deep breath, he quickly changed the subject. "Hey, I think it's cool that you wrote that book. My dad wanted to use it against you at trial, but I told him he would end up looking stupid."

"Does your dad know you're here? What does he say about this?"

"Not yet. But you'll probably hear him yelling when I tell him."

The door burst open and Gabby, red-faced, ran in. "I'm thirsty. Can I have a Coke?"

"No, have some water," I said.

Susan followed behind her. "Did Andrew say what needed to be said?"

Ashley headed to the kitchen. "Yeah, we're done."

I turned to Susan. "Can I offer you something to drink? Coke?

"No fair!" Gabby said from the kitchen.

Andrew was standing awkwardly by the door. "I'll be in the car."

Susan waved him off. When we were alone, Susan touched my arm. "Cassie, I've wanted to call you about a few things. First, Andrew. He really has done some soul searching about what he did. We're both going to talk to his dad tonight."

"I don't envy you."

She shrugged. "It'll be okay. I also wanted to tell you I loved *Wild Rose*. I can't believe you found the time to write such a great book while working full time and keeping up with your girls. Then to keep it a secret."

"I almost said something to you when you were at the bookstore. I was nervous thinking you'd recognize me."

"You fooled me." She smiled. "I really admire you. I wish I were organized enough to pull off something like that. I've decided to go back to school to get my teaching certificate." She paused. "Maybe I'll take a photography class."

"That would be fun," I said.

"You've inspired me to do something more with my life," Susan said. "If you could write a novel, work full time, and be a great mom, maybe I can, too."

Wild Rose

– From Chapter 22

Rosemary couldn't decide what to wear to her settlement conference with Sarah and The Fakers' attorney. She dug deep into her closet, pulling out clothes and throwing them on the floor. Sarah told her to look professional but not overdone—no blue jeans.

Hugh rolled over in bed, sleepy-eyed, and asked her, "What are you looking for?"

"I don't own a piece of clothing that looks professional."

"Why don't you wear my personal favorite, your birthday suit?"

"Thanks, but I don't think that would help my credibility."

Hugh got out of bed and pulled Rosemary to him. "Well, no matter what you wear, you'll look beautiful."

She smiled. "Will you be here when I get home?"

"Can I be? Alone?" Hugh asked, surprised. "I get out of my last class at three." He was in college working toward a degree in music. His wild side was tamed by the demanding schedule.

"I'm not sure when I'll be done. Let me give you a key so you can let yourself in."

He looked closely at her. "You're joking? You trust me with a key?"

"Yes. I may need a strong shoulder this evening."

"I've got two."

Rosemary arrived at Sarah's office, glad that Hugh would be there later. He'd been staying with her almost every night, using the excuse that her place was quiet so he could study. He'd matured since starting school, and had been a comfort with the rock tour photos and Colten's death.

She checked her image in the rearview mirror. No makeup, her linen shirt was already wrinkled, and her black pants were probably too casual for the law firm.

Sarah greeted Rosemary warmly and took her to her office. "Nate and his attorney are waiting in the conference room. You can hang here, and I'll come in periodically with updates. I've prepared a few posters." Sarah grabbed three charts. "This one shows the danger of drug overdose and the effects on the brain."

"You're going to say I'm brain damaged?"

"I'm saying these drugs can cause physiological changes." Sarah displayed two more posters. "The other charts outline the emotional and monetary damages to you."

Rosemary almost fell over when she saw the dollar amount.

"Are you going to ask for that amount of money?"

Sarah gathered the posters together. "I'll demand that amount. They'll offer less. We'll probably settle close to that. That's why I wanted you here—to approve any offers."

Rosemary fell back on a plush sofa in Sarah's office. "That's a lot of money."

Sarah dramatically batted her eyelashes and put a hand to her chest. "Less my fee, of course."

"Am I doing the right thing?"

Becoming serious, Sarah said, "Rosemary, don't stress about taking money from them. Not after what they took from you. Capisce?"

Rosemary nodded.

Sarah's eyes twinkled. "Let me go feel these guys up and see what they're willing to offer." She giggled at her joke. "Make yourself at home. Do you want some coffee?"

"Sure. Extra strong, please." Rosemary was surprised how quickly the case had moved. "Don't these things usually take longer than this?"

Sarah called her assistant to bring in coffee. As she hung up, she said, "The reason we're moving so fast is I promised not to file suit until we talked settlement. They don't want to drag this out. However, if we don't settle, I'll start moving hot and heavy, taking depositions and fact finding. I'm not sure they're willing to face that much scrutiny, especially with the The Fakers' new found success. She walked to the door. "Sit tight. I'll be back soon. Ciao!"

The Faker's attorneys offered less than half of Sarah's demand. She told them to take a hike, and she'd see them in court.

Rosemary was more than happy with the money, but Sarah said they were blowing smoke. "If they offered that much so soon they'll meet our demand by the end of the week. If I don't hear from them by then, I'll file suit.

Hugh prepared a delicious dinner of fettuccini and salmon, heavy on the wine.

"This is yummy. Not only can you sing and dance, but you can cook, too!" Rosemary said through a mouthful of food.

"And don't forget, I'm making straight A's" He toasted her with his wine. And I'm incredibly cute."

"You know, I'm proud of you for going back to school.

Honestly, I wasn't sure you'd follow through with it."

"I wasn't either, but something clicked when I started going to classes. I need to give my dad the credit for that. He encouraged me, no, forced me, and told me he'd pay my way, even if I studied rock and roll. There's so much I didn't know about music."

Rosemary put her fork down. "Well, I hope my career is salvageable."

"Of course it is. Think of your talent. That's what matters. Then consider the money from the lawsuit. It'll buy you time."

"I'd rather keep my name. It all feels cheap." Rosemary stirred food around on her plate. "I'd really like an apology."

"It sounds like you'll get an apology in the form of money." Hugh touched her hand tenderly. "Hey, did you hear Bonnie Bunnie is going to host a sex therapy talk show on late night?"

"No way!" Rosemary looked at Hugh, surprised. "From children's programming to sex TV?"

"See? There is hope." He raised his glass again and winked. "Given her ventriloquist abilities, it should prove to be an interesting show."

Chapter Forty Eight

"...If you believe, clap your hands!"
~ *J.M. Barrie*

Now that I was finally "out," I was having the time of my life.

I had a publicist to help me schedule interviews, photo sessions, and book events. I was away from home more now than when I worked full time. My family thought it was cool and we managed to take a few family trips tied in with book signings.

Rita still kept close tabs on me but had relaxed a little while fielding offers for book and movie deals.

Through it all, Mitch and I continued to work on our marriage. He was trying hard to keep the family together and was consistent seeing Dr Ogden. I met Mitch at Dr. Ogden's office late one afternoon after a photo session and a luncheon I'd been invited to attend as a guest speaker.

I ran to him as he waited outside in the heat. "Sorry I'm late."

"Considering how much she charges, every minute counts." Mitch held the door open for me. "I told the girls we're having family night, whether they want to or not."

"I think that's a great idea. Let's eat in, ignore the phone, and play Scrabble."

"You never could spell."

"Oh, yeah? Didn't I beat you last time?"

"No, that was solitaire."

We stepped into Dr. Ogden's quiet anteroom where maroon and dull shades of blue screamed calm.

"Too bad the walls aren't padded. This room would drive me crazy if I were in it long." I'm afraid to sit down for fear of being rendered mute."

Mitch shrugged. "I didn't notice."

The door to Dr. Ogden's office swished open and a whispered voice told us to come in. "How are you today?"

"Sorry we're late. Cassie's schedule has been demanding."

I couldn't tell if Mitch was being sarcastic or sincere.

We took our seats across from her. I was grateful the office had a lot of windows to brighten the intended soothing mood.

Dr. Ogden clasped her hands in front of her and looked over her glasses. "How was your week?"

I didn't feel like talking. Luckily, Mitch spoke up first. "I've spent time thinking about our marriage, you know, the kids, the whole relationship thing."

"You have?" I was surprised Mitch came out of the starting gate so strong. He usually complained about coming here.

"Yeah." He looked at me. "The other day I was driving in my car, listening to some old songs. It reminded me of when we first met and started dating. All of a sudden, I got scared thinking about losing you and the girls."

"What are your thoughts?" Dr. Ogden asked me.

I shot her a glance.

Mitch went on. "Cass, I screwed up. I know that now. Before, I thought you were to blame—"

"Wait a minute." I interrupted. "How was *I* to blame? As I recall, *you* were the one who left."

"Let me finish." He tapped the arm of his chair nervously. "It was easier to believe you were too busy, that you never gave me the time of day. Now I realize I wasn't putting effort into our relationship. Work wasn't going well, and I never put blame on myself."

"Go on," I said.

"Suddenly I realized what was at stake. You, the girls..." He held his hand up. "Listen, Cass. When I saw Ashley lying in that hospital, comatose, it hit me hard. I realized how important you all are to me. I've never been so afraid of losing anything. We have too much together to throw away. We're a family."

"What are your thoughts?" Dr. Ogden directed the question to me.

"Oh, shush," I teared up.

She gasped and unclasped her hands. "This is good. I'm seeing anger."

I rolled my eyes. "Mitch, I understand what you're saying, but you really hurt us. I want to keep the family together, but I keep having flashbacks of seeing you with that woman."

"I've thought about what I would have done if the tables were turned. Pulverized the guy, probably." He sat back in his chair and gazed out the window. "I hope it's not too late for us."

I was crying. "I don't know if it is."

"I remember the first time I laid eyes on you in college." He looked at me. "You used to walk across the courtyard every day at the same time. I always made sure to be there, playing Frisbee, hoping you'd talk to me."

"I didn't know that."

"You never noticed me. It wasn't until I threw my Frisbee directly at your head you even looked up." He grinned. "I swear, I didn't mean to hit you so hard."

"I remember. I didn't know a Frisbee could cause such a big bruise." I rubbed the spot on my forehead where it had hit all those years ago.

We laughed.

"You never said you waited for me." I was touched.

"I was afraid you'd think I was a wuss if I told you. You know, needy." He faced me and took my hand in his. "And, as they say, the rest is history. We have so much together, a life, two beautiful girls...too much to let go of, because...because I was stupid. I want to make a real effort to stay together. I need you."

"What if I thought you were a wuss anyway?"

He shrugged and gave me a mischievous grin. "I *am* trying to find my sensitive side."

I laughed. But then became serious. "We have made a life together, a good life. But, I don't know, Mitch." I let go of his hand. "There's also a lot of hurt."

"You're right. But please, I want you to think about us trying. I'll take whatever I can, whenever I can get it with you and the girls. I promise to be here for you." He studied me, sadness in his eyes. "You know, Cass, I'd do anything if you'd look at me the way you did twenty years ago."

That point speared me. Maybe real romance had been there the whole time, but I hadn't known where to look. I'd lost sight of my life trying to live it.

I'm not sure what happened, but the light in the room shifted. I looked at Mitch differently. The sun's rays passed through a cloud and shone over him seeming to illuminated his soul. Wisps of radiance highlighted the hairs on his strong arm like a smoldering sage fire. I felt a stirring. Mitch's obsidian eyes read mine, hungry, desperate. A rush of balmy desire spread through my body, hot flames teasing from inside out. I pictured him, all those years ago—his dark, smiling eyes and long, brown hair falling over his chiseled face. I remembered the Frisbee coming straight at my head, hitting me with such force I saw stars, twinkling, raining sparks of light. I saw them again today as I looked long and hard at him.

He must have sensed my mood because he pulled me forcefully from my earth toned chair into a sturdy, manly embrace. The layers of pain began to unfold gradually, like the delicate, velvety petals of a flower, responding to the hot, torrential shower of passion. Each soft leaf opened gently to his familiar touch, resonating with a pressing, blistering need.

"Oh, my! This *is* good." Dr. Ogden's hands flapped, as if they were unsure where to land. "I can *see* what you're thinking."

His mouth found mine, and we kissed hard and deep. His tongue danced, begged, and penetrated.

I took a deep, trembling breath. "Mitch, we still have a lot to work on." I pressed my body close to his engorged desire.

"But this is a good start."

I looked at Dr. Ogden. "Since we're only twenty minutes into this session, can we get some of our money back?" I winked at Mitch. "We could use it for a hotel room."

I could feel his eyes on me. "I love you, Cassie."

Wild Rose

– FROM CHAPTER 23

Rosemary - Ten years later:

"Rosie, where are my socks? I'm late."

"I don't know. Check your feet first and work back. Do I look like your mother?" Rosemary walked into the bathroom and pushed Hugh from the mirror, so she could see herself.

Hugh tried to kiss Rosemary's neck as she brushed her hair. "If my mother looked like you, I'd still be breastfeeding."

She popped him on the butt with her brush. "Stop it. Remember, you're late." She pulled on a pair of old jeans that had been slung over a towel rack.

"Work can wait. It always takes a long time to set up the studio before we start recording anyway."

She slipped on a button down cotton blouse. "What are you singing today?"

"Some jingle for a bread commercial." He began to dance around the bathroom, singing. "'Put your buns in the oven and wait till they rise...yeah, yeah, yeah.' Hey, maybe I'll make a lot of dough today."

Rosemary couldn't help but laugh at him, half-dressed and barefoot, as he danced around the cramped space. "What time will you be home? I was hoping we could celebrate our five year anniversary."

"I've already made dinner reservations." He grabbed her

from behind in a bear hug and looked over her shoulder at their reflection. "Can you believe it? Five years as Mrs. Rosemary Christi-Hardick. Gosh, it only seems like four years and three hundred and sixty four days ago. Where does the time go?"

Hugh had proven to be wonderful and attentive.

He turned her to face him and kissed her tenderly. "I guess I'll have to sweep, mop, and clean the house for you to prove it."

"It'll take more than that." She returned his kisses. "You'll have to cook, too."

"I'm cooking now." He unbuttoned her shirt, his hands moving deftly.

She caressed his back."How late can you be?"

"If we don't hurry, I may come early." He pressed close to Rosemary, pushing her onto the bathroom counter. The mirror began to steam from the searing heat of their love.

Rosemary pulled him close, ready for him.

Their bliss was interrupted by wails of,"Mama! Dada!" coming from the baby's room.

"Oh, no," Hugh groaned and wilted. "Timing, it's all in the timing."

"Sorry. I'll get Davis, you take a cold shower." She kissed him playfully. Buttoning her shirt, she called to her baby, "Coming, sweetie."

"Almost," Hugh said to himself sarcastically, as he leaned over the bathroom counter.

She went to get their son from his crib.

"Hugh, come here, and bring my camera."

He walked into Davis's bright room and handed Rosemary her Nikon.

"I have to get a picture of this." She set the aperture and began shooting Davis, sleepy-eyed, as he hugged his Winnie the Pooh bear. "Have you ever seen anything so adorable?" she cooed.

"Dada," Davis whispered.

Hugh picked up his son and hugged him.

Because of the large settlement from The Fakers, Rosemary was able to work less making sure there was plenty of time for family snapshots. She hugged both of the men in her life. "Hurry home, so we'll have family time together before dinner. And later there's a Colten Garrison movie marathon on HBO. We'll make a night of it."

Hugh tossed Davis in the air then caught the giggling, squealing baby.

She edged closer. "Stop! You might hurt him."

"Don't be a worry wart. Hey, I've got a better idea for tonight. Why don't we cancel the dinner reservations, you can record the movies." He rolled his eyes, making it clear he was not interested in Colten's old films. "We'll have dinner by candlelight, and we'll try to make another one of these little guys." He snuggled both Rosemary and Davis close.

"Sounds perfect. Now take Davis over by the window and let me get some pictures of the two of you."

The End

Chapter Forty Nine

"If you can walk, you can dance. If you can talk, you can sing."
~ Zimbabwe Proverb

"Come on, kids. It's a pizza and game night." I walked into the house with Mitch, still tousled from our "afternoon delight." It was the first time we'd been together since his affair.

Gabby skipped into the living room. "Mommy, can Angela come over to play, too?"

"No, honey. It's just us tonight. We're not answering the phone or watching TV."

"What if Bradley or Teresa calls? I need to talk to them." Ashley leaned against the door. "Why is your hair messed up?"

"We...uh...were driving with the windows rolled down." I smiled at Mitch, who gave me a quick neck kiss.

"Oh, gross!" Ashley squealed.

"Gross? Can't I kiss your mother?" Mitch grabbed me and kissed me dramatically. "Come on, girls, you're next!" He chased them around the room.

Gabby giggled at the chase. Ashley was cool but happy as she dodged him.

It was nice to have the family together, laughing. Mitch and I still had bigger issues to deal with, but after our session today, I knew we should make an effort to work on our family.

I'd fallen in love with him once. We'd vowed to stay together in front of God and family all those years ago. As I watched Mitch play with the girls, I knew what we had was worth fighting for. It was still hard thinking of his affair, but I forced those thoughts down. It was too destructive. I needed to be unselfish for the girls and to learn and grow from this. I heard an inner voice, sounding very much like Mom, telling me this was the right decision.

Mitch talked more that afternoon about our marriage than he had ever before. I believed he was willing to work on our relationship. If not, I had the peace of mind that I could survive. There was comfort in the knowledge I could rely on my own means to support Ashley, Gabby, and myself. That confidence was reassuring.

As I was ordering pizza, the other line rang. Forgetting about the no phone rule for the evening, I answered. It was Rita.

"The publisher's thinking about another printing. Cassie. Let's get you scheduled to visit other cities this month. You're booked on some regional news shows starting next week."

"All right, Rita. I'll need to put the dates in my calendar. We were just getting ready to eat dinner. Also, we're scheduling trips to Disneyland and Atlantis this summer." My dreams of treating my family was now a reality. "Maybe we can schedule some interviews around those dates."

"Okay. I'm in Dallas. Plan to come into my office tomorrow morning. We need to go over your schedule and talk about your next book. If we don't keep you out there, I'm afraid you'll be forgotten. You'll wind up changing bedpans again."

I still hadn't officially quit the hospital but continued as a PRN. For some reason, I wasn't ready to break those ties. There was security there that I wasn't willing to give up. I had stepped down from the supervisor position and recommended Adam. He declined because he liked working with patients more than management. Jennifer jumped in and took the job. She was handling it nicely. "Okay, Rita. But I haven't started on another book. I'm still dealing with the issues of *Wild Rose.*"

"Well, I suggest you work on an outline tonight. If we tell your audience you're working on a new book, they'll be looking for it."

I suddenly had a revelation. "Rita, I think I have an idea."

"Yeah, go on."

"What do you think about a story of a working mother, one who wants to spend more time with her children and follow her dreams, so she writes a blazing bodice ripper under a pseudonym? The novel becomes a huge bestseller, but she's afraid to be found out by her family and friends for having written it. Then she finds her own daughter reading it. She goes to book events incognito until she's eventually discovered and has to deal with the issues." I paused to let the idea sink in. "It could work."

Rita snorted as she laughed. "Don't be ridiculous. Cassie. You can do better than that. Really," she scoffed. "A book like that would never sell."

"Don't let it end like this. Tell them I said something."
~ Last words of Pancho Villa

ACKNOWLEDGEMENTS

Writing is a journey that works best with good people. I'm grateful for the help I had in bringing the story together. Thanks to my wonderful writer's group all amazing authors: Jean Reynolds Page, Ian Pierce, Mary Turner, Kathy Yank, Christopher Smith, Lou Tasciotti, Jill Sayre, Adrienne LaCava and Mandy Montane. And, of course, J. Michael McClary (Devil Dog), who brought new insights to the story. I really should credit them as co-authors considering how much they helped shape *Dance Like You Mean It*.

Readers: The fabulous authors Kathleen Kent and Jean Reynolds Page for their kind comments. Cherryl Duncan, who always gives me the confidence to write. Julie Dee, Karen Huston, Mary Misdom, Jane McGregor, Lilly Davis, Cindy Jones, Lori Reisenbichler, and Cindy Corpier. Best muses: Brigitte Kelly, Cherryl Duncan, and Donna Holmes.

My publisher, Melissa Carrigee.

For Mom, who never got to read this but inspired me to never quit and always told me that I could do anything I wanted if I worked at it. Cheers, Mom. This is for you.

My daughter Alexandra, who is my light and joy and will never be allowed to read this because of the sex scenes. And my husband, Terry, thank you for understanding when I'm always running off to write so I can do something about the voices in my head.

And, especially, to the readers. I am indebted to you all.

ABOUT THE AUTHOR

When not writing, Jeanne Skartsiaris also works as a sonographer. Prior to that, she was a medical/legal photographer for a plaintiffs' law firm. She attended creative writing courses at Southern Methodist University. Also the author of *Surviving Life* and *Snow Globe,* she lives in Dallas, Texas.